THE PRETEND CHRISTMAS BRIDE

L. STEELE

*For the good girls who
love a morally grey man
who'll t1e y0u up and
worship y0u like
the goddess y0u are!*

*Because you asked,
here's a count of relevant words:
The 'F' word = 96 times
The 'p' word = 55 times*

*No of times he calls her **"my wife"** = **87 times**
No of pages with groveling = 50!!!!*

*Chapters with sp1cy scenes
Ch. 23, 25, 26, 29, 30, 31, 32, 33, 35, 36,
37, 40, 41, 48, 49, 50, 51, 52, 53, 55*

SPOTIFY PLAYLIST

Pray - Jaden Hossler *(L. Steele's note: I see this as Edward's anthem)*
Jealous Guy - The Weekend *(L. Steele's note: This... this song... is everything Edward feels for Mira)*
All the Good Girls Go to Hell - Billie Eilish
Ceilings - Lizzy McAlpine
Maria Maria – Santana ft. The Product G&B *(look up the Fabio Rodrigues cover too)*
Wake Me Up When September Ends - Green Day
New Year's Day - Taylor Swift
Old Money - Lana Del Ray
Lithium – Evanescence
Somebody Else - The 1975
Something in the Way – Nirvana
Sleeping Beauty Waltz – Tchaikovsky
Angels & Demons – Jaden Hossler
Whispers – Invadable Harmony
Fallen Angel – TIX

SUN SIGNS

Edward Chase - Scorpio

You are deep, emotional, and loyal.
You are single-minded in achieving your goals.
You can be painfully honest and obvious in your intentions.
You can be mistrustful, possessive, controlling and jealous.
You are aggressive when looking for vengeance.

Mirabelle 'Mira' Young - Pisces

You are a hopeless romantic.
You are kind, intuitive, and very giving.
You experience intense emotions in the heat of the moment.
You are creative and imaginative.
You have a big heart and respect honesty.

1

Mira

"You're with child?" I yelp, then flush when everyone at my friend Gio's wedding turns to stare at me. We're at the bookshop her husband gifted her, because that's where Gio wanted to hold the ceremony. And the brew of choice? Coffee. Also, there are cupcakes, because what else do you need when you're a smuthead getting married in your favorite space? Talk about marriage goals. Tiny, the Great Dane, who's currently being dog-sat by one of Gio's friends, parks himself next to me. He looks at me with melting eyes, and I swear, he has the only sympathetic gaze in the house.

I tighten my grip on the mug of coffee in my hand, flash a smile at Gio, and say, "I mean, *you're going to have a baby*!" I take a step forward and stumble across Tiny's flag-like tail. *Oof!* The cup goes flying from my hand, and the contents spill over a man standing nearby. The cup bounces off his chest and hits the ground, then spins away.

"What the—?" He glances down at the coffee stain he's wearing across the front of the tailor-made jacket which, by the way, molds his shoulders while his pants cling to his powerful thighs.

My heart stutters. My pulse booms at my temples. I draw in a sharp breath, and under the bitter whiff of coffee is the sharp tang of something more complex, something spicy and savory and so laced with that tingle of electricity, it arrows straight to my center. My toes curl, and goosebumps pepper my skin. I glance up and into his face, and tawny-brown eyes blaze at me. The anger in them cuts through the noise in my head. I flinch, take in the mess that was once what I'm relatively certain is his ten-thousand dollar three-piece suit. I should know the price; it's the world of privilege I come from, too. Which indicates he can afford another with ease. But to see the loathing in his features, you'd think otherwise. I manage to get a hold of myself and gasp, "Oh god, I'm so sorry."

I remove the scarf from around my neck and dab at his suit lapel, then at his thigh then—*stay away from his crotch. Not his crotch*—I brush my scarf over the impressive packet between his legs. His thigh muscles bunch. Anger vibrates off of his big body, and I flinch, retrieving my arm.

"Am I always such a klutz? I'm not. Do I often ask questions of myself aloud and reply to them? Only when I'm nervous." I chuckle, making sure to keep my eyes averted. "What comes first, though? Being nervous leads me to being a klutz? Or does being a klutz make me nervous? Or maybe one leads to the other in an endless feedback loop." I nod. "Yep, that's what happened. Which is why I tripped over Tiny's tail. But Tiny didn't mean to cause the accident, did you?" I look down at Tiny.

The dog woofs, then head-butts me. The momentum causes me to tumble forward. The man catches me around the waist. I look up, and this time, when our gazes meet, gold fire sparks in his eyes. A lick of fire, a whip of mahogany, a sheen of amber—all polished to a burnished, searing flame that could burn you on contact. The air between us seems to ignite, drawing in all the oxygen in the room. I try to breathe, but my lungs protest. I sway, and his hold on my waist tightens. His jaw hardens. The sharp contours of his cheekbones lend a stark, almost cruel quality to his features. I've never met this man before, but I've heard about him from Gio. Edward, that's his name, and he's a former priest. He walked away from the church and embraced a life in pursuit of money—or so I heard from the girls—not that I tend to gossip. Okay, maybe a little.

When you don't have a choice in your future, you take pleasure in the little things in life. And gossip happens to be one of those treats I refuse to deprive myself of. Besides, I want to know why he walked away from what was, surely, his calling. It takes strength of conviction to become a priest, but to then leave it behind? Why would he do that? On that count, my girlfriends were mum. It's his story to tell, they said. Which led me to speculate, it had to have been because of a woman. Did he break up with the church to be with her? Though, from what I've heard, he's single. So, does he still think of her? And why is my mind racing at a million miles an hour? Why are my palms sweating, my stomach twisting and turning? Why is my heart banging into my chest like thunder crackling across the skies before a storm?

A heavy weight pins me in place. I can't move. Can't speak. Caught up in the tractor beam of this man's gaze, I'm a butterfly trapped in a bell jar. Then Tiny woofs, and both of us jump back from each other.

"Sorry, sorry, oh my god, I am so sorry." I wave my hands in the air. "And I sound like I'm a broken record, stuck on repeat. You do know what I mean by a record, right?" I peer up at him. "Of course, you do." I take in the threads of grey at his temple. "You're older than me—not dinosaur age, but close to it. I mean you're not Santa Claus old. No way I'd mistake you for him though, given your build is much more stream-lined. Not to mention, your whiskers are jet black. Although, this time of the year is the most wonderful time, don't you think?" I beam at him because... *Who doesn't love Christmas?*

"I hate Christmas," he snaps.

This guy, apparently. Just my luck. Of all the men I could have spilled my coffee on, it had to be the grumpiest, growliest, meanest...sexiest looking man I've ever met.

His diamond-hard jaw grows more rigid. A nerve throbs at his temple. Fish on a tricycle, it should frighten me, but honestly, he's too yummy-looking. He can glower at me any time. He can fix me with those intense golden eyes and make my panties melt with his smoldering gaze.

The tension coiled in his muscles thickens the air between us. I swallow around the ball of lust in my throat and attempt a smile. "Just so you know, I didn't mean to imply you're ancient. I mean, you're, what, twenty years older than me?"

He scowls.

"Okay, fifteen, at least." I cough. "Not that I don't like older men. I have a soft spot for them." I shuffle my feet. "No, no, not that kind of soft spot. I find older men much more confident. You know what you want, and don't hesitate to get it. You guys have your shit together, you know?"

His scowl deepens.

"I don't mean I find you attractive. Not that you're not good-looking. You have that whole tall, dark, and intense look going on, which I admit, is a turn on. Not that *you* turn me on."

The blood drains from my face.

"Oh my god, I didn't mean to say that. Also, whoa—you'll have to dry-clean your suit. I'll pay for it, of course."

Utter silence follows my proclamation. Even Tiny is quiet. Guess I shouldn't have offered to pay? Maybe, I should have kept quiet. But his demeanor is daunting. Why is he standing there, silent, except for his body language, which screams his displeasure? A muscle works above his jaw. If he grinds his teeth any harder, he's going to crack a molar or two. Why is he so annoyed? It was an honest mistake, after all. "At least the coffee was decaf," I offer.

Someone titters— then turns it into a cough. Someone else chuckles, then manages to stifle it. But the man in front of me stays silent. His shoulders are bunched, and the tendons of his neck stand out in relief. He might as well be carved out of stone but for the rise and fall of his impressive chest.

I shuffle my feet. "You're not saying anything. Why aren't you saying anything? Are you pissed-off? Oh god, you're pissed-off. I'm sorry, you make me nervous. Can you tell? Haha, I tend to fill the silence when the person I'm talking to stays quiet. I do like to talk; ask anyone. The only time I clam up is in church, because it would be rude to talk while the —" *don't say priest, don't say priest*—"priest," *oops*—"is talking…"

I had *not* meant to say that out aloud. *No shit, Mira. Why did you think of the P-word in his presence? You know you have no filter between your brain and your mouth, or where he's concerned, between that space between your thighs and your mouth. No, don't think of how moist you are down there. Not right now.*

Edward's shoulders swell. The tendons of his throat are so pronounced, he's beginning to resemble the Hulk. Only his face is utterly emotionless, which is, frankly, terrifying. I gulp. At my side, I sense Gio trying to smother her laugh, but I don't dare look at her. I draw in a ragged breath and want to turn and run out of there. But one thing I'm not is a coward.

It's why I didn't run out on my family, either. That would have hurt them too much. Instead, I bargained with them—a few months of freedom in exchange for returning to the fold. Helplessness squeezes my chest. Any day now, I'll get the call and have to go back home, to the arranged marriage that will follow. Until then—I can live life the way I want.

I found work at a preschool, made enough to rent my own apartment, and everything was going well. Until it went out of business. But I'm going to find another job soon. I'm not going to give up and go back home. Not until my father calls for me. I have the strength to face my uncertain future, knowing I won't have control for much of it. But this, here? In this moment, I hold the power.

I straighten my spine. "I didn't mean to talk about your past. I was warned not to. Not that I'm a gossip—" I pause. "Okay, maybe a little." I hold up my thumb and forefinger. "And only because gossip is good for you. It helps to de-stress. And you look like it would help if you were to relax. I'll bet you keep it all locked up inside. Which makes you a prime candidate for a coronary. Not that it's any of my business. It's your heart, after all."

"Heart?" he asks in a dark voice.

"The organ that beats in our chests? On the other hand, looking at your grim-faced countenance, I'm guessing you don't have one." I squeeze my eyes shut. "I've crossed the line, haven't I?"

When I look at him again, his expression veers between fascination, disgust, and anger.

"Okay, that's it. I will not speak anymore. I'll wipe you down and be on my way." I lean forward, then brush my scarf over the lower part of his jacket which covers his crotch. And again. His thigh-muscles coil. The fabric of his pants stretches until I'm sure they're going to pop at the seam. I sense his gaze boring into the top of my bent head, but I don't dare look up.

"You done?" he finally growls through gritted teeth. And his voice— it's gravelly and hard, and carries the promise of all the delicious, unforgivable things he could do to me. And I want him to.

I swallow around the ball of emotion in my throat. "It's not getting any better, is it?" I ask in small voice. "No, it's not. Am I making it worse? Of course, I am." I slowly tip up my head and meet his gaze. "Can I make it up to you?"

His lips thin, he looks ready to bite my head off, then a cunning look comes into his eyes.

"How are you at obeying orders?"

2

Mira

"Orders?" I blink slowly. "What kind of orders?"

Not the kind you read in your smutty books. Definitely can't be those kinds of orders.

The skin around his eyes tightens. "What are smutty books?" he rumbles. My nerve-endings spark. Oh my god, that caramel-velvet voice of his brushes up against my skin, and every cell in my body seems to come alive. *Also, no, no, no, did I say the S-word aloud?*

"I meant, slutty books." I cover my face with my hands. "I said that aloud, as well, didn't I?"

I peek through the gaps in my fingers in time to see him nodding slowly. He doesn't say a word, though. He merely glares at me like I'm a puzzle to solve, or maybe, an annoyance, or an irritant, or a pest he'd prefer to swat away.

The silence stretches. Our gazes catch. The air between us crackles with awareness. The fine hairs on the back of my neck rise. A heavy feeling pushes down on my chest. I swallow, and my throat feels like it's lined with sharp glass. *What's happening to me?*

"Do you always say whatever comes into your mind?" he asks in a voice that's both detached and curious, in the way a scientist might be while observing an animal in the wild.

I frown. "Of course, not." I wave a hand in the air, striving for casual. "Only when I'm nervous. Not that I'm nervous now. And do you make me nervous? Of course, not."

"Also a liar." He drags his thumb under his lower lip, and my gaze is drawn to his mouth. Gorgeous mouth. Hard mouth. A mean upper lip that hints at his authoritarian nature. That puffy lower lip that might signify his pursuit of pleasure. A hedonist. A savage. A fiend. He's all of them. Does that make him a heartless monster? Or a merciless lover? One who seeks gratification, but not in an instant way. This man would wait months…years, if needed. This man would pursue what he wants with a singular focus. And oh, to be at the receiving end of that intensity.

What I'm facing now is a tiny insight into how it would be if he were to get fixated on me. I shake my head. Fixated? I don't want that. Not at all. I don't know this man. All I know is the passing reference to him within the circle of my girlfriends, whose husbands he's a friend of. I've never seen him with a woman, though.

"I've never seen you with a woman." *What the—!* "Did I say that out loud?" I ask weakly.

His features harden until they look like they could be carved from a diamond-hard material, whatever that's called.

"Oh, shit," Gio says in a soft voice from behind me.

Indeed.

"Umm, sorry? Did I say something wrong? Of course, I did. But why is it wrong? I have no idea. No one has ever seen me with a man before today, either. So, it's not odd not to be seen with someone of the opposite sex. By the same token, it's allowed for a woman to have friends who are men and a man is allowed to have woman friends. Besides, you're no longer a priest, so…" I swallow, for he's leaned forward on the balls of his feet.

It's a slight movement, but it brings him close enough for his spicy scent to crash over me. A tingle of electricity runs up my spine. It's as if I've been bathed in a cloud of aphrodisiacs—oh wait, those are his pheromones! A-n-d my stupid stomach goes into free fall. "Sooo, what I'm trying to say is, it doesn't matter if you have women friends. Or girlfriends. Or ladyloves, as they called it in the regency era. I mean, you look stuffy enough to belong in an historical romance. All you need is a ruffled shirt..." I hum thoughtfully. "Yep, a white ruffled shirt, which would stand out against your skin and be the perfect foil to your cut-glass cheekbones. Does that mean you're good-looking? Of course, not. I mean, if you smiled a little more... Now —"

"Smile?" he asks in that dark, dangerous voice, and that swirling sensation in my belly intensifies. My toes curl. Goosebumps pop on my skin.

"Smile," I say in a dazed voice. "You know, when the sides of your mouth curve up because your sense of humor is tickled, or when you feel the urge to show your appreciation of a situation, like this." I project my most confident, school-picture-day smile. "Not that either of those have crossed your mind for a decade."

"How do you know that?" he asks in a curious voice.

"Oh, b-b-b-because your lips have been set in a firm line since I saw you earlier. And there's this wrinkle between your eyebrows which seems to have been etched in permanently, and then the frown-lines that radiate out from the corners of your eyes, which are, no doubt, because you're old — er," — I cough — "older and distinguished. Anyway, you have that dark-cloud-brewing-over-your-head look that only adds to your charm. From far away. I mean, it's understandable you don't have a girl-friend or any significant woman in your life. You look like you're angry at the world, and there's an internal war going on inside, and you're all scowling and brooding and menacing. Which is all fine in a smu — I mean, romance novel. But in real life, no one wants to be around a man who's an alphahole."

"Alphahole?" He says the word as if he's trying it on for size, and it fits. Speaking of fits, from the looks of it, he'd need an XL condom, given the size of the resting-package at his crotch. A-n-d, my gaze slides downward. It...it's bigger than what it was earlier, so the tent under that coffee-stained fabric is... because he's aroused? Am I thinking in ques-tions? That's a first. That's how rattled I am in his presence.

Tiny woofs. I jerk my chin up to find this tempting package of yum is looking at me with a glint in his eyes.

"Was I caught in the act?" When he only raises an eyebrow, I continue, unabated. That's me, I keep digging that hole. "I was. So what?" I tip up my chin. "A man can stare at a woman's chest, but a woman can't ogle a man's package?"

One of my girlfriends — Summer? — gasps, before turning it into a cough.

"Hear, hear," Gio calls out.

Someone else titters, then the sound cuts off.

I don't dare look around the room, though. Can't take my gaze off those tawny eyes of his—burnished gold, glistening copper, hard like topaz gemstones. They could sear me, look right through me to decipher my secrets. They could turn soft like melted butter which… is not me. He's an unfeeling brute, a vicious beast. The devil incarnate. The kind of man who'd be all wrong for me.

Besides, I don't like him. I don't like the fact I can't read him. I prefer someone who's open and honest with his feelings, who can be sensitive to my needs. This man… He'd break me down, then leave me. I'd be better off keeping my distance from him.

"Oh, look at the time." I raise my hand and pretend to gasp at my empty wrist—*no, I don't wear a watch, but so what? It's the intent behind my gesture that counts, right?* "I need to be someplace else, somewhere urgent. Nice meeting you, Mr. Former-Priest who shares his name with the man whose side I was not on in Twilight."

I turn to leave, when he drawls, "Team Jacob, are you?"

I pause, then scowl at him over my shoulder. "Is that a problem for you?"

"Is it for you?" he shoots back.

"Of course, not."

"Good." He nods with satisfaction. "Remember, you asked how you could make things up to me?"

I nod slowly.

"Come work for me."

My jaw drops. "You're kidding."

"Am I?" His eyes glint.

My heart crashes into my rib cage. This is a joke—him asking me to work for him. Only, it doesn't feel like that. His harsh features indicate he has not one funny bone in his gorgeous, sexy, chiseled out of granite, body. And to have him as my boss? This brooding, unfriendly, severe man, this…dark, handsome in an uncompromising manner man, who'd relish ordering me around, is not something I want. Of course, not.

"Of course, you are." I turn to face him. "You don't know me. You have no idea of my qualifications. Why would you want me to work for you?"

When the expression on his face doesn't change, I swallow, spare a glance around the room, and find no one willing to meet my eyes.

"You *are* joking?" I ask in a small voice.

He tilts his head. "What I am, is offering you a job."

"A-a job?" I manage to choke out.

"I assume you need one?"

"What makes you think—" I shut up because there's a knowing look on his features. *What gave it away?* I'm still a plus-size woman. Never mind, I've been surviving on dry ramen for the last week, ever since the preschool went bust. My body shows no signs of losing these stupid curves. Good thing Gio had already moved out of the apartment when I lost my job. There's no way I would have wanted to bother her with my problems or allowed her to buy my food. And I know she would have insisted. It's not that I don't want to burden her, because I know money isn't an issue for her and Rick, but I'm too ashamed to admit I need help. I need to do this on my own. But what hurts the most is not being able to see the kids I used to take care of.

Between my aching heart and my empty stomach, I've only managed to make it to two interviews, both for jobs I didn't get. I'm running out of options. And there's no way, I'm calling up my family. My stepmother and half-sisters would be only too happy to tell me, again, I'm a failure. I had enough of that when I lived with them. I am not subjecting myself to that misery again. So yeah, I need a job.

He sees the expression on my face, and a flash of satisfaction colors his before he schools his features back into a mask. He reaches into his suit pocket and pulls out a card before handing it to me. "Be at my office, eight a.m. Monday morning."

3

———————

Edward

"You think she'll turn up?" Sinclair spots me as I bench press twice my body's weight. My chest squeezes down, my shoulders scream in protest, my biceps threaten to tear apart, but I ignore it. Breathe through it. In and out.

"She will."

"And if she doesn't?" He assists me as I push the barbell up and over my head.

"She will," I grunt.

"There's a chance she won't."

"If she doesn't, there are more fish in the sea, but she will." I lower the weight down to my chest, hold, then he assists me as I hoist the barbell up again. The tendons on my throat strain, and my triceps feel like they are being shredded. I push the barbell up and hold. And hold. Sweat runs down my temples, between my pecs. My stomach muscles harden, my thighs contract. I push my feet into the floor and brace. Brace. *You need to bear the weight. Bear the mistakes of your past. Bear how you were abandoned by your parents when you needed them most. Bear how she decided you were not the one.* Not that I blame her. Baron would be—has been—a better husband for her. And now, they have a child. A family. Moisture trickles out from the corners of my eyes, joining the beads of sweat on my face.

"You okay, mate?" Sinclair murmurs.

"Why wouldn't I be?" I begin to lower the barbell down, and he doesn't let go. He helps me as I push up and through the pain again. *Work through it. Keep riding it. At some point, you'll find the calm in the center of the storm.* At some point, I'll figure out my life's purpose.

It's the only reason I took the meeting with my grandfather. My father's father, who I never met before. Never even knew existed. Imagine my surprise when he called me and introduced himself. My father never spoke about him.

After the incident, the communication with my parents broke down. They were at a loss for how to deal with what had happened to me. And I took refuge in whatever helped me find oblivion from the emotional pain I was carrying—am still carrying—inside.

I almost hung up, but he pleaded with me to meet him. Just once. Ten minutes of my time. I finally agreed because, why not?

Being the General Manager of the London Ice Kings has given me some focus. Working with Rick Mitchell, the captain of the team, we steered the team to victory in the League. From being the underdogs to one of the highest paid teams in the world, and in one season. It was unheard of. I'd accepted the position as a favor to Knight, the owner of the team. But in working toward a greater goal, I discovered some measure of satisfaction. You can take the priest out of the church, but you can't take the need to help people from him. It's also the reason I agreed to my grandfather's request.

"You've been through a lot in the past week." Sinclair helps me ease the bar onto the rack. I draw in a breath, feel my heart thunder in my chest, and the blood pounds in my ears, drowning out all thoughts for a few seconds. It's the main reason I work out. Pushing my body in a way I can't push my mind. Controlling how much I can lift in a manner I never can control my thinking.

All those restraints, the limitations I imposed on myself. I lived my life according to the directives of the Church. Found some modicum of peace in the routine, the daily prayers, the sermons... All the while, knowing the storm brewing inside me would break loose, and ignoring the warning signs. Until it did. I sinned, and punished myself by leaving the house of God.

Unmoored, I left everything behind. I travelled until I managed to ground myself. And by the time I returned? It was too late. She had turned to Baron. And they were—they are—happy together. And me?

The empty shell that constitutes me, Edward Chase, lives from moment-to-moment, not quite sure what I wanted out of life. I feel un-needed, unwanted, useless to everyone, even myself. Maybe, that's why I grasped onto Grandfather's ask. Maybe, I could be of help to someone, after all.

I don't need a shrink to tell me I'm going about this all wrong. I don't need a shrink to tell me the person I see when I look in the mirror is not the person I was. Or the person I want to be. I don't need my friends to point out I'm on a one-way trip to a crisis again. Hell, I'm living from one crisis to another internally. Every minute I get through without doing something I'll regret is a win. As is the deal I made with my grandfather. It gives me a reason to…keep going.

I sit up, then reach for my bottle of water and chug from it. I lower it and raise a shoulder. "I'll live."

"For how long?" he asks softly.

"For however long it takes, I assume."

He searches my features. "I'm worried about you."

I bark out a laugh. "Since when did you start going soft?" I raise a hand. "Forget I said that. All six of you are married, and most of you with kids… Who'd have thought?"

His mouth curves in a smile, the kind I never thought I'd see on Sinclair fucking Sterling's face. The meaner they are, the harder they fall, apparently. The seven of us are united by an incident that changed our lives forever. And each of my friends went through their journey and found their soulmates. That's not my path, and that's okay. I'm happy they're happy. All of them. Including Baron. He makes her happy, and in her happiness is mine.

"Speaking of,"—he tilts his head—"what time is your girl coming to the office?"

"Not my girl, merely a—"

"Cog in the wheel?" His smile grows sly. "A piece in the puzzle. A—"

"Stepping stone to my larger plan? Yes," I say dryly.

"Hmm." He snatches up a bottle of water, twists open the cap and chugs from it.

"The fuck does that mean?"

"Nothing. Why should it mean something?"

I frown. "No, of course not, but if you have something to say—"

He caps the bottle, then wipes his hand over his face. When he lowers his arm, his eyes gleam. "It would be lost on you. Ergo, you need to learn your lessons yourself."

"Thanks. And to think, I'm the one who gave the sermons."

"You know what they say? Even a doctor needs another when he's unwell."

I lower my eyebrows. "Are you saying—"

"Nothing. You do you, Ed. Find your way. I have every confidence that you will."

I snort. "What-fucking-ever."

He laughs. "The classic rejoinder of a man who's at a loss for words. Also,"—he nods toward the clock on the wall—"you need to rush if you don't want to be late."

I *am* late but not for the meeting with her. I left instructions with my HR manager to get her settled in. I'm on my way to a much more important meeting. When I walk into the conference room adjoining my new office, the five men in the room turn to glare at me. Once again, I'm the outsider, but I prefer it this way. They're brothers. Some of their blood runs through me, but I've never met them before today.

"Knox." I jerk my chin toward the man standing in the far corner. The sunlight streaming in casts his face in shadows. The other four are at strategic positions around the conference room. None of them are seated. And I'm sure their locations weren't chosen by chance. These five are united in a way that tells me I am the opposition. The enemy. The one who came in from the cold to take over their business. The one chosen by their grandfather to take over as the CEO of their company.

"Edward." Knox tips up his chin. "Or should I call you Priest?"

There's a challenge in his tone—one I don't rise to. I've come across enough men who've decided it's best to go on the offensive when they're backed into a corner, as my half-brothers, no doubt, are at this moment.

"I prefer Priest."

"Yet, you left the church?" This from Ryot who's standing closest to me.

"Funny how you only value something when you don't have it anymore," I murmur.

"Like your girl who's not your girl anymore?" Tyler, the brother standing on the other side of the table drawls.

Anger squeezes my guts. My pulse begins to race. "Better than not knowing your child was not your own."

The moment the words are out of my mouth, I regret it. I raise my hands.

"Sorry, that was a low blow."

Tyler's jaw tics. A nerve pops at his temple. He folds his fingers into fists and takes a few steps forward, as if he's about to jump over the table and hit me.

But the brother standing near him—Connor—moves forward and touches his shoulder. Tyler seems about to shake it off, but the other man says, "Don't. Arthur won't be happy if you fuck up this meeting."

Arthur. So they do refer to our grandfather by his first name? He's the chairperson of the company, so it stands to reason it's easier for all concerned to call him by his name at work, and he asked me to do so the one and only time we met. But I'd have thought when they were among family, they'd refer to him as Grandpa? Or Grandad? Not that he looks like either of those.

Tyler lowers his arms to his sides but continues to glower at me.

The fifth man who, so far, stands in one corner of the room reading, looks around, then snaps his book shut and walks over to the table. From my research, I know that Brody is the quietest of the five, and the one I know the least about. He keeps to himself and does not participate in the day-to-day running of the company. The only reason he's here is because Arthur asked him to come.

Brody pulls out a chair, and seats himself. The rest of the brothers look at him, their expressions ranging from anger to frustration. All of their gazes are tinged with stubbornness. Do I really want to take over the company and deal with their egos, not to mention, the roadblocks they'll put up to obstruct any plans I want to execute?

If it's a challenge I'm looking for, being the GM of the London Ice Kings provides me plenty—or rather, did provide me plenty—right until the time they won the League, and on their first attempt. I played a role by helping to put the team together, but the glory belongs to the players. And they won the championship.

I have the option to continue as GM, but I'm ready to hand that off. I paved the way for someone else to take over and build on the foundation I set up. That's me. I prefer to do the hard work, the dirty work, the work that requires the most obstacles to be overcome. And once that's done, I move on.

The only time I stayed consistent was when I was part of the church. The routine, the discipline, and the regulations ensured I could focus on the only thing which mattered—my devotion to the Lord. And then I left it behind, and with it, my ability to have a focal point in my life. I hoped being the GM of the Ice Kings would provide me with that anchor, and it did. Briefly. But something was missing. The position always felt temporary. I loved building something with the team, but like I said, something was missing. Something I hope I'll find as the CEO of the Davenport group of companies.

It's why I accepted Arthur's offer to take over this role. The fact that it means working with my half-siblings is something I've both been looking forward to, while also dreading it.

It's not every day a man finds out he has an entire biological family he never knew anything about. Turns out, my biological father and my mother had an affair, and when she broke things off with him, she didn't realize she was pregnant. By the time she did, she was married to my adoptive father, his older brother.

My biological father went on to marry and father my half-brothers.

My adoptive father, who is technically my uncle, fell out with his family, changed his surname to his mother's maiden name, and never spoke to them again.

But when Arthur found out about my existence he wanted me to rejoin the family business. He also wants to groom me to become his heir.

Now, I glance about at the faces of my half-brothers, then pull out the chair at the head of the table and drop into it. The men stiffen. None of them move for a few seconds. Then, Knox steps forward into the light. I take in the scars on his face as he crosses over to the chair at the other end of the table.

He sits down, and once his brothers follow suit, he leans forward in his seat. "You have something to tell us?"

4

———————

Mira

"He had nothing to say to you?" Gio scowls up at me from the screen of my phone.

I shake my head. "I didn't see the man the entire day."

She taps her finger to her cheek. "Maybe he was busy? He is the CEO of the company."

"And he asked me to get to his office for eight a.m., which I did, but he wasn't there. He palmed me off to his HR manager who onboarded me. She also told me one of my roles, get this, is to ensure his favorite coffee is stocked, as well as his sparkling water."

"So he did instruct someone to show you around?"

I pop a shoulder. "There was no reason to ask me to report for eight a.m. if he wasn't going to be around."

"But the office hours are from eight a.m. to five p.m.?"

"Eight a.m. to eight p.m." I grimace.

"He's a workaholic." She shrugs.

"I don't want to work for him."

"So don't."

"Don't think I have a choice. I need this job."

"Join me. I've resumed PR for The London Ice Kings. Also, the bookshops are booming. I need someone who can help manage the workload."

"I don't know anything about PR," I protest.

"You don't know anything about being an assistant."

"How difficult can it be? I have experience taking care of three-year-olds. Surely, pandering to the needs of a CEO can't be as challenging?"

"You have a point." Gio pushes the hair back from her face.

Since she married Rick, she's taken to wearing her hair down. She also seems less stressed; there are no wrinkles on her forehead. She's glowing with health and seems a lot more relaxed. "Most men, in my opinion, don't develop beyond being five years old anyway. You need to treat them like they're children. Humor them, but also don't hold back the truth from them. You have to be upfront, but also selective, when necessary. It's a fine balance."

I chuckle. "Is that how you manage Rick?"

"Now, there are always exceptions to the rule. Rick was one of them. Nothing I said or did could sway the man, stubborn as he is. He's one of the only men I've met who's so secure in himself, he wasn't threatened by my self-confidence. That's what made me hate him, at first, but also intrigued me enough to find out more about him."

There's a soft smile on her face. Almost as if talking about him has conjured him, I hear Rick's voice in the background.

"Do you have to go?" I ask.

"Not until you tell me what you're going to do next."

"Not much I can do. It's noon, and I'm stuck here behind this assistant's desk. I have a ton of emails which have landed in my inbox. I've tried to reply the best I can, but without his direction, I'm not sure how much further I can go, and—"

A baby's shriek breaks the silence of the office.

Gio frowns. "Was that—"

"A child, yes." I glance around the floor. This is the executive floor, so it's only the senior management who are here, along with their various assistants behind desks similar to mine. And no one seems to be bothered by what I've heard. Maybe, it's from someone's computer or phone? But it didn't seem that way and—there's another cry, and this time, the sound doesn't stop. And yet, nobody else on the floor seems to be reacting.

"I need to find out what's happening. I'll talk to you later, Gio." I disconnect before she can protest, then rise to my feet, pocket my phone, and walk in the direction of the crying child. As I pass each cubicle, I find people glued to their computer screens. Many are wearing earphones; others are typing into their tablets. No one seems curious about the child's crying. I pass an empty conference room, then a few offices with more executives staring at their screens. Gosh, this place is as cold and severe as my new boss. I reach the end of the floor and peek into the last cubicle to find the HR manager, the one who inducted me, changing a baby's diaper on her desk. The kid begins to cry in earnest.

"Not a fan of her diaper being changed, huh?"

Adela, the HR manager, shakes her head. "She hates it. I had to bring her in because the babysitter called in sick. I was hoping she'd sleep for most of the day, but clearly, I didn't think things through."

Just then, the baby flings out her leg and hits a pen holder which crashes to the floor.

"Andrea, no. Stay still. It's almost over, I promise." She manages to remove the used diaper, folds it and looks around for a place to deposit it.

"Here, give it to me." I grab it from her and head to the restroom that's in the hallway behind the cubicle.

I'm back in a few minutes and find Adela has finished changing Andrea's nappy, but the kid is still crying. She presses the child into her shoulder and rubs circles over her back. "There now, hush, baby. Everything is fine. You're fine."

The infant cries louder.

A man pops his head around the adjoining cubicle. "Keep it down. We're trying to work here. Also, you shouldn't have brought the kid here. You know this is a child-free zone."

"You think she had a choice?" I scowl at him.

He looks me up and down. "You're new, I take it?"

"I'm Edward's Chase's new assistant."

"Well, I'd say good luck, but it's not going to help where Priest is concerned. As for you"—he turns to Adela—"I hope you have your CV brushed up. You're going to need it."

I open my mouth to tell him off when a hard voice interrupts, "Ms. Young, am I paying you so you can waste your time babysitting?"

5

———————

Edward

"Firstly, any time spent baby-sitting is not a waste. Babies are our future and take priority over anything else." She plants her hands on her hips. "Secondly, you haven't yet paid me, and thirdly—"

The baby's wails rise to a crescendo.

"—you're scaring the little mite."

With that, she flounces toward my HR manager and holds out her arms. The other woman hesitates; the baby screams louder.

Someone pops his head out of his room, while another woman looks over her cubicle. Both notice me and retreat without a peep. In the week since I've taken over as CEO of the company, my reputation has been cemented as someone not to be messed with. Except for this sprite of a woman who turns her back on me.

My HR manager hands over the baby to my new assistant. She rocks the kid, soothes it, but the child only cries louder. She pats the little one's back but the infant screams.

"Oh, for heaven's sake." I stalk over to her and hold out my arms. "Hand over the kid."

She gapes at me. "You?"

My HR manager looks at me with an expression of shock.

"I was a priest. I know how to calm a child," I say through gritted teeth.

The infant solves the problem by jumping into my chest. I hold the kid close, then rub ever widening circles over her back. Her crying slows down, turns into hiccups, then stops. The baby draws in a deep breath, and her eyelids flicker down. I smooth down the wisps of soft curls on her head, then rock her for a few more seconds, before I hand her over to my HR manager.

"Thank you," she whispers.

I nod, then turn to my assistant, in time to catch the dreamy expression on her face. Hold a child in your arms, and every woman in the vicinity takes it as a sign you're ready to procreate. Something I've sworn off. "Ms. Young, don't keep me waiting again," I snap.

She blinks then straightens her spine, "I'm the one who's been *waiting*. I came in at eight a.m., as instructed, but you weren't here." She smooths her hand down the skirt she's wearing. One which clings to her curves and outlines her full figure. Her hips are the most enticing I have ever seen. As for her thick thighs which stretch the fabric of her skirt? I'd do anything to squeeze them apart and—I stiffen, then curl my fingers into fists at my sides. She wore that skirt on purpose, knowing how tempting she'd come across in it. She squeezed into it, knowing exactly the effect it'd have on me. But I'm not going to give into my base instincts. I will not be distracted from my goal of becoming the CEO of this company. I resisted my impulses when I was a priest. Surely, I can do the same now?

"I've done what I could with your email inbox, but I need some direction." She sets her jaw. "And I couldn't stand by while the baby cried. Also, I had my phone with me so you could have contacted me anytime." She pulls out the device and waves it around.

I arch an eyebrow at her, and she blinks rapidly. "Surely, you didn't expect me to stand by while Adela needed help with her child."

"Speaking of"—I turn to my HR manager—"you're aware children aren't allowed in the building?"

"What?" my assistant screeches in horror. "No children in the building?"

I glare at her. "Look around you, Ms. Young. This is a workplace."

"So? People have families. And working women like Adela need babysitting facilities so they're assured their children are taken care of while they're at work."

"Does it look like I'm running a charity, Ms. Young?"

She juts out her lower lip, and my dick twitches. A zing of lust sizzles up my spine. I stiffen. There is no room for a woman in my life—not since the one I wanted decided I was not for her. I made a vow, then, never to be emotionally involved again. It's one I don't intend to break. Definitely not for a curvy woman who streaks her hair purple and with a figure like she's channeling Marilyn Monroe.

"Companies which provide childcare have seen productivity soar by fifteen percent," she announces.

"Is that right?" I drawl.

She raises a shoulder, then sighs. "I don't know if it's a fact, but I do know women need all the help they can get. And by going that extra mile for your employees, you'll ensure they stay loyal to you."

"I pay them. That's more than enough. If they don't like it, they can leave, as can you—" I stab my finger over my shoulder.

My assistant stiffens, "If I hadn't seen you with the baby, I'd believe you were an insensitive ass, but now—"

"Now?" I incline my head.

"Now, I know you *are* one, you—"

"I'm so sorry, this is all my fault," my HR manager cuts in, "my babysitter cancelled today, and I knew I had to get into work to complete the staff-training. I thought I'd get through things while she was asleep, but then she woke up. Then, I had to change her. And then, she started crying." She swallows. "I'm sorry, Mr. Chase, I know it's against the rules. It won't happen again."

I nod, "Emergencies happen, and we can't always predict circumstances when it comes to children, so I'm willing to overlook the incident. This time."

"Of course," Adela says stiffly.

"It's not what I want to do, but I have to set an example, you understand? If it happens again, I'll have to compensate for the drop in productivity by taking it from your salary."

My assistant gasps. "And will you pay her extra if productivity goes up?"

I shoot her a look. She scowls back, but thankfully, stops speaking.

"It won't happen again." Adela pats the now sleeping baby on her back, then turns to my assistant. "Thank you, Mira, you're a lifesaver."

My assistant smiles. "Anytime."

I make a warning noise at the back of my throat.

Of course, she ignores it. "What's your daughter's name?" she asks.

"It's Andrea," the other woman replies softly.

"I predict Andrea's going to sleep for at least another hour, enough time for you to get through whatever's urgent."

The HR manager shoots her a grateful look, then walks back toward the makeshift bed she has for the baby.

Silence descends. Mira stiffens then slowly turns to me. "I guess I can't delay any longer?"

I tilt my head.

She heaves another sigh, then lowers her chin to her chest. "Fine, whatever. I know you're pissed off. But I'm not going to say sorry."

"Good."

She jerks her gaze back to my face. "Did you say, good?"

"You passed your first test."

Her jaw drops. "Did you say, test?"

I raise a shoulder. "If you want to work as my assistant, you need to stand up to me."

She blinks slowly. "I thought you wanted someone who follows orders?"

I tap my fingers against my chest. "You arrived at eight a.m. today, didn't you?"

"Another test?"

I fake a yawn. "Enough of this prattle." I turn, walk a few steps forward, then turn back and scowl. "Are you waiting for a special invitation, Ms. Young?"

Her mouth firms, but she follows me down the corridor and into my office. I walk over to the floor to ceiling window that looks out over the River Thames. In the distance, the circle of the London Eye cuts a swathe through the rain. The dome of St. Paul's Church is almost hidden by the low hanging clouds, except for a curve at the top bared like the shoulder of a shy bride.

"You love this city, don't you?" she asks from behind me.

I nod before I can stop myself. *The hell?* I never talk about my likes or dislikes with my friends. Definitely not, with my employees. During the time I was General Manager of the London Ice Kings, I kept a strict demarcation between my personal life and my professional one. I prefer to keep my preferences and my secrets to myself. A hangover from the days I was a man of the cloth, maybe, but it's served me well. This way, I can keep my life straightforward. No emotions, no connections, nothing that could result in getting hurt.

The incident when I was a boy changed me forever. Then there's the broken heart, which I'm still not over. Which is why I've done away with messy sentiments. No more allowing myself to feel a connection with others. I did that when I was a priest.

I opened my heart to her, and she chose someone else. I don't hold it against her. How can I? I left her, with no explanation. She was right in choosing my best friend over me. He can give her everything I can't—emotional security, a grounding influence, the stability to put down roots and start a family. I curl my fingers into fists.

Last I saw Ava was at a gathering with Baron. She was glowing, and he had his arm around her. They looked at each other with adoration. And their love created a cocoon which enclosed them in their happy space. Surrounded by people, they remained separate, a unit tuned into each other's presence.

Then I knew, I'd done the right thing by walking away. I stepped aside so the two of them could be happy. And something inside me grew peaceful, knowing they were. I made the correct choice…for them. So what, if I'm to spend the rest of my life alone?

"Edward?"

I blink, then pivot to face her. "Whether I love this city or not is not your concern. You're here to do a job. You'd best focus on that, so you don't lose it."

Her mouth firms. "I haven't said I'd accept the role."

6

Mira

"Where are we again?" he drawls.

"We're in your office, why?"

"I rest my case."

He brushes past me and heads toward his massive desk.

"What do you mean?" I follow him.

"Let's cut the bullshit. You need this job to pay your rent." He slides into his armchair, his back straight. That soldierly poise of his hints at the strict control with which he lives his life. I can almost imagine him as a priest, at the pulpit, wearing the robes, standing upright and sermonizing to his congregation. None of which gives him the right to pass judgement on my life.

"Who told you that?" I jut out my chin. "It can't be Gio, or any one of my friends, for that matter."

"Does it matter?"

"Did you overhear me talking to them? No, that can't be. I know I tend to run my mouth, but no way, would I have turned to them for help."

"Why not?" There's a note of curiosity in his voice, but the expression on his face is bored, like this entire conversation is a chore.

I stiffen. "Does it matter?"

A spark of something lights his eyes, but he extinguishes it quickly. "I didn't get to be where I am in life without reading body-language. And yours indicated you were desperate at the event yesterday."

"I'm not desperate," I protest.

He stares at me steadily, and I hunch my shoulders. "Maybe, a little. No doubt, you saw me scarfing down the cupcakes at Gio's wedding yesterday. But they were free, and I hadn't eaten breakfast yesterday. Also, I ended up having ramen for dinner last night. Not that I'm—"

"Have you had breakfast today?"

I blink. "Why do you care?"

He continues to hold my gaze, and damn, I don't stand a chance. Those tawny eyes of his bore into me, and I'm sure he can read my mind.

"I ate breakfast," I say in a firm voice. My stomach chooses that moment to rumble. The sound seems to echo in the room, and I flush.

Without breaking my gaze, he picks up his cell phone, presses a key, and holds it to his ear. "Send in lunch for me and Ms. Young." He places his phone down on the table, then points to the chair opposite him. "Sit." The light glistens off the watch on his wrist.

I shake my head. "No, thank you."

"We need to go over your duties."

"Still haven't said I'm accepting the job."

His chest rises and falls. "I'm paying you £10,000 a month."

"What?" I squeak. "Why would you pay me that much?"

"Trust me, you'll earn every penny." His lips curl.

I scowl. "I'm not going to sleep with you, if that's what you're after."

He looks me up and down. "No fear there. You're not my type."

My jaw drops. "Were you born this rude?"

"No, it's a skill I've perfected over many years."

Wow, okay. "If you're going to be this obnoxious—"

"I haven't even started, Ms. Young."

"Mira."

"Excuse me?"

"That's my name."

"I know what your name is, Mirabelle."

I pick up my jaw off the floor, again. "H-h-h-how d-d-did you…."

"Mirabelle Young, living temporarily in a one-bed room apartment in Hackney. Father is Cyril Young, the CEO of the Young group of hotels. One of the most successful and wealthy families in the world."

My gaze widens. I open my mouth, but he holds up his hand. "Before you ask any predictable questions, I make it my business to know everything about people before I hire them."

"So, when you saw me yesterday at the gathering, you already knew about my background?"

He hesitates. "I had my investigator get me a file on you and —"

"You have a file on me?" I yell.

"I have files on all of my employees. It's standard HR procedure to do a check before you hire someone. It's why I didn't ask you for references."

"It's an intrusion of privacy, is what it is."

"Not when all your information is in the public domain."

I blink, then realization dawns. "My social media networks."

"Shouldn't have set your settings to public." He clicks his tongue.

I cross my arms over my chest. "Do you take pleasure in belittling people?"

"I don't care one way or the other."

I throw up my hands. "What *do* you care about?"

"That you do the job you're paid to do."

"Don't you want to know why I'm looking for a job, despite my father being one of the richest in the country?"

"Nope." He makes a popping sound at the end.

"You must also be aware my only experience so far has been working in a preschool."

"Where you also helped with the admin and running the place. In the short months you were there, you not only helped hands-on with taking care of the children, but also streamlined the processes. Too bad the owner didn't have deeper pockets. If he'd managed his cash flow wisely, the nursery would exist today."

Chills run up my arms, and I skim my suddenly sweaty palms down the fabric of my skirt. I struggled to zip it up this morning, and the jacket is a little too tight at the shoulders. That's what happens when you shop at the second-hand outlet. I can only find my size in the plus-sized brands, which are currently out of my budget, so I knew I'd lucked out when I found a half-way decent-looking ensemble in the thrift store. Unfortunately, it's one size smaller than what I normally wear. I thought I'd looked professional when I saw my reflection in the mirror. But with his piercing gaze on me, and that inscrutable expression in his eyes, I feel like I'm back in high-school and being rebuked by the principal. Though none of them looked anywhere as delicious as the glowering man on the other side of the desk.

"You seem to know everything about me."

"I know enough." He looks me up and down. There's a peculiar look in his eyes, which he banks again. "Only what's needed pertaining to your job. In my position, I need to be careful who I allow in my proximity."

"You've only taken this job recently, I understand?"

His gaze narrows.

"I heard from our mutual friends—"

"Friends?" he drawls in a tone which indicates he doesn't have many of them, which, given his attitude so far, is not surprising.

"I meant, the girls who are married to your friends. And I know you're close to the Seven—"

"What do you know about the Seven?" There's that hint of lazy curiosity in his voice again, one that signals he finds this entire conversation amusing.

My stomach tightens, but I force myself to relax. *You do need this job. Besides, it's only going to be for a few months.* That's as long as my family is going to let me be. And no way am I borrowing money from my friends or admitting defeat and returning home before that. This must be a test, his version of an interview. Yes, that's all it is.

"I know the Seven co-own 7A investments. They each are on the list of multi-billionaires on the continent. I know they're rumored to have links to the Mafia, so they know about all the big deals in the country. I know that six of the seven are married, leaving only one, who is among the most eligible bachelors in the country. And that person is you."

When he doesn't react, I'm emboldened to add, "I also know your half-brothers aren't too thrilled that you'll be taking over."

He seems taken aback by my knowledge.

"I do my research, too." So what if my primary source of information is The Daily Mail and Cosmopolitan? I have my ear to the ground as far as celebrity gossip is concerned, and the Seven used to grace the tabloids, until they found their ladyloves. Except for Edward—though speculation is rife that it won't be long before he settles down, considering his new position is that of the CEO of Davenport Industries. As for him not getting on with his half-brothers, that was a calculated guess. I may not be a cut-throat corporate shark, but even I know when an outsider is given the top position, the ones on the inside tend to be pissed off.

"Why is your surname different from the company you manage?"

"Didn't your research reveal that?" he drawls.

Heat flushes my cheeks. "My sources aren't as thorough as yours. All I know is your grandfather is Arthur Davenport, a business legend. I also know that, while he is estranged from your parents, he's decided to make you the CEO of his group of companies."

He doesn't seem surprised by the scope of my knowledge. "Did your investigation also reveal that Arthur wants me to get married?"

"He does?" I blink.

He nods. "Question is, do you have what it takes to be my wife?"

7

____

Edward

"You mean, do you have what it takes to be my husband, don't you?"
She huffs. "Also, if that was a marriage proposal, it sucked,"

"But you're considering it," I declare with satisfaction.

"No, I'm not."

"If you weren't, you wouldn't have mentioned it," I point out.

"What do you— Wait... You— I—" Finally, she throws her hands
up. "Aargh. Even if I were considering it, which I'm not, you'd be the
last man I'd marry."

"Oh?"

"Oh, *yes*." She tips up her chin. "You're too arrogant, too unfeeling,
too conceited. You're the kind of man—"

"—you'd prefer to fuck you."

Color flushes her cheeks. "Excuse me, did you use the F-word with
your employee?"

"Get used to it."

"You're breaking every rule in the employee handbook," she
informs me.

"I'm paying you enough to look past it."

She rubs at her temples. "This is all too much. I'm definitely not going to marry you. In fact, I'm not even sure I want to work for you—"

"Yet, here you are."

"You caught me at a vulnerable time." Her shoulders slump. "I suppose, that's what makes you good at your job. You see an advantage and move in. It's annoying; except, a part of me can't help but admire it, too." A determined look comes into her features. "I want to be more like you."

"No, you don't."

She sets her jaw. "Yes, I do."

"Trust me, you don't."

"You don't understand. You're confident and in control of your destiny. You can do what you want, when you want, how you want, and no one's going to stop you."

"Who's going to stop you?"

She opens her mouth, then seems to catch hold of herself. "Doesn't matter."

"Of course, it matters. Everything you say or think matters."

She flushes a little. "That's not a very professional thing to say."

You make me forget what it is to maintain a professional relationship. In fact, I'd rather we skip the professional etiquette and head to the more personal stuff and —what the—! I stiffen. *Why is it that talking to her tempts me to break the vow I made to myself?* In the three years since my last relationship, I haven't been with another woman. I haven't been interested in much else, except spending time on my own. I used to hang out with the Seven, but it became too painful to see Ava with Baron, so I reduced the amount of time I spent with them.

After leaving the church, and after fucking up the opportunity I had with Ava, I travelled the world, searching for a challenge, a focus, anything to get my mind off what I could not have. It's what led me to accept the post of the General Manager for the London Ice Kings, and now, the role of the CEO of the Davenport group of companies.

Perhaps that's what she is—a challenge. Is that why I haven't been able to get her out of my mind since I met her?

"You'd prefer for us to keep our relationship professional?"

"Is that a trick question?" She frowns.

"You want control over your destiny. This is me giving you the chance to define this relationship."

She rubs at her temple. "You're confusing me. There shouldn't even be a choice here. You're my boss. I'm your assistant, who's been working for you for less than a day. Of course, I want our relationship to be professional."

"Okay."

She seems taken aback. "That's it? Okay?"

"You seem disappointed."

"What? No." She shakes her head. "It's the right thing. The only thing possible between us is a professional relationship, after all."

I look up at her. "If you're going to work for me, the first thing you need to do is remove the idea that anything is 'impossible' from your vocabulary."

She thinks it over, then shakes her head again. "I disagree. Certain things are not done."

"Like what?"

"Like fraternizing in the workplace, for one."

"If you'd bothered to check the employee contract, you'd know that there is no clause that prohibits employees from engaging in a relationship. As long as it doesn't impact their performance, I don't care."

Her gaze narrows. "Everything has a consequence. You can turn a blind eye to everything but the money you're making, and it's only going to end up hurting you."

"Worried about me?"

She scoffs, "You can take care of yourself."

"But who's going to take care of you?"

She folds her arms across her chest. "I don't need you looking out for me."

"You're my employee. Of course, I'm going to look out for you."

"You don't seem to have the same interest or concerns about anyone else."

"That's because they are not you." *What the—? Where did that come from?*

A wrinkle appears between her eyebrows. "What do you mean?"

"That I ensure nothing impacts the bottom line. Ergo, I do what's needed to create an environment that results in optimal efficiency."

"I'm still not sure—"

There's a tap on the door before one of the kitchen staff wheels a food trolley into the room. "Where would you like this served, Mr. Chase?"

I rise to my feet and walk over to the seating area on the right side of my desk. "Here is good." I gesture to the coffee table.

He slides the two covered plates on either side of the table, then whisks off the dome shaped covers. "Enjoy." He half bows, then spins around and leaves.

Mira rises to her feet but makes no move to approach the food.

I take a chair and gesture to the settee on the opposite side.

When she stays unmoving, I tilt my head. "You need to eat."

"I don't understand you." She locks her fingers together in front of herself.

"What's not to understand? I ordered us an early lunch, since you didn't eat breakfast."

"But I told you I ate."

I stare at her.

"Well, anyway, that's not the point. What I don't understand is, why do you care whether I've eaten or not?"

"Because it's going to be difficult for you to focus on an empty stomach."

The sound of her stomach growling fills the room. She flushes. "Fine, have it your way." She stomps over, throws herself onto the couch, then stares at the food.

"It's not poisoned." I reach for my fork, scoop up some of the black truffle risotto from her plate, bring it to my mouth and wipe the tines clean. I glance up to find her gaze fixed on my lips. I run my tongue across the seam of them, and she swallows. I chew, swallow, then scoop up more of her risotto and offer it to her. "Open."

She raises her gaze to mine, then slowly parts her lips.

"Good girl," I murmur.

The pulse at the base of her throat kicks up. *Oh, she likes that.* I slide the fork over her tongue. She closes her mouth around it, and when I pull it back, the tines are clean. She chews, and her gaze widens.

"Good?"

She nods.

I scoop up more of the food and hold it to her mouth. Then watch as she closes her lips around the fork, as she flicks the tip of her pink tongue around the tines and picks off the food, as she chews and swallows. I place the fork down, then reach out with my fingers.

She flinches.

I pause. "You have a bit of food at the corner of your mouth."

"Oh?" She sweeps her tongue to the right-hand corner of her lips, and my cock, which already thickened from watching her eat, jumps in excitement. *Interesting.* This reaction of my body to her every move is fascinating. And unwelcome.

"Is it gone?" she asks in an anxious voice.

"May I?"

She hesitates, then nods. I close the distance to her face, scoop up the cream on the left corner of her lips, then bring it to my mouth and suck it off.

She draws in a sharp breath. "Why did you do that?"

"Do what?" I transfer the fork to my left hand, pick up my knife, and cut into the duck's breast on my plate.

"You fed me with your fork, then picked up the smidgen from my lips—"

"And swallowed it?" I shrug. "It was a reflex."

"Oh."

"Also, you're not eating."

She watches me for a few seconds, then picks up her own fork and eats a few mouthfuls. "You ordered risotto for me and duck for yourself."

I nod.

Her features light up, "You knew I'm vegetarian?"

"You mentioned it in the employee forms you filled out."

"Oh." She deflates a little and continues to eat.

"Thanks," she murmurs. When she's done, she places her hands in her lap. "That was delicious. Thank you, again."

"Don't expect me to feed you lunch every day; this was a one off."

Her lips stiffen.

"I order you to make sure you have your breakfast every day from now on."

"You order me?" Her gaze widens, "Who are you to order me?"

"Your boss."

"And if I don't want your job?"

I lean back in my seat and nod toward the door. "You're free to leave."

She glances toward the exit, then back at me. Her blue eyes spark, and color flushes her cheeks. She glowers at me, her features set in a mutinous expression.

"That's what I thought." I rise to my feet, head back to my chair and busy myself with the document open on my computer.

Footsteps sound, then she walks over to stand on the opposite side of the table. "Are you going to tell me what else is expected from me?"

"Your task list is in your inbox, Ms. Young, along with my expectations of the role. I assume you're able to read?"

She makes a strangled sound at the back of her throat.

My lips twitch. This has got to be the most fun I've had since preparing for my sermons. The thought wipes the smile off my face.

I managed to put the days of my being a priest behind me. I managed not to think of the absolute calmness which filled me then. How I was so sure I'd found my calling, my purpose... Only to find, it's not for me. And I haven't allowed myself to think back in such detail to that time in my life. I thought I'd managed to put it behind me and move on, but all it took was one conversation with her, and the gates to my past have been pushed open. My hard-won control over my thoughts has never been this tested. I was right. She is a test, a provocation, a problem poised to flush out the weakness in my defenses. And I'm not going to let her win. I'm going to resist her. I'm going to use her to strengthen my resolve. I will not be swayed from my path. I will not give in to this temptation. I will stay true to my promise to never be involved with anyone.

"I take that as a yes?" My voice comes out in a snap.

She flinches, then juts out her chin. "Thank you for sending through my job description. I promise I will not bother you with such trivial questions again."

She turns to leave, I call out, "Oh, Ms. Young? The zipper on your skirt is undone."

8

———————

Mira

"Oh, my god! What did you do?" My friend Abby cackles from the couch. We're in the townhouse she shares with her husband Cade. He's the captain of the English cricket team and currently on a tour of Australia.

"What could I do?" I look into the depths of my glass of Pinot Grigio. "I hauled ass out of there, then ran to the ladies room and checked."

"And," Gio interjects, "was your skirt unzipped?"

"Yep," I say sadly. "I must have tugged on the zipper a little too hard while I was trying to pull it on that morning. It must have broken at some point, and I didn't realize it."

"Oh, no," Summer, Sinclair's wife, gasps. "You were wearing a skirt with a broken zipper all that time?"

"Don't remind me." I tilt the wine glass to my mouth and polish off the liquid. The alcohol slides down my throat, hits my stomach and sets off a pleasant warmth. I hold out my wineglass.

Gio tops me up, then herself. "I can't believe he pointed that out to you."

"It might have been worse if he hadn't. I'd have ended up flashing the world. This way, I only flashed him. I hope."

"Oh, honey, I am so sorry." Summer rises from the couch and walks over to me. She hitches a hip on the arm of the chair I'm seated on and touches my shoulder. "I can only imagine how mortifying that must have been."

"It was." I press my head into her arm. My family is not the most demonstrative, to say the least. My ma died when I was little. My father married again, and my stepmother and half-sisters, have never been welcoming to me. Surprisingly, it worked in my favor when I wanted to leave home. My stepmom sided with me—probably because she wanted me out of her hair. Definitely, because she wanted me to get into trouble, in the hope I would spoil my chances of making a good marriage.

How I wanted to be able to do that, too. But I couldn't break my father's heart that way. Maybe he wasn't always available to me, but he loves me, in his own way.

That's me, the responsible girl, at heart, even though a part of me wants to break free and rebel so much. I tried to please my stepmom, went out of my way to be friends with my half-sisters, but that invisible barrier that comes from not being blood seemed to always be between us. The three of them were a unit, and I was always on the outside. I thought I'd never find my tribe, until I met Abby and her girlfriends. They adopted me, and for the first time in my life, I feel like I belong.

"Learn from it and move on, honey." Summer runs her fingers though my hair. "Don't dwell on it, or it'll drive you a bit crazy."

"I have been going around in circles in my head," I admit.

"I hope you, at least, flashed Priest properly," Gio drawls.

Abby spits out the non-alcoholic beer she's been drinking. She's six months along and glows with that radiance that pregnant women seem to exude.

"Really, Gio?" Summer says mildly.

"He probably got a glimpse of my stockings." I try to shrug in a nonchalant manner. *OMG, he saw my pantyhose, and probably a hint of my panties through the material.* "Though, I doubt it made any impact on that man." I glance up at Summer. "Has he always been this…inscrutable?" Of all of us in the room, she's known Edward the longest.

Summer straightens and slips into the armchair next to mine. "He's always been the quietest of the Seven, and the one who always seemed the most wounded from within."

"So, he was like that even before he left the priesthood?"

"He was, maybe, more hopeful when he was a priest." Summer twirls a lock of hair about her fingers. "He seemed to have a purpose then. But after what happened with Ava—" She firms her lips.

"Ava?" I frown.

She lowers her hand to her lap. "Pretend you didn't hear that name from me."

"But—"

"It's not my place to tell you, Mira. You understand that, right?"

I purse my lips. "I understand, but don't agree."

"Did she break his heart?" Gio asks.

"Is he still carrying a torch for her?" Abby muses.

Summer merely shakes her head. "Not fair guys. I don't want to speculate about his love life—"

"Aww, where's the fun in that?" Gio protests.

Summer sets her jaw. "It's Edward's story to tell," she insists.

"Well, give me something." I lock my fingers together in my lap. "He's my boss. It'll help me manage him better, considering it's so difficult to read him."

Summer seems conflicted.

"I need this job so I can prove to my family, and to myself, I can be independent. And I can't do that unless I have an advantage."

She glances around at our faces then sighs. "There was an incident," she finally says.

"An incident?" I frown.

She shuffles her feet. "When the Seven, including Edward and Sinclair, were in school, something happened. It's how they formed a bond that's lasted all this time."

"You're saying something affected all seven of them when they were young, and that's how they forged their friendship?" Gio narrows her gaze.

Summer nods. "And that's all I'm going to say."

"Aww, not fair," Gio begins to protest, but Abby pipes in, "I think Summer's right. Whatever happened to Edward, it should be his prerogative to share or not."

I take another sip of the wine. "I know you're right, but given how uncommunicative he is, not to mention how mean he was to me, it probably means I'll never find out what happened and"—my phone chirps from my bag —"and I guess that means I'm going to have to find another way to survive on the job."

My phone stops, then starts again.

"You going to get that?" Gio stares at my bag. There's a feverish look in her eyes. Woman has her own phone strapped to her palm, and thanks to her PR background, leaving a phone unattended is akin to a worldwide disaster.

"Fine, you can get it for me," I offer.

"Oh, thank you!" She springs up, pulls my phone from my bag, and holds it out to me.

I look at the screen and groan. "I don't want to answer it."

"Yes, you should."

"No, I don't want to." I sink back further into the chair.

"Don't be such a coward; it's only a man."

"Is that what you thought of Rick, when you first saw him?"

Her expression changes. "So, he's not just a man?"

"I didn't mean *that*."

My phone stops buzzing.

"You did compare your boss to her husband," Abby points out.

"It was a slip of the tongue."

"Like how your zipper slipped down your skirt?" Summer murmurs.

"You too?" I cry. "Girls, honestly, my boss is a hottie, but I am not attracted to him. I'm not."

"Then why didn't you answer the phone?" Gio looks at me with knowing eyes.

My phone starts buzzing again, and when she holds it out, I take it from her. "Hello!"

"Ms. Young, what's the use of having a phone if you don't answer it?" His hard voice sets off little tingles that slither straight to my core. I will not be turned on by the velvety depth of his tone, or that clipped British accent of his which brings to mind frosty mornings, and dewdrops on grass, and the clopping of horses on paved stone. *Lay off the historical romance books, Mira. This is Edward, your boss, the rudest man you've ever met.*

"Oh, sorry, uh... I had the phone in my bag... Which wasn't near me. I find holding a phone in my hand is so distracting, especially when I am with my friends and want to concentrate on them instead of on my device. It's such a shame people prefer to sit at the same table and focus on their phones instead of on the person opposite them, don't you think?

It's alienating, instead of bringing people together. You should know. You were a priest, so you must have seen how people are finding themselves even more alone, despite all the ways technology has enabled us to keep in touch. Imagine if they came to you for counsel and you happened to be on your phone instead of guiding them and..." I swallow down the rest of my sentence then squeeze my eyes shut. "I'm sorry I was prattling on, wasn't I?"

The silence on the phone could be the kind you face when you walk into a haunted house at an amusement park, right before the creepy crawlies reveal themselves in the light. I swallow. The silence stretches.

"Um… You there, Mr. Chase?"

"You done, Ms. Young?"

I open my mouth to reply, then don't dare let any words emerge from my lips because I might not be able to stop myself from another word vomit. I don't normally let my sentences get the better of me. Not really. It's this man whose presence and absence both disturb me in equal measure. I content myself with a nod, not that he can see it, but he must sense it, because he says in that stern tone of his, "I'm picking you up in thirty minutes."

9

Mira

"Some advance notice would have been appreciated." I scowl at the man in the driver's seat. Of course he'd drive his own car. He's too control-ling to put his life in someone else's hands. A reluctant admiration fills me. He truly is the master of his life. A position I'd give anything to be in. Right now, I'm at his beck and call though.

When I complained, he reminded me that I signed away my life when I agreed to work for him. I'm sure he's doing this to test me, too. I might look weak, but I have more mettle than he imagines. Doesn't mean I'm going to take his springing this trip on me without making my displeasure known. Not that my questions have brought forward an answer from him. He focuses on the road in front of us. I glance out the window and notice we're on King's Road. At this time of the night, the high-end boutiques and yummy-mummy cafes are closed. He turns off the main street, and I notice the sign for Chelsea Pier.

"Are we taking a boat?"

He doesn't answer. I risk another glance at his profile, then wish I hadn't. Illuminated by the lights from the dials on the dash, the gold in his eyes glints like that of a predator. A beast at the top of the food chain, who is the master of all he surveys. His hooked nose and square jaw, once again, bring home how much his profile resembles that of the regency heroes I'm so fond of. Only, he's wearing a fresh three-piece suit with a new tie. This one is a dull gold, and the color lends a burnished glow to his skin. His well-cut jacket accentuates his biceps, and when he turns the wheel into the parking bay in front of the dock, I can't help but notice his thick fingers, the blunt fingernails, the capable way he steers the vehicle. He was born to rule, to command.

I can't imagine any woman turning this man down. How was he before he had his heart broken? Before he walked away from the priesthood? How was he with his flock? Was he good at giving advice? Is that why he prefers not to talk much now? Or is it only because I don't know him too well? Is he different with his friends? Although, from what Summer mentioned earlier, he hasn't been socializing much with them, either. The man's an enigma, a mystery which intrigues me, but which I doubt I'm going to be able to solve anytime soon.

Moonlight glints off the water of the Thames and he pulls to a stop in front of a jetty. He switches off the engine, and except for the ticking of the engine cooling, it's silent. The lights of the jetty illuminate the wooden boards, and at the far end, I notice a motorboat.

"A little late to be cruising on the Thames, isn't it?"

"I need to remind you that you signed an NDA, Ms. Young."

"An NDA?"

"A non-disclosure-agreement." His tone carries a touch of boredom, which rubs me the wrong way.

"I know what an NDA is."

"But you didn't read it before you signed it."

"Of course, I did."

He slowly turns his face in my direction. "Are you lying, Ms. Young?"

"Of course, not."

He reaches into the inside pocket of his jacket and pulls out a sheaf of papers. "I suggest you read it properly before we leave."

I shoot him a curious look, then take the papers from him. He flips on the interior light, and I take in the letters on the sheets. He's helpfully highlighted some of the passages, and when I read them—for the first time, I admit—my jaw drops.

"D-d-does…it say a-anal?"

"Not only."

I race my gaze across the page. *Ball gag, fellatio, edging, whipping, choking, dominant, submissive.* "Double penetration?" I squeak.

"Could be with two dicks or with one real dick and a vibrator."

"Vibrator." I swallow around the word.

"Surely, you've used one before, Ms. Young?"

"Of course." I lie around the ball of nervousness in my throat. "What does this have to do with me?"

"It has everything to do with you." He takes the sheets from my nerveless fingers and turning, slides them onto the back seat.

"I… I am your assistant."

"And the only other person who has so much access to me."

"O-k-a-y?"

"Other than Tiny, of course."

"Of course. Speaking of, where is he?"

"He gets seasick," he declares.

I blink slowly, "Tiny, your Great Dane, gets sea-sick?"

"I'm dog-sitting him. Also, the mutt can down a bottle of expensive champagne without any problem, but get him on a boat, and he begins to puke. So, I had to leave Tiny home today. Which works in your favor. It means we'll only spend half the night on the ship."

"The ship?"

He nods toward the windshield. I look through it to the lights I noticed in the distance, but which I now realize *is* a ship.

"You don't get seasick, I assume, Ms. Young?"

I shake my head.

"Ever been on a boat?"

"I'm from Brooklyn. Of course, I have."

"Brooklyn, huh?"

"And what am I doing in London, you ask? It's the furthest I could get away from my family."

"Don't get along with them?" His tone is mildly curious.

"My dad's okay. But I wanted to be on my own. Find out what I like and don't like, before —"

"Before?"

I bite the inside of my cheek. "Never mind."

"Never cut off your thoughts like that. If you have something you want to say, do it with confidence."

I blink. I've never had anyone tell me that. With my father, I've always minded my words because I don't want to disappoint him. With the rest of my family, I've preferred to keep my thoughts to myself because I don't want to upset them. With my friends growing up, I hid my true sentiments because I wanted to fit in. It didn't help I went to a private school where everyone was too busy trying to keep up with the latest trends. It all seemed so empty, so pointless. I bottled it all up, until one day, I rebelled in spectacular fashion.

For the first time ever, I skipped school to hang out with another girl. The funny thing is, she wasn't even my best friend, just someone who always seemed so 'with it'. So when she invited me out, I couldn't refuse. We were caught smoking pot and chugging down beer in her car. Looking back, it seems like a relatively innocent escapade. It's not like I was caught having sex. But my father was so disappointed.

The worst part? He didn't scold me. He simply drove me home in silence and told me to go to my room, and that made it so much worse. I vowed not to ever let him down again. Yet, here I am, an ocean away, in the car that smells of that dark spiciness and ozone with my boss, and I'm about to find out what the sexual acts I read about in the NDA mean in real life. This…is not what I had in mind when I wanted to claim my freedom. This is not what I envisioned when I said I wanted a say in how I live my life… Did I?

He must see the apprehension on my face for he arches an eyebrow. "Scared, Ms. Young."

"Please call me Mira."

"Ms. Young, don't change the topic."

I blow out a breath. "I'm not sure if I want to do this."

"Do what?"

"This." I stab a thumb over my shoulder to where he tossed the NDA. "Whatever it is."

"You don't have to take part in anything. You simply need to be with me and take notes when I tell you to."

"Take notes about the s-s-sex acts you mean?"

"About the kink you're going to witness, yes."

Heat flushes my cheeks. "You said that word simply to get a reaction from me."

He pauses to think, then nods. "You're right, I did."

"At least, you don't lie."

"Unlike you."

I set my jaw. "I am being honest when I say I don't want to witness sexy—huh—kinky stuff."

He stares at me steadily. His features are inscrutable, but there's a bend in his lips which indicates he's amused by this conversation.

"There's nothing funny about this situation."

"Except for the fact you're curious about said acts. Except, you've always wanted to know about kink but never had the courage to find out. Except, you can't wait to get out of this car and accompany me to the yacht, but you don't want to admit it."

"I don't."

"Hmm." He taps his fingers on his wheel. "Slide your fingers into your panties."

"What?" I stare.

"You can, of course, leave the car, and I'll have someone drive you home and we may never speak of this night."

"And I'll still have my job?"

"You will."

The expression on his face indicates he expects me to take the easy way out. The rebel at heart, who's headed for an arranged marriage, and who's never had the guts to seize the opportunity when it was presented to her, wants to prove him wrong. And I was so sure I wanted control of what I would do next. *What am I going to do next?*

I straighten my legs, then raise my hips to hitch up my skirt. It takes some wriggling to pull it halfway up, but finally it's bunched up my thighs. Good thing I noticed a tear in my stockings earlier and took them off. Or a bad thing… Depends on your perspective. I have to admit, it's with relief I slide my fingers down the front of my panties. My breath hitches. Fish on a bike, I'm soaking wet.

"Exactly." His voice is calm.

I search for any traces of triumph or satisfaction in his tone, but I only hear a methodical intent in them. It's as if he wants to prove a point and knew he wasn't going to lose. He baited me, and I walked into his trap. I could, of course, get out of the car and leave…but that would mean walking away from his challenge. I'd be conforming to the image my family created for me. Following through would mean, when presented with the opportunity to create my own experiences, the kind I could draw on later when I was trapped in a marriage I don't want, I'll have some satisfaction that I embraced my deepest desires. The kind the man next to me seems to bring out in me. The kind I heard gossiped about among my girlfriends, and to which I nodded along, pretending a first-hand knowledge I didn't have. The gap in my skillset is one I could fill now. He's giving me the opportunity to find out how it would be to feel my fingers inside of myself while he watches. When I still hesitate he stiffens. I sense the change that comes over him.

"You're a virgin," He declares.

"What? No." I jerk my chin in his direction, then gasp, for he's staring at me. And his amber eyes glow with a look of such intensity, I'm sure he's going to reach over and curl his fingers around my neck and pull him to me and—

"Touch your clit," he orders.

I don't comply.

"You do know where your clit is?"

"Of course, I do." He said it to rile me. He's trying to manipulate me… And I am going to let him. This time.

I circle the swollen bud between my moist pussy lips, and frissons of electricity zip out from the contact. "Oh," I gasp.

His gaze intensifies. "Run your fingers around it again."

I do. The pin-pricks of sensations deepen. Moisture bathes the area between my legs. My thighs quiver, and my toes curl.

"How does it feel?" he asks without moving his gaze from mine.

"Like…a storm is gathering in the most intimate part of me." *Like I've never realized what my body was meant to be used for. Like I want to be used by you. Like I want you to close the distance to me and replace my fingers with your thick ones.*

The air in the car grows heavy. The tendons of his throat stand out in relief. The muscles of his jaw flex and I realize he's not as much in control as he'd like to think he is. "Pinch your clit," he snaps.

A tremor of heat zips under my skin. I hold the tiny swollen nub between my thumb and forefinger, and when I bear down, a volley of sparks charges to my extremities. My nipples tighten. My scalp tingles. I throw my head back and moan. I hear the sound and realize how needy it is. It also turns me on more.

"Do you want to squeeze your tits?" he asks in that low heavy voice which courses another flurry of butterflies through my veins.

I nod, then begin to remove my fingers from my pussy, when he clicks his tongue. "Did I give you permission to do so?"

I shake my head.

"As a punishment, rub your clit."

The thought of the friction where I need it most is almost too much to bear. "I can't."

"You can. You will. Do it, Belle."

Wait? He has a nickname for me? A glow ignites deep within. I replace my fingers with the heel of my hand. The first stroke sends a surge of sparks spiraling down my legs. I groan, continue to swipe, and an avalanche of goosebumps covers my skin. My entire body shudders. My fingers tremble. "I can't. No more."

"Once more," he commands.

A whimper spills from my lips. I squeeze my eyes shut, draw in a breath, another, then brush up against my throbbing clit. This time, flames lick my nerve endings. A trembling begin at my toes, steps up my calves, my thighs, circles my lower belly, my pussy. "I think I'm... I'm going to—"

"You will not come without my permission."

"What?" I open my eyelids, turn to him. "Why?"

He merely jerks his chin. "Bring your fingers to your mouth and suck on them."

My breath hitches, my gaze caught by his fiery eyes, the look in them so insistent, I know I can't disobey. I raise my fingers to my mouth and suck on them.

"How does it taste?"

"Sweet, complex and tangy, with an underlying saltiness." I hold out my fingers. "Do you want to taste?"

10

Edward

Fuck, yes. The sweet scent of her arousal wafts over to me, and my already thickening cock extends further. My blood drains to my balls, and my thigh muscles are so rigid, I'm sure I'm going to split my pants. I've never wanted anything as much as I want to lick the glistening ends of her fingertips. And if I do, I'm going to hell.

I swore never to fall for another woman. Yet here I am, in an enclosed space, with the most dangerous woman I've encountered since *her.* Maybe even more than *her.* I can't remember feeling this out of my depths with *her.* But Belle… She is a constant surprise.

Mirabelle Young, daughter of one of the most powerful families in the world, a woman whose purple streaked hair indicates she's trying to change what's in her control — ergo, she can't change many of the bigger things in her life. The woman who's twelve years younger than me — not twenty, or fifteen, as she'd guessed. The woman whose beauty struck a blow to my chest the first time I saw her, so much so, those big blue eyes of hers had seared themselves into my soul.

The creamy expanse of her neck had made me want to dig my teeth into the skin and mark her where her shoulder met her neck; the flare of her ample hips had invited me to dig my fingers into them and hold her still as I bent and swiped my tongue across her cherry blossom mouth. She's perfect. From the top of her blonde hair, whose shine not even the purple streaks could hide, to the imprint of her nipples that can be seen through the layers of her blouse and her jacket, to the thick thighs that beg me to wear them as earmuffs—to sink to my knees and push my face into the delectable treasure between them. Fact is, since meeting Ms. Mirabelle Young, everything about my carefully structured life has been upturned.

The force of her beauty touches that dead organ in my chest, the one I thought would never revive—indeed, did not want to be revived. Her presence is grace and light, with an awkwardness that awakens my protective instincts. It's why I offered her a job as my assistant. This way, I can watch out for her. I can make sure she's safe. But I cannot allow myself to develop feelings for her. I cannot act on this attraction I feel for her. Besides, if she sees the truth of the man I am, she'll hate me. She'll never want to see me again. My only role is to ensure she's protected. That what happened to me as a boy never happens to her.

When I showed her the NDA, I was sure it'd discourage her from accompanying me on this little sojourn. But Little Miss Gorgeous—whose face I almost jerked off to twice today—surprised me... Again. It made me want her more.

Not to worry; I can resist her allures. I stayed celibate as a priest. Until I didn't, and see how that worked out for me. Nope. I'm not falling for a woman again. And definitely not for her.

I step out of the car, hit the electronic lock, then walk around to open her door. "Ready?"

"Always." She tucks her handbag under her arm and brushes past me, only to trip on a crack in the pavement.

My heart slams into my ribcage. I grip her shoulder and straighten her.

"Do I have Tiny to blame this time? Of course, not," she mumbles. She tries to pull her arm from mine, but I tighten my grip.

"You can let me go."

"Can't have you breaking your neck on my watch." My voice comes out harsher than I intended.

She winces, then a shudder grips her.

"You're cold."

"Don't be ridiculous," she huffs.

"What did I say about lying?" I glare.

She pales, then slowly, nods. "I am…a little."

I shrug off my jacket and place it about her shoulders. It's big enough to envelop her completely and comes to mid-thigh. She burrows into it. Then, as if unable to help herself, turns her face into the collar and sniffs. She draws in a long breath, holds it, then sighs. Then, as if she realizes what she's done, she whips her head around in my direction. "Did I sniff your jacket?" she bursts out.

When I nod slowly, the color on her face deepens.

"I… I didn't." She bites down on her lower lip, and goddam her, I feel the tug in my groin.

I step away from her. Pretending not to notice the disappointment on her face, I stalk forward, without waiting for her.

I sense her surprise, then hear the clopping of her heels as she hurries to keep up.

We reach the waiting motorboat. The man at the wheel nods in my direction. I jump down into it, then turn and, without asking for permission, grab her hips and haul her down. The warmth of her skin sinks into my blood. My cock thickens, and my balls tighten. She draws in a sharp breath, and I have no doubt she feels the connection, too.

Fuck. I thought I was being clever when I invited her to join me as my assistant. I hoped I could keep a few steps ahead of this—whatever it is she's doing to me. I thought I was being clever by taking the lead and nipping this attraction in the bud. I took that entire 'keep your enemies close' dictum to heart. Apparently, she's not the one I need to be worried about.

It's me and my reaction to her that I need to control. And I have the rest of the night to prove to myself how wrong it was to have anything to do with her.

"Sit." I point at the bench set into the side of the boat, then heave a sigh of relief when she complies. I grab a life-vest and place it about her shoulders. She begins to protest but I shake my head. "That's non-negotiable. I will not risk your life, Belle."

She looks between my eyes then nods. "What about you?"

"I'm good."

"I will not risk your life either, Edward." She sets her jaw.

A frisson of heat squeezes my chest. I bat it aside, then reach for another life-vest and shrug into it. Then, I take a stance beside her. Not because I want to act as her shield from the wind, and definitely not because I want to make sure she's safe. She's a grown woman; she can handle herself on a boat. The vessel leaps forward, and she lurches with it. I grip her arm until she finds her balance again.

"Thanks." She tilts her face up. Her hair flows across her features, and before I can stop myself, I've pushed the strands behind her ear.

In the moonlight, her blue eyes turn a translucent silver.

"Beautiful Belle," I murmur.

"Excuse me?"

I shake my head, stare ahead, but don't let go of her.

"I like it when you call me, Belle." She whispers the words, and I shouldn't hear it above the breeze, but I do. Only, I pretend I don't.

When the motorboat reaches the stern of the larger ship, the driver cuts the engine, then throws the line to one of the waiting crew on the yacht. He secures it, then signals that we're good to climb aboard. The man moves toward Mira, but when I glare at him, he pauses.

I reach for her and help her onto the boarding ladder. When I follow her up, I realize I made a mistake. From my vantage point, I have a clear view of her pear-shaped bottom in that too-tight skirt outlining her lush curves. My fingers tingle, and the blood roars in my ears. I raise my arm, needing to touch her twitching arse, then stop before I make contact.

Why is my control so fraught around her? Why does she reduce me to the most basic of instincts? Why does she turn my emotions inside out? Why does she affect me so? Why did I decide to bring her here? I thought I'd punish her for daring to tempt me, yet I'm punishing myself by her proximity. She reaches the yacht, and the steward helps her aboard. When he touches her, a burst of anger sweeps through me. I don't question my need to hurry up and reach her. I step between them, and steward's arm drops away. He looks between us, then lowers his gaze, signaling he understands my unspoken sentiment.

I shrug out of my life-vest, then help her slide off her own. I hand it over to the steward. He accepts it, then half bows his head, "Everything you asked for is ready," he assures me.

"Belle, are you ready?" I rap on the door to the room she disappeared into. I told her she'd find fresh clothes laid out for her. She protested, but I glared at her, and she paled. I softened then, and told her, since I'd spoiled her evening with her friends, the least I could do was make it up to her. She finally relented and walked inside to change.

That was half an hour ago. Truth be told, I'm getting impatient. I want to see how she looks in the clothes I chose for her. I want to see her features—those plump lips, those rosy cheeks, the vulnerable column of her neck, the pulse that beats at the hollow of her throat. Every part of her is enticing and alluring, and I want... No, need to smell her and see her and be in her presence again.

"Open up." I bang on the door. "If you don't, I'm going to break this down and—"

The door swings open. I stare.

11

—————

Mira

"I'm not sure this looks good on me." I run my hands down the silken fabric of the dress which clings to my curves like it's a second skin.

He runs his gaze from my feet, now clad in six-inch-Manolo Blahniks, up the gown which sweeps my ankles, over the slit which bares the length of my leg up to almost the top of my thigh, to the flare of my hips which are molded by the glossy material, to where it dips in the front to bare the valley between my breasts. His gaze stays there for a few seconds, and by the time he meets my eyes, I'm flushed to the roots of my hair.

"This wasn't made for someone with my figure," I burst out.

He frowns. "What do you mean?"

"Don't pretend you can't see it."

"Can't see what?"

"This." I gesture to myself. "I'm overweight. I always have been. Nothing I do has helped me get rid of the extra pounds I'm carrying on my body."

He slides his hand inside his pocket, which pulls the fabric across his crotch tight. It outlines the bulge which I'd noticed the time I spilled coffee on him. It only seems bigger… Ugh, I have no business noticing these things about my boss. Except, he's the one who asked me to get myself off… And I obliged.

How am I going to face him in the office tomorrow? How am I going to get through the rest of this evening, for that matter? "Forget it. I changed my mind. I need off this boat. Can you arrange for me to leave, please?" I turn away, but he curls his fingers around my wrist. A flare of sensations run up my arm. My nipples tighten. A thousand little bees have taken up residence under my skin. I sense him draw a sharp breath, then he releases me.

"Look at me."

The authority in his voice forces me to comply. I slowly glance over my shoulder to find he's looking at me with a strange fervor, one that raises the hair on the back of my neck. I'm trapped in the vortex of gold, which are his eyes.

"You are the most beautiful woman I've ever seen, and I don't say that lightly."

"Oh." I swallow.

"You're a real woman, earthy, sexy, voluptuous."

"You mean, I'm fat." I swallow.

"I mean, you're gorgeous. You're curvy, shapely, full-figured, as Mother Nature intended you to be. The swell of your hips mirrors the beauty of spring, the dip of your waist and the thrust of your tits, hint at the passion within, your luscious thighs promise that softness which is your appeal. Your eyes, your lips, your flushed cheeks, your every inch radiates the appeal of a siren calling to every man in the vicinity."

"Everyone, except you."

"Especially me." His throat moves as he swallows. He raises his arm, then pauses, before curling his fingers into a fist and tucking it back into his side. "You're perfect as you are, and never let me catch you saying otherwise."

I hold his gaze and sense the seriousness in his eyes, the sincerity writ in every hard angle of his body, the honesty which laces his expression and I know he means everything he said. "Thank you," I say softly.

He nods. Then slides his hand into his pocket and holds up a strip of leather with a circular disc in the center. "What's that?"

"Turn around."

I do so without hesitation, his earlier words having cut through any doubts I might have had about coming on board this yacht. He places the piece of leather around my throat and hooks it at the nape of my neck. I see our reflection in the mirror on the wall ahead, and the bees under my skin seem to take wing. Edward, in his black three-piece suit and golden tie is the perfect foil for the flaxen color of my dress. He's tall, stern, all straight lines and angles and dark shadows. I'm a glittering, glowing, shining bundle of sparks. His fingers brush my neck, and goosebumps crowd my skin. He looks up and meets my gaze in the mirror. The air thickens, pulsing with unsaid emotions. There's a wrinkle between his eyebrows as he peruses our reflection. I touch the engraving on the disc that nestles at my throat. "Is this a—"

"Fallen angel," he nods.

"It's pretty," I muse.

"It's essential, so everyone here knows you're mine."

A hot sensation stabs into my chest. "I'm y-yours?"

"For the next few hours. It's necessary."

"Necessary?" I frown. "Why would it be necessary?

"You told me it was necessary, not that it was a collar."

We're in the grand hall of the yacht. The light is low, and there's music on in the background. It's very faint and rhythmic, and filled with pounding, pulsing beats which surround me in an intimate, soothing, yet edgy ambiance. He led me through the hall without touching me, but making sure I was close to him at all times. We passed a few couples, and the men eyed me with interest, until their gazes alighted on the band around my neck. At which point, they turned their attention away. That's when I'd realized the necklace signified possession. I should have felt like an object—I *did* feel like an object—but I was being seen as *his* object, and somehow, that gave me pause.

Edward ushered me to a couch in a corner. A waiter served us. A glass of sparkling water for me and a glass of whiskey for him. When I asked for alcohol, he said he preferred me to have my wits about me. Which wasn't exactly reassuring. Also, I didn't notice him giving the waiter an order which means he must have messaged ahead.

Before I can ask him about it, I notice a woman halfway across the room. She's on her knees, next to a man who's seated on a couch. He's talking to a woman in a leather jumpsuit.

The kneeling woman has a strip of leather around her neck with a circular disc on the side. That's where the resemblance to my accoutrement stops. There's a chain hooked to her choker, the other end of which is in the hand of the man next to her. He's talking to the leather clad woman while she stays with her chin lowered to her chest. She's motionless, but for the rise and fall of her chest. She's wearing far less than me, and her skirt rides up high, enough for me to see the moisture glistening on her inner thighs. My face grows hot. She's aroused. And I'm embarrassed on her behalf.

"You don't need to be embarrassed. She's content." He takes a sip of his whiskey.

"How would you know?"

"Look at her face. What do you see?" He places his glass on the table in front of us.

"It's not polite to stare." The words come out in a prim tone, and I wince. The gap between me and this man has never seemed as insurmountable as now in this space. A very exclusive space which you have to be invited to, and only if you are of a certain profile, or so Edward informed me earlier. It's not about the money you have. It's about your ability to be discrete. Everyone here trades in something which entitles them to be here. When I asked Edward what he bartered, he stayed silent. I didn't bother to pursue that line of questioning. See? I'm learning fast. He only answers if he wants to, and he can't be swayed. I can only speculate, so I decided not to waste my time on it. I was too busy taking in the scene around me.

"She wants you to stare at her. She wants the world to know she belongs to him."

"You're a man. Of course, you'd say that."

He blows out a breath. "You're just like the rest—quick to pass judgement. Quick to view everything through a narrow moral compass, when the world is much more complex."

"You should know. You're the one who turned your back on your calling, after all."

His entire body goes rigid. The tension that always seems to cling to him intensifies. The static in the air shoots up, and the hair on the back of my neck straightens. "I'm sorry," I whisper without meeting his gaze, "that was uncalled for."

"Life is complex, Belle. It's not what you expect it to be. You think you have it all planned out, and then something happens that destroys everything you believed in. Suddenly, your past and the choices you made haunt you. The future's a long road, with an end you cannot see. And your present? It digs its claws into you and refuses to let go, no matter how painful your everyday is."

Tears prick the backs of my eyes. A ball of emotion chokes my throat. The bleakness in his voice drips onto my skin like acid and burns me to the bone.

"What's this?" He reaches forward and scoops up the moisture on my cheek. "Are you crying?"

If I didn't know him better, I'd say his voice carries a note of wonder, but this man is not capable of such emotion. More likely, he's laughing at me. And I'm not going to risk looking at his face to find out.

"Are you, Belle?"

I sniffle. "I didn't mean to. It's just…you sound so lonely."

"I enjoy being on my own."

"Yet here you are." I gesture to the large hall which is now considerably fuller than when we came in.

"This is a way to connect to the only part of me I still recognize."

"Which part?"

'The one I knew I always had but which I refused to acknowledge all that time I was a priest. The one that resulted in my losing everything I once held dear."

I stiffen. "You mean—"

"I mean, you haven't looked at her face and told me what you see yet," he interjects.

Of course, the moment it seems like he's opening up, he has to change the topic. Which is good. I don't want to get to know the man behind the facade. The man who's emotionally wounded. The man who's hurting and refuses to share it with anyone. The man who's an enigma…

Which I want so badly to solve. I focus my attention on the woman who hasn't moved from her perch on the floor. She's been kneeling all this time on the wooden floor without a word of complaint. Her hands are clasped in front of her, her gaze lowered. The light is dim in the space, but there's enough for me to take in her relaxed features. The slight upward turn of her lips. The man next to her runs his fingers through her hair, and she trembles. She licks her lips, and when he drags his knuckles over her cheek, her mouth opens. I'm not close enough to hear it, but I'm sure she's panting. She's even more aroused and she looks "blissful."

"She is."

Only when he replies, do I realize I said the word aloud.

"But he's demeaning her, by making her kneel, and not paying any attention to her," I protest.

"Is he?"

I bring my gaze back to his face and pout. "Of course, he is. She may seem happy, but looks can be deceiving."

"Everyone who is here is here by their own choice."

"But I—" I'm about to say I'm not, but he did give me a choice. And it was my decision to be here, too.

He nods.

"It doesn't seem right. Why should she be chained? Why is he treating her like—"

"His possession?"

His rough voice forming that word turns the flesh between my thighs into molten lava. I begin to cross one leg over the other, but he shakes his head. "Don't."

"Why not?"

"Because I want to smell your cunt."

12

Edward

"What did you say?" she gasps.

"I want to smell your—"

"I heard you," she says hastily, "But did you have to use the C-word?"

"Did it turn you on?"

Her pupils dilate. Her breathing hitches. She seems taken aback, but also, she obeyed me. She's a natural submissive. Doesn't mean she's compliant. And the deepening azure of her blue eyes tells me she's going to deny my statement. She's feisty, likes to stand up for herself, and isn't easily cowed. She's curvy and perfectly formed, but only a fool would take that to mean she's malleable. This woman may not know what she wants yet, but she'll stand up for herself. She's diffident about her figure—but that's only because she doesn't realize how stunning she truly is.

She's spirited, plucky, a ray of light which illuminates those parts deep inside of me that I haven't wanted to examine closely. She…makes me want things I was sure were not in my future. She urges me to ignore the limitations I've put upon myself. She tempts me to break the rules I've decided to live my life by. She…is turning me into someone who's obsessed with her every move, her every breath, her every gesture. She makes me want to find out her every thought, her dreams, her deepest desires…and fulfill them. She makes me want to own her, keep her, possess her, make her *mine.* My belly churns, my heart slams into my ribcage, sweat pools under my armpits, and I rise to my feet. "Come on."

She rises to her feet. I indicate she should follow me. I march across the floor, retracing our steps out the door to the stairs. Taking them two at a time. I reach the landing and wait for her to catch up. She's panting by the time she reaches me. "What's the hurry?"

"You'll see."

I motion for her to go ahead, then curse myself once more when I'm unable to keep my gaze off her luscious behind as she climbs the next set of stairs. The twitch of her butt, the rhythmic sway of her hips, the pull of the fabric across her arse-cheeks, the way her waist flares out to meet her fleshy bottom… My throat closes. My mouth dries. The blood drains to my groin. I reach down and adjust myself, then follow her to the top of the flight of steps. I brush past her, cross the floor and hold open the door on the far end. Her footsteps are soft on the carpet as she approaches. She walks into the room, takes in the rectangular table, the chairs set around it, and the man standing on the far side with his back to us and looking out of the window onto the lights of the city visible in the distance.

"Is that?" She comes to a standstill. "No, it can't be."

I walk past her, pull out a chair. "You'd better sit down for this."

She doesn't take her gaze off of the older man. His shoulders froze when he heard her voice, but he doesn't turn to glance at us.

"Dad?" The color fades from her cheeks. "Is that you?"

He turns and her gaze widens. "What are you doing here?" She swallows.

He looks like he's about to say something, then he shakes his head. "I'm sorry, Mirabelle." His tone is clipped.

"Sorry for what? Why are you in London?"

"Belle, sit down," I order.

She shudders visibly, then manages to tear her gaze off of her father, and walking over, sinks into the chair. I push it in. My fingers graze her shoulder, and goosebumps scatter over her skin. I stay with my head bent, drawing in her sweet apple blossom scent. My cock extends further, and I straighten. This is not the time to be sporting a hard-on, especially not in front of her father. Not that the man particularly cares for her. If he did, he wouldn't have come to an agreement with me.

"What's happening?" She addresses her question to him. "Why are you here?"

"You mean, why is he here in an S&M club?" I drawl.

Her father flinches. His cheeks redden, but he manages to hold his silence. Good thing, too, because nothing he says can justify what he's about to tell her.

"Dad?" she prompts him. "What's going on?"

He rubs at his temple then slowly lowers his hand. "You know, I love you, Mirabelle, don't you?"

"Of course, you're my father." Her tone is impatient.

"And you know I want what's good for you?"

She sits up straighter. "What is it? You're scaring me. Is everything okay? Is it your health? Are you sick? Is that what this is about?"

His features take on a stricken look. "Nothing's wrong with me, honey." He swallows. "I'm here because"—he looks at me, then back at her—"because…"

"If it's not you—" She tilts her head. "Is everything okay back home?"

His features soften. "Only you'd be kindhearted enough to ask after your stepmom and sisters, even after the way they've treated you."

I lean forward, and before I can stop myself the words are out: "What do you mean? How did they treat her?"

"It's nothing." She waves her hand in the air.

"I know I've never openly taken your side, and I apologize for that." His lips turn up in a sad smile before he raises his gaze to mine. "My wife was threatened by Mirabelle from the moment she saw her. And after the birth of our daughters, that sentiment only grew worse."

"Dad, stop," Belle bursts out.

"I'm telling the truth." He glances at her. "It's not like I haven't been aware of how the three of them have tried to make your life miserable over the years."

Every muscle in my body tightens. *Why does it matter to me that she hasn't had an easy life? Why do I feel this angry that someone upset her, that her own family distressed her?* My stomach churns. *Why do I feel her pain like it's my own? If only I'd been able to prevent the emotional scars she carries from her growing years. If only I'd actually been there to help.* I draw myself to my full height. "Your wife and your daughters were unfair to her, and you did nothing?"

The violence in my tone must be evident, for her father holds up his hands. "I accept the blame. I knew they weren't being kind to her. I should have stepped in, but my head wasn't in the right space."

"Of course it wasn't. You'd lost a wife," she interrupts.

"You lost your mother," he replies.

Belle begins to speak again, but he shakes his head. "I thought I was doing the right thing by getting married again. I hoped she would be a stabilizing influence in your life. I was too consumed by my grief to put things right. I hoped to make it up to you by finding the right match for you, but I've failed you again."

The skin across her knuckles whitens. "What do you mean? You said you'd wait until the year was out. You said you'd give me a year to live my own life before you called me home."

He winces. "I said you could live your life until I called on you to come back home."

"And I asked you for a year."

"I never promised that. I agreed to let you go on the condition you'd return when I asked you to."

"Is that why you're here now?"

"I'm here because"—he swallows—"because—"

"Because he's arranged your marriage."

She looks at me, confused. "He has?" She leans back in her chair and locks her fingers together. "Dad? Is this true? Have you...have you decided who I'm going to marry?"

He nods but doesn't raise his gaze.

"Who is it?" she asks in a low voice.

He stays silent.

"Dad, please." She swallows. "Is it...is it someone I know? Is that why you're not speaking? Is it someone I don't like? Is it—"

"It's me."

13

Mira

"What?" I jump up so quickly my chair almost topples over, except he grips it and straightens it.

"What do you mean, it's you?"

He rounds the conference table until he's standing on the opposite side of the room from me.

"You know what I mean."

"No, I don't." I turn on my father who's examining the carpet at his feet, because apparently, that's more interesting than confronting the future that lies ahead for me.

"Dad, what's he saying?"

My father sets his jaw. His lips thin but does he speak? Of course, not.

"Dad? Please, say something, please."

My plea must get through to him for he slowly raises his eyes, and then I wish he hadn't, for the expression on his face confirms my worst fears. "No, no, no, no."

"I'm sorry, Mira." An anguished expression comes over his features. "So sorry."

The fact that my father called me Mira, a name he's eschewed in favor of the more formal Mirabelle, confirms to me everything Edward said is true. That, and the fact my father looks torn. Cyril Young is too set in his ways. Too confident in his ability to make money, to steer the des*tiny* of his company and his employees and his family, to ever show any emotion or resort to niceties. The fact he apologized to me earlier is a sign the deal is done, and while he may not be in favor of it, as evinced by his reluctance to tell me about it, the fact is ,he's here. And we're talking about my future—*my* future—like it's a business transaction.

"How much did he pay for you for the deal?"

My father flinches, but he doesn't deny it. *He. Doesn't. Deny. It.*

"No." I begin to shake my head. "No. No. No." My knees give way. I sink down into the chair, and suddenly, Edward's standing next to me. He snatches up a bottle of water from the table, twists open the cap, pours it into a glass, and offers it to me. "Drink."

I shake my head.

"Belle," he lowers his voice to a hush, then holds the glass to my lips, "drink it. Now."

I take the glass, ensuring not to touch his fingers, then take a sip, another.

"Drink all of it." There's a command in his voice which insists I·obey. I drain the water like the dutiful wife-to-be that I am, then place the glass on the table with a soft thunk. *Is this my future? To obey him? Is that why he's committed to this alliance?*

"Why?" I address my question to my father. "Why him?"

My father's shoulders stiffen. There's a look on his face I can't quite interpret. One that's a mixture of anger and irritation and helplessness. I've never known my father to be helpless. Never known him to be this silent. It's as if he's unable to form the words. "The least you owe me is an explanation."

Next to me, Edward stays motionless. His attention is on me. I feel his gaze on my face like he's run his knuckles down my cheek. Heat suffuses my skin. The hair on the back of my neck rises. It's like I'm caught in a quagmire of emotions that's pulling me under.

"Dad,"—I swallow—"tell me."

He blows out a breath. "I needed the money."

"Money?" Of everything he could have told me, that was not what I expected. "You are a billionaire many times over. Why do you need the money?"

"I *was* a billionaire many times over." He looks away, then back at me. "A few of my investments in the last six months did not deliver the way they should have. I lost a lot of money. Enough that when Chase, here, approached me, I couldn't say no."

"You approached him?" I turn to meet Edward's gaze and flinch. The full impact of those smoldering embers which are his eyes sends a shiver of anticipation—no fear, it has to be fear—down my spine. I see the answer in his expression and a slow burn starts somewhere deep in my belly. "Why?" I clear my throat. "Why me?"

"Why not you?"

"There are so many other women out there. Anyone who would fit the bill and would gladly become your wife."

"I chose you."

Something hot coils in my chest. Satisfaction? Pride that he wants me? I could deny it, but the fact is, a part of me is taken aback that he decided on me—the plus-sized woman who's never had a chance to have a boyfriend, or managed to hold down a job long enough to know what it's like to be independent and live my own life. The woman who never knew the love of a mother. Whose own father decided her only worth was to barter her into an arrangement.

"I didn't choose you." I tip up my chin.

My father exhales sharply. He begins to say something, but Edward shakes his head. My father falls silent. That's a first. I've never seen him not win an argument, but apparently, today is a day for firsts.

The skin around Edward's eyes wrinkles, then a divot appears on the left side of his mouth, which is how I know he's smiling. Yeesh, I've worked for him only a day and I already know how to interpret his expression.

My father shuffles his feet. He begins to say something, when Edward nods his head toward the door without taking his eyes off of my face. "Leave."

"What?" My father blusters.

"You've served your purpose. It's best you go while you're still able to walk."

"Are you threatening me?" my father snaps.

"I should do more than that for your being a silent spectator to the emotional agony she was subjected to. In your home. In front of your eyes."

"B-b-b-but—" my father begins to stutter—another first, I've never heard him stutter, ever — but Edward shuts him down.

"You'd best get gone before I show you just how angry I am. And I don't want to do that, not when it's bound to upset my future wife."

Future wife. Wife? He said WIFE. My breathing grows shallow. Strange tingles make their way down my extremities.

I want to turn and take in the expression on my father's features. I want to see the regret on his face. I want to hear him admit that he did wrong by me. But a part of me is afraid that I wouldn't see that if I looked at him, so I won't. The way he allowed them to treat me is something I've never dared acknowledge to myself before today. Oh, I hoped he'd come to my rescue, that he'd tell my stepmother and half-sisters that I was a part of the family and needed to be treated with respect. I hoped, but never thought the day would come when he'd actually admit he wasn't fair to me. Not only did he do so today, but he also apologized to me.

And it's because this man put him in a position where he was no longer the most powerful man in the room. Where he was beholden to someone else... And you know what? He's beholden to me. I could have refused the wedding, and where would that have left him? I could still refuse the marriage, but that would mean my father would suffer financially. And while I've wanted him to show me his love, even though he never actively defused the situation with my stepmother and sisters, there was never any question he loved me. I can't stand by and let him face financial ruin. Not while I can make a difference and help him. Before this, I've never had the chance to contribute to our family. This is my chance to impact the outcome for my father in a positive fashion. This is my chance to... Marry this man who's fascinated me from the moment I set eyes on him. I don't know him well, but he's not a stranger. As the saying goes, better the devil you know than the one you don't, right?

"Mira, I—"

"You need to leave. Right now," Edward says in a voice which sounds casual but which has a steely undertone to it.

My father hesitates, then I sense him getting a hold of himself. "You'd better take care of her."

"You can bet I'll take a damned sight better care of her than you ever did."

"That's not fair. She's my daughter—"

"She's not yours anymore. She's mine."

14

Edward

Mine. Mine. Mine. The word ricochets around in my mind before swooping down to my chest where it sets off a fireball of sensations. How strange. I've never felt this, alive, this apprehensive, this nervous, and also…angry. I curl my fingers into fists at my sides. *How dare she walk into my life and turn it upside down? How dare she make me feel the emotions I locked out of my life? How dare she stare at me with those big blue eyes with hurt swimming in them and trailing down her cheeks? Fuck!* That ball of sensations in my chest shoots off flames which zip to my fingers, my toes. Every part of my body seems to come alive. Like a seed sprouting through the ground, the individual sentiments make themselves known.

I'm aware of her father walking out of the room. The door snicks shut. I go down on one knee, then scoop up the trail of moisture. I bring it to my mouth and suck on it.

She gasps. "What are you doing?"

"Why are you crying?"

"I'm not." She swats at her cheek. "At least, not on purpose." She bites her bottom lip before whispering, "No one's stood up to my father for me before today."

"I'm sorry for what your family put you through."

"It wasn't that bad." She half smiles. "I had a roof over my head, and designer clothes, and a team of staff who made sure my every need was taken care of."

"Everything except your emotional needs," I murmur. *And what do I know of that? Why am I unable to stop myself from comforting her? You can take the priest out of the church. You can even try to unlearn everything that you stood for by traveling around the world and trying to lose yourself amongst strangers... But it only takes a full-figured goddess with tears in her eyes to bring out that tenderness inside you which you thought you'd managed to wipe out completely.*

"He wasn't a bad father. He was just lost without my mother."

"You're defending the man who signed away your future in return for money?"

"Was it a big amount?" she murmurs.

"A few billion dollars."

"At least, it has a lot of zeroes." She chuckles, but the sound is weak.

"A lot of zeroes," I assure her.

"And you're the one he made the deal with."

"Does that make you angry?" I search her features.

"I'm angry that I'm unable to disobey my father." Her lips tighten. "I'm angry I was born into a family that believes in arranged marriages to further their business interests. I'm angry that the little time I thought I had to be independent and have a normal life was taken from me. As for the rest, I'm confused."

"Confused?" I tilt my head.

"I'm confused you asked me to work for you and you gave me a job. I'm confused how you connected with my father. How you knew he was in trouble, how—" She must notice my expression, for she slowly nods. "Of course, you knew. You have money and power and connections. You knew he was in trouble. You knew you could barter a deal with him."

"I need a wife. And contrary to your declarations, you do need a husband."

"I do not." She scowls.

"If it weren't me, it would be somebody else. Better a man you've already met than a complete stranger."

She blinks, then tips up her chin. "That's what I'm trying to tell myself. But I don't know you, either."

"A problem that's easily solved."

"What do you mean?"

"We'll get to know each other after we're married."

"And love, what about that?"

"I don't believe in love."

"Because you already gave your heart to someone else?"

I narrow my gaze. "I see you've heard about my past from our mutual friends?"

She shakes her head, then stops herself. "Only a little. It wasn't that I asked; it was mentioned in passing that you had your heart broken."

I firm my lips. I want to deny it, but that would be lying. And that's the one thing I don't do. The habit of always telling the truth, no matter the consequences, is one I haven't been able to shake. I settle for not saying anything, which she interprets correctly in the affirmative.

Her forehead wrinkles. "So, what I heard is true."

"My past is of no consequence to you."

"How can you say that when it will impact my future?"

"All you need to know is that your father and I came to an amiable agreement, and he has agreed to my proposal of marrying you."

"Do I have a choice in this?" There's a bitter note in her voice.

"You know the consequences of refusing."

"So, that's a no?"

I rise to my feet then pull out a chair and sink into it. "That's a—this relationship can work to both of our advantages."

"How's that?"

"You'll be my wife in name only."

"Meaning?"

"You'll take my name, you'll marry me, you'll wear my ring on your finger. You'll be civil toward my family. As far as they're concerned, this is a real marriage. But we will not sleep in the same bed."

"We won't?"

"I have no interest in having sex with you."

"You...you don't?"

"I'll take care of my needs...elsewhere."

"You mean in this club?" She gestures to the room.

"I'll be discreet, of course."

"Of course." That bitterness is back in her voice, and for some reason, that bothers me.

"You have no interest in being my wife, Belle. But you want to save your father from bankruptcy. You also need money to keep a roof over your head."

She begins to protest, and I cut in, "You and I both know if I hadn't offered you a job as my assistant, you'd have had to return home. This way, you don't need to stay under the same roof as your family again."

She sets her jaw but doesn't deny the facts.

"I am compelled to get married to ensure my grandfather confirms me as the CEO of his group of companies. This is a win-win, as far as I'm concerned."

"I can only see losses in my future."

"How's that?"

"I'll be stuck in a loveless marriage, with no intimacy. No intimacy,"—her features pale—"which means, no children."

"You want children?" I stare.

"Of course, I want children. The only reason I'd consider this marriage if I could have children." She sets her jaw. "I know this might sound lame, but I've never known a time when I didn't want to be a mother. In fact, it's the reason I decided to pursue a career in childcare. It's one way to be in the company of kids throughout the day. It's probably not the most ambitious of dreams, but—"

"Don't put yourself down. Your dreams are important, and you deserve to give them life."

"I... I do?" Her lips part.

I nod slowly. A soft sensation invades my chest. Belle, big with my child. Belle, playing with my son or daughter, taking them to school, making breakfast for them. Belle, holding him or her in her arms and—I shake my head. "You can still have children."

"How—oh!" The wrinkle in her forehead vanishes. "You mean, by IVF."

"If that's what you decide."

"And if I decide I don't want to be married anymore?"

I lean forward in my seat. "I'm afraid that's not possible."

"Meaning?"

"Once you marry me, you can't leave me. You'll be mine for the rest of your life."

"So, I marry you and that's it. I'm stuck with you?"

"Don't overwhelm me with your enthusiasm," I drawl.

She flushes. "You know what I mean. One day, I don't know you.

The next, you're my boss. And now, you're saying you want to be my husband, but not in the true sense of the word."

"There are worse options out there."

"So you keep saying."

"I'll make sure you have your independence. You can continue to work for me."

She frowns. "But wouldn't that be conflict of interest?"

"It's my company." I raise a shoulder. "Besides, we'll be married only in name, so—"

"So—" She swallows. "No sex."

"None."

"And I can stay in my own flat?"

"You're my wife; you'll have to move in with me. We'll share the same suite—"

"But—"

"We'll have our own rooms."

"So we won't share the same bed?" she says slowly.

"I sleep best on my own."

She locks her fingers together. "Can I think about it?"

"Afraid time is running out." I pull back the sleeve of my shirt and look at my watch. "My grandfather wants me married within the week."

"The week?" she squeaks.

"Is that a problem?"

"It's just… Things are moving very quickly, and I haven't said 'yes' yet."

Not that she has a choice, given her father has already committed her to the marriage. She knows it. I know it. But I'm enough of a gentleman to play along...for now. If an illusion of having a choice is what it takes for her to say yes, then I'm more than happy to humor her.

I tap my fingers on my thigh. "What are you waiting for?"

"I... I have some questions." She shuffles her feet.

"Shoot." I settle back in my seat.

"Why did you bring me to this club?"

"So you'd be aware of the inclinations of the man you'll be marrying."

"You mean BDSM?"

Not bad, she managed to get out the words without fumbling over the vocabulary.

"Among other things."

"You wanted to show me your needs are…a little extreme?"

I can't stop my lips from twitching. "Those are your words, not mine."

"So this was a test?"

"Maybe?" I yawn.

"Why hire me as your assistant?" The wrinkle between her eyebrows deepens.

I want to lean forward and smooth out her brow a-n-d nope, not going there. *Why do I feel so compelled to soothe away her worries?* I set my jaw. "I told you already. You needed a job. I did need an assistant. Besides, what better way for you to find out more about my habits than working with me in such close proximity?"

She rubs at her temple. "But when did you decide you wanted to marry me? Did you know about my father having business troubles already? Did you—" She searches my face. "You knew who I was when we met at Gio's place."

I nod.

She firms her lips. "You've been planning this since then?"

"When I met you, I needed an assistant. You're trusted by my friends. And I trust my friends, so it felt right to offer you the job. Turns out, I also need a wife, and—"

"You decided I fit that role, too?"

I wipe my thumb under my lower lip. "You're single. And when I had you investigated, I realized who you were."

"So, all the pieces fell together," she says flatly.

"It seemed the logical next step. You'll have to sign a contract, of course."

"I… I do?"

I nod. "Only you and I will know the real state of this marriage. To everyone else, we decided to get married because we're in love."

"So we met, and you decided I was the one, and we got married within a week?" She scoffs.

"When you know, you know." The words come out with more certainty than I intended. And for some reason I believe it, too.

She must, too, for her eyes widen. "You sure you used to be a priest and not an actor?"

I tilt my head. "A priest has to be an actor to take the pulpit, and an actor might well be a priest when he's on screen."

"How do you mean?"

"An actor is the mirror of the audience's desires. He or she accepts it without judgement, and in turn, grants them absolution."

She searches my features and hers soften. "Also a poet."

I hold her gaze and ensure my own are steely. "You must be mistaken."

She looks at me a second longer, then nods. "I must be."

I reach for my phone and message a number, then slide it back into the pocket of my suit. "The contract is for everything I outlined, including a non-disclosure agreement. Everything I've told you today is confidential."

"So you don't trust me?" She scoffs.

"I asked you to marry me, didn't I?"

"Only because I happened to be convenient. Not to mention, you had leverage over me." She wraps her arms about her waist.

"The NDA is a deterrent. So, if you're tempted to tell your friends, it will stop you."

She jerks her chin up, and I take in the guilt in her eyes.

"It's normal for you to want to consult with someone else on this, but I'm afraid I can't allow that."

"You can't?"

I shake my head. "Time is of the essence. As is the timing. I understand it's all sudden, but you need to trust me on this."

"How can I trust you when you used my father's circumstances to coerce me into a wedding?"

"You can leave, of course."

"We both know that's not an option." Her lips turn down. Her eyes grow haunted.

I want to go over and pull her into my arms and tell her everything is going to be okay. But that would be lying. And I don't say anything I don't mean. *Also, why am I so affected by her?* All the more reason to get through this sham of a wedding, make sure my grandfather and half-siblings believe in the veracity of my marriage, and then I can get on with my life.

There's a knock on the door, and a suited man walks in. He looks between us, then places an envelope in front of me. I nod, and he leaves.

She stares at the envelope with a look of apprehension. "What's that?"

"The agreement outlining our marriage of convenience." I pull a pen from the inside pocket of my jacket, then slip a sheaf of papers from the envelope and slide them over to her.

"Do I have to sign this right now?"

15

Mira

"You're marrying him?" Abby pales. "You barely know him."

I glance out at the pouring rain. It's a Saturday, so I didn't have to go to work. Gotta hand it to Edward. He planned it out so we didn't have to meet at work this morning. He gave me eighteen hours to arrive at a decision. Eighteen hours to make a decision that's going to impact the rest of my life. Should I be grateful he gave me this much time? Or is this a way for him to pander to me, safe in the knowledge I'm going to comply? Definitely the latter. Edward's too smart. He knows I will agree to his proposition. He knows I don't have a choice in the matter. This—giving me a few hours—is him creating an illusion I am in control when I'm not. A chance for things to sink in, so I'll go into this arrangement more willingly.

"Are you sure about this?" Summer asks quietly.

No. But of course, I can't tell her that.

The girls are in my tiny apartment. Abby and Summer are on the couch. Penny, has taken the sole armchair, and Gio's pulled up one of the barstools from the kitchenette. I've been too restless to sit still. I was moved that my girlfriends turned up so quickly, but I also knew it would be pointless telling them I was okay when it was clear from the expression on my face that I'm not.

Edward dropped me off at my apartment building yesterday. Neither of us spoke a word. He focused on driving, and I focused on trying to get my thoughts together. I barely slept last night. When dawn broke, I made myself a cup of tea and wondered how I was going to get through the coming few days. *How am I going to get through my life?*

Other than my father, the rest of my family won't care about my marriage. I want to talk things through with my friends, but I signed the agreement last night, which means, I have to keep the details confidential. The minutes ticked on, and with every passing hour, my panic increased. When Gio called me, I tried to appear normal, but she must have seen something in my expression because the next thing I knew, she was at my doorstop, followed by Abby, Summer, and Penny.

"His proposal was very sudden," I murmur.

"No shit. I knew he was up to something when you spilled coffee on him, and he responded by asking you to work for him. And now he wants to marry you." Gio looks at me with suspicion. "Is he holding something over you? Is that why you agreed to be his wife?"

I glance away, not wanting her to see the confusion in my eyes. Edward is one hell of a good actor, but I can't say the same about myself. And these are my friends. And now, I'm lying to them.

"It's nothing like that. I...uh... I fell in love with him. It's why I'm marrying him."

"You met him a week ago," Gio points out..

"It was love at first sight." I hear the defensiveness in my voice and wince. That isn't very convincing. Judging by the silence behind me, none of my friends believe me, either.

"If you're in trouble, you can tell us," Penny says in a soft voice. "We can help you. Our husbands—"

"Wouldn't hesitate to use their billions to rescue me from a sticky situation, I'm aware." I turn to face them. "And I appreciate the offer. But honestly, it's nothing of that sort. He... He loves me." *Don't look away. Don't look away.* I lower my eyelashes, and Gio instantly jumps to her feet.

"You expect us to believe that grumpass took one look at you and decided you were going to be his wife?" She stabs a finger in my direction.

I raise my gaze to hers and nod firmly. In this, at least, I'm not lying. The truth in my eyes must convince Gio, for she seems taken aback.

"It's not that I don't believe in insta-love. I'm the living embodiment of it, after all, but getting married to him within the week you go to work for him?" She shakes her head.

"I know it's a little rushed—"

"Try very rushed." Gio scowls.

"Give the girl a chance to speak," Abby admonishes her.

Gio firms her lips but continues to stare at me with a speculative look in her eyes.

"Is this what you want?" Summer searches my features. "Is it, Mira? Because if you have your heart set on it, then of course, we're in your corner."

"But if that asshat is holding something over you—" Gio begins.

"Didn't you agree when Rick asked you to marry him? And you knew him for a short period of time.

"I met him months before he asked, but yes, I only got to know him properly for a week before I agreed." She tosses her hair over her shoulder. "I suppose, I shouldn't be lecturing you about the need for caution, but I worry about you, Mira. You're—"

"Innocent?"

"In a good way. You're the best of us. You have a heart that is swayed so easily."

"Doesn't mean I'm stupid." I set my jaw.

"I didn't say that. I only mean, you lead with your emotions. You're the woman who volunteers at the senior citizen's center when you're not taking care of kids at the preschool."

"Nothing wrong with volunteering." I tip up my chin.

"But you went above and beyond the call of duty. You started a knitting club so those old ladies had something to look forward to."

"Only because they love reading smut, as do I."

"Wait, you started a smut club for grannies?" Penny gapes.

"And one grandpa, if you want to be accurate, but yes. We meet weekly and knit and talk about spicy books. You should hear them. Their vocabulary of four-letter words puts the rest of us to shame."

Gio chuckles. "That's what I mean. You're smart and sexy. You light up any room you walk into, Mira. While Edward—" She shakes her head. "Is not the easiest man to be with."

"Maybe that's why they work," Penny says slowly.

Silence descends.

"What?" She looks around the room. "It's why Knight and I are so good together. He's a grumpy-face, and I can't stop myself from having a smile on mine" She curves her lips to demonstrate.

"It *is* probably why I'm so attracted to him," I admit.

"Hmm." Gio shifts her weight from foot to foot. "Edward's a complex man."

"That's putting it lightly." I half laugh.

Abby taps the arm of the couch. "I think we all agree that our relationships with our respective husbands did not begin in the most traditional of ways—"

"—but it turned out well, and we're very happy," Abby murmurs.

"Blissfully." Summer nods.

"Doesn't mean you have to agree to marry him," Gio points out.

I set my jaw. "But what if I want to?"

"Do you?" Summer asks.

I nod slowly.

"If you do, then make sure you negotiate with him, before the wedding." Gio brushes off a speck of dirt from her Prada jacket. "Make sure you get what you want out of it before giving in to him."

"Like what?"

"Money? Houses. Whatever you want out of it."

"But how—" A knock on the door interrupts me. I glance toward it; so do the girls.

"Don't you have an intercom system?" Penny frowns.

"I do." I begin to walk toward the door when whoever is at the door knocks on it again. I look toward the peephole, then step back and pivot around to face them. "It's him."

"Who?" Gio asks.

"Edward," I whisper. Not that he can hear my voice through the door, but he's right there on the other side of it. "What should I do?" I wring my hands. "I'm not ready to see him.

"Belle?" He bangs on the door again. "I know you're in there."

I freeze, and I'm sure the look on my face is that of pure panic, for Gio rises to her feet. She marches past me and grips the door handle, before turning to me. "Should I tell him to leave?"

I shake my head.

She sighs. "You want me to buy you some time?"

I nod.

"Why don't you go on into the bedroom?"

"Thank you" I race past the other girls.

Behind me, I hear her throw open the door. "Edward, what are you doing here?"

16

Edward

"I'm here for Mira."

"Hmm." Gio purses her lips. "What are your intentions toward her."

I glance past her to where the other women look at me with varying expressions of displeasure and mistrust.

"Can I come in?" I hold up my hands. "I mean no harm."

"That's debatable." She purses her lips, then finally, stands aside.

I stalk past her and into the center of the rom. "Ladies." I tilt my head. "I'm glad Mira has friends looking out for her."

"Can we say the same about you?" Summer asks in a serious tone.

Of everyone in this room, I've known her the longest. I attended her wedding to Sinclair. I've seen the bond between them grow. Sinclair loves her more than his own life, and she reciprocates their sentiment. She's aware of my past. Of the incident that binds Sinclair and me and the rest of the Seven together. No one else in my family knows the true extent to which that incident scarred me. It's a secret, known to us, and now the wives of the Seven.

I keep my arms loose at my sides and nod. "You can."

I hold her gaze, and she must read the sincerity in my eyes, for her shoulders relax.

"She's my friend, Ed," Summer murmurs.

"I'm aware."

"Don't hurt her."

"I won't," I hear the vehemence in my tone. "I'll do everything to protect her."

"Including from yourself?"

I blink. *That's the plan.* The problem is, when I'm around her, I don't act in character. I tend to become unpredictable and unable to keep my gaze off of her. I'm also not able to stop my mind from wondering how it would be to have her under me, to bury myself in her softness, to have her scent wipe away the images from my past, to allow her voice to lead me out of the maze I am stuck in.

And I can't allow that to happen. I can't let myself fall for her. "I'll do everything in my power to give her what she needs."

She frowns. "That doesn't answer my question."

I square my shoulders. "Her happiness is important to me. I will ensure she is taken care of, that she wants for nothing, that all her wants are met—"

"Including her emotional ones?"

I hesitate. "I will do everything in my capacity to give her what she needs."

Summer rises to her feet and walks over to stand in front of me. She scans my features. "I know you've been through a lot, Ed. You deserve a chance at happiness. Mira can be the catalyst to help you move forward with your life, if you'll let her."

That's what I'm afraid of. That's what I have to guard myself against happening. I incline my head. "Do I have your blessings?"

She looks between my eyes, then nods slowly.

"If you do anything to upset her, you'll have me to contend with," Gio snaps.

"And me." Penny stabs her forefinger and middle finger in the direction of her eyes, then at me.

"And me." Abby gives me a considering look from the couch.

I look between the women and nod. "You won't need to because I'd punish myself if I did anything to make her unhappy. Now, can I go in and see my wife-to-be?"

Gio stalks past me, and raps on the bedroom door. "You ready to meet this asshat, honey?"

A few seconds pass, then the door opens. Mira stands in the doorway. She turns without meeting my eyes and walks away. I move past Gio, step inside the room, and shut the door behind me. I lean against it, cross my arms over my chest, and watch as she stands at the window with her back to me.

"I have a surprise for you."

She stiffens.

"Don't you want to know what it is?"

She shakes her head.

I stalk toward her. She hears me approaching and stiffens but doesn't turn to look at me. I pause behind her; then, because I can't stop myself, I lean in and sniff her hair.

She turns and stares at me. "Did you sniff me?"

Busted. "Me? Do I look like the kind of man who'd sniff you?"

The skin between her eyebrows wrinkles. She looks uncertain, but at least, she's looking at me.

"You said you have a surprise?"

I hold out my hand, palm face-up. She looks at it warily.

"I promise, I won't bite." *Yet.*

She places her left palm in mine with reluctance. I slide my other hand into my pocket, pull out a ring, and slide it onto her ring finger.

"Oh, my god, is that… Is that a—"

"Engagement ring."

She swallows, then slowly raises her hand. She tilts it this way and that. The light from the window bounces off the sapphire in the center. The diamonds surrounding it reflect the blue. Together they deepen the color of her eyes into a shade you'd only find in the depths of the Mediterranean.

"It's gorgeous." Her chest rises and falls. "And it fits."

"Of course, it does."

She looks up at me. "How did you know my size?"

"You are mine. I know everything about you."

The skin at the corners of her eyes crinkles. She scrutinizes my features like she's trying to solve a puzzle, then her forehead smoothens. "It's because you need to convince your family our marriage is real."

It's because I have this compelling need to know everything about you. What makes you smile; what makes you laugh? What makes you worried or scared?

What you like; what you hate? Why you always manage to bring the sunshine with you wherever you go? "Can't slip up. This is my one chance to make sure my grandfather confirms me as the CEO of the company."

"Is that so important to you?"

"Is that a question?"

She opens, then shuts her mouth. "Money isn't everything. Nor power. There's more to life than just trying to build your business empire."

"Been there, done that. All there is to life is money and power. It's what allows you to control your future."

"You don't believe that."

I incline my head.

She searches my features, then lowers her hand to her side. "Just because you had your heart broken once—"

"That is not up for discussion," I growl.

Hurt flares in her eyes.

My heart stutters. I'm unable to guard myself against her responses. I want to draw her close and tell her everything, and then what? I'll never break my vow to not allow anyone else in my life again. It's not right to give her false hope when I intend to always keep that emotional distance between us. I firm my lips.

She takes in the expression on my face, then squares her shoulders. "I am going to be your wife—"

"Fake wife."

"But real in front of everyone else."

"What's your point?"

"I need to know enough about you so I can ensure no one, especially your family, can question our relationship." She thrusts out her lower lip in that expression I'm coming to recognize as stubbornness, and damn, if that doesn't make me want to close my mouth over hers, dig my teeth into her lower lip and—

I clamp down on my errant thoughts. "You're right."

"I am?"

I nod. "It's why you're moving in with me."

17

Mira

"This is your room. Mine is next door; the ensuite connects both rooms."
He stands at the entrance to the bedroom, one hand braced on the door-
frame. It's a posture that declares his masculinity in no uncertain terms.
When he said I needed to move in with him 'right now,' he meant it. He
coerced me to pack what I needed in an overnight bag. He assured me
the rest of my stuff would be sent over soon.

Then, he hustled me past my friends, who looked at us open-
mouthed in surprise. He gave me just enough time to tell them I was
fine, and that I was relocating to his place until the wedding, which is in
approximately five days. Gio spotted the engagement ring. When she
pointed it out, my friends gathered around me while Edward waited
nearby, impatience writ in every angle of his body. Abby congratulated
me, and Summer said she couldn't wait to help me choose my wedding
dress. She's also recommended a wedding planner, who she said would
contact me. Penny said her friend, Amelie's company would do the
catering.

Only Gio remained unconvinced. She made me promise to call her if

I need any help. I hugged them all, managed to keep the tears from falling, and left with Edward.

And I know, he mentioned we'd have separate rooms, but looking around the space, which is almost as big as my entire one-bedroom, I'm overwhelmed. I'm getting married in a few days, to a man I don't know. And no one except me, him, and my father knows why. A shiver grips me, and I wrap my arms about my waist.

I hear footsteps, and the next thing I know, he's draped his jacket over my shoulders. The scent of woodsmoke and that faint tingle of electricity surrounds me at once. It's as if I'm surrounded by Edward. I'm not sure if I like him, but I could bottle his scent and sniff it all day. Not that I'll ever admit that to him. I snuggle into his jacket. The weight of his hand on my shoulders sends a flush of heat over my skin. I shiver again.

"You're cold. I'll turn up the heating in the room."

"No, I'm good, I—" I begin to protest, then turn to find he's pulled out his phone.

He plays with the screen. "All done."

"You're able to control the temperature of my room with your phone?"

He raises a shoulder. "I want to be sure you're comfortable."

"Right."

"I'll give you a tour of the apartment tomorrow."

"I wouldn't have envisioned you living in a penthouse." I nod toward the lights of the city which shine outside the floor-to-ceiling window.

"Why not?"

"You seem like a man who values history. I thought you'd live in a Victorian townhouse. Or in a heritage building."

A strange look comes into his eyes, then he banks it. "You don't know me at all."

"Which is why you asked me to move in with you before the wedding, so we can get to know each other."

He tilts his head.

"When do we meet your family?"

"Tomorrow."

"What?" I gape. "I… I'm not ready."

"You'll be fine."

"Easy for you say. You're not the one on display."

His features soften. "My grandfather will be relieved I'm settling down. As for my half-brothers, their opinions don't count."

"How can you say that. Aren't they family?"

"I'm the odd one out."

"Why is that?"

"Their father, who is also my biological father, didn't know of my existence until a few months ago. My mother fell pregnant with his child, but never told him. She broke up with him and married my uncle, his older brother, who adopted me. My adoptive father was estranged from his family. He changed his surname to his mother's—"

"Hence, your surname is Chase, while your family surname is Davenport."

He nods. "My grandfather, Arthur, found out about my existence a few months ago. He realized I was his oldest grandson and wanted me to take over as the CEO of the family."

"And you agreed."

"I want to make him happy." He raises a shoulder.

"You also need a goal, a focus in your life, and this gives you an anchor."

Once more, that strange look flickers in his eyes—it's a combination of puzzlement and surprise. Once more, he banks it, and his features take on that mask of polite disinterest. The one I'm coming to hate.

"If this is going to work, you have to be truthful with me."

"Are you accusing me of lying?" he asks in a low, hard voice. My core instantly clenches. My nipples perk up. When he uses that voice, it's as if he flips a switch somewhere deep inside me that controls my feelings of arousal.

"You don't lie, Edward."

He blinks.

"But you *are* evasive."

His gaze grows hard.

"I know the episode in your childhood hurt you, and then—"

"What do you know about the episode?" That uncompromising tone of his voice is like a diamond edge.

I manage not to flinch, manage to tip up my chin and peer into his face. "Just that it affected you and your friends. I don't know any of the details."

He searches my features, then slowly nods. "I'm not ready to talk about it."

"I understand."

"Do you?" He sets his jaw.

"Of course, I do. You're not a sharing kind of person. So, for you to say that you're willing to allow me to get to know you is huge. You're not as beyond redemption as you think you are."

A muscle pulses at his temple. "And you're the one who's going to redeem me?"

"I am going to be your wife."

"Only in name."

"So you keep telling me. It's as if you're trying to convince yourself." I look between his eyes. "Is that what this is about? Are you worried you're going to fall for me, Edward?"

His features shutter.

"Are you?" I ask again.

He sets his jaw and shoves his hand into the pocket of his well-cut pants in a gesture I'm beginning to see as a tell. "I will not fall in love."

"Will not?"

"I took a vow after my last...run-in with that particular emotion... that I won't allow it in my life again."

"You took a vow?" I ask in a dazed voice.

"Love is not for me."

"But you do love your friends. I know you're close to Sinclair and the rest of the Seven."

He nods slowly. "The seven of us have been through a lot. We have a bond that cannot be broken. I suppose, I do have a depth of feeling for them. Is it love?" He raises a shoulder. "Maybe. As for romantic love? That will not figure in my life again."

"Why is that? Don't you owe it to yourself to be happy? Don't you—"

"I promised myself not to fall for anyone again."

I gape. "You promised yourself?"

"And that's all you need to know."

"Wait, that's not fair. You—"

The door is pushed open, and Tiny pops his big head around the corner. He looks between us, then shoves the door open the rest of the way. He walks into the room, past Edward and plants his rump near me. He looks up at me with his melting brown eyes—so different from my fiancé's. Tiny may be a mutt, but there's something in his eyes that's heartfelt and soft, like he carries his heart in his eyes. My fiancé, on the other hand? Carries his emotions buried behind so many walls… And while I may have seen some flickers of emotion in his gaze, they've been few and far between. As if sensing the turn my thoughts have taken, Tiny makes a whining noise.

"Aww, did you miss Eddie? Is that why you're here?" I reach over and scratch Tiny behind his ears. He makes a purring sound and leans into my touch.

"Did you call me, Eddie?" His voice is shocked.

I risk a look at his face and find an incredulous expression there. It's so unexpected, I laugh. Tiny lets out a small bark at that. "He agrees." I nod.

"Agrees with what?"

"That it's the first time I'm seeing you taken aback."

"Hmph." He firms his lips and schools his features back into that emotionless mask.

"You don't fool me." I point my forefinger at him.

"Do I want to know what you mean by that?"

"Just that you're not as impassive as you make yourself out to be."

He seems taken aback, again, then inclines his head. "I decided a while ago there was no place for feelings in my life."

"We've established you feel something for your friends and also, for Tiny here."

Tiny woofs, then turns his soulful gaze on Edward. My fiancé scowls at the dog, then sighs. "Yeah, okay, that mutt has a hold of my heart. But that's it. There is no space for anyone else in my life."

Nice. Now I'm in queue behind a dog. No matter, it's a Great Dane who's so intelligent he might well be almost human, I'm not as important as he is to Edward. He must realize how his words sound, for he stiffens. "I didn't mean —"

"You did."

"You are my fiancée," he offers.

"Fake fiancée."

"Real to the outside world."

"But it's a charade."

"It is," he agrees.

"Okay." A heaviness tightens my chest. I wrap my arms about my waist, feeling so very lonely.

I thought when I got married, even if it was an arranged marriage as my father wanted, perhaps, I'd find companionship in it. Perhaps, I'd have my children make up for the loss of a true partner. And sure, I could technically still have kids, but the entire process is going to feel so clinical. I hadn't thought as far as sex with my future arranged husband... But maybe, a part of me had hoped he'd fall in love with me. That we could find love on the heels of the arrangement. Guess I was wrong. Tears prick the backs of my eyes. I look away. Tiny senses my sadness, and rising up on his feet, he brushes his head gently against my hand. I pat his head, then give in and lean forward to kiss his shaggy head.

Edward clears his throat and I look up. He has strange expression on his face but I'm too exhausted to decode it.

"What time do we leave tomorrow?"

18

Edward

"May I take your coat, Sir? Madam?" Otis, my grandfather's butler looks between me and my fiancée. I slide my coat off and hand it to him, then ease Mira's coat from her shoulders. I place it over his arm.

"This way please." He gestures toward the hallway that leads to the dining room.

"I can see myself in, Otis. Thank you."

He seems taken aback, then nods. "Of course, Sir."

I barely slept last night. And when I finally fell asleep, it was to images from my past. I broke my vows, walked away from my calling. I'd searched for that elusive peace, which I'd fooled myself into believing I had when I was part of the church. It's only after I left, I realized I'd been running all my life.

I'm still running now—except I've come up against a woman who threatens to stop me in my tracks. I don't like it. It's a feeling I don't relish. I don't want to be faced with the proof of my own vulnerability. And all it took was a pair of baby blues and a lusciously curvy figure on a woman who's all sunshine and rainbows, despite her own unhappy past. A woman who places the happiness of her father before her own.

What kind of person would push her dreams aside and bow to the call of duty? She reminds me of the man I thought I was. The man who put his vocation before anything else; the man who believed in the greater good; the man who wanted to redeem others.

He walks into the cloak room adjoining the hallway, leaving Mira and me alone. She glances up at the ceiling, which is three stories above us. The skylights are dark, but in the mornings, light pours into the entryway. In the center, two staircases curve toward each other to meet on the second-floor landing. Above that, the rooms on the third floor look down on the entryway. A massive chandelier descends from the roof, and the lights shine off the stained glass that adorns the windows on the first floor. The floor is made of marble, and there are satin drapes on the walls, interspersed with paintings of some of the great masters — all originals. The overall effect is that of wealth — the kind that has been in a family for generations. My parents weren't poor — not materially — but my grandfather's wealth makes them look like small business owners.

"I forgot it's almost Christmas." Mira walks toward the Christmas tree set between the two staircases. The focal point of the entranceway, it's almost as high as the roof and is lit up with Christmas lights and ornaments. The scent of pine is heavy in the air, but as I approach her, I detect her light, apple-blossom perfume below it. I come to a stop behind her, then lower my head and discreetly sniff. She doesn't notice it, too intent on taking in the decorations.

"It's gorgeous," she murmurs.

"It is," I murmur, looking at her.

"I loved opening my gift on Christmas morning. It was the one time my father was around, and I knew he'd always have something I loved."

"Gift?"

She turns to me. "Yes, my father would buy me a gift."

"What about your —"

"Stepmother?" She shrugs. "We always pretended it was from her too, but it was obvious she never gave me much thought. Given a choice, she'd have sent me off to boarding school so I wouldn't be around, and definitely not for Christmas morning. But it was the one thing my father refused to agree to. He'd promised my mother he'd keep me close. He also knew how much my mother had loved Christmas. And while he never had time for me otherwise, he made sure I knew I was loved during Christmas. What about you? Do you love Christmas?"

"I don't believe in Christmas."

There was a time when I did, but when I left the priesthood, I also turned my back on the rituals, and that's all Christmas really is.

"What?" She pivots to face me. "Are you serious?" She sees the expression on my face and her jaw drops. "You are serious."

"Always."

"You don't say?" she says in a droll voice.

"It's the one time of the year I ensure I'm away from this city."

"Christmas is the best time of the year in London. I arrived in this city last December and found it all lit up. There were decorations up in shop windows, the pubs were festive, people on the tube smiled at each other. I thought it was the most cheerful place on earth. Then came January, and I realized it's the only time of the year people walk around with smiles. But my first impressions remained. I ended up falling in love with the city anyway. Now I can't wait for December and the festive season. It's the one time of the year everyone in London seems almost happy."

"Exactly."

"Jeez"—she shakes her head—"should've guessed you're a Grinch."

"He's a chip off the old block, all right." Arthur's voice reaches us. Then my grandfather draws abreast.

"Edward." He nods at me.

"Arthur." I nod back.

"You made it."

I half smile. You don't turn the old man down. I haven't known Arthur Davenport that long, but even if he hadn't been my grandfather, his authority is writ large in everything he says and does. He's not the kind of man you say no to easily.

"You must be Mirabelle." He turns to Belle.

"Grandad." She closes the distance to him and throws her arms about his shoulders. "I am so happy to meet you."

Arthur stiffens. His gaze widens, and he gapes at me. If I didn't know better, I'd say the old man is shocked. And it takes a lot to shock him. I manage to keep the smile off my face, then watch as my grandfather recovers himself. He pats Belle on the shoulder. "It's nice to meet you, too."

She steps back and beams up at him. "Call me, Mira."

"Hmm." He scans her features. "I can see why Edward fell in love with you."

"Oh, but he's not—" she begins.

I cut her off. "I hope we didn't keep you waiting."

"You did"—he shoots me a glance—"but since you were showing Mira around, you're forgiven."

Belle laughs, a happy sound that infuses warmth into my veins.

"When Edward told me he was getting married, I was sure he'd decided to ask the first eligible woman he came across to be his wife. I'm relieved to see he's been much more discerning."

"Umm—" She shuffle her feet. "I... We...."

"We're very in love, Grandad. When I saw Mira, there was no question I was going to marry her. Your condition that I get married before I can be confirmed in my role as CEO spurred me to pop the question."

Arthur holds out his right hand, and when Belle places her left palm in it, he raises her fingers and kisses her engagement ring. "You gave her the ring your grandmother left you?"

"This is your grandmother's ring?" She glances at me in shock.

"It's the reason I found out about his existence," Arthur adds.

She tears her gaze away from mine and frowns. "I'm not sure I understand."

Arthur hooks her arm through his, then leads her down the hallway. I bracket her in from the other side.

"When my wife passed away last year, I was gutted."

"I'm so sorry for your loss," she murmurs.

I shoot him a glance in time to see his eyes shadow. "Thank you. I appreciate it. Greta and I were married for fifty-five years."

Her gaze widens until those blue eyes seem to fill her face.

"Seems like a long time, but it went by in a flash." Arthur's lips curve. *Holy shit, the old man smiled?* In the little time I've known him, I've never seen the hint of softness on his face, but a few seconds with her, and he's already in a better mood. Seems I'm not the only one susceptible to her sunshine nature.

"Time is funny." I narrow my gaze on him, then continue, "When you're having fun, it speeds by, and when you're dreading a deadline, it seems to be roaring toward you."

Arthur nods. "I'll bet the two of you can't wait to get married. It must seem like an impossibly long time until the ceremony."

I frown at my grandfather. Did he mean...? Nope, he means we're in love and can't wait to get married, and it seems like a long way off in the future, though it's only a few days.

Belle hesitates, then shakes her head. "You're wrong."

"I am?" He knits his brows.

I narrow my gaze on her. *What the hell is she doing?* Before I can say anything, she hooks her free arm through mine, and rubs her cheek against my sleeve. "Every day with Eddie is the best day of my life. He's so warm, so caring, and he has a great sense of humor." She beams.

I do? I blink.

"Oh, honeykins, you have a wicked, tongue-in-cheek wit, and your jokes crack me up." She pats my shoulder.

I stare at her, unsure of where she's going with this.

"Oh, Sweetie, you have such a sense of humor. I've never laughed so much as when I'm with you. In fact, the amount of tears I've shed—"

I growl loud enough for only her to hear me.

"—due to finding your jokes funny… Perhaps, I'm the only one who does, but you've made me burst out in hysterics until I cry, Eddie." She flicks an imaginary tear from the corner of her eyes.

She called me Eddie, again. I'm aware I'm glowering at her, and in front of Arthur, but what-fucking-ever. *No one calls me Eddie and gets away with it. Except her, apparently. Time I put an end to that.* I open my mouth to set her straight, but Arthur cuts me off.

"That's what my Greta used to say."

I manage to tear my gaze from that of my fiancée long enough to take in the wistful look on Arthur's face.

"She always found my jokes hilarious. Even after all those years of being married, she'd laugh at my jokes. She liked to say she was the only one who found my jokes funny after all that time." He swallows then turns to me. "I'm glad you took my advice to heart."

"Wouldn't dream of doing otherwise." I can't stop the note of sarcasm in my tone.

His shoulders tense. There's a flicker of anger in his eyes before he bats it away. "Then you also won't dream of turning down an old man's wish?"

It's my turn to stiffen. "Depends on the wish. I've already agreed to not only take on the role of CEO but also to settle down, as you dictated."

He doesn't seem satisfied by that. "You were wise to acknowledge when someone gave you good advice. All I ask is you do one more thing for me."

I scowl.

His forehead furrows.

I am only just beginning to get to know this man, but I see the same stubbornness in his expression that I recognize in myself. My footsteps slow; so do his and Belle's. We come to a stop at the threshold of the library he's been walking us to—not the dining room, as I'd originally envisaged.

"I think I've done enough. I—"

"G-Pa, can I call you G-Pa?" Belle chimes in.

Arthur shoots me a final look, then glances down at her upturned face. "I would like that very much. And both of you would make me very happy if you agree to my last wish. I don't have many days left on this earth, after all."

Why that canny so-and-so. The man has a strong enough constitution, he'll probably outlast all of us. My scowl deepens. I open my mouth to tell him off, but Belle cries out, "Of course, G-Pa." She turns to me. "I'm sure there's no harm in agreeing to what he wants."

I glare at her. Her color fades, but she firms her lips. The two of us lock gazes. The air between us heats. The pulse at the base of her throats kicks up and moves as she swallows. Another wall I've built around my heart crumbles, and a slow beat drums at my temples. If Arthur weren't here, I'd teach her never to defy me. My fingers twitch. I reach down and tuck a strand of her hair behind her ear. Her pupils dilate. She sways toward me. I begin to lower my head when Arthur declares,

"I want the two of you to marry right now."

19

Mira

"What?" Edward whips his head around to look at his grandfather. Whatever he sees there has him turning to look at the conservatory. And that has him tightening his jaw. He's gritting his teeth so hard the muscles of his jaw flex. I follow his line of sight, take in the group gathered inside, a-n-d, the breath whooshes out of me.

"We...we're getting married, right now?" my voice comes out shaky.

"Why wait until next week, when you can tie the knot now?" G-Pa's tone is satisfied. He glances toward us, then seems to falter. "I hope it's okay I invited your friends and arranged for an officiant?" He waves a hand toward the be-spectacled guy I don't recognize at the far end of the library in front of the lit fireplace.

"I assume you didn't want a priest presiding, Edward?"

"Nice of you to take my wishes into consideration." His tone has a biting edge which cuts through me.

"You're welcome," G-Pa says in a mild voice. "Mira, I arranged for your friend to get your wedding dress made."

"My wedding dress?" I ask faintly. *What is happening? Are we getting married, right now?* Given I recognize the people in the room who're all dressed up in their finest and who're looking at us with big smiles on their faces, I'd say my question is rhetorical. *But I'm not ready.* I wasn't ready for getting married in a week. And I'm absolutely not ready to get hitched within the hour. I tighten my hold on Edward's arm. He must feel the pressure of my grasp, must sense the nervousness that, no doubt, vibrates off of me like I'm an off-balance washing machine on the spin cycle, for he places his big warm hand over mine, and it's at this point, I notice my fingers are freezing.

He lowers his head to mine, and under the pretense of pressing a kiss to my temple, whispers, "Breathe."

I try to comply, but my lungs burn. I shake my head. This must be a dream. We're getting married. *Right now. Right. Now.* My guts churn. A bead of sweat slides down my back. My muscles seize up.

"Take a breath for me." His hard voice cuts through the chaos in my head.

I suck in air, and this time, oxygen rushes to my head, and I sway.

He tightens his hold on my hand. "You will not faint."

His voice is harsh and emotionless, and exactly what I need right now.

"Keep breathing," he orders.

I do as he says. Focus on my breathing. In-out-in.

"Good girl." The words are spoken in a low voice only I can hear. My toes curl, and heat courses through my belly. I blink and manage to focus on the faces of the people in the room. Summer and Sinclair, Penny and Knight, Abby and Cade, Gio and Rick—the eight of them stand clustered in a corner. The women wear expressions that range from happiness to concern.

On the other side of the room are five men I don't recognize. Four of them wear dark suits; three of them with ties. The fifth wears jeans with a leather jacket and has his hair slicked back. All of them are broad-shouldered. The tallest of them has a scarred face which adds to the menacing air about him. He's glaring at us, as are his brothers—they're definitely brothers. Which means, these are the half-brothers Edward mentioned. He wasn't kidding about them hating him. The air around them might as well be painted black, thanks to the contemptuous vibes emanating from them.

A little distance from them is a very pregnant Karma with her husband Michael's arm about her. When she catches my eyes, she walks forward. "I have your dress ready for you. I hope you don't mind, I estimated your measurements, but I think you'll be happy with the results." She turns to Edward. "I'd like to take her away so she can get ready. No woman likes to be caught unawares on her big day." She shoots an admonishing look at G-Pa. "You're lucky to be getting away with this."

"Oh, pffft!" G-Pa waves his hand in the air, and the gesture is so authoritative, so much like Edward's, I have a snapshot from the future when Eddie's as old as him, and every bit as stern and forbidding, and only allows himself to unbend for our granddaughter.

Our granddaughter? Holy shit, we're not yet married, and by all accounts, I'm not going to be able to bear him a child unless I go the IVF route—which, I have to admit, I'm not completely comfortable with. But I may not have much choice if I wanted a baby of my own—and my mind is totally future-casting here by imagining a future where we have grandkids.

I must make a noise because all three of them turn to me.

G-Pa surveys my features and furrows his brow. "Are you okay my dear? I hope this wasn't too much of a surprise. I thought, since you two were getting married in a few days—"

"In a full six days," Edward growls.

"—in less than a week, we could short-cut the process and have the ceremony today."

"Why would we want to short-cut something like this? You could have asked," Edward says in a hard voice.

"Would you have agreed?" his grandfather turns to him.

"That's not the point." Edward scowls, "Maybe Mira had a dream wedding planned, and you're cheating her out of it. Besides, it's only six days away, I don't understand the reason for the hurry?"

G-Pa's face falls. "I'm so inconsiderate. I only thought of myself and how much I did not want to wait a day longer. At my age, every day is the equivalent of a year, and who knows if I'm going to be around when the two of you tie the knot. I wanted to be present for my oldest grand-son's wedding."

"You're not in danger of dying anytime soon," Edward says drily.

I jab my elbow in his side. "That's not very nice."

"I'm sorry, truly. I hadn't thought of the fact it would deprive you of your dream wedding." G-Pa turns to me, "We can stick to the original plan and—"

"No, it's okay," I say around the ball of emotion in my throat. "It's not like I had a vision of what I wanted my wedding to be."

"You didn't?" Eddie blinks.

"I didn't." I tip up my chin. Knowing I was going to have an arranged marriage, I was too stressed worrying about who I'd end up marrying to plan the perfect wedding ceremony in my head. Not that I'm going to say that aloud in front of G-Pa.

"Hmm." Eddie surveys my features. "All the more reason to hold the wedding as planned in six days so you have time now to plan and—"

"No, really, it's fine. It doesn't matter to me if it takes place now or six days from now." *It's inevitable, after all, so maybe it's best I get it over with.*

He frowns. "Are you sure about this?"

"I am." I hold his gaze.

"I apologize, my dear. In my excitement to get the two of you married, I didn't take your feelings into consideration." G-Pa holds out his hand. I glance at it. Then, with reluctance, release my hold on Edward and place my palm in his. G-Pa's big gnarly hands engulf both of mine. "I did not mean to trample all over your dreams—"

"You're not."

"We can move the wedding to the original date, in six days—"

"Actually, I think it's better to have it today. You've gone to the trouble of planning everything, and all of my friends are here, and I think I'd rather not spend the next few days stressing over what is to come." *Besides, I don't have the energy to plan anything. The fact that someone else has stepped in and taken care of the arrangements is a weight off my shoulders.*

G-Pa, doesn't seem convinced.

"I mean it." I squeeze his hand. "I'd like to get married today."

"Don't feel compelled to agree," Eddie interjects.

"I'm not." I raise my gaze to his. "Unless, of course, you'd prefer to wait another six days to get married?"

He blinks, then slowly shakes his head. "I'd prefer we get married right away."

"It's settled then." I turn to G-Pa.

His eyes glisten with tears. He raises my hand to his face and kisses my fingertips. "You're an angel. I'm aware how all of this must be a surprise for you. I thought I had five grandsons. After my wife's death, I read a letter from her that told me about Edward. Our daughter-in-law swore her to secrecy, but my wife wanted me to do right by him. When I learned I had another grandson—my oldest—I realized a part of me always knew. I wanted to ensure he got his share of the inheritance. And when I met him, I could sense how deeply unhappy he was."

Edward makes a sound deep in his throat, but G-Pa ignores it.

"My son and his wife want nothing to do with me. I hoped they'd attend his wedding, but as you can see, they're not here."

"Neither are mine, by the looks of it," I say softly.

"I'm sorry. Your mother said it was too last-minute and too far to travel, and they had other plans. I suggested changing the time but…

"…but she declined…"

He nods sadly, then brightens. "But I'm here." G-Pa's eyes, more grey than brown, yet so much like Edward's, turn intense. "And I want to thank you for already changing him."

"Me?" I look at Edward, then back at his grandfather. "I've done nothing."

"By simply being who you are and being here, you've set events in motion."

"O-k-a-y?" I'm sure he's mistaken, but I guess this is not the moment to argue with him.

"The two of you have so much in common, my dear."

"We do?" I burst out.

"No, we don't," Edward says at the same time.

"Your stubbornness, to begin with." G-Pa smiles.

"Look who's talking," I say lightly.

"It's a family trait, which is why you'll fit right in."

Tears prick my eyes. I've never felt this welcome before. He's the patriarch of the family, and when Edward spoke about him, I sensed that he might be much more aloof and standoffish, but I was wrong. G-Pa, for all his faults—and I'm sure he has many—has opened his arms and his heart and made me feel at home in a way my own father hasn't done in a very long time.

I pull my hand from his, then throw my arms about him and hug him. "Thank you," I whisper.

I sense him clearing his throat, then he pats my back. "I should be saying thank you for your agreeing to marry my grandson."

I sniffle, then lean back and look up into his face. "Actually, he should be the one saying thank you to me.

Edward growls.

G-Pa laughs.

"I assume you took care of the paperwork needed for the marriage to go ahead?" Edward cuts in.

G-Pa snorts. "The Registrar General is my golfing buddy."

All right, then.

Karma smiles, then places her hand on my shoulder. "Shall we get you dressed?"

20

Edward

"The fuck am I doing?" I stare at my reflection in the mirror. Arthur made sure to get me a brand new suit, in the style I favor, and it fits me, too. The bastard thinks of everything. I knot my tie, then swear when it comes out wonky. I untie it, try to knot it again, fail. Anger squeezes my chest. I curl my fingers into fists, and am about to let it fly when I hear a familiar drawl. "The cool emotionless Priest losing his temper? That's a first."

Sinclair draws abreast and meets my gaze in the reflection. "Need some help?" He nods toward my tie.

When I don't answer, he steps around between me and the mirror and begins to fasten my tie. "There; all done." He nods in satisfaction.

"Thanks," I murmur.

"Do you remember when I got married?"

"That was what, two years ago?"

"Nearly three." His lips curve. "Remember how nervous I was?"

"I'm not nervous."

"Of course, not," he says in a soothing voice.

"Don't humor me, Sin."

"I wouldn't dare, Priest." He raises his hands. "All I'm saying is, it's natural to feel unnerved. A man doesn't get married every day."

"I shouldn't be getting married in the first place." I glance away.

"You deserve to be happy. You deserve a second chance."

Do I? I pivot and walk to the window of Arthur's manor. No other way to describe it. It's a ten-bed Victorian home perched on a hill in the center of Hampstead Heath. It has its own private driveway and swimming pool, and underground parking garage. Also, a home theater, a gym, and a den, which is where my half-brothers retired to wait for the ceremony to start. My entire life has turned upside down in the space of a few months. A family who largely hates me, except for Arthur—and he has his own selfish reasons for wanting me to take on the business. A fiancée who I should have never put in this situation. The only blessing is I have the company to focus on. Power and money—the two things ingrained into me as wrong when I was a priest. The two things I crave more than anything else now.

Wait. I can't lie. Now, there's her. She's quickly becoming my new obsession. It doesn't take rocket science to tell me I was wrong to offer her a job, in the first place. I wanted to keep her close, in the hope of controlling the damage she could do to my focus; but this time, I calculated wrong. I should have walked away from her. Instead, I invited her into my life, and she accepted. And I'm going to pay the price for it—

No. Once we're married, I can put distance between us, and everything can go back to being the same.

"You can't keep blaming yourself for what happened," Sinclair's voice sounds over my shoulder.

"Is that your expert opinion?" I scoff.

"When I met Summer, I was a heartless bastard." He stands abreast.

"Still are," I point out.

He ignores my comment and nods toward the city. "My only goal then was to amass as much money and power as I could, hoping to fill that void inside of me."

His words are so close to my earlier thoughts, I stiffen.

"Then, Summer swept in, with her pink hair and her optimistic nature, no matter that she'd been dealt some tough cards in life. She showed me it's okay to not always be uber-focused on my goals. She made me realize there's more to life than chasing the next billion. The thrill of seeing her smile is more satisfying than the next merger, more exciting than another acquisition. She's the only person who knows the truth about Max."

"Max, your Whippet?" I shoot him a sideways glance. "What about him?"

His mouth kicks up. "That's between us."

I shuffle my feet. A sliver of tension coils in my belly. I'm not jealous of his happiness. I'm not envious about his contentment. Or his absolute certainty that Summer is his soulmate. I had mine and I lost her. And Belle?

She deserves better than a man who'll never be able to love her the way she should be loved. Only, I'm not selfless enough to let her go. I can't have her. But I will not let anyone else have her, either. Does that make me a selfish bastard? I never claimed otherwise. I have more in common with my grandfather than he'll ever know.

"The reason I'm going all emo on you is because you need to pull your head out of your arse and recognize the good thing you have here."

"I'm not cut out for marriage." I rub the back of my neck.

"Who is? But then, the right woman comes along, and you willingly tie yourself to her, clip your wings, and remind yourself she's always right."

"Sounds torturous." I wince.

"With the right woman, there's a certain contentment, a peace of mind, a knowledge that she's your better half, that she rounds out your edges, compliments your strengths. It's the two of you against the world. A unit. And then you have kids, and everything changes again."

"Sleepless nights, and all the bullshit that comes with it." I roll my shoulders.

"You're only looking at it from the outside—"

"It's all I can do."

"You're choosing to ignore the obvious upsides."

"There's none— Oh, wait… In my case, I get to consolidate my role as the CEO of the Davenport group, so there's that."

"Money was never your motivator." Sinclair frowns.

"It is now."

"You're the last person to be power-hungry."

"People change."

"The Edward I knew was the most loyal, the most ethical of all the seven of us."

"And look where that got me."

"So, you got your heart broken. Shit happens. You deal with it and move on."

I squeeze my fingers at my sides. "You're beginning to piss me off," I growl.

"Good. I'd rather you *feel* those emotions you've bottled up inside since the incident."

"I don't want to talk about the incident."

"Or the fucking betrayal you feel you committed in leaving the church?"

"I had my reasons." I set my jaw.

"And have you shared them with anyone?"

I glance away.

"Thought not. It's not healthy to go through life without sharing what happened with someone else."

"Baron knows what happened." I swallow. It's difficult to talk about the man who was my best friend once without that familiar pit opening up in my belly. I thought I'd gotten over what happened, but the ghosts were merely lying in wait under the surface.

"Have you spoken to him or Ava since you returned to London?"

When I don't reply, his forehead creases. "You have to meet them at some point."

"Not if I can help it."

"We move in the same circles. He's one of the Seven; it's unavoidable."

"I've managed to avoid them this far."

"You can't do it forever," Sinclair points out.

"I don't see why not."

He sighs again. "Perhaps, being married will help you move on."

If being torn apart inside is how it feels to do so, then I'm not so sure.

"It will get better, Edward." He puts a hand on my shoulder.

If it were anyone else but Sinclair, I'd shake it off. But after I decided to limit my interactions with Baron and Ava, I ended up spending more time with him. The rest of the Seven are busy with their wives and families, and while they went through the same experience as Sinclair and I did, there's always been a kinship between us because Sinclair, like me, has other demons to deal with.

"They have a child." I swallow.

There, I've said it aloud. It's the first time I've acknowledged it to myself. I want Ava and Baron to be happy. I wish them well—*I do*—but when I found out Ava was pregnant, it gutted me. That's when I realized I might not get over what happened for a long time. That's when I knew every time I felt I was healing, it was merely my emotions lying in wait to ambush me again. That's when I vowed to find myself a new focus. Something to channel all my energies into, so I could occupy my every waking moment with something other than my past.

I need to move on. I know that, and the only thing that seems to help has been throwing myself into something bigger than me. First, as the General Manager of the London Ice Kings, and now, as CEO of the Davenport group. It's a temporary solution, but if it helps me move forward, I'm not complaining. It's also why this marriage is important. It's the only way for me to ensure Arthur hands over the decision-making power to me.

"I know you're hurting Ed, and I wish you didn't hide it. It's not healthy for you."

I snort. "You're beginning to sound like one of those new-age self-help gurus."

"And you're ignoring the obvious."

"Which is?"

"You need her, Edward, more than you realize."

21

Mira

"You ready?" Gio looks at me closely.

I tighten my grip around the bouquet, Rachel—the wedding planner—thrust into my fingers.

"I hope you don't mind that we worked with your soon-to-be grandfather to pull this wedding together overnight?" Summer asks softly.

My friends are standing with me in the guest room we took over. After G-Pa's announcement, things were out of my hands. Karma whisked me here, with my friends in tow. I was helped out of my clothes and into the gown that Karma had chosen and altered to fit my measurements, so it was ready for me in less than twenty-four hours.

"The only other time I had to stitch a wedding dress faster than this was my own," she murmurs.

I shoot her a sideways glance. "You stitched your wedding gown overnight?"

She laughs. "Let's just say, I was not a willing bride."

"And Michael, he—"

"Kidnapped me and forced me to marry him, yes."

I blink. "But the two of you are—"

"So happy? Yeah." She rubs her massive belly. I swear, the woman seems about ready to pop. She winces, and Summer touches her shoulder.

"You okay, sis?"

"Of course." She waves a hand in the air. "Baby's kicking, is all."

"And everything else is fine? Your heart—"

"It's all good," she insists.

I heard about Karma's heart condition and how being pregnant put her in the life-threatening zone. But Karma was adamant about carrying another child.

"At least, sit down." Gio drags a seat over and Karma sinks into it.

"Thanks, that's much better." She places her hands on her belly and surveys my mermaid dress. "If I'd had more time, I'd have designed you a more spectacular one. But given the urgency I had to go over the dresses I had in stock and choose one and alter it to your measurements."

"This is perfect." I turn around, glance over my shoulder and take in how the neckline dips down almost all the way to the crack of my butt. "Is it too sexy?"

"Nope," Gio says with conviction.

"The long sleeves down to your wrists and the modest neckline that only hints at your cleavage make the entire effect even more startling." Summer nods.

"And sexy." Gio's eyes gleam. "Priest is going to swallow his tongue when he sees you."

"I doubt he'll even notice," I murmur. I rub my fingers lightly down the silky fabric. I mentioned to Karma that I'd always wanted an unusual wedding dress. To consider it my last stand at being independent. I wanted to break from what's customary and have a dress in a shade of purple for my wedding. She'd used that as a guide and while the dress looks different from a normal wedding dress, her genius is such that the pale lavender color is both demure and sexy, at the same time.

"Oh, he'll notice all right." Summer laughs.

"You do realize, he couldn't take his gaze off of you earlier," Karma says slowly.

"What do you mean?"

"He went all protective when Arthur announced the wedding was today. If I'm not mistaken, he was upset on your behalf."

I don't comment. I sensed the same, but my thoughts were all over the place, so I wasn't sure.

"Arthur swore us to secrecy. I was tempted to break it, but the man has so much power and connections—" Gio shakes her head. "I should have told you what he was planning."

"I don't think it's advisable to go up against a man like Arthur," I say slowly.

"But it's your wedding, your life, Mira." Gio takes my hand in hers. "If you don't want to go through with it, say the word, and we'll get you out of here."

"We're on your side," Summer says softly, but there's a hint of steel in her tone.

"Only you know what's right for you." Karma rubs her belly. "No one knows what's happening in a relationship except for the people involved, so if this isn't what you want—"

"I do." I draw in a sharp breath. "I know it seems strange. But I believe Edward has—feelings for me—" It's half true. He's not impervious to my presence, as he's demonstrated, but he's good at hiding behind that wall he's built around himself. "I know he's not very demonstrative—"

"That's putting it kindly." Gio snorts.

I half smile. "But if it weren't Edward, my father would want me to marry someone else."

"You did mention arranged marriages are a norm in your family," Summer says slowly.

Gio stiffens. "Are you marrying him because you love him or because you think he's a better option than someone else your father would choose for you?"

"A little bit of both, I don't know. I mean, my father did choose him." I touch the petals of the flowers in my bouquet. "I think Edward will make a good husband. He's not very demonstrative, but I don't think he's the kind of man who'd knowingly hurt me."

"You sure?" Summer touches my arm. "The offer stands… If you want to call off the wedding—"

"—we'll march right out and tell Arthur." Karma nods.

"He doesn't scare us," Gio says with a fierce look in her eyes.

I sniff. "You girls are the best friends ever. I appreciate the offer. Truly. But I want to get married."

There's a knock on the door and Rachel the wedding planner, pops her head in. "Are you ready?"

I stand at the threshold of the library. Earlier, I got a glimpse of the skylight, the stained glass windows set high up in the walls, the floor-to-ceiling books, and the massive fireplace on the far side, before G-Pa's announcement scattered my thoughts. As venues go, this is exactly the space I'd have chosen to have my wedding. And my wedding dress could not be more perfect. It's only the bride-groom I'm not sure about.

"Love you, babe." Summer kisses the air next to my cheek—so she doesn't smudge my make-up, which she applied earlier—then pushes the door open and steps onto the aisle lined with the candles on either side. I draw in a breath. With the other lights in the room dimmed, and flower placements which were set up in the short time I was away, the space seems magical.

"You look incredible. Ed is a lucky man." Karma squeezes my shoulder, then follows her.

We agreed they'd be my bridesmaids. I'm so lucky to have my friends with me.

"You sure you don't want me to escort you down the aisle?" Gio scans my features with her all-seeing eyes.

"Actually, I was hoping you'd give me that privilege." G-Pa steps up on my other side.

Gio looks from me to him, and her forehead furrows. "I'm not sure—"

"I know, it's a little unusual, I'm from the groom's side, after all, but if you'd indulge an old man a little more, it would be my honor." G-Pa's features are serious. There's a plea in his eyes that goes straight to my heart. This man is responsible for my sudden change in status, from a single woman, to an engaged woman, to a soon-to-be married woman, not to mention, it's because of him that my year of freedom is being cut short. So, why is it, I can't seem to hold a grudge against him?

"Mira?" Gio frowns.

I clear my throat, then tilt up my chin. "I think I would very much like that G-Pa."

"You sure?" Gio touches my arm. "I can accompany you on your other side."

I half smile. "I'll be fine, I promise."

"You sure?" She looks toward the aisle. I follow her glance and spot Rick waiting for her.

"I'm sure." I give her a big, genuine smile. "Go on, your husband is waiting."

She leans in and air kisses me near my cheek. Then, with a last scowl at G-Pa, she leaves.

"Your friends are protective." G-Pa holds out his arm, and I hook mine through it.

"So are you," I murmur.

He pats my hand. "If I could've, I'd have given you more time to prepare for the wedding. But it seemed fortuitous that all of my grandsons agreed to be here under my roof at the same time. I wasn't sure if or when that would happen again. I didn't want to let the occasion go to waste. Also, I want to see Edward married." He looks between my eyes. "Do you understand?"

"I do." I swallow. "I can tell you love Edward very much."

His features soften. "I see a lot of myself in him. Of all my grandsons, he's the one who's had it the roughest."

I take in the troubled expression on his face and realize he knows about the incident. I could ask him about it, but that doesn't seem right. No, I need to wait for Edward to tell me, when he's ready. And he will be. He has to be.

"You want him to be happy."

"I know he'll be happy." He squares his shoulders. "Shall we?"

22

Edward

"Your grandfather never ceases to surprise," Sinclair murmurs. He's my best man, along with Knox, my oldest half-sibling. If Knox was surprised, he didn't show it. He merely nodded, then fell in line behind Sinclair. He's pissed off at this turn of events because it confirms I'm the CEO and not him. He hasn't spoken a word to me since that tight-lipped nod. I'm surprised he agreed to be my best man. I felt sure he would refuse me. Maybe, it was Arthur's presence that compelled him to assent. Although, from what I know about Knox, he's not the kind to be intimidated by anyone, not even our very charismatic grandfather. But then, he's had a relationship with Arthur which has lasted for the dura-tion of a lifetime. He can take liberties with the old man I can't. And it's not because I'm daunted by him. It has more to do with the fact he's newly-found family, and someone who already seems to understand me more than my own parents.

How would it have been to have had him in my life when the incident happened? Would he have helped me out? Would he have guided me in navigating the after-math of that one event that changed the course of my life? If he had been there, would he have stopped me from becoming a priest? Would that have meant I'd still be with Ava? At least, now, I'm able to refer to her by name, which is something I haven't been able to do for a long time. Having Belle in my life is changing me already, and in ways I'm not ready for.

"You're not going to turn and watch your bride approach?" Knox growls.

I stiffen and stare forward into the flames. The hair on the back of my neck prickles, and I sense her approach. My heart sends up a clamor in my ribcage. My pulse rate heightens. Every cell in my body is switched on and aware of her approach. And I want to. *I. Want. To.* And yet…if I do… If I see her face and take in her figure, I'll be a goner. The sense of events running away from me squeezes my stomach.

"Edward," Sinclair's voice cuts through my thoughts.

It's going to look suspect if I don't turn toward her. And the entire point of this charade is to convince my new family that this spectacle is genuine. I lengthen my spine, square my shoulders, turn… And the breath whooshes out of me.

She's a vision in lavender, the fabric clinging to her curves and stretching across her thighs with every step she takes. It embraces her lush figure until, in a dramatic sweep, it falls to her toes. Her purple-streaked hair is loose and in long curls. It streams out over her shoulders. The blonde strands catch the candlelight and gleam like burnished gold with threads of copper shot through it. And her eyes—the blue is deeper, almost indigo, taking its cue from the color of her gown.

In one hand, she holds a bouquet of white and purple flowers. The other hand is curved into the crook of my grandfather's arm. The old man took it upon himself to escort her down the aisle. He seems to be enamored with her, in their very first meeting. Enough to walk her to me himself. On the other hand, he's probably making sure the two of us are hitched without anything coming in the way.

Arthur reaches me, then places her hand in mine. "You keep her happy, boy," he says in a stern voice, before stepping back.

I tilt my head, unable to take my gaze from her features. The perfect arc of her eyebrows, the curve of her eyelashes, the tiny nose, the rosebud lips, the flushed cheeks—she's beautiful, ethereal. A goddess. And I'm a sinner. She's pristine. I'm tainted. I'll never be good enough for her. I release her hand, then turn toward the officiant. He begins the ceremony, and the words wash over me.

I must say the right things, for suddenly, he's asking us to exchange rings.

I glance at Sinclair, who jerks his chin in the direction of the aisle. Good thing, I acquired the rings after I proposed the arrangement to her.

Sinclair insisted I hand the rings over to him so he could hand them over to me at the wedding. And he knew about the wedding being pushed up. Obviously, all my friends did; that's why they're all here. I make my displeasure known to him. He shrugs. Looks like Arthur got to him, too.

I turn to find Tiny walking toward us. He's holding a cushion in his mouth, and it holds the two rings I chose. I assume he thought it fitting to have the Great Dane be the ring bearer. Which, judging by Belle's joyful exclamation of, "Tiny," was the right thing to do.

She bends and scratches his ear. He makes that mewling noise at the back of his throat, and she giggles. The sound is so fresh and young and innocent, my heart stutters in my chest. She should always sound like this. Happy and carefree, not weighed down by the past, like I am.

Tiny looks up at me with reproach in his eyes. I scowl down at him, and he makes a growling sound. Nice, now a mutt is telling me off at my own wedding.

I take my ring, hand it over to Belle, then take her ring and straighten. I wait for her to hand her bouquet over to Gio who's hovering nearby. When I hold out my hand, she places her palm in mine. I slide the ring onto her finger. It's a platinum band studded with blue sapphires, the companion to her engagement ring. She slides a platinum band, devoid of any stones, onto my left ring finger. When she glances up at me, her eyes are wide, her color pale. The pulse at the hollow of her neck draws my attention to the creamy expanse of her neck.

I want to sink my teeth into the curve where her shoulder meets her throat and mark her. I want to throw her over my shoulder and march her out of here so no one else will dare take in her delicate beauty. I want to—break the vow I made to myself to never have feelings, to never get involved in a relationship again. My throat closes. My heart rate soars. And when, from a distance, I hear the officiant say I can kiss my bride, I don't hesitate. I close the distance to her, wrap my fingers around the nape of her neck, and draw her up on her tiptoes. Her blue eyes dilate, her lips part—in surprise, I'm sure—but it gives me the perfect opportunity to close my mouth over hers.

23

Mira

I expect his kiss to be cold and biting and hard, and it's all of that, and so much more. His hold on the nape of my neck. The assuredness in his grasp, the way he hauls me to him with complete confidence, how he slants his mouth across mine, thrusts his tongue inside my mouth to dance over mine, how he then…slows…slows… Like we have all the time in the world, like we're not in front of our friends and his family, like he's not my arranged husband, like I'm his real wife… Wife. I'm *his* wife. A shudder runs down my spine. He must sense it, for his hold on the nape of my neck tightens. He runs his tongue across the seam of my lips, and my nipples tighten. My heart drops to the place between my legs. My core throbs. He softens the kiss even further, until his lips barely brush mine, until we're sharing breath, and his gaze, which hasn't wavered from mine since he captured my mouth, intensifies. Sparks of gold and silver light up his eyes. It mirrors the million little sparks bursting under my skin. I'm burning up from the inside, melting into a puddle at his feet. My knees give out. I sway, and he wraps his other arm about my waist and pulls me into his chest. My arms are around him. He tucks my head under his chin. I close my eyes and draw in a breath of pure, unadulterated Edward. The tension in my muscles fades; the throbbing between my legs increases. The sound of our friends clapping reaches me. Oh god, I forgot where we were. I try to pull away, but he doesn't let me. He holds me in place and rubs soothing circles over my back. A sigh of relief leaves my lips.

"Better?" he rumbles from somewhere over me. When I nod, he finally steps back, but continues to hold me about my waist.

Then he notches his knuckles under my chin, tips up my face, and surveys my features. Whatever he sees there must satisfy him, for he nods, then turns, guiding me to face the room and the group.

He leads me up the aisle, and our friends surround us.

Summer reaches me first. She clasps my shoulders and kisses me on both cheeks. "That was beautiful!" she sniffs.

Karma is next. Her swollen belly between us, she squeezes my shoulder, then leans in and whispers, "I hope both of you will be very happy."

Then it's Penny, then Abby, and finally, Gio. She holds out the wedding bouquet, and I take it from her. "Since most of us here are married, you might want to hand this over to Rachel. She's the only one not married."

I nod.

She leans in and kisses my cheek. "That was a very convincing kiss."

I feel myself blush, then nod.

"Is he taking you on a honeymoon?"

I blink, but before I can reply, there's a woof. Then Tiny pushes his way between Gio and Rick, who's congratulating Edward.

"Hey, baby, you played your role so well." I bend and rub him behind his ear. He woofs again and wags his tail with such force, he brushes against G-Pa who's walked up to congratulate us.

Gio steps aside, and G-Pa takes my hands in his. "That was beautiful." He blinks the tears from his eyes. "Edward is very lucky to have you in his life."

"I'm lucky to have him in mine," I murmur.

My husband must hear my words, for his muscles stiffen. He continues to accept the felicitations from his friends. Then, it's his half-brother Knox's turn. He jerks his chin toward Edward. "Congratulations."

Edward nods. "Thanks."

"Just because you're married and fulfilling the terms of Arthur's agreement doesn't mean I accept you as the CEO."

Silence descends as, one-by-one, people stop talking and train their attention on the exchange.

G-Pa slowly releases my hands. He looks between the two half-brothers but doesn't say anything. Apparently, he wants to see how this exchange will proceed.

Knox shoves his hand in his pocket. "I won't make it easy for you during your honeymoon, either."

"There is no honeymoon," Edward drawls.

G-Pa stiffens.

Gio gasps.

I'm not sure what I expected, but I think a part of me, somewhere, assumed there'd be a honeymoon. Isn't that what people do when they get married? But this is a fake wedding. And that's my fake husband. Let's ignore that he kissed me so I felt it all the way to my toes; it was all pretense.

Knox looks taken aback. "No honeymoon, huh?"

G-Pa looks at Edward with something like suspicion in his eyes. "You're not taking your wife for a honeymoon?" His forehead furrows.

"I'm the newly appointed CEO. I can't take time away from the job."

"Don't forget, you continue to stay CEO only if you consummate the marriage," G-Pa snaps.

"What?" Edward's usual mask-like features unwind enough for the shock to show in his eyes.

"What?" I squeak.

"Why do you seem surprised?" G-Pa looks at Edward steadily. "Were you planning otherwise?"

"I'm surprised because I didn't expect my grandfather to interfere in my personal life to this extent."

"Welcome to the family," Knox says drily. Then he steps toward me. "I assume it's okay to kiss the bride?"

Without waiting for Edward's response, he bends and kisses me, not on my lips, but so close, he might as well have.

There's a growl from Edward, and the next minute, Knox is shoved away. "Get away from my wife." Edward wraps his arm about my shoulder and pulls me close.

Knox's lips twist. It's not a smile so much as a grimace. Then he glances at G-Pa. "You have your answer; he has feelings for her."

"Did you plan this?" Edward growls at G-Pa.

"Give me some credit." G-Pa scowls at Knox. "You will apologize to your brother —"

"Half-brother," Knox sneers.

"And his bride," G-Pa thunders.

Knox glowers at G-Pa, then clears all emotions from his features. When he looks at me, he's wearing a mask that rivals Edward's. They might protest at the fact they're related, but clearly, they are, given the trait of masking emotions runs in the family.

"I'm sorry if I embarrassed you, Mirabelle." He smirks. "Though I'm not sorry I kissed you."

There's a low snarl, then Edward shoots out his fist and catches Knox in the side of the jaw.

24

Edward

"For someone who's quite controlled, you sure lost it." My wife bathes my knuckles. We're back home after that shit-show.

To say Arthur was not happy with my behavior is putting it mildly. He glared at me, then pivoted and walked out of there with Tiny on his heels.

When the Great Dane refused to leave Arthur's side, I decided to let him be. Apparently, the mutt has not only taken to my grandfather, but has also decided to adopt the old man as his current companion. Besides, the old man could do with the company. Then, there was Knox. The satisfaction on his face made me realize he'd been baiting me, and I had fallen for it. I lost my control for the first time since... Since I found out *she* was in love with my best friend.

Then, Knox left. My other half-brothers didn't bother to congratulate me. Except for the youngest, Brody. He's the only one who came up and congratulated me and my bride. Then he, too, left. Sinclair and our other friends gathered around us. He wanted to call a doctor to have my knuckles looked at, but I had refused. Instead, I told them Belle and I were leaving.

I should have apologized to them for the disaster of the evening, but all I could think of was to get out of there with her. To make sure no one else could see her in that dress. That possessiveness I always feel around her seems to have multiplied since I slipped the ring on her finger.

I need a little time and distance to understand why I reacted the way I did. I needed...to get my emotions back under control and back in the box I've sealed them in for so long. I turned away all other offers of help. I looked around for Tiny, but the pooch had decided to follow Arthur out. Apparently, I was also a shit dog-sitter; the mutt decided to cross over to my grandfather's side. I shoved the thought aside and hustled Belle out of there.

She managed to toss her bouquet to the wedding planner and then, we were out of there. I drove us home, then went to my room. She followed me and insisted on cleaning my bruises. It seemed churlish to protest, so I let her. When's the last time someone took care of me? Perhaps, after the incident, when I found myself at the hospital. And then, it was the impersonal touch of the nurse. Belle's touch, though, is gentle. She drops the blood-stained cloth, reaches for the antiseptic and glances at me from under her eyelashes. "This is going to hurt."

I don't reply.

"Do you want some whiskey to help with the pain?"

When I stay silent, she firms her lips, then pours the antiseptic over the torn skin of my knuckles. I hiss out a breath, but the pain cuts through the remnants of anger. My mind finally slows down. I look on as she holds my palm between her much smaller ones, then she bends her head and blows on it. The burning sensation fades. When she looks up at me, our gazes hold. Color flushes her cheeks. The air between us heats. Her lips part, and I can't take my gaze off her mouth. She swallows, and the pulse at the base of her throat accelerates. When I raise my free hand and dig my fingers into the thick strands of her hair and tug, she shivers. When I pull my bruised hand from her grasp and press my thumb to her lower lip, her breath hitches.

"So fucking gorgeous." I drag my thumb down her chin, the column of her neck to where her pulse flutters like a pinned butterfly. I continue down to where the neckline dips at her cleavage. She shudders. I hook my thumb in the cloth and tug. The delicate material rips.

She gasps. I expect her to cry out; instead, her pupils dilate. A low moan bleeds from her lips.

"So fucking alluring. You come across as all virginal, but you have a dark side."

She draws in a sharp breath, but doesn't contradict me.

I slide my fingers inside her wedding dress and cup her breast, and goosebumps shiver up her skin. I pinch her nipple between my finger and thumb and when I tweak it, she cries out. The sound arrows to my groin, and my cock extends.

"So fucking beautiful. You're a siren I can't resist, despite my best efforts." I urge her down to her knees. She goes willingly, then looks up at me. There's complete trust in her eyes. A submissiveness I knew she possessed, but seeing her at my mercy, waiting for me to command her, shoots a thick arrow of lust up my spine.

"Unzip me," I order.

"What?"

"You heard me."

She looks like she's going to hesitate, then reaches up and undoes the button of my waistband. When she lowers the zipper, the sound of the slider over the metal teeth is loud in the silence.

"Take it out."

She hesitates. Her cheeks are pink; a fine sheen of sweat beads her upper lip. Nervousness is writ in every curve of her body, and fuck, if that doesn't entice me more.

"Don't keep me waiting, Belle."

She reaches inside my briefs and curls her fingers about my length. The blood drains to my groin. "Fuck." I tighten my fingers in her hair.

When she inches my briefs down enough, my cock springs free.

"Oh, my god." She stares at the throbbing length. I follow her gaze to where the bulbous head of my length stares back at her, the crown an angry purple, pre-cum clinging to the slit. The contrast between the dark skin and her pale pink-tipped fingers, which don't meet around the girth, intensifies the throbbing ache at the base of my spine.

"You're so big," she whispers.

My shaft twitches in response, and her gaze widens.

"So hard." She squeezes me from crown to base and back, and I almost come.

"Open your mouth," I snap.

She glances up at me, a trace of fear in those eyes mixed with need, and it's my undoing. The pressure in my balls intensifies.

I ease her face forward until her lips graze my cock. Shockwaves spiral through me. "Bloody hell." And I haven't even slid my dick inside her mouth.

She holds my gaze, then flicks out her tongue and licks the crown.

A groan vibrates up my chest.

She blinks, then sweeps her pink tongue around the rim of the head, and my entire body shudders. A small smile curves her lips, then she opens her mouth.

25

Mira

I part my lips to take him inside my mouth, but he's already pushed my head forward, and his dick slides across my tongue. My heart rams into my ribcage, and my pulse rate sprints like it's running a marathon. The throbbing between my legs accelerates in tandem. My entire body has turned into an oscillating pendulum, each swing taking it closer to breaking point. The muscles of his shoulders flex under his jacket. He's still dressed in his three-piece suit with the tie knotted around his throat. Every part of him is covered except for his cock, the crown of which is in my mouth. I guess you could say that's covered too. I curl my fingers around the base, and when I squeeze, a growl emerges from his lips. His golden-brown eyes catch fire, and a bead of sweat slides down his temple. He's affected by the blowjob I'm giving him. A flood of triumph pools between my legs.

I open my mouth wider, and he pulls me forward enough that his cock hits the back of my throat. I gag. Saliva drips down my chin, and tears squeeze out from the corners of my eyes. His chest rises and falls, and a flush steals up his cheeks. Other than that, his features are inscrutable. His shoulders could be carved from granite, the muscles of his body so coiled with tension, he could be the spring of a wound-up clock.

He pauses with his dick pushed into the back of my throat, the girth so wide he's pushing against the walls of my mouth. I swallow and he heaves out a breath. The nerve at his temple pops. He digs his fingers deeper into my hair and maneuvers me forward. And when I open my mouth wider, a flicker of satisfaction laces his features. He slides down my throat. "Good girl."

My toes curl. Moisture drips down my thighs. He releases his hold on my hair, only to wrap his fingers about my throat. He pulls me back, enough that the tip of his cock rests between my lips. "Breathe through your nose," he instructs.

I do.

"Once more."

I draw in a breath; my chest rises and falls.

When I exhale, he tugs me forward, and his cock sinks down my throat. My gag reflex kicks in. I swallow it back, and I must be doing something right, for a growl rumbles up his chest. He increases the pressure around my throat, enough that my lungs burn. I can feel his cock press against the sides of my throat. I feel the length of his cock encased in the column of my neck. And the sensation is like nothing I've experienced in my life—which is not saying much, seeing how woefully inexperienced I am at anything related to sex.

I may have read spicy romance books and managed to sneak a peek at porn videos online when I was sure I wouldn't be found out. None of that prepared me for how demeaning it feels to be on my knees servicing him. Nothing equipped me for how erotic it would feel to be used by him. *Take me. Treat me like your possession. Do to me, anything you want. Whatever will bring you pleasure. Manipulate my body. Utilize my flesh. Fill my holes the way they have never been before. I am yours to do as you please. Only yours.*

He must sense my thoughts, for his jaw hardens. A muscle flares to life below his cheekbone. His gaze is harsh, but the fire in his eyes tells me he's feeling everything right now. It's the first time he's given me a glimpse of the molten, churning miasma of conflict he carries within him.

And I should be upset with him for taking my mouth like this. No warning. Nothing to tell me he was going to use my body, and yet—there's a strange sense of power in knowing it's *my* body causing him to lose control again. I'm the reason he lost his temper earlier. Slowly but surely, Edward is opening up—despite himself—and it's thrilling and humbling at the same time.

So much control holds him back. How will it be when he finally loses himself completely? His cock thickens further, filling my throat, pushing down on my tongue. Tension vibrates off of him. I sense his body shudder and know he's close. That's when he pulls out, only to pinch my nipple. He tweaks it, and the jolt of pain cuts through the jumble of sensations. All of my senses seem to sharpen. I glance up at him, his cock once more poised at my lips. He releases my tit, only to haul me up to my feet. Then, without releasing his hold on the nape of my neck, he hooks his fingers in the already torn front of my dress and rips it all the way to the hem. A part of me thinks I need to protest. It's a Karma West Sovrano creation, which must be worth thousands.

"I'll buy you many more." He pushes aside my panties and shoves two thick fingers inside me. I gasp, try to squirm away, but he holds me in place. He begins to weave his fingers in and out of me. I'm so soaked, there's a slurping noise as he thrusts in and out of me. It seems to please him, though, for he gives me a barely perceptible nod. It's not like I had anything to do with it. My body's a kite, and he holds the reel which controls the string.

He adds a third finger, and a whine spills from my lips. It seems to spur him on, for his movements intensify. Every time he shoves his fingers inside me, my entire body jolts, and I rise up to my toes with the force of his thrust. When he pulls it out, I settle back on my heels. In-Up-Out-Down, the rhythm echoes through my body. The next time he plunges inside me, he curves his fingers and hits a spot deep inside me. Sparks of sensations oscillate to my extremities. My knees knock together, and I sag, impaling myself further on his digits.

And when he presses his thumb into the swollen bud of my clit, I cry out. I grab hold of his shoulders, and he watches me closely as I sweat and pant and moan and plead with him. The words are garbled. I dig my fingertips into his jacket, and feel I'm poised on the verge of something big, something new, something so different and yet, so familiar. Something the primal part of me recognizes, but my mind and my body can only guess. The trembling shoots up my legs, my thighs, and squeezes down on my belly, only to zip up my spine. And I'm going to—

He pulls out his fingers. In one smooth move, he stands and turns me around so I'm forced to grab the edge of the counter. He pulls off the remnants of my dress then tears off my panties. I cry out but hold his gaze in the mirror as he fits his cock to my opening. He stays poised there, one pulse. Another. Then, he impales me.

26

Edward

"Eddie," she cries out my name. The sound goes straight to my cock, and I grow bigger, harder, more insistent. I need to pause. I need to give her time to adjust. I dig my shoes into the floor, tighten my thighs, and wait. Wait. Her pupils are dilated, and there's only a circle of blue around the black. Her mascara has streaked down her cheeks, a dribble of saliva drips from her chin. The remnants of her dress are on the floor, and her left tit is out of her bra cup. Her color is high, and her hair is a cloud of spun gold with violet streaks about her shoulders. She looks used and messed up and yet, there's an innocence to how she licks her lips, a stubbornness to how she refuses to break the connection of our gazes.

She's stubborn, has a tenacity I'd have never guessed, and has the most gorgeous curves I've ever laid my eyes on. She's a goddess, a siren, a vixen—and an innocent. How could I have gotten so lucky to have found her? How could I have resisted her? How can I let her come any closer, when she's already wriggled her way under my skin?

"You're so fucking tight, so hot; your cunt is a work of beauty," I growl through gritted teeth.

She opens her mouth, but before she can speak, I pull out and thrust into her again. Her entire body jolts, and she cries out. I wait until her breathing slows again, until her eyes clear, and she, once more, holds my gaze. I pinch her clit, and she shudders. I begin to rub that hard little knob, and she wriggles and writhes, but I hold her in place. I strum her pussy lips and am rewarded with a gush of moisture between her legs. I pull back slowly, stay poised at her opening, and this time, when I plunge forward, she throws her head back, showing me the length of her neck. I begin to fuck her in earnest. In-out-in. Each time I sink into her, she shudders and cries out. Each time I pull out, she whines. Her little noises, her groans and whimpers drive me over the edge. I rub her clit, and her eyes roll back in her head. I tilt my hips, piston forward and into her, touching her deep—so deep inside, I almost come. With a growl, I manage to hold back, then lean down and press my cheek against hers. "Open your eyes."

She cracks open her eyelids, and I look into her eyes as I slowly, inch by inch, bury myself inside her one last time. I flick her clit and command, "Come," and she shatters. A high-pitched whine emerges from her lips as she shudders. Her knees give out, and I hold her up as her body twitches and jerks with her climax. When she closes her eyelids and slumps, I pull out. When I look down, I notice the blood on my cock. *What the—?*

I lift my hand, notice the stain on my fingers. *A virgin? Of course, she's a virgin. She was told she was going to have an arranged marriage.* Most likely, she was instructed to keep herself unsullied. And I sensed it. My subconscious sensed it, but I was too caught up in my own ghosts to acknowledge it. I thought I felt some resistance when I took her but put it down to my size. And she didn't tell me. *Why didn't she tell me? Maybe, because you had your cock down her throat, you bastard.* I hold her limp body close, manage to pull up my briefs and pants and zip up, then scoop up her limp body and walk over to the bath.

I lower her to her feet, balance her, and run a bath. When it's half-full, I shut off the water, divest her of her bra, then lower her into the tub. I keep her upper body upright and run a washcloth over her face, her breasts, down between her legs. My still hard cock strains against my pants. My balls are so hard, they weigh a ton. I acknowledge the need, the blinding desire that still runs through my veins, and watch it as it infiltrates every pore of my body. I'm good at punishing myself. It's the one thing I learned in my days as a priest that's stuck with me, and

I've become an expert over the years. Practice makes perfect, after all. When I raise my gaze to her face, I find her eyes are open.

"You didn't come."

I tilt my head and continue with my ministrations, trying to keep my actions as clinical as possible—like that's possible with her? Especially not with the massive column between my thighs, and my balls, which are as hard as the iron I pump in the gym. I finish up, throw the cloth aside, then reach down and lift the plunger. The water begins to drain. I rise to my feet and hold out my hand. She grips it and I pull her up, then grab a towel and drape it about her shoulders. I wipe her down quickly, trying not to glance at the column of her neck, or her plump breasts, the dip of her waist, the curve of her belly, and the alluring mound below. I wrap the towel around her, then lift her in my arms.

"I can walk," she protests.

I carry her to my bedroom, lower her to her feet, and pull back the covers. "Get in."

"This is your room," she points out.

When I don't reply, she firms her lips. "I thought you said you didn't want us to share a bed."

"We're not going to share a bed."

"But—"

"Why didn't you tell me you were a virgin?"

She glances away. "I…thought you knew."

I rub the back of my neck. "If I had been thinking straight, I might have guessed and gone slowly." I shake my head. "Get in the bed, Belle."

"First, tell me why you didn't come."

I blink. The mouth on her. The very sexy, hot hole that was my undoing. That is, until I was ensconced in her pussy. This woman isn't afraid to go toe-to-toe with me. Unlike my employees. It's refreshing and invigorating and—I will not think about how much I want her right now. I reach over and tug on the towel so it slides off of her.

"Oh!" Her cheeks turn pink. A flush creeps up her chest. Her embarrassment fuels the lust in my veins. My cock throbs, a burning sensation extending out from my groin. She glances down at my crotch and swallows. "You're still hard."

"And you're not yet in bed."

She scowls, then slides in under the cover. I pull it up until she's covered all the way to her neck, then sit down next to her on the bed. "Are you sore?"

Her flush deepens. "A little."

"I wish I'd known this was your first time. If I had—"

"You wouldn't have made love to me?"

"I wouldn't have fucked you," I agree.

Her face falls, and a hot sensation stabs at my chest. I'm too attuned to her. Too sensitive to her needs. Too responsive to her change in emotions. She glances away, and when she looks back at me, her gaze is haunted. "Is it fucking if you didn't come in me?"

I shrug.

"The only reason you made lo—penetrated me is because you needed to consummate the marriage."

I incline my head.

"And you married me because you want G-Pa to confirm your position as the CEO."

"You knew this already, Belle," I murmur.

She bites the inside of her cheek. "Knowing it and living it are two very different things."

"Are you having second thoughts?"

Why am I asking her this? It's not as if I'm going to let her go. Especially now.

My fingers tingle. I want to reach over and push back the hair from her face. I want to crawl into bed with her, turn her over and pull her into me. I want to spoon her, watch her as she falls asleep, then wake her up by crawling in between her legs and eating her out until she comes again… I want…what I can't have—the kind of intimacy that comes from having confidence in another. That emotional oneness that means you never have to second guess yourself when you're with them.

I want her sweetness to soothe my hard edges, her innocence to throw me a rope so I can climb out of the dark place I've descended into, her sunshiny nature to illuminate the blackness I've held close. I'm changing, and it's all because of her. I want to push her away, yet I find myself circling back to her, always. I want to teach her how it could be to open herself up and offer herself to me. I want her to know the satisfaction of putting her trust in me. Of allowing me to wring every last drop of desire from her body, of fulfilling every wish of her soul. The ecstasy she'd feel giving herself to me, comfortable in the belief she can stop me anytime. The exhilaration that comes with letting me push her boundaries, believing in me enough to put her faith in me.

Faith. I'm asking her for the one thing I've lost. I no longer believe in the greater good. I'm no longer sure there's a higher power. I'm no longer convinced of the purpose that guided me for most of my life. I'm a stone sinking slowly in a river of depravity. I lost my moorings and found her, and it threatens every principle I've sworn to live my life by since *her*. I cannot...will not let this woman turn my life upside down. But I also cannot bear to see her hurt.

"Belle? Do you regret marrying me?

"Would it matter?"

"I'm not going to let you walk away..."

She scoffs. "I didn't think you would."

"I'm also not sorry I took your virginity."

Her jaw drops.

"Nor for the pain I caused you."

She gasps. "Christ-on-a-bus, don't hold anything back, will ya?"

"It's best you find out what kind of a man I am."

"A hurt, broken, emotionally unavailable, sadistic dominant?" She scoffs.

I look at her with interest. "You're beginning to understand me."

"I liked you better when I merely thought of you as recovering from a broken heart."

"That's a very romantic picture of me; afraid the truth is not so black and white."

"Oh, you're nothing but shades of grey." She peers up at me, and her blue eyes are clear and bright, the gaze of someone who doesn't have to carry around the burdens of a lifetime.

"And black." I set my jaw. "There are parts of me you don't want to come in contact with."

"The very fact you're warning me off, tells me more about you."

I smooth the covers under her chin. "And what will you do when you're disappointed? What will you do when you realize you'd have been better off if you'd never met me?"

27

Mira

"And that's the last you saw of him?"

Summer pats the little boy who's fast asleep in his crib. I wrapped up work, then came to her place. She was putting her son to bed, and I stayed with her as she spun a story for him, something involving dragons and space travel and rockets, complete with hand gestures which had entranced him. He resisted sleep; they always do. A couple of times, he closed his eyes, and we were sure he'd drifted off, only for him to open his eyelids and cry out as soon as Summer started to move away. But she persisted, and he finally fell asleep. We've stayed just to be sure he doesn't move. And she strokes his back in rhythmic beats that have me curling up in the armchair and burrowing my cheek into the cushion.

"Haven't exchanged a word with him since, and it's been a week."

She gives me a strange look. "Don't you two share a room?"

"Um… Yes." I change my position, looking for a more comfortable spot in the chair. "But I fall asleep before he comes to bed, and he's gone before I wake up." It's a lie, I know. But you can't expect me to tell her

I'm not sharing a room with my new husband, can you? I love my friends but draw a line at sharing such intimate details with them.

"And you work with him, so you see him in the office?" She pushes the hair back from her baby's forehead, a soft smile on her face.

"He's been busy in meetings, and communicates with me through emails," I murmur.

"So he spent your wedding night with you, but then he was gone?" she asks slowly.

"Something like that." I don't want to go into details about what happened that night. That my husband let his control slip and fucked me, but he didn't come inside me. It still counts as consummation, though; I looked it up online. The Oxford dictionary defines the completion of a marriage by an act of sexual intercourse, which is defined for these purposes as complete penetration of the vagina by the penis, although ejaculation is not necessary. So there you have it, ladies and gents. My husband has made it clear to me he 'fucked' me and did his duty by consummating the wedding. And now, he's making it clear he doesn't want anything to do with me.

I thought I could catch him in the office, at least, but he's made sure to stay ensconced in his room in meetings.

He turned the glass wall between his office and my desk into an opaque sheet, so I can't look in. The symbolism isn't lost on me either. And when it was time for lunch, he asked the receptionist to bring it to him. She, with the long nails and false eyelashes that graze her forehead. I hated her slim figure and pixie haircut on sight. Hated her even more when she came out smirking and walked by me without a second glance. *Bitch.*

"Guess he must be busy?" Summer rises to her feet, then bends and tucks the covers around her son.

"I suppose." My voice isn't convincing.

She kisses her son on the forehead, then straightens and leads me out of his room. She pulls the door half shut, and we walk down the stairs into the kitchen. She pulls out her phone, makes sure the app linking to the baby cam is active, and places it on the island, then busies herself making us both herbal tea. I slip onto the stool and watch her pour the hot water into the cups. She slides one over to me, then sits on the stool next to me. "I know you got married in a hurry—"

"Which is putting it mildly."

"But as you know, I believe in love at first sight, so I'm not as surprised as some of the others."

More like lust at first sight on my side, and convenience at first sight on his, but I don't say that aloud.

"I know you and Sinclair, too, had a rushed courtship—" I begin to say, but she laughs.

"He thought my father was responsible for what happened to him and Edward and their friends. He wanted revenge, so he blackmailed me into marrying him."

"What?" I gape.

She shrugs. "I needed the money he promised in return. It was a logical arrangement, only—"

"You fell in love."

"He fell first." She laughs. "Then he fell harder. He'd wanted me all along, but didn't know how to express his feelings. So, he hatched this very convoluted plan to marry me. All to avoid talking about his emotions. Sound familiar?"

"It does. The only difference is, Sinclair loved you. Edward? I'm not so sure. He sees me as a convenience. I was the first eligible woman he came across, and he had to fulfill his grandfather's conditions in order to retain his role in the company, and—" I firm my lips. "Oh, shit, I just gave everything away, didn't I?"

She looks at me with soft eyes. "Nothing I hadn't already guessed."

"But I signed an NDA. Please don't say anything."

She makes the motion of zipping her lips.

"So you knew all along this was a marriage of convenience?"

"I could tell he has feelings for you—"

"He does not," I protest.

She merely smiles in that enigmatic manner women who are at peace with themselves, who've been through this merry-go-round and decided to get off, have.

"I was there when he was pissed on your behalf with his grandfather. Then, he beat up his half-brother because he dared kiss you too close to your lips, without his permission."

I wince. "That's just him being all possessive...because I'm his 'wife.'" I make air quotes. The light from above flashes off of my rings. She glances at them.

"He gave you his grandmother's engagement ring."

"Only to make sure everyone believes in this make-believe relationship."

"But it's not make-believe for you, is it?"

I begin to nod, then scowl at her. "Sneaky."

She laughs. "And you always wear your heart on your sleeve. I like that about you, Mira. I like that a lot."

"Doesn't help when you're trying to play a game with your husband and you don't know the rules."

"Make up your own."

I frown. "What do you mean?"

"He's attracted to you, Mira. He can't take his gaze off you when you're with him. He's possessive about you—"

"Which makes no sense; I'm his wife in name only."

"So test him."

"How?"

"Use his weakness."

"He's Edward, the emotionless robot who's convinced he can't be redeemed. He doesn't have one," I grumble.

She continues to look at me with a meaningful look on her face.

"What?"

When she only gives me a small smile, I sigh. I take a sip of my herbal tea, then place the mug on the coffee table.

"I suppose his one indication of fallibility is losing his temper with Knox," I admit.

And the fact he lost control and fucked me on our wedding night. He was unable to resist me. Of course, he had to do it because G-Pa made it a condition—the marriage had to be consummated. Still, he didn't have to actually do it. He could have lied to G-Pa, and everyone would have believed it. But apparently, he's not a liar. Which is good, right? It means he'll be truthful with me, as well. I draw in a breath. "You're saying I should play on what seems to be his vulnerability and use it to get a reaction from him?"

28

———————

Edward

"I don't care how risky it is. I've decided we're going to take over the company." I glance between Knox and Sinclair. We've spent most of the morning trying to find a way to combine the forces of the Davenport empire with that of 7A—the company I co-own with Sinclair and the rest of the Seven—to launch a joint takeover. It's a deal set with mine-fields and egos that could send the entire acquisition into a tailspin. It took Knox and Sinclair four hours to conclude the deal's not doable.

"I don't accept no for an answer," I growl.

Sinclair leans back in his chair. "Neither do I, old chap, but some-times, the writing is on the wall."

"And this is one of those times," Knox says in that gravelly voice of his. The sunshine streaming in through the floor-to-ceiling windows illu-minates every single dip and cranny of the scars on his face. I can take credit for the newest one on his temple. Not that it takes away from his appeal. If anything, it seems to have increased his popularity with the women-folk, most of whom tittered and stared at him as we walked through the maze of cubicles earlier.

Thankfully, my wife wasn't at her desk. She went out for an early lunch. I know this because I moved things around to make sure she was out when my half-brother prowled in, along with my best friend. Now that I've shut Baron out of my circle, and because, except for Sinclair, the rest of the Seven are either traveling for work or with their family, I've found myself spending more time with him. Given the joint history of the incident which binds us, there's a level of trust I share with Sinclair that should make this joint venture successful. But of course, Knox—that douchebag—has his own interests to protect.

"If you'd bother to look at the figures, you'd see we turn a profit in twelve months," I snap.

"With losses for six of those."

"The higher the risk, the higher the return." I shrug.

"Like your marriage?"

Anger squeezes my guts, my fingers tingle, and I curl them into fists and try to rein in the burn that eats through my veins. He's trying to provoke me. I know that. I also know G-Pa is watching to see how I settle in—at work and with my new bride.

He called to say he'll be making an announcement soon, confirming my role as CEO, but he hasn't mentioned when he'll do it. Meanwhile, Knox will use every dirty trick to show I'm not fit. And it's important to me to get my grandfather's approval. My parents didn't give two shits about me, whereas my grandfather—even if it had been for his own selfish needs—decided I'm his heir. And I'm not going to fuck it up. I don't need a shrink to tell me this only highlights another issue in my psyche. In addition to the ones I already carry around, but whatever. I have a right to this company, and I'm not letting go of it.

"Something you want to tell me?" I narrow my gaze on Knox.

He leans back in his seat and shrugs. "Not really."

"I do." Sinclair scowls at me. "Don't be an arse, Ed. Don't go making choices that will endanger the company when you're not thinking clearly."

"Who said I'm not?" I lower my voice to a hush. Not that it has any impact on Sin. Motherfucker's as alpha as they come.

"The fact that you're here, instead of taking your gorgeous wife on a honeymoon, is enough of a giveaway that you're not in the right space."

"Don't fucking talk about my wife."

Knox flicks an imaginary piece of dust from his tailored jacket. "Don't get your knickers in a twist. Just stating what I see."

"What I see is a lost opportunity. I'm going to push this deal through, with or without you." I set my jaw.

Knox inclines his head. He doesn't seem disturbed by my announcement. "Well then, my work here is done." He rises to his feet and nods at Sinclair. "Sterling." Then without another glance at me, he prowls toward the exit. He heads out, and the door snicks shut behind him.

"Why do I get the feeling there's something up his sleeve?"

"Why do I get the feeling you're about to commit career suicide?" Sinclair sighs.

"Don't you trust my judgement?"

He scrutinizes my features. "Frankly, not in the state of mind you're in at the moment."

"Nothing's wrong with my state of mind."

"It will be when you find out Knox is talking to your wife." He jabs his thumb over his shoulder.

I glance toward my computer screen, showing a live feed of her desk outside my office, and stiffen. He's right; there's Knox, leaning a hip at my wife's desk. He says something, and Belle throws her head back and laughs.

He continues to talk, while she leans over to grab a paper and write on it. He says something else, and she looks up at him with a soft expression about her eyes. I gape. *What the hell is happening? I look up at the window separating us, to be certain I'm not seeing things.* That's when she reaches out to touch his arm and—"What the fuck?!" I jump up so quickly, my chair topples over. I race out the door, and before she can withdraw her hand, I grab his arm and twist it, throwing him aside. "Get away from my wife."

<hr>

"You are crazy, just crazy!" She fumes at me.

After I went caveman and pulled Knox away from her, he didn't retaliate. Much to my disgust, he smirked, dusted off his jacket, and left. He didn't say a word, but the smug glitter in his eyes told me I'd allowed him to provoke me again. He turned and prowled off. Sinclair shook his head at me, told me to rethink the acquisition before I went through with it, then he asked Belle to take care of me and left. I marched back into the office, and she followed. I told her to leave; she'd planted her hands on her hips and scowled at me. I mirrored her stance and glared back. She didn't look away. Interesting. *My little Belle is finding her spine.*

"I think you need to leave." I jerk my chin toward the door.

"I think you're avoiding me," she bursts out.

"What gave you that idea?"

"The fact I haven't seen you or spoken to you since our wedding night?"

"I've been busy." I shove my hand in my pocket. Technically, not a lie, because I've thrown myself into work.

"Too busy to spend time with your new wife?"

"New fake wife."

"Not so fake after you took my virginity." She tips up her chin.

"I told you, I'm not apologizing for it."

"I'm not looking for an apology, but you're not talking to me, either."

"Did you expect me to whisper sweet nothings and tell you how gorgeous you look because"—I look her up and down, taking in the purple dress nipped in at the waist to accentuate her sumptuous figure—"you know you do."

She blushes. "I'm not looking for compliments."

"I'm making a statement."

She looks at me with confusion in her eyes. "Only you can deliver praise and look like you don't mean it."

"But I do."

"I know you do, but your face—" She shakes her head. "The expression on your face says you don't care."

"Because I don't?" *That's it, buddy, keep telling yourself that.*

Her lips tighten. "You're an asshole."

"And I can't stop thinking about your other virgin hole."

Her color deepens. "I didn't come in here to be insulted." She pivots and flounces toward the door. I slip my phone out of my pocket and swipe my finger across the screen. There's a clicking sound. When she reaches the door, she pushes at it, but it doesn't open. She turns and frowns at me. "Open this door."

I yawn.

Her eyes flash silver blue lightning at me. "Edward, open the door," she says through gritted teeth.

"That's not the name you used when I was inside you."

She swallows. "This is not funny, Ed."

"First, call me by the name only you do."

"You mean, douchewaffle?"

I almost allow myself a chuckle. Almost. My life is way more fucking entertaining when she's around. I can watch her all day—which I do, whenever I get the chance, anyway—and not be bored. Every action of hers entrances me. Every word that comes out of her mouth enchants me. Her scent bewitches me. Her curves captivate me. Everything about her has held me in thrall since the day I first saw her. Since she came into my life, it's turned into a patchwork of technicolor. I want to resist her, but my defenses are crumbling. It's pissing me off, but the more I try to put distance between us, the more thoughts of her invade my mind. As for my body? Every part of me remembers how it felt to be buried inside her. My cock thickens, and my thigh muscles harden. I widen the space between my legs, then crook my finger at her. "Come 'ere."

29

Mira

His voice is hard with that mean edge that propels a zing of sensations up my spine. When I hesitate, he lowers his arms to his sides.

"Come. Here. Belle."

I set my jaw, "And if I don't?"

"You know you want to," his tone softens. "You know you want me."

I don't. I don't.

"You do." He states the fact without malice. The expression on his face is confident, but his gaze is tortured. It's as if he senses the struggle going on inside me and recognizes it, and maybe that's what makes me place one foot in front of the other. When I come to a stop in front of him, his eyes flash.

"Say my name," he demands.

The rasp in his voice makes my insides melt. My breath stutters. My scalp itches. He's not touching me, but the way he rakes his gaze over my features, down the thrust of my breasts, to the space between my legs, he might as well be.

Then he sinks down to his knees, and I cry out. In seconds he's shoved my skirt up around my hips, leaned in, and pushed his face between my legs. My knees buckle; my head spins. He inhales a deep breath, and every pore in my body seems to breathe fire.

"What are you doing?" I say breathlessly.

"Smelling my wife's cunt," he snaps, "you have a problem with that?"

"N-noooooo!" The word is pulled from my mouth, for he's clamped his teeth around my clit and tugged. Shockwaves bolt up my spine. My fingers tremble. My heart rams into my chest and I'm sure it's going break out of my ribcage. He slides his big hands around my butt cheeks and fits me snugly over his mouth. Then he begins to lick me through the fabric of my panties. The combination of the smooth silk combined with the lapping sensation of his tongue is sheer torture. I dig my fingers into his hair and tug. "Edward, please Ed."

He makes a growling sound at the back of his throat, then slides his palm down the back of one thigh. He applies pressure and I raise my thigh. There's a ripping sound and he throws my leg over his shoulder.

"Fish on a turbocharger," I cry out.

There's a huffing sound, then he looks up at me. "Your swearing is very creative, but you don't want to use the Lord's name in front of me."

I glance down and the sight of his head between my thighs propels another burst of goosebumps over my skin. "Sorry." I swallow, trying to get my thoughts together. "I didn't realize it offended you. Especially since you're a former-priest—"

"You're mistaken."

"I am?"

"I don't believe in Him anymore."

O-k-a-y. "What do you believe in then?" The question is out before I can stop myself. His jaw hardens.

"I believe in myself."

"And love?" I know the answer, and yet I have to ask. *Stupid, stupid. Why did I have to open my big mouth?* My worst fears are confirmed when his features close further.

"It's not for me."

I try to pull away, but he holds me in place.

"Don't be angry. You knew the score before we got married. You knew I wasn't cut out for a relationship. You knew we weren't going to sleep together."

"So I'm good enough for you to penetrate me—"

"It's not going to happen again."

"—but I'm not good enough for you to make a sperm donation?"

His jaw tightens. "This what you want to be discussing now when I have my head up your skirt?"

"You started it, Buster."

"And I'm finishing it." With that, he shoves my panties aside and stabs his tongue inside me. My eyes roll back in my head. I hold onto him as he begins to thrust his tongue in and out of me. In-and-out, in imitation of how he penetrated me with his cock. It's not as thick or as long as his cock, of course... And, as if he's reading my mind, he swipes his tongue up my pussy-lips and curls it around my swollen clit, and at the same time, he stuffs three fingers inside me. I whimper, and it spurs him on. He moves his fingers in and out of me, continues to worry my clit. Then he adds a fourth finger a-n-d... I was mistaken. I love his cock, but the combination of his fingers and his tongue is so very wicked. He laps up my core, curls his fingers inside me, and the orgasm rams through me. It sweeps up my thighs, folds around my center, then zooms up my spine. It explodes somewhere at the back of my eyes, and I forget how to breathe. Then, I hear a keening sound and realize it's me crying out. The ecstasy fades away to be replaced by a glowing warmth. I'm aware of him rising to his feet. He scoops me up in his arms, walks around the desk and sits down with me in his lap. He holds me close, and I cuddle into him. I breathe in the familiar scent of woodsmoke shot through with that sharp tang, the way the air smells before a storm, which is so uniquely him. "Eddie," I whisper.

He tightens his arms around me. I push my ear into his chest and the bang-bang-bang of his heart gives away his state of arousal. That, and the length of concrete digging into the space between my naked asscheeks.

"My panties—" The word comes out as 'pahntiieesh,' and I realize I'm slurring.

"Shh, don't worry. I have some spare ones here for you."

"Hmm, okay." I cuddle closer, then snap open my eyes. "You have spare panties for me in your office."

He doesn't reply, and I interpret that correctly as an affirmative answer.

I glance up and meet those amber eyes of his. "Why do you have spare panties for me in your office?"

He tilts his head.

I sigh. "Did you know I was going to come in here, and that you were going to—"

"Make a mess in my lap?"

"What?" I wriggle this way, then that enough to catch a glimpse of the damp spot on the front of his pants. Heat flushes my cheeks. "I didn't mean to—"

"I'll wear it as a badge of pride."

I blush deeper, and the hard column underneath me extends further. "You still haven't come."

"I haven't come in two years."

30

Edward

Fuck, fuck. Fuck. Didn't mean to blurt that out. And since when do things slip past my control? Since when do I ensure there's an entire wardrobe change for a woman in the closet in my office? Since I met her. Since I got married to her. Since I feel this responsibility for her. This deep tenderness and need for her. This desire to make love to her. This compulsion to dominate her. To ensure she is always high from the pleasure only I can bring her. To mark her flesh and dig my teeth into the curve of her shoulder, to look into her eyes as I bury myself inside of her. To teach her who she belongs to. For she is mine. *My wife. My life. My love. Fuck… I can't have fallen for her in such little time.*

I wanted to keep her at arm's length. Instead, I can't stop myself from holding her in them. Close to me. Against my chest where I can smell her, feel her softness against me, assure myself she's safe and cared for. My pulse rate accelerates further. A bead of sweat trails down my spine. *I can't let myself feel so much for her. I will not break my vow. My self-control is the only thing I have left, and I will not willingly relinquish it.*

Some of my thoughts must show on my features—another first—for she cups my cheek. "Eddie, what's wrong?"

I want to tell her. I want to tell her why I can't be a better husband to her. Why I can't give her what she wants. Why I'll never be the man she deserves. Why I will not break the vow I made to myself. Why I'll never demand she submit to me, though every inch of me craves to feel her come apart, bit by bit, around my cock. I want to see her shudder as I bring her to the edge. I want to play her body like it's an instrument made for my pleasure. I want to do the most degrading, filthy things to her and watch her fight back before the inevitable capitulation.

She holds the power to destroy me; a power she's snatched from me without trying. She's more dangerous than the incident that changed me. Bit by bit, she's peeling back my layers, and revealing the man I'd hoped to become. I want to be everything for her…but can't. *I can't.*

"I can't."

"What?" She frowns.

"I can't do this."

"Do what?"

"This—you, me… It's not worth it."

She swallows. "I… I'm not sure what you mean."

I begin to lower her to the ground, but she throws her arms about my neck and clings. "Eddie, please talk to me. Don't shut down."

When I don't respond, she bites her lower lip, and of course, my dick instantly stabs against the restraint of my pants. Everything about her is designed to tempt me, to allure me and seduce me. I thought I could control myself around her — Ha, the joke's on me.

I thought I could resist her. Instead, I'm falling for her. I need to put distance between us again. I need to ensure there's no opportunity for me to be enticed by her.

Once again, she must read something in my gaze, for alarm flits across her features. She scrambles up, and pulling her skirt up further, she straddles me. "Eddie, no, don't do this." She pushes into me, so her breasts are flattened against my chest. Those hard nipples of hers dig into my jacket, and despite the layers between us, I can feel their outline against my chest, can sense the beating of her heart like it's my own. Can intuit the confusion that grips her, the appeal, the craving, the concern in her eyes. And that's my undoing.

"I don't deserve this. I don't deserve you."

"Why do you say that? Why do you beat yourself up so? The little time I've spent with you has shown me you're not the persona you project to the world. You're not hard, or emotionless; quite the contrary.

You feel so much." She slips a hand under my jacket, and my heart thuds against her palm. "You're real, and vital, and alive, and there's so much inside of you. You have so much to share with the world. You care deeply, Edward—too deeply—and that's the problem."

My pulse rate surges, and my stomach goes into a spiral, "I have no idea what you're talking about."

"Yes, you do. You feel everything. You see everything. You're so instinctive, so intuitive, so sensitive. You know exactly how I feel, which is why you stopped yourself earlier."

"I fucked you once… Without coming inside you, I might add. And only so when I tell my grandfather the deed is done, I'm not lying. And you think you know me?"

She winces, and of course, my heart stutters, but I push aside the pain.

"You're my husband."

I shrug. "We've been married for a little over a week."

"You don't have to spend time with someone to know them. I mean, you do"—she shakes her head—"but I trust my instincts, and they say you're not as mean or as ruthless as you make yourself out to be."

"Your instincts are wrong this time."

"I don't believe you. If I were wrong, you'd have fucked my ass, like you intended to, but you stopped yourself."

I stiffen. "Don't second guess me."

"Isn't that right? You wanted to do it, but you knew it would hurt. You knew I wasn't ready, so you stopped. Instead, you gave me pleasure —so much pleasure. You're a giver, Edward. But you think it's a weakness. So, you try to hide it behind all that bluster."

I yawn.

"Don't do that." She firms her lips.

"Do what?"

"Pretend you don't care, when the way your heart is racing, the way your eyes have turned bleak, the way the muscles of your shoulders bunch and your chest-planes tense, tell me the opposite."

Fucking hell, how does this woman see past the barriers I've erected against the world? How does she see into my soul every single time? How does she read me so clearly, when no one else has in the past? How can she, with a few words, destroy the remnants of my control?

"I don't know how much more plainly to tell you this, but I. Don't. Care."

She sets her jaw. "You're lying."

"I never lie." *And I did. For the very first time in my life, I lied. I. Fucking. Lied.* Something inside me splinters—the last bastion that has held back my shadow self, the partition I laid down to ensure the darkness inside me never peeked out. The last time I gave in to the darkness inside, I lost everything. And this time… This time, I'm going to lose her.

I squeeze her hips with enough force that she gasps. Whatever she sees in my face makes her gulp. "E-Eddie… You're scaring me."

"Good."

"I… I think… I need to leave." She tries to slip off, and I laugh.

Her gaze widens, and her blue eyes deepen until they're sheets of the deepest aquamarine. "You… You laughed? I've never seen you laugh. It should be reassuring but, it…it's not."

"Glad you're smarter than you look."

"That's not fair. You're saying that to hurt me."

"I haven't even started, baby."

She swallows. "You won't do it, Edward. I know you're not as heartless as you portray yourself."

"This heart might beat"—I slap one hand over hers, which is still inside my jacket—"but it's not capable of loving anyone."

Her features crumple, then she gets a hold of herself. "I know you don't mean it. I know you, Edward. I've seen you with Tiny—"

"A mutt—"

"The way a person treats a pet says everything about them. Everything. And you"—she searches my features—"you are all heart."

"What I am, is so hard that I can no longer wait to have your virgin arse."

31

Mira

He's being salacious in his choice of words so he can shock me. And I am shocked. And aroused. His dirty talking voice rockets a buzz of lust to my core. My thighs tremble, and my scalp tingles. He must sense the effect on me, for a look of interest comes into his eyes. "You like that, Belle?"

"Of course, not. Why would I like it if you're purposely being filthy in your speech."

"Because—" He shoves his hand between my legs and cups my bare pussy.

I gasp.

"—I can feel the moisture drip down your thighs and dampen on my crotch. I can"—he draws in a sharp breath—"smell your arousal intensify. I can—" He shoves two fingers inside me.

I whimper.

"—feel you clench down on me because you're empty. I can—" He pulls out his fingers, only to run them up the cleavage between my asscheeks.

I flinch, try to pull away, but he smears the moisture on my forbidden entrance.

"Edward," I groan. "Please. Edward."

He continues to hold my gaze, continues to tease my puckered hole. I instantly tense, and he leans in and runs his nose up my throat. "Your scent drives me crazy. You smell of sweet apple blossom and innocence, and it makes me want to mess you up."

"It's my shampoo." Goosebumps pepper my skin.

"Your shampoo?" He nuzzles my jawbone, my cheek, up to the corner of my eyes. It's almost sweet and gentle and romantic and so like the man I know he is inside. My muscles slowly unwind. A warmth steals up my limbs. I sink into him, feel my legs go lax, my thighs, my butt-cheeks... In a flash, he slides a finger inside me and past the ring of muscle in my back hole.

I gasp and bear down on him. "Edward, Ed." I dig my fingers into his hard shoulders. "Please, Ed."

"Shh, I promise, you're going to enjoy it."

"I'm not yet."

"You will." He continues to whisper kisses over one eyelid, between my eyebrows, the other eyelid, down my cheek, to the shell of my ear. When he flicks his tongue inside, I shiver. When he bites down on my earlobe, I moan. And when he continues the path down my cheek to the other side of my lips, I can't stop myself from turning to meet his lips. For a second, we stay there, gazing into each other's eyes, his lips touching mine, our breaths mingling, being shared, our eyelashes almost tangling. Something flickers deep inside. Those silver sparks I've seen before, joined, this time, by flashes of gold, sparkling, almost festive. "It's like it's already Christmas," I whisper.

His lips twitch, then he brushes his mouth over mine once, twice. The third time, I sigh, and he slides his tongue between my lips. He licks the seam, and my nipples tighten until they're pinpoints of need. He drags his tongue over my teeth and, fish in a train, those fires on my body, which are never too far from the surface, ignite again. I'm burning up, little pinpricks of need clawing at me from inside. I whine, and his body tenses. I lean in and push my tits against his chest, and a shudder grips him.

He's destroying me, but I have the power to tear him apart, too. This knowledge is an aphrodisiac that skyrockets the lust in my veins. I wrap my arms about his chest and force my muscles to relax. One-two-three,

I bite down on his tongue, and his entire body turns granite hard. The tension thrums off of him, the heat spooling off of his chest and slamming into mine. I gasp, and he absorbs the sound, then tilts his head and deepens the kiss. He drinks from me, ravages my mouth. As soft as his kisses were earlier, this is all inflexible and demanding, with a touch of meanness that is so very him. Both sides are him. The tenderness and the ruthlessness, the gentleness and the ferocity, the compassion and the brutality.

He showed me the first without wanting to, and the latter... He wants me to see it, feel it, sense it, imbibe it. Like he did when he took me to the BDSM club, he thinks if he shows me his hidden depths, I'll panic. That I'll run and hide and never want to be in his vicinity.

What he doesn't realize is I'm made of sterner stuff. I'm a survivor. I've learned to depend on myself. I persevere. I don't give up easily. I hope. And yes, I pray. And I believe. In him. In us. Most of all, I believe in myself, and it's time he saw that, too.

I slide my hand over his jacket-covered arm down to the back of his broad palm, and then his fingers.

I fit a second broad digit to my back hole and urge him on. His gaze widens, then a look of determination sweeps over his features. Without taking his eyes off of mine, he pushes his finger inside.

A slight pain threads over my nerve-endings. Nothing I can't bear, though. And the fullness... It's a little uncomfortable. Okay, very uncomfortable, but he doesn't move. He stays that way, allowing me to adjust to his size. We stay silent, communicating with our eyes, then he brings his other arm up and wraps his fingers about the nape of my neck. It's a gesture of complete confidence, of domination, of ownership, a sign that he can do what he wants, a signal to my body to turn to a melting gooey mess. It's comforting and arousing and sends a signal to every part of me that I'm ready. *I'm ready.*

"I'm ready," I whisper.

He nods. "Good girl."

Oh, my god, that's it; I'm undone. A small sound escapes my lips, and that's enough. His gaze crackles, his forearm bunches, and he begins to move his fingers in and out of me, in and out. Widening me, loosening me up, preparing me for him. And I want him. Oh, my god, I want him so very much. I want everything he can give me. Everything. And more. I want so much more. "Edward, please."

This time, when he smiles, it's a curve of his lips that has nothing to do with pleasure. It's an expression of satisfaction. Of approval. I've passed some test I didn't even know he'd set. I open my mouth to ask; but before I can say anything, he stands up, lowers my feet to the ground, spins me around, and bends me over his desk. I blink and realize my cheek is pushed into his desk, and my ass is up in the air. Then he kicks my legs apart. There's a ripping sound and my already torn skirt splits further.

"You're an animal," I gasp.

"Finally. Took you long enough to recognize it."

He shoves my skirt up as far up as it will go, so it's bunched under my armpit, then he urges my arms to my sides, curls my fingers around the edge of the desk.

"You good?"

I nod.

"Hold on tight."

"What—" A line of pain zips up my spine. It takes me a minute for my brain to catch up with my nerve cells. Then I yell, "Did you spank me?"

"Yup." His big palm connects with my left cheek, then the right, then the left, before he pauses. "I spanked you four times."

"What are you—" I yell again as he brings down his palm, alternating between my asscheeks, four more times. Four slaps, four more zings of pain that skitter to my core, curl around my clit like a lasso and pull tight. I moan and pant and curse. He laughs. The bastard laughs. I've never seen him enjoying himself so much.

"I hate you," I say through gritted teeth.

"Not yet."

He rubs his palm across my throbbing butt cheeks, and the contact sends another swish of sensations bursting up my spine. My brain cells feel like they're melting. Everything around me seems to sparkle. He seems to have brought the Christmas spirit to life without lights, a-n-d I might be a tad high on whatever reaction he's eliciting in my body. Heat covers me. The edge of his jacket chafes my backside as he bends over me. He pushes my hair away from my face and stares into my eyes. "How are you feeling?"

"I'm fine," I say in a dreamy voice.

He wraps his fingers, once more, around the nape of my neck. I sigh. I like when he does this; I like it a lot. He draws long strokes down my back over my blouse and skirt, down to the base of my spine, and up again.

Warmth seeps into my shoulders and my arms, and the muscles of my back unwind. I stretch under him, feeling like I'm a cat, feeling my lips stretch up in a smile. He bends and presses his lips to mine, and it's soft and sweet and hard and demanding, all at once. *Jeez.* "Where did you learn how to kiss like that?"

"It's you," he murmurs into my mouth. "You make me want to show you how good it can be when I make love to you."

"Hmm." I smile. *He said 'make love to you.'* My gaze widens. I open my mouth to ask him…when something fat and blunt teases my forbidden hole.

32

____

Edward

Only when the words are out of my mouth, do I realize what I've said. And that she heard it, and that there's no turning back now. I tried to show her my true self, and I let the truth slip out— dammit—the very reason I lost my composure, the very reason I lied earlier. And now, it's all out there. And I know she's going to ask me about it, and I'm not ready to talk about it—not now, not for a while. So like the coward I am, I tilt my hips, push forward, and breach her.

"Eddie," she cries out. No one's ever called me by this nickname, and hearing it from her lips sends the blood draining to my cock. My cock thickens impossibly more, pushing up against her walls. I wait, wait, allow her to adjust to my size. Then, when the trembling in her body recedes, I propel my hips forward and bury myself inside her.

She groans.

So do I.

And because I can't stop myself, because I'm falling for her—and my heart knows it, though my brain hasn't yet caught on—and because she's so fucking gorgeous laid out in front of me, and because her lips are a better taste, better than any liquor I've ever drunk, I lower my head and press my mouth to hers again. She parts her lips willingly, and I ease my tongue over hers. The taste of her is potent and sweet and complex and innocent, all mixed into one. It goes straight to my heart and ties a lasso around it, then heads to my cock. My shaft twitches. I draw of her breath, lick into her mouth, absorb her whimper, and when I straighten, she looks at me with so much trust, that ball of sensation in my heart expands until it bleeds into my skin and covers my entire body. I hold her gaze, then lock my fingers around the nape of her neck. "Do you trust me?"

She nods.

And it undoes me, all over again.

I reach down and around her, then begin to strum her pussy. Color flushes her cheeks, and she moans. Her muscles relax even more, and I slip deeper inside her. "You're so tight… So hot… So perfect." I grit my teeth and allow her to adjust, once more, to my intrusion.

I continue to play with her pussy lips, circle her clit, and when I slide my fingers inside her cunt, she moans. "It's too much. You're filling me up. I can't take any more."

"You can," I say with complete confidence in her. "You will. You're my Belle."

"And you're a beast," she moans.

I like that name even more, though I don't say that aloud. Instead, I rub her clit with the heel of my palm. "Open up and let me in, baby."

She willingly widens her legs further. I continue to slide my fingers in and out of her, and when I add a fourth finger, she shudders.

"Ohgod, ohgod, ohgod," she chants. I don't stop her. Even if I don't want to hear His name from her lips. Whatever she wants, whatever she needs, It's hers.

Except me. I can't give her myself. Not more than what I've already shared.

But I can make her come one last time. I pull out but stay poised at the rim of her back entrance. She shivers, and when I propel myself forward, I slide all the way in. My balls slap against her slit, and the entire desk shakes. A glass crashes to the ground, but I don't stop. I pull out, once again, and still holding her gaze, push into her. I bury myself to the hilt, hitting that spot deep inside her.

"Oh—" she gasps. "Oh my—" I release my hold on her neck, squeeze her hip and position her at the right angle. This time, when I push into her, I hit that spot again. She opens her mouth, but no sound comes out.

But I know. I know she's close. She's almost there. Her back curves, her thighs clench, and she squeezes down on my cock and my fingers. I pull out and push forward, again and again, and when her pupils dilate until only a circle of blue is visible, and the skin over her knuckles is stretched white, and that tell-tale shudder spirals up her hips, I lean over, place my lips above hers and command, "Come."

"You didn't come, again."

She shoots me a sideways glance. I keep my gaze focused on the road ahead. After she shattered under me, I pulled out, then scooped her up in my arms, and took her into the ensuite. I helped her out of her clothes and, brushing aside her protests, cleaned her up. Then, I showed her the walk-in closet I had built especially so I could store clothes for her. She seemed taken aback by the range of clothes—all in her size, including the underwear.

"You bought all this?" she asked.

When I nodded, her gaze widened. "It's not easy to find plus-size clothing; it must have taken you a lot of searching to find this array of clothes."

"It was worth it. You're worth it." I helped her out of her clothes, and while she stood naked, I worshiped her with my eyes. I stored every curve of her body in my mind—her heavy breasts, the nip of her waist, the flaring of her hips, and those fleshy thighs that haunt my dreams. I wanted her to sit on my face, so I could take my time and make her come again. I wanted to crawl up her body, settle between her legs and finally, *finally* bury myself inside her. I almost lost my resolve and did just that, but at the last moment, I managed to tear myself from her. I left her to find a suitable change of clothes.

She chose a below-the-knee skirt, a blouse, and a jacket in a peach color that turned her skin to ivory.

She's so fucking beautiful, my wife. If only I could give her the kind of love she deserves. For the first time, I'm wondering if marrying her was a mistake. I didn't want anyone else to have her. I was selfish. *I am selfish.* I've spoiled her life, and I have to make up for it.

Once she was ready, I hustled her out of the office, not caring that it wasn't even five p.m. As I steered my wife toward the elevator, the receptionist shot me an alarmed look. When I didn't acknowledge it, she jumped to her feet and walked over to me. "Are you okay, Sir? You've never left office this early before."

"I wasn't married then. I am now."

Belle draws in a sharp breath.

My receptionist ignores her and takes a step in my direction. "If you need anything else — ?"

I squeeze my wife closer. "I have everything I need."

This time, Belle turns to me, a question on her features, which I pretend not to notice.

I hustle her into the elevator, then hold her close as the elevator doors close on the receptionist's crestfallen features.

"I think she has a crush on you," Belle teases.

And I'd like to crush you in my arms, is what I want to say, but I don't.

We ride in silence for a few more seconds, then she turns to me, "Is it true you've never left the office this early before?"

I nod.

"You didn't have to leave early because of me."

Yes, I do. I want to spend every second of every day with you. The first time I saw you, my heart hurt, and the throbbing in my groin has become a permanent fixture. My balls need to be drained before it gets to be too much. Too bad, I'm not going to indulge myself.

Something of my thoughts must be revealed in the stance of my body, for she stiffens, then scans my features. "Edward, have you taken a vow of abstinence?"

33

Mira

"I'm no longer a clergyman, as you're aware." He continues to focus on the road.

"But you said you haven't been with any woman for a while, and whenever we make love—"

"You mean when we fuck—"

"You used the word 'love,' earlier."

"What?" He frowns.

"You said—"

"I know what I said, and it was a slip of the tongue."

"I thought you said you don't lie?" I narrow my gaze on him.

He tightens his fingers on the wheel and continues to drive. "I don't. Except when I'm with you, apparently."

I blink. I hadn't expected to hear that. "Are you saying—"

"People say all kinds of things when they're having sex."

"We weren't having sex; you didn't come."

"I made *you* come… And hard, as I recall."

On cue, my backside smarts. I shift around, trying to find a more comfortable position. I try to be discreet about it, but he notices it, of course, the bastard.

"Does your butt hurt?"

"What do you think?"

"I think I enjoyed seeing my palm print etched into your arse."

Oh, my god, what is it about him saying arse in that British accent of his that has me all hot and bothered again? "I don't know what game you're playing—"

"Not a game."

"—but I'm not going to be put off by you demonstrating your kinky side."

He blinks. "My kinky side?" he asks slowly.

"Spanking me, then the, uh—backside entry."

"You mean anal?"

My flush deepens. I'm not a prude. I've read enough super-spicy novels and listened to even more of them, so of course, I know my way around the smutabulary, but I've never been able to say that world aloud. Never mind the fact that, an hour ago, my husband's monster cock was up my ass. Oh, shoot, I *am* a prude.

"Exactly," I say in a prim voice. "Since you took me to the BDSM club, I know you're not vanilla in your preferences."

"Not vanilla?" There's something in his voice that makes me cast a quick glance in his direction. The divot to the left of his mouth tells me he's finding this entire conversation amusing.

"It's not funny," I protest.

"It's not," he agrees.

"Then why are you smiling?"

"Because you think what I did to you was kinky."

"It was."

"You have no idea," he says in that voice that has more than a hint of darkness to it.

A ripple of heat squeezes my belly. "You mean, that was the beginner's level introduction to smutty sex?"

"I mean, that was the pre-kindergarten level introduction to my depravity."

"Oh." I know my mouth is open and that I'm staring at him, but it's the first time we've had an open conversation about something... So what, if it's about his perversions.

"So you have, uh…different tastes, but you haven't been with a woman since…"

"Since I left to go traveling, two years ago."

"You…you haven't been with a woman in two years?" I stare.

He merely stares at me.

"But you go to the BDSM club."

"And as you've experienced firsthand, I don't have to ejaculate in order to indulge my debaucheries."

Oh, my god! The heat in my stomach expands into a full-blown forest fire, which instantly spreads to my extremities. My lower belly clenches, and I squeeze my thighs together to tamp down on the yawning emptiness.

"For someone who was a virgin until a week ago, you sure relish the dirty talk," he murmurs.

"Only when it's you doing the dirty talking."

He chuckles, then seems to realize what he's done, for he wipes all expression from his face.

"It's okay to laugh and smile and cry and show emotion. You are human, after all."

"And it's because I allowed myself to be human, because I chose to give in to my emotions, that I'm here today."

A hot sensation stabs into my chest. It's as if he's plunged a burning rod into my heart. He seems to realize what he's said, for he scowls. "I didn't mean —"

"Yes, you did. You're regretting that you married me."

"Not for the reasons you think."

"So you *do* regret marrying me."

He steps on the accelerator and the car speeds up. "I never regret my actions."

"Expect the time you gave in to your emotions and lost the woman you loved."

Tell me you don't love her. Tell me you love me. You said it earlier; just say it aloud again.

But he doesn't. The muscles at his jaw line flex, but he stays silent, focuses on the driving. In another ten minutes, we drive up in front of his townhouse.

We stay in the car; the silence stretches, then he states, "I'm not the man you think I am." His voice is emotionless. "I'm not a knight in shining armor. I'm not Prince Charming."

"No, you're the beast, the villain. You're Hades, and Severus Snape, and Loki, rolled into one."

"Severus Snape?" He frowns.

"Point is, the darkness in you is what I find so attractive."

His jaw tightens. "You don't know what you're talking about."

"Sure, I do. I know that every time you look at me, you feel something, but you're so convinced you'll never own your emotions again, you won't admit it."

"It's why you should have never married me, Belle." His tone is serious.

And when I search his features, I realize he believes it, too. I swallow hard. "I married you of my own free will."

"Did you?" There's something in his features, an expression I can't interpret.

A cold sensation spirals down my spine. I shiver, then shove it aside. "I did," I say in a firm voice.

"What you got a taste of in my office is not even a starter course."

"I'm not scared, Edward. I want to be your main and your dessert. I want to be your eight-course meal."

He scoffs, "You, the newly deflowered virgin… You have no idea what you're talking about."

"No, don't do that." I cut my palm through the air. "Don't patronize me. I am not a child."

"You were one not too long ago."

I shake my head. "You don't get to diminish me. I know what I'm doing."

"Do you?"

"I do. I knew what I was taking on when I left home and moved to a new city. I knew what I was doing when I agreed to marry you."

"You didn't have a choice."

"I could have refused you and my father. I could have walked out."

"But you didn't."

"That's right." I straighten my spine. "I chose the tough route, because it was my responsibility to help my father. I don't shirk my duties."

"So that's what this is?" He looks me up and down. "You want to sacrifice yourself at the altar of my depravity because you want to live up to the duty of being my wife."

"Yes." I tip up my chin. "I won't shirk from my obligations."
"You have no obligation toward me."
"How can you say that? I am your wife."
"And I will not corrupt you further."

34

Edward

"Why are you not with your wife?" Arthur frowns.

"Because I didn't want to miss poker night." I focus on my cards, while well aware of the suspicion in his eyes.

I'm not doing a good job of playing the newly-married husband desperately in love with his bride. In fact, I'm screwing up my role so badly, even my grandfather believes something is wrong.

"For a man enjoying post marital bliss, you seem strung tightly," Knox drawls.

Asswipe is trying to get another response from me, and this time, I will not give in to him.

I accompanied Belle to the door of the townhouse, made sure she was in safely, then instructed my housekeeper to cook dinner for her. I had no interest in the poker game, but I did want to see my grandfather face-to-face. He still hasn't confirmed me as CEO, even though I'm in charge of all the key decisions of the company. I'm not going to bring it up with him, of course. I'm more strategic than that.

It's why I asked Sinclair to invite Arthur and Knox for his weekly poker night. Our mutual friends who'd normally attend are out of town.

It's the perfect opportunity to get facetime with the old man, without asking for a meeting. As for inviting Knox? It's a chance to demonstrate I don't hold a grudge.

I hoped to get a reading on my grandfather. But from what I'm seeing, he's not very happy with me.

"I'm taking my wife on our honeymoon over Christmas," I declare.

"You are?" Arthur looks up from his cards.

"I have a property in Cornwall. Very picturesque and isolated…and romantic. The perfect way to spend Christmas."

Arthur's features relax. "That sounds like the ideal getaway."

"It is."

"I'm pleased you're taking your duties as a husband seriously. If the wife's happy, everything else in your life will fall in order." He nods.

I incline my head to show I agree with him.

"I assume you'll do this properly and not work while you're away?" Knox murmurs in a casual tone. Which doesn't fool me at all. Mother-fucker will try any which way to take control of the company.

"Oh, I'll make sure I'm connected to the internet while I'm gone. Remote working and—"

"Absolutely not. You need to focus on your wife and your marriage completely while you're gone. It's very important you make it your priority."

"Oh, I can still attend meetings. The takeover we spoke about in conjunction with the 7A company—"

"Will be taken care of," Arthur declares.

I glance at Sinclair, but his expression indicates he has no idea what Arthur is talking about.

"The takeover is in a delicate phase." Sinclair looks up from his cards. "We'll probably sign the deal during the last week of December, and as the main signatory, it makes sense for Edward to be on the calls and—"

"—it's not right to disturb the man, no matter how important he is, on his honeymoon."

"But he's the key decision maker," Sinclair points out.

"Which is why I'm bringing in someone else with signing powers."

I stiffen. There it is, then. The old man never did intend to hand over the running of the company to me. He may have made me CEO, but he was never going to let me have veto power.

Knox throws down his cards. "Now, that's what I'm talkin' about."

He leans back in his seat. "You've made the right choice, Gramps. I won't let you down."

"Of course, not." Arthur's eyes gleam. He's hiding something, all right. He reaches over and scratches Tiny behind his ears. The Great Dane yawns. He welcomed me like an old friend when I walked in today, then abandoned me to take Arthur's side. There's a bond between the two of them which Arthur clearly relishes. When Tiny decided to stay with Arthur, I was worried about the mutt being shuttled around between homes, but I'm realizing Tiny has a mind of his own. He decides who's going to be his dog parent, and right now, he's adopted my grandfather as the adult in his life. He's softening up the old coot too, going by how Arthur smiles at the group.

Come to think of it, he's not the only one thawing. First, Tiny; then, Belle. Between the two of them, my life has been turned upside down.

Footsteps sound, then a man walks into the room. He's tall—as tall as me, six feet three inches, at least—broad shouldered, muscled in a way that hints at time spent doing physical work, and not just the gym kind. This man spends time working with his hands. He's wearing a black suit, which stretches over his physique and indicates its tailor made for his dimensions. His dark hair is peppered with grey at the temples.

I take in all of this, but what holds my attention are his features. They are so familiar. So like Knox's and like my grandfather's. He's... *Nope, can't be.*

"Arthur." The new guy nods in my grandad's direction.

"You don't mind, I invited Nathan here to join your poker night, Sterling?" Arthur phrases it as a question to Sinclair, but his tone makes it clear, he isn't asking for permission so much as informing.

If Sin is surprised, he hides it well.

"Of course." Sinclair rises to his feet, pulls up a chair, and slides it into the space between him and me.

"Thank you." Nathan slides into the seat, then jerks his chin at Knox, who's been glowering at him from across the table.

"You must be Knox," Nathan murmurs.

"The fuck are you?"

"I'm your oldest half-brother."

"What the fuck?" Knox throws his cards down on the table. "Is this a joke, Arthur?" He turns to our grandfather. "Because if it is—"

I scan Nathan's features and see the truth in his eyes. "It's not a joke, Knox."

"I want to hear it from Arthur," Knox says without taking his gaze off of our grandfather.

Arthur pets Tiny one more time, then turns to face Knox. "This is Nathan Davenport, my oldest grandson."

"I thought *he* was your oldest grandson." Knox jerks his chin in my direction.

"So did I." Arthur looks at me with an apologetic expression. "I found out about him at the same time as Edward. I reached out to Nathan and Edward at the same time, but Nathan never replied."

"I was traveling." Nathan shrugs.

"And now, you're conveniently here, in time to claim a part of the family fortune?" Knox growls.

"I'm independently wealthy." Nathan's lips twist, "I'm here because —"

"I asked him to come," Arthur interjects. "Turns out, before your father met Edward's mother, he had a son with his childhood sweetheart. She was sixteen when Nathan was born. Your father refused to step up to his responsibilities."

"What a surprise." Knox snorts.

"Greta paid off Nathan's mother, so she could leave with him and bring him up far away from us."

Nathan's jaw tics, but he doesn't comment.

"Apparently, your father knew if he came clean to me, I'd disinherit him. Greta didn't want that for him either. The two kept this a secret, but Greta wanted me to do right by Nathan."

"How did you find him?"

"His mother didn't keep her promise. She couldn't help but name your father on his birth-certificate." Arthur glances around the table. "Nathan grew up with the Davenport surname."

"A name I never wanted to be associated with. A name I should have gotten rid of the first chance I had," he says in a matter-of-fact voice.

"But you didn't." Arthur turns to him. "Family ties, dear grandson, can't be broken that easily."

"You trying to convince yourself or me?" Nathan drawls.

"You're here, aren't you?" Arthur puffs on his cigar.

"Grandma sure kept a lot of secrets from you." Knox lowers his chin to his chest.

Arthur's shoulders tense, then he seems to get a hold of himself. "And she wanted to make amends for it.

"By asking you to split the family fortune amongst those who don't deserve it?"

"You will apologize to your brother," Arthur booms.

"That's half-brother, and I will not," Knox shoots back.

Arthur sighs. "When you reach my age, you'll realize, family is all that matters."

"Good thing I'm not your age yet," Knox sneers.

Nathan looks like he's about to say something, then firms his lips.

"Any other long-lost relations we need to know about?" Knox tips up his chin in Arthur's direction, "Any other 'grandsons'"—he makes air-quotes—"lurking in the background with whom we'll need to split control of the company?"

"No grandsons," Arthur murmurs.

"But there are *others*?" I ask.

"My oldest son is Edward's adoptive father. And you're aware of my middle son, your biological father." He directs this statement at me and Knox before looking around the table. " The one you haven't met is my youngest," he murmurs.

"I knew it." Knox slaps his hand on the table with such force, the cards jump.

Arthur purses his lips. "We, uh…had a falling out, which caused him to leave home. It also resulted in me wiping all traces of him from my home, which is why you didn't know of his existence. I'm sorry to say, I hurt your grandmother deeply with that." The old man swallows.

"You're hurting us with these revelations," Knox points out.

"I promised Greta, on her deathbed, I'd reunite my family." He sets his jaw.

"More like, you're setting us up for a fight with all these new entrants," Knox mutters under his breath.

"And where is this long-lost uncle?" I ask slowly.

"I haven't been able to track him down. Maybe, he wants to stay hidden." Arthur pats Tiny's giant head.

"Maybe he *should* stay hidden." A nerve throbs at Knox's temple. "You expect us to accommodate yet another relation—no offense, Edward—"

"None taken." I shrug.

"— and slice up the family fortune because you've decided to make up for your sins in your old age?"

There's silence, then Arthur blows out a breath. "I understand how difficult all of this must be for you, especially when you were groomed to be my heir-apparent. Your father was a loser. The only good thing he did was sire you boys. I thought long and hard before bringing in first, Edward and now, Nathan, but it's for your own good, Knox."

Knox snorts.

"You're not made to be the CEO. Yet," Arthur declares.

Knox's jaw tics. "Don't hold back, Gramps," he growls.

Arthur holds up his hands. "I know, you're upset. But I promise you, when you look back, you'll understand it was for your own good."

"That's what they always say," Knox says in a bitter voice.

"You'll still be on the board of directors and lead on one of the smaller companies—"

"I just won't be CEO," Knox snaps.

"You'll never lack for money," Arthur points out.

"I just won't have the power." The tendons of Knox's throat bunch.

"I've given you a foothold in the company. When you prove yourself, you can climb the ladder like everyone else. There's nothing keeping you from staking a claim to be the CEO."

Knox stares at him steadily, "And he has the experience I lack? That's what you're trying to say, aren't you?"

Arthur lowers his chin to his chest. When he speaks, it's in a matter-of-fact tone, "Edward's had a few knocks in life, enough to make him worldly-wise. Nathan joined the navy and has been posted all over the world. He has experience making decisions involving the lives of people."

"Navy, huh?" Knox glares at the new guy.

Nathan tilts his head.

Arthur looks between us. "I realized it wasn't fair that I put the entire burden of leading the company on Edward, given he's just gotten married."

Motherfucker. The old man asked me to marry in order to ensure my inheritance. Now, he's using it as an excuse to hold it back from me, as well. I thought he was canny…but he's positively Machiavellian.

Arthur's features are all innocent as he turns to Knox. "I don't have much time left—"

Knox makes a rude noise, which all of us ignore.

"—and when your grandmother died, she left me information on not only how to track down Edward, but also Nathan."

"And you didn't think it important to mention it to me?" I ask mildly.

"It came as a surprise to me, too. I only found out a few days ago," Nathan offers.

Arthur pretends to be hurt. "I hope you boys are not going to gang up on me. I merely want what's best for the family, and for the empire *I* have built from scratch."

No missing the emphasis on the 'I' there.

"It was your grandmother's wish that I bring all her grandchildren together, and that they have a vested interest in working together to grow the business," Arthur continues.

"Decision-making by community never works," Knox warns.

"Oh, you don't have to worry about that." Arthur lays his cards down on the table face-up—a Royal Flush, no less. "The veto power rests with both Edward and Nathan."

Knox draws in a sharp breath.

Sinclair raises his eyebrows.

Arthur looks very pleased with himself.

This…is unexpected. It's not what I had in mind when I decided to make being the CEO of the Davenport empire my focus. This…changes things. Considerably. Anger squeezes my chest. A cold sensation percolates through my blood. I trusted Arthur—perhaps naively, I realize now. I hoped I would find in him the sense of family I hadn't had with my own parents. I miscalculated. Once more, I've allowed my emotions to rule me, and it has come to bite me in the arse. Lesson well learnt.

"This is bullshit." Knox jumps up to his feet. "You are going senile, old man." He stabs a finger at Arthur. "And you"—he turns to Nathan —"can go to hell."

He pushes away from the table, grabs his jacket off the back of his chair, and stalks out.

We sit there in silence for several moments.

"Now that that's out of the way,"—Sinclair grabs the bottle of whiskey—"who can I top up?"

<hr>

"You're pissed." Sinclair half carries, half drags me up the steps of my townhouse.

"What I am is pisshhed… Pissshhed… Pishhhhhed offfffff." My words are slurred; I can hear them as if from far away. This is not being drunk. This is…medicinal. *Yep, that's all it issssshhhh. Fuck, I'm slurring in my head now, too.* I miss the next step, stumble and would fall face first if Sinclair doesn't grab my shoulders and straighten me.

"Fucking hell, Priest, what's wrong with you?"

"Whatssssh wrrrrong is that I trusssted that fucker."

"You mean Arthur?"

"Ar—fucking—thur… My fucking grandfather. I shhhhhouldn't be surprised; my parents didn't give a fuck about me, eeeeither. And after the incident, if it hadn't been for B-B-Baron, I wouldn't've sssshurvived."

"Have you spoken to him at all?" His voice softens. "You guys were the best of friends and—"

"I don't need him in my life. In fact,—" I push away from him, stumble, but manage to find my footing. *Why the fuck is the door swaying in front of my eyes?* I put one foot in front of the other, reach the door, and am about to knock when it swings open. The most beautiful woman in the world, aka, my wife, stands there. She's wearing a pair of yoga pants that cling to her thick thighs, and a tiny T-shirt that outlines her gorgeous breasts. Heat tugs on my lower-belly. My cock thickens. Not that drunk, then.

"Wife, you're fucking gorgeous."

"And you're pissed." She slaps her hands on her hips, and her top tightens further. Now, I can see those sweet nipples outlined against the fabric, too. I lean in, intent on taking a bite of those gorgeous double-D tits; only, I lose my balance and stagger. She throws her arms about me. I bend and take a long sniff of her hair. Apple Blossom. Any remaining blood drains to my cock. My head spins. I begin to topple over. She yelps, sways. My knees begin to give way, when a firm hand under my bicep pulls me to my feet again.

I shake my head to clear it, pull away from Sinclair, then brush past her and step inside. I'm dimly aware of Sinclair supporting me on one side. Then, she slides her arm about my waist from the other. I lean my weight on Sinclair and tuck her closer under my arm.

"Alright, let's get you to your room." Sinclair urges me forward. One step at a time, one foot in front of the other. *Why is everything so blurry?*

I hear a voice singing from far away. Weird; it's a familiar voice, but what-fucking-ever. There will no longer be any emotions in my life. That much is clear. Then, we're climbing up the stairs, down the hallway, into my bedroom. The mattress floats up to meet me. I spin on a cloud of white and grey and blue and red. So much red. Anger, pain, suffering. I draw in a breath, and my lungs burn. It's dark, so dark.

There's a groan; someone else is there with me. I try to open my eyes, but realize I'm blindfolded. Try to move my arms, and realize my hands and legs are tied. I begin to struggle in earnest, trying to break the ropes that bind me, but they seem to tighten with my efforts. My muscles burn, my heart pounds in my chest. Sweat pours down my face. Pain screeches up my arms, and I realize the restraints are cutting into my wrists.

Let me go, I didn't do anything wrong. Let me the hell go. Oh god, oh god, why am I here? Help me, Lord. If I get out of here, I'll forever be grateful. I'll make sure I don't run away from school again. I'll be a good boy, I promise. Please, God, please. Tears squeeze out from the corners of my eyes. Wetness drips onto my lips. *Help, help me, please don't punish me like this please.*

"Edward."

I need to get out of here. I didn't do anything wrong. I didn't. Don't punish me, I beg you.

"Ed, Eddie."

There's a rustling sound as the door creaks open, followed by footsteps. I try to move my arms and legs but realize I'm tied up. The space around me lightens, enough for me to make out another figure tied up not far from me. I blink until the person's features come into focus. It's Baron. Fuck. I strain at my restraints, but they don't give. The footsteps come closer; I try to push away from it. Arms reach for me, and I strain away. "Don't touch me. Don't fucking touch me. Don't."

"Eddie, it's me!"

I snap my eyes open. Baby blues meet mine. Thick eyelashes, flushed cheeks, rosebud lips. I draw in a shuddering breath, and the scent of sweet apple blossoms coils deep in my chest.

"Ed,"—she swallows—"you were dreaming."

"And now, I'm not." In one swoop, I've flipped her on her back on the bed and slammed my palms on either side of her head.

35

Mira

"Eddie." My heart crashes into my rib cage. "Ed, are you okay?"

He doesn't answer. He's planked over me, so his weight is not on me, but his big body is so close, the heat from him crashes into me and sinks into my blood. It feels like I'm in a sauna. Sweat breaks out over my upper lip. "Edward, it was a dream."

"But *you're* not," he says in a hard voice, which is darker, meaner than how he's sounded before. My pulse rate leaps. My pussy clenches. *I should not be aroused by the viciousness in his voice, but I'm learning, I'm not the woman I thought I was. I enjoy it when he looks at me like I'm an object made for his pleasure. I adore it when he manipulates my body to bring himself satisfaction. I'm positively giddy when he touches me like it means nothing to him. What does that say about me? Is that why I was attracted to him right away, because I sensed the darkness in him? Because it touched that part deep inside of me which I'd hidden but somehow known existed? Known I was waiting for someone like him to flick a switch and let out the pleasure seeker inside of me?*

"I'm not," I say softly.

"You're *my* wife."

"I am."

"And you are *duty-bound* to do everything I ask of you."

I swallow. He's repeating my words back to me, but from his mouth, they take on a darker meaning. Goosebumps dot my skin. A jitteriness twists my lower belly. Moisture bathes my pussy, and it takes everything in me not to whine with fear and anticipation...and need. *Oh god, I'm turning into a puddle of want under him.* And the way his nostrils flare, he senses it.

"Will you, Belle?" he growls. The sound is harsh and demanding, and it rips through my defenses. That melting puddle I am turns into a seething ache. One that can only be satisfied by him.

"Yes," I croak.

He bares his teeth in response. I shiver. Another thing different about him. He's allowing his emotions to show on his face, something I've hoped for, but also... It's so unexpected. It turns him from that cold, unemotional man into someone whose control has snapped. Someone who feels everything intensely. Someone I knew existed underneath the seemingly detached front he's always presented. But there's a difference between knowing it and facing it. He's let the beast inside out to play and I...am the recipient of the consequences.

"And you'll do anything I ask."

I nod.

"Anything?"

He tilts his head, an inquiring look in his eyes. The angle of his head, the way he's watching me closely, the way those amber eyes of his gleam, he could be an apex predator, stalking his prey. Another jolt lances through me. I brace myself, and nod again, then cry out when he drops his head and drags his nose up my cheek.

"Your scent drives me crazy. It makes me want to throw you down and rut into you. It makes me want to throw you over my shoulder and carry you away where no one else can see you. It makes me crazy, and I hate it. I fucking hate how you make me want things I shouldn't."

There's a thread of desperation woven through that darkness in his tone. It gives me the courage to dig my fingers in his hair and tug. He straightens and glares at me. His gaze is so hard, so filled with lust, my heart almost stops, then starts again. It also spurs me on to declare, "Good!"

His gaze widens, then a resolute look comes into his eyes. "I'm going to use you. I'm going to do things to your body, you could have never imagined in your wildest dreams. I'm going to stuff your holes and you're going to take everything like a good girl."

My toes curl. My breath hitches. I begin to pant and can't stop myself.

"I'm going to have you begging and writhing and wanting to come, but I won't let you."

I swallow.

"Not until you've forgotten who you are and where you are, and all you know is my touch, my gaze on you, my fingers inside you, my cock throbbing in your cunt, and you're crying for release and then... Perhaps, I might consider it."

"You...you're cruel," I moan.

"And you love it."

"And you have a big ego."

"And the balls to go with it." He lowers himself and the evidence of his arousal nudges the cleft between my legs. He's so big, so heavy... And I've felt him inside of me, but somehow, he feels thicker, more swollen, more solid, more everything.

"I want you inside of me. I want you to come in me."

His gaze flickers. "And I want to see you cry. I want your tears to cleanse the burden of my past. I want your innocence to dissolve the darkness in me. Can you do that for me, Belle?"

There's a plea in his voice, which is strange. He's promising he's not going to be easy on me, and... I don't want him to be. I want him to come to me unvarnished. Show me who he really is. I want the unadulterated version of him. I want everything he can give me. I want him. HIM.

"Yes." I nod slowly. "Yes, I can do that." Then, I reach up and slap him.

36

______

Edward

My head snaps back. The pain slices through my head, spikes my blood stream and ignites my need. My cock is so hard, I'm sure I'm going to come any second.

She raises her hand again, and I grab it, twist it over her head, then do the same with her other. I transfer her wrists to one hand; the other, I wrap about her neck and squeeze. "You've done it now."

Her gaze widens. The blue is now a deep indigo, which is almost black.

"Do you want me to punish you again? Is that it? Do you like my handprints on your butt? Do you like pain?"

Her lips part.

"You a pain slut, Belle?" I look between her eyes. "You trying to provoke me into hurting you?"

"Why don't you find out?"

My muscles bunch. Every pore in my body seems to come alive. "You don't know what you're asking for."

"You don't know who you married." She holds my gaze, her own steady. "I don't back down. I don't frighten easily. And I never give up. I know who you are, Eddie. Deep down, I know you're not the hardened indifferent man you portray to the world. I know how much you're hurting. And I want you to share it with me. I want you to use me and pleasure me. And yes, I want you to take from me so you heal. But it's not all altruistic. I want you to show me how it can be with you. I want you to wring every last orgasm from my body. I want you to give me so much pleasure, I can't think of anything else but you, I—"

I swoop down and close my mouth over hers. I kiss her hard, I mean to punish her for her impertinence, for provoking me, for being there for me when I woke up from my nightmare, for stealing my peace of mind from the first moment I saw her. For…agreeing to become my wife. For becoming…mine. Mine. *Mine.*

I deepen the kiss, and when she moans, I swallow the sound. I release my hold on her throat, only to cup her tit and squeeze. She shudders. I pinch her nipple through her camisole, and her entire body jolts. The beat of her heart thuds faster against my chest, and I feel each thud like it's my own. I'm drowning in her. I'm losing myself. And this time I can't… I won't stop it.

I soften the kiss. I share breath with her, lick her mouth, press my lips to hers, and she melts into me. I continue to kiss her, taking my time, learning the shape of her mouth, the cupid's bow of her upper lip, the softness of her lower lip, the way she sighs and makes that little noise at the back of her throat that sends a spear of heat to my groin. And when she groans, I slide my tongue over hers, and the taste of her fills my senses. Her scent surrounds me and every pore in my body seems to open to absorb more of her. When I finally pull back, her features are flushed. Her hair a cloud of purple-streaked gold about her shoulders, and her mouth is swollen.

"Open your eyes."

She raises her heavy eyelids to reveal dilated pupils. A fresh burst of need tightens my belly. Without breaking the connection, I pull up her camisole, then bend and close my mouth around an erect nipple. I bite down and she cries out.

"Oh, my god!"

I release it with a pop, and when I suck on her other breast, she writhes under me. "

"It's too much. I can't take it. I can't."

I release my hold on her hands, only to slide down her body. When my face is level with her crotch, I slide my finger in the waistband of her lacy underwear and snap it. I pull it free, then press my face into her pussy and breathe her in.

She shudders, digs her fingers in my hair, and tugs. Pin-pricks of awareness travel to my cock. My balls harden, and the ever-present tension in my groin shoots up. I slide my hands under her hips and urge her legs over my shoulders. Then I begin to eat her out. —her slit, her pussy lips, that throbbing button of desire between them. She whimpers, tries to pull away, but I hold her in place. I continue to ravage her cunt, thrusting my tongue in and out of her sopping wet channel. She whines, shudders, squeezes her thighs around my face, smothering me with her flesh, her touch, her scent, and fucking hell, I'd die happily right now. I squeeze her ample butt cheeks and she arches into my touch. Thrusts her pelvis up so my tongue dips deeper inside her. Fat drops of her cum slide down my chin, and when I nibble on her swollen clit, she mewls. More moisture squirts from her slit and I lick it up.

A trembling sweeps up her legs. "Please Eddie, please," she cries out.

I know she's close, so I tear my mouth from her cunt, crawl up her body and kiss her. "Taste yourself."

She licks her lips and her cheeks flush further. "I'm sweet?" she whispers.

"Like honey, or nectar, an aphrodisiac that makes me want to lick your every hole."

"Oh." She pants.

I reach down, and because I fell asleep in my slacks, I lower my zipper. When the blunt head of my cock nudges her opening, a trembling grips her.

Once more, I urge her to lock her ankles around my waist, then rise up on my knees to get traction. I slide a cushion under her to elevate her hips, then in one smooth thrust, I impale her.

37

Mira

The breath squeezes out of me. He's bigger than I remember, and thicker. I'm spread around him, pinned to the bed, and he's pushing against my channel walls. I was so wet, he slipped in easily and yet, his girth is such that flickers of pain travel to my brain.

"It hurts," I gasp.

"You knew it would."

"I'm not scared."

"You should be." With that, he thrusts his tongue between my lips and drinks from me. His cock throbs inside of me, and the sensations that ping through my blood signal the pleasure that's on its way. He kisses me until all my attention is focused on where his lips meet mine and his tongue mates with mine. It's a single-minded worshipping of my mouth, which wipes all thought from my head. Then, without breaking the kiss, he pulls back until he's poised at the rim of my slit. When he breaks the kiss, I survey his features.

His cheeks are flushed. His eyes are alert. He surveys me closely, and this time, when he propels his hips forward and breaches me, the entire bed jolts. He slides inside all the way to the hilt, and I'm sure I can feel him in my throat. He stays there, watching my face, taking in every expression I'm unable to hide.

And when I part my lips, he slips his thumb inside my mouth. I suck on his digit and his eyes blaze. He drags his wet thumb down my chin, my cleavage, to the space between us. He circles the part where his cock is plugged inside me, and I can't stop the mewl that slips from my lips. He plants his hands on either side of my head and pulls out slowly enough for me to feel every throbbing inch of his length. His next plunge sends a shockwave of sensations up my body, and he doesn't stop.

In-out-in, his movements speed up. Each time he sinks inside me, he hits that secret spot in my core. Sweat breaks out on his beautiful shoulders, and the tendons of his throat stand out under his skin. His features are so stark, they seem lined with pain, and his gaze has an almost helpless quality to it. He continues to fuck me, never breaking the connection of our eyes, and it's so intimate. More intimate than anything I've ever encountered in my life.

I dig my heels into his back, feel the planes of his back give and flex with each move. I dig my elbows into his shoulders, locking my arms about his neck. Like a machine, he continues. His body is a blur of motion, a power drill that has only one goal. Taking us to the top, together.

"Come with me," he orders. His body is wound so tightly, every inch of his body seems to be carved from stone, the muscles under his skin taut, the expression on his face strained. The heat of our bodies melds and traps us in a furnace of mutual desire. Then he slides his hand under my butt, into the cleavage between my ass cheeks, and when he slides it inside my forbidden hole, the climax blazes up from my toes. It shoots up my legs, tightens around my core and zips up my spine. I arch my back, open my mouth and when I cry out, he's there. "Now," he growls.

And I shatter. The orgasm bursts behind my eyes, the white noise a roaring in my ears. The climax seems to go on and on. When I begin to float down from the high, I realize he's still inside of me.

"Open your eyes as I come inside you, wife."

I manage to prop open my eyelids and hold his searing golden gaze. He fucks into me one last time, then his gaze widens, the flames inside his eyes flare into a shower of gold and silver, and with a low roar, he pours himself inside me. His body shudders, and his shoulders quiver. I hold onto him, tightening my grip as he empties himself. When he begins to slump, I tighten my grasp about him. He buries his face against my neck, and I turn my cheek into his sweaty hair. I inhale that edgy, spicy scent of his and fill my lungs with Edward.

"I'm too heavy." He begins to move, but I refuse to let him up.

"Stay. I like your weight on me."

The aftershocks convulse through him — or that might be me. At this moment, we feel like the same person. His muscles grow heavy, and when his body twitches, I realize he's fallen asleep. I close my eyes and drift off.

Something wet licks between my legs. My nipples tighten. Sparks prickle along my skin. I moan, then gasp when a sucking sensation on my clit fans the sparks to flames. I crack open my eyes and look down long enough to glimpse his head between my thighs. Holy shit, the sight of his dark hair in contrast to my white skin, the intensity with which he's focused on eating me out, the way he squeezes the backs of my thighs as he holds them apart, create the most carnal sight I've ever seen.

"Eddie," I moan.

It seems to spur him into action. He rises up on his knees then stretches out next to me. He turns me so my back is to his chest, pulls me in snug, then urges me to bend my knees. "What're you doing?"

In response, he turns my head and kisses me. The taste of me and him intertwined together fans the flames that run through my veins. And when he nudges his cock into my slit, they become a forest fire. He slips inside me, filling me, stretching me in that pain-pleasure way. He brings his hand up to squeeze my nipple, and my pussy clenches.

"You're so fucking perfect," he whispers against my mouth. Then rocks into me, then again. He presses tiny kisses up my cheek, then to that erogenous zone behind my ear. He ravishes the column of my neck and slides his hand down my stomach.

I flinch.

"What's wrong."

"Nothing."

"Tell me," he orders.

"It's—" I swallow. "I've never had a flat stomach. I'm not exactly thin."

"You're perfect."

Tears prick my eyes. "Nice of you to say that, but a size sixteen is not everyone's idea of beauty."

"It is mine." He leans back so he can look into my eyes. "You are my idea of beauty."

His cock twitches inside me as if to punctuate his words.

"And you call yourself emotionless."

"Except when I'm with you. You get under my skin—with your sweetness, your gentleness, your gorgeous curves, and your beautiful mouth."

"And you don't like it."

"I don't." He lowers his head until his mouth hovers over mine. "I love it."

I walk into Edward's office and come to a stop. He's standing at the window, his back to the room, his phone held to his ear. It's snowing outside. A reminder that Christmas is less than a week away. It's my favorite time of the year, but in the rush of events that have swept me in their wake over the last few weeks, I haven't been able to focus on it. I have to get him a gift; but he doesn't believe in Christmas. Did he believe in it when he was a priest? Of course, he must have. Will he ever get over what had happened? I'd like to think last night is an indication that he might.

He came inside me twice, then woke me up, once again, before dawn when he slid inside me. He didn't seem to be able to get enough of me.

He was so gentle that last time, so tender. He brought me to climax and it almost felt dreamlike, suspended as I was between that half-asleep, half-awake state. He came inside me again, and I drifted off to sleep.

I woke up when he brought me breakfast in bed. He'd already showered and dressed. He kissed my forehead and told me he was leaving for the office. He said I could take the day off, but I wasn't able to stay away. I wanted to be near him.

Then, there's also the fact that he didn't take off his clothes when he made love to me. And it was making love. He could call it by another name, but he wasn't fooling me.

I take in his tall form, dressed, as always, in his three-piece suit. He was dressed in a similar one last night—when Sinclair helped him up the stairs and onto the bed, where he passed out, fully dressed.

I've never seen my husband naked. He turns and sees me. His lips curve in a smile, one that reaches his eyes. It lights up his features, making him look so much younger. Is this how he looked before her? Before he left the church? Before the incident?

He pockets his phone and stalks toward me. I'm aware of the answering smile which curves my lips.

He reaches me and takes in my features. "Sleep well?"

"Did you?"

"The best." His smile widens.

"I missed you." I curse myself as soon as the words are out. Because it's true and because I don't want to come across as clingy and because... I don't want him to sense how much in love with him I already am.

A strange expression crosses his features. "You shouldn't be so open with your feelings," he says in a guarded voice.

I scoff. "I know you missed me, too. Saying it aloud does not minimize your standing as an alpha-male."

"Thought you said I was an alphahole?" His eyes gleam.

"And you take it as a compliment?"

"Isn't it?" He smirks.

Fish on an e-scooter, this is the first time he's smirked. And it's hot. So hot, my panties just melted, and I'm wet all over again. Good thing he didn't use that particular weapon against me earlier or I'd have never been able to resist him. The sun rays glint off his hair, which is so dark, there's a blue hue around it. His tawny eyes are a brilliant gold. The sense of power that clings to him is so potent, I almost orgasm spontaneously. You'd think having slept with him would lessen his appeal, but it's only made me even more conscious of how attracted to him I am.

There's a knock on the door. It opens, and Edward glances over my head. The color fades from his cheeks. "Ava?"

38

———————

Edward

She walks in, and I wait for my heart to jump into my throat. Wait for my pulse to speed up, for that familiar hollowness to squeeze my stomach… But I experience none of that. Of course, I'm surprised, but that's due to the unexpectedness of her visit. Seeing her does not hurt me the way I thought it would to see someone I once loved. I know then, I'm over her.

I glance down and see the shocked look on my wife's face before she composes herself.

"Ava, how lovely to meet you." She walks forward and holds out her hand.

Ava shakes it. "You must be Mira."

"I'm Edward's—"

"Wife." A smile curves her lips. "I was so happy when I heard he'd married."

"Right." There's a note of caution in Mira's tone. And something else…something like fear. It's what propels me to draw abreast with them. I look from my future to my past.

"What can I do for you, Ava?" I manage to keep my voice steady.

Her presence isn't affecting me the way it used to; doesn't mean I'm not reeling with images from my past. Images I've kept locked away in a place I haven't visited in a long time. I hadn't looked at another woman since her, not until Belle. Now, here she is, in my office, and it doesn't hurt the way it did when I last saw her with Baron. Still, I haven't forgotten the fact that she chose my friend over me. And the fact that I made love to my wife last night; the fact I allowed myself to break my vow of abstinence, my promise to never be involved with another woman—I curl my fingers into fists. Belle crumbled my defenses. And now, my past is here to confront me.

"I tried to reach you." She wrings her fingers. "I know you don't want to talk to me, but"—she looks from me to Mira then back at me—"but we need to speak."

"I'm not sure there's anything left to say."

"It's about Baron."

When I hesitate, she holds up her hand, "Please. Five minutes; that's all I ask."

"I... I'll leave you two to catch up." Mira begins to leave, but I grip her shoulder. "Mira, this isn't what you think it is."

She looks from me to Ava, then back at me. "If it were, you'd better believe I wouldn't stand for it." She nods at Ava. "I hope we can get to know one another. Maybe we could get a coffee?"

"I'd love that," Ava replies with another smile.

Mira walks out the door. I watch her leave, and when I turn to Ava, she has a knowing look in her eyes.

"What?"

"You love her."

"She's my wife."

"You. Love. Her." Her eyes gleam.

"Of course, I do."

"I'm so happy for you, Edward." She begins to reach for me, then hesitates. "I came to tell you, you need to move on, but I'm happy to see this was a wasted trip."

"It was." The words come out shorter than I intended. Enough for her to peer into my features. "You're still angry with me and Baron."

"What gave you that impression?"

"The fact that you never attend any of the gatherings with your friends? That you avoid us all?"

"I've been busy." I raise a shoulder.

"And now you're married. You should bring Mira around so she can meet us."

"I intend to take her on a honeymoon first."

Her features light up. "That's good. She seems like an amazing woman."

"She is." I glance toward where I can see her seated at her desk through the glass-wall of my office. *Why do I miss every moment apart from her?*

"I really am pleased for the both of you," Ava murmurs.

"Thank you." I incline my head.

She bites the inside of her cheek. "It's not my place but... Have you told her about the incident?"

I stiffen, then draw myself up to my full height. "You're right, it's not your place to ask that question."

She flinches. "I'm sorry. Really, I am. But I had to ask. Especially since Baron still has nightmares over what happened. And this, after years of therapy."

"Baron agreed to therapy?" I blink. The Baron I knew was as adamant as me on not relying on anyone else for help—well, other than each other. We always had the other person to talk to when things got hard.

And I cut him off. And turned my back on his friendship. I had to. It was the only way I could get through that phase of my life. Strangely it doesn't bother me now, to think of him and Ava together. Is it because I found Belle? Because she fits me in a way that makes any other relationship in my life pale in comparison?

"He did, after I pleaded with him." Her features soften. "I'm not saying it's the answer, but it has helped him find some measure of peace."

"How is he?" I ask in a cautious tone.

"He's good." She scrutinizes my features, then sighs. "I wish you'd call him; he misses you. Not that he'll admit it to me, but I know he does. You two were closer than brothers, and you both have been together through so much. He's tried to reach you so many times, Ed. I wish"—she swallows—"I wish you'd give him a chance."

Guilt seizes me. I haven't answered his calls or his emails. Sure, I wanted them to be happy, but I couldn't bring myself to witness it first-hand. But the lack of reaction to seeing Ava assures me thoughts of her no longer hold sway over me. The only woman who occupies my mind now is Belle. And it's been her from the moment I saw her. Ava and I were never meant to be. I suspected it, but meeting Belle has shown me, there's only one woman for me. Her.

"Goodbye, Ava."

"You'll call Baron?" she pleads.

I hesitate. "I'll think about it."

"That's all I ask."

I walk Ava past Belle's empty desk—*where the fuck did she go?*—and see her off at the elevator. When I return, Belle's desk is still empty. I push open the door to my office and walk inside to find Belle standing behind my desk. She's staring at my computer screen, a wrinkle between her eyebrows.

"There you are; I was worried when I didn't see you at your desk earlier."

"Is that why you have a camera trained on me?"

I stiffen, then force myself to move forward until I stand next to her. I follow her gaze to the screen, knowing what I'll see. A quadrant view. One of which shows her empty desk. I forgot to shut down the view when I took the phone call earlier.

"I can explain." I touch her shoulder, but she pulls away.

"Why would you do that?"

"There are cameras all over the floor," I murmur.

"Are you tracking anyone else?"

"Of course, not."

"So for all these days, you were watching me. While I was outside your office door and doing my work, you kept an eye on me?"

"I wanted to make sure you were safe."

"Safe?" She throws up her hands. "I'm in the office. What could happen to me?"

"Things aren't always what they seem. You think you can trust someone, but really, they're putting on a front."

A wrinkle appears between her eyebrows. "What are you talking about?"

I cut my palm through the air. "It doesn't matter."

"Of course, it does. This is about you, Edward. About your past, about your experiences that hold you back. And you promised you'd share them with me."

"And I have."

"If by that, you mean, finally consummating our marriage properly—"

"I came inside you. I haven't allowed myself that release in two years. That doesn't give you the right to plumb into my past."

"Does she know about it?"

"If you mean Ava, yes, she does. Baron told her."

She firms her lips. "So she knows things about you, which your own wife doesn't."

"You don't have to worry about her."

"I saw your face when you saw her; you were shocked." She swallows.

"Only because I wasn't expecting to see her."

"What did she want?"

"She came to tell me to move on, but I told her it was a wasted trip."

"Oh." She blinks rapidly.

"I told her she needn't have bothered to come."

"Whys that?"

"Because she's my past. I expected it to hurt to see her, but it didn't. Seeing her proved to me I'm over her."

"You are?" Her expression softens.

"Now, I realize you're the only woman for me. I knew that from the moment I saw you, but it's not something that was easy for me to accept. For too long, I've been focused on keeping my emotions to myself. I didn't want to be involved with anyone else. I didn't want anyone else in my life."

"You don't want me in your life, either."

"I confess, I didn't. I resisted it for a long time."

"And now?"

"Now, I know there is no future for me without you."

Her features soften. "Then you'll tell me about the incident?"

39

Mira

"I can't." He turns and stalks to the window again.

"Why not? Don't you trust me?"

"It's not that." He drags his fingers through his hair. "It's not something I speak about to anyone."

"But I'm your wife." I move toward him.

"Just because I came inside you does not entitle you to know everything about me."

I stop so suddenly, I stumble, then manage to right myself. "That's not fair," I whisper.

"I'm sorry," he says without turning around to face me. "I didn't mean it that way."

"But you don't think of me as your wife in the real sense, either."

"I already told you, you're the only woman for me."

"But you won't tell me about the incident?"

"I—" His shoulders rise and fall. " I can't. I don't talk to anyone about it."

"Maybe you should. Maybe you need to see a therapist about it and—"

"No. Absolutely not." His spine goes ramrod straight.

"It's not a sign of weakness to speak to a therapist."

He doesn't answer.

"Edward, I don't know what happened to you, but you're not over it. You're still dealing with the fallout of it. It's colored your life so far. It's what caused you to lose…her."

Not that I'm complaining, but I'm not going to mention that.

He turns his head so I can see him in profile. "You're psychoanalyzing me?"

"Only because you don't want to go to a professional. When she married your best friend, you swore off women. You didn't sleep with anyone for two years. You were, technically, celibate. That's… unusual."

"That didn't stop me from watching others masturbate," he says in a harsh tone.

I flinch.

"That didn't stop me from touching other women and making them come, either."

"You're saying all this to hurt me. And I know you're doing it because you're hurting inside."

He turns to face me, and his features are, once more, schooled into that mask I've named his 'Priest face.' Not that I knew him when he was a priest, but I imagine that's how he came across to his congregation. All stern and upright and erect a-n-d…

No, that did not make me think about his cock. Not at all. This is not the time to have images of how his big, fat dick felt inside me. How he squeezed my tits and slide his finger into that forbidden part of me. How he made me come, and then how he allowed himself to orgasm inside me. How it felt to receive hot streams of his cum. Fish in the street, these are not the kinds of X-rated thoughts to have when we're having a serious discussion. Not to mention, when he's all but admitted he doesn't regard me as his wife in the truest sense of the word. "And am I allowing myself to be distracted by salacious thoughts? Of course, not."

His gaze narrows. "You're distracted by salacious thoughts? About us?"

"Of course, not." I redden.

"That's what you said aloud."

"So?" I tip up my chin.

"So you were thinking about last night and how I wrung orgasms from your body?" There's a knowing glint in his eyes.

"Fine." I throw up my hands, "I was thinking about how you made me come, and yes, I said that aloud. But it doesn't change the fact that you're unable to tell me about the incident. It's what made you who you are. It changed your life forever, and you can't share it with me."

The light in his eyes banks, and his features harden. He's switched back to his hot priest persona. *How sad is it, that even though he can't share his past with me, even though he prefers to keep so many of his thoughts and emotions to himself, even though his unfeeling demeanor is back, I find it sexy? He's hurting me, and I'm no less attracted to him. Where's my survival instinct when I need it?*

"Don't ask me to do that. It's something I'd prefer to forget, to move on." He scowls.

"And have you? Either forgotten it, or moved on from it?"

His jaw tics.

I look between his eyes, "You can't bury what happened and pretend everything is fine when it's not. You can't move forward until you resolve the issues associated with what happened."

"And have you moved on from the fact that your father traded your future for his company?" He sneers.

"You know, I haven't." I glance away then back at him. "The difference is, I've talked about it and shared my feelings with you. I didn't try to keep anything a secret."

"Not all of us can be so perfect." He curls his lip. "Not all of us can go around wearing our heart on our sleeve and sharing our emotions with the world."

I stiffen. "Not all of us are unfeeling jerk-holes."

He raises a shoulder. "Never pretended otherwise."

I rub at my temple. "I know you're lashing out at me because you're hurting."

"I'm simply stating a fact. As for my hurting, you don't have to worry; I have ways to manage the fallout from it."

My heart leaps into my throat. The blood thuds at my temples. "What do you mean?"

"I have good coping mechanisms. It's how I've survived this far, after all."

"You're talking about the BDSM club?" I swallow.

He inclines his head. "You don't have a problem if I go without you, do you?"

"And if I did?" I set my jaw. "I'm your wife. We're married. And you're telling me you're going to a BDSM club without me?"

"And since I've broken my 'vow of abstinence'"—he makes air-quotes with his fingers—"there's nothing to hold me back, is there?"

Anger squeezes my guts, and the band around my chest tightens. I try to draw in a breath, but my lungs burn. *How dare he taunt me with that? How dare he treat me with such little consideration? How dare he break my heart? I will not stand for it. I allowed my family to walk all over me. I kept my father's best interests at heart, but that doesn't mean I intend to put up with his bullshit.* "Was I a dutiful daughter? Yes, I was. Did I want to be a dutiful wife? Yes, I did. But you know what? Fuck that."

His gaze widens. I realize it's the first time he's heard me swear aloud. *Well, watch out, buster, there's more where that came from. I refuse to take this insult lying down. I refuse to allow my ego to take a beating. I refuse to hand over my power to anyone else.* "So, you're going to the BDSM club, hmm?"

"That's what I said." He yawns, then pulls back the sleeve of his expensive jacket and glances at his $10,000 dollar watch. "Look at the time. I need to get going. As for you, you need to get back to your desk. You need to cancel the rest of my appointments for today. I'm going to be busy with other things." One side of his lips curls.

Fish-on-a-stick, if he thinks I am going to stand aside and let him leave, he is so wrong. I shrug out of my jacket, and it falls to the ground.

"What are you doing?" He frowns.

In answer I reach behind, unhook my skirt, then shimmy it down my thighs. I kick it aside, then look up to find his gaze is fixed on my legs. Color smears his cheeks. A nerve throbs at his temple. He seems entranced by my little strip-tease. Not the finest or most coordinated, I admit, but that hasn't stopped him from curling his fingers at his sides into fists.

"Belle," he says in that deep, hard voice of his. There's a thread of anger, a threat running through it. A shiver squeezes my legs. My nipples tighten. *Do I know what I'm doing? Of course, not. But my instinct says I'm on the right track. Am I pissed off with him for saying he'll go to the BDSM club? You betcha. And am I going to teach him not to throw that in my face again? What do ya think?* I grip the hem of my blouse, pull it over my head, and when I lower my arms, I gasp, for he's standing in front of me.

"You…sure move like your namesake."

His gaze is fixated on my chest. I'm wearing a bra, but it's see through. Which means, he can see my nipples stand to attention through the sheer fabric. He licks his lips.

"Don't you want to ask who I'm talking about? No matter, I'll tell you. It's Edward from Twilight, the vampire who glows in the sun. He moves really fast, like you did."

"Thought you were a Jacobite?" His voice is low and hard, and the promises hidden in there slingshot a trembling to my core.

"I... I think I'm converted." My fingers twitch, and the blouse slithers to the floor.

A muscle works at his jawline. His features are rock hard. I don't know what he's thinking, but when I glance at his crotch, the massive tent there gives me an idea. I've felt his cock inside me, but honest to god, the watermelon he's sporting makes me take a step back.

He slowly raises his gaze to my face. "You shouldn't have done that."

"I'm just getting started." I reach behind me, unhook my bra, then I toss it at him. He swoops up his arm and catches it. The cool air sweeps over my naked breasts. That's the only reason I'm sporting goosebumps on my chest. It has nothing to do with how his gaze is fixed on my tits. Or how my nipples are diamond hard, or how my panties are so damp, I could probably wring moisture from them, or how those sparks, which are never far from the surface when he's around, have flared to full-blown flames.

"Belle," his voice is thick. The skin over his knuckles is stretched white. He seems to be holding onto his control by a thread, and fish-in-a-kettle, it's the most erotic thing I've ever seen. That this gorgeous, handsome, emotionally-wounded man who's practiced self-control most of his adult life is so close to going into a tailspin, thanks to my strip-tease, surges a rush of power through my veins. I slide my fingers into the waistband of my panties. His chest rises and falls. I begin to slide them down, not taking my gaze off of him. I'm rewarded by his shoulders swelling, pushing at the fabric of the jacket he's wearing, so I'm sure it's going to pop at the seams. I relish the movement of his throat as he swallows. The way his chest rises and falls, how he stares at my core, waiting for it to be revealed, as I slowly slide my panties down my hips, my thighs, my legs. I step out of them, and his entire body goes still. That's when I straighten and toss them at his face.

40

———

Edward

Without taking my gaze off her damp, pink pussy, I catch her panties, and bring them to my nose. A deep whiff, and that apple blossom scent of hers, laced with something tart, sinks into my blood. My already thickened cock strains against my pants. One last whiff, ignoring the pulsing sensation that grips my balls, I slip her panties into one pocket, then wind her bra around my fingers. Her gaze widens. I raise my fingers and twirl it. She hesitates, then slowly turns in place. When her magnificent butt is facing me, I touch her shoulder. Goosebumps snake down her back.

I sink to my knees, dragging my stubbled chin across the curve of her butt. A whine spills from her lips, and a slash of fire sears my groin. *Fuck!* I rise to my feet and walk over to perch on edge of the desk. "Turn around."

She trembles, then complies.

"Crawl to me."

She gapes. "What?"

"Don't make me repeat myself," I warn.

She swallows, then tips up her chin, and in a graceful move, lowers herself to her hands and knees. Then, holding my gaze, she crawls forward. With each move, her gorgeous breasts swing, her butt twitches, and her thighs quiver. The color on her features deepens and extends down her chest. I widen my legs, and when she reaches the space between them, she pauses. Her face is level with my crotch. *Perfect.*

"Sit back on your heels."

She does. I'm instantly entranced by the golden triangle between her legs. I ease my foot between her knees. She shudders but obeys and slides them apart. A-n-d there it is, between those pink pussy lips, that knob of Venus, that little sugar-plum, that devil's doorbell, her clit.

"Fold your hands behind your back."

A mutinous look comes into her eyes. "If this is your way of punishing me—"

"It's my way of taking what my wife is offering."

"Oh." She blinks.

"Now, do it." I lower my voice to a hush. She pales. The muscles of her arms twitch. Then she slowly locks her fingers behind her back.

"Good girl."

A groan boils up her throat.

"You like it when I praise you?"

She nods.

"You like it when I touch you?"

She nods again.

"You like it when I fuck you?"

She frowns. "You know, I do."

"Good, because from now on, you need to earn all three."

"Excuse me?"

"You heard me."

I slip my booted foot up the valley of her thighs, and when I press into her core, she gasps, "Eddie."

I begin to rub on her clit, stroke up and down her slit, again and again. When I withdraw, the tip of my boot glistens.

"So wet. Can't wait to feel my cock inside your weeping cunt, hmm?"

She swallows, then presses her lips together. My wife likes to defy me. How sweet. It gives me more to work with. It inspires me to show her how it can be when she finally surrenders to me. Oh, I don't want to break her. I merely want her to put her trust in me. I want her to hand her body over to me willingly, secure in the knowledge that I'll always know what she wants. I'll always treat her like the queen she is. I'll always ensure she's taken care of. That she never lacks for anything. That she's always pleasured and secure, that she has the power. One word from her, and I'd stop this.

"If you want me to stop, say so."

She blinks.

"You can always leave."

"And you'd go to the BDSM club?"

I glance away, then back at her. "You were right. I said it because I wanted to get a rise out of you. I would never touch anyone but you, Belle. You should know that. You are my wife. My. Wife."

Her lips part, and her chin trembles. "Do you mean it?"

"The only lie I've ever told in my life, was to you, and it didn't feel good. I'll never tell anything but the truth, from now on. But I also need time."

"Okay," she whispers.

"Okay." I widen my stance to accommodate my throbbing arousal. "If you want to leave, now would be a good time."

"And you won't go to the BDSM club?"

"I won't."

"But if I stay, you won't let me come?"

"Not until you earn it."

"What do I have to do to earn it?"

"Stay and find out."

She nods slowly. "Okay."

Thank fuck. I release the breath I was holding. If she'd refused, would I have let her leave? Probably not. Good thing she'll never find out.

I lower the zipper on my pants, reach inside my boxers, and take out my cock.

Her lips part. Her pupils dilate. Her gaze is fixed on how I stroke my swollen shaft from base to crown, and again. Pre-cum glistens on the swollen head. I scoop it up, reach forward and smear it over her lips. She licks it up, then opens her mouth again.

"Good?"

She nods.

"Good." I cup the back of her head, then position my cock between her lips. I tug her forward, and my shaft disappears into her mouth. *Fucking hell, I've never seen a more erotic sight.* The feel of her moist tongue grazing the underside of my dick draws a groan from my lips. I grit my teeth, trying to tamp down on the rising tension in my belly, but the feel of my wife's mouth as she licks around the rim of my cock, the sensations it rockets to my extremities, surely warrant a poem dedicated to it.

I pull back, and when I push in again, I hit the back of her throat. She gags; drool drips from her chin. A trail of moisture slides down her cheek leaving a black trail in its wake. It's so perfect, I almost come in her mouth. I squeeze the base of my cock to hold back my orgasm, then pull back again. "Open wide," I order.

She complies, and this time, when I push forward, I slide down the warmth of her throat. It's tight and hot and perfect. She's perfect. And she's my wife. *Mine.* My balls draw up, and the pressure at the base of my spine curls in on itself, growing harder, higher and when she swallows, I know I can't hold back. I pull back, and the climax boils up. A roaring sound fills my ears, and I come.

41

Mira

He paints his orgasm on my face, my mouth, my tits. He comes and comes, and there's so much cum, it drips down my chin and clings to my nipples. He holds me in place with his grip on the back of my head, but even if he didn't, I wouldn't move. This… He's given me power over him. He's used my body, and it brought him so much pleasure, I know for a fact, he wouldn't have been this open and he wouldn't have let himself be this vulnerable with anyone else. *So why can't he tell me about the incident? Why can't he share what happened to him? Why is he holding himself back? And why has he never taken off his clothes in front of me?*

He squeezes out the last of his cum, then reaches down and massages it into my cheeks, across my mouth, down my throat, and around my breasts. His cock twitches, and by the time he raises his gaze to mine, he's hard again.

"You're gorgeous," he murmurs, and tucks a strand of hair behind my ear. "You deserve better."

"I want you."

"I'll never be able to give you what you want."

"I don't believe that."

"Believe it." He tucks himself inside his briefs and zips himself up, then pulls me to my feet. He hauls me to him, fits his mouth over mine and kisses me. There's a desperation to how his lips close over mine, a yearning to how his tongue tangles with mine. An anguish to how he holds me close, a sea of agony to how his thighs push into mine. When I place my hand over his heart, it's galloping with all the emotions he'd never allow himself to reveal. And when he releases me and peers into my eyes, I glimpse the regret in them before he shuts me out.

"Don't do that, don't hide what you're thinking. Don't conceal whatever thoughts are going through your mind. Don't brush aside the sadness, the fears, whatever it is that feels too big for you to face alone. We'll do it together."

He doesn't respond.

"Edward…" I cup his cheek. "Talk to me."

He looks at me through that mask of the hot priest again. "I think we need to take a trip."

"A trip?" That's the last thing I expected him to say.

"I promised Arthur I'd take you on a honeymoon."

"A honeymoon?"

He rubs his thumb across my mouth. "So you can earn your orgasms."

I glance at the flakes of snow that float down, only to melt when they touch the car. Outside, the Christmas lights on Regent Street light up the city. The display windows of the shops show off their festive decorations. There are crowds of people on the sidewalk. Families, children, everyone is out shopping. I can make out the shop windows of Hamleys —the biggest toy store in London—and the throngs of kids with their parents milling around outside. One day, when I have kids, I'll be able to buy gifts for them, put up a Christmas tree at home, and surprise them on Christmas morning with their presents. Of course, I do need to get pregnant first. I cross my fingers. Hopefully, my time will come before too long. It has to. Meanwhile, I'll have to make do with the gift I bought for Eddie, which I have hidden in my handbag.

We left the office an hour ago. He hasn't told me where we're going. When I asked, he said it was a surprise. Before we left, he led me to the ensuite and told me to shower. When I emerged with a towel knotted between my breasts, he gestured to the walk-in closet.

I opted for a skirt and a full-sleeved blouse, teaming it with a wool-lined leather jacket. Combined with a scarf, gloves and a hat, I was ready to go. He looked at me with approval when I strode out, then wrapped up the call he was on.

When I asked about clothes for the trip, he said it was all taken care of. Then, he ushered me to his Jaguar, slid into the driver's seat, and we were off.

Now, I reach over and fiddle with the dial of the radio until I find a favorite radio station. The notes of WHAM!'s "Last Christmas," as interpreted by Ariana Grande, fill the car.

I begin to hum along to it.

"You really do like Christmas?" He shoots me a sideways glance.

"You really don't?"

One side of his lips quirk. *Hooray! That's a win.*

"When you smile, your entire face changes. You look younger and innocent."

His eyebrows draw down. "But I'm not."

I glance away. *Why did I have to go put my foot in my mouth?*

The music changes to Mariah Carey's, "All I Want for Christmas."

He winces.

When I reach over and shut off the music, he doesn't protest. We drive in silence, and once we cross the city limits, he relaxes a little.

"You must have celebrated Christmas when you were a priest?"

He hesitates, and I'm sure he's going to stay silent, but then he nods. "It was a special time of the year, when the spirit did seem to infect the congregation. It changed the tone of the prayers. There was something magical about the hymns. The one time when the veil between this world and the next seemed to thin enough to feel the presence of The Other."

He lapses into silence, and I swallow around the ball of emotion in my throat. "That was almost poetic."

"That's when I was a believer."

"What do you believe in now?" The words are out before I can stop them. Because I need to know what it is that drives this man. When he walked away from his calling, how did he cope? By his own admission, he was unmoored. *What is he holding onto now? How does he move from one day to the next when what he once put his faith in doesn't exist anymore?*

When he doesn't answer, I touch his shoulder. He flinches, and it's as if someone slapped me. I begin to retreat, but he grabs my hand, then brings it to his mouth and kisses it, before placing it on his knee. "Sorry, I'm still getting used to having someone else in my space, in my life."

"You didn't think it through when you decided to marry?"

One side of his lips lifts. Another almost-smile. *Whoo-hoo, that's a score right there for me.*

"I hadn't thought it through when I asked you to marry me. I didn't realize how you were going to turn my world upside down. How you were going to occupy space in my mind, my thoughts... My heart."

I freeze. "Did you say—"

"My heart, yes. I swore not to lie to you anymore, remember?"

"So you do have feelings for me?"

"Isn't that evident?"

"But you still don't trust me enough to take your clothes off in front of me?"

42

Edward

"Don't ask that of me… Yet." I tighten my fingers around the steering wheel. *Haven't I unbent enough? Haven't I shared more with her than with anyone else, including Ava? Except perhaps, Baron.* He knew the boy I was. She knows the man I've become. I've allowed her a peek into my thoughts, I've confessed to having feelings for her. *What more does she want?*

"I'm sorry, I shouldn't have pushed you." She begins to pull her hand back, but I hold onto it. I slide my fingers through hers and she seems to relax a little. "I never thought you'd ever come out and tell me you have feelings for me, and I know how difficult that must be for you."

"Do you?" I ask, not because I don't believe her, but because I'm genuinely curious. *Could this woman understand, when I've tried and failed at that task so many times myself?*

"Yes." She nods. "Yes, I do. You think I'm young and naive, but I am wise in the ways of the world. I saw how it tore my father apart when my mother died. How he tried to do his best when he married my step-mother. How he hoped to replace the mother-shaped hole in my life and the wife-shaped one in his with another family, despite knowing it would never work. She was gone, and nothing we did could alleviate the pain that was left behind. And when he realized he had only worsened the situation, he retreated into his business. He poured his love, his feelings, his desires into it… Which is why I couldn't say no when he asked for my help to save it."

My shoulder muscles stiffen.

"He replaced my mother with his work, with building this empire which he was going to hand over to someone else one day, anyway. Not me or my half-sisters, because we weren't interested in running it, but to a stranger. And when I realized that it would be you, it felt right."

I release my hold on her hand and place it back on the wheel. *It was wrong. I shouldn't have done it, but how can I tell her that? When we're beginning to establish the foundations of a fragile trust that we'll need if we're going to build this marriage? No, I shouldn't tell her the truth behind what happened yet. Not until I'm sure she'll never leave me.*

"I met you and knew you were the one. Okay, not me, but my subconscious knew. And I fought it because I was all set for an arranged marriage, after all. But when my father said he wanted me to marry you, I knew it was a sign. All the pieces were falling into place. Of course, it had to be you to run my father's company. It was always you, Eddie."

I'm aware of her gaze on my profile, of the yearning in her features, of the love that shines in her eyes and, like a coward, I don't turn. If I do, I'll be lost. If I do, *all* will be lost. If I do, I'll have to confess to her everything that I set in place to bring us here. And I'm not ready yet. *She's* not ready yet. I need to find a way to tie her to me, so she'll never leave. I need some kind of assurance that when I share the extent of my machinations, she won't have a choice but to look past it. I need a guarantee, but what?

The silence stretches. I'm aware when she finally turns to look forward. She places her hands in her lap. A few more miles pass, we pass a road sign, she looks at it, then turns to me. "We're going to Cornwall?"

"Penzance." I nod.

"I've always wanted to go there," she exclaims.

"It's one of my favorite places," I murmur. *Another thing I've never told anyone. See, I'm sharing more of myself.*

"The scenery is so beautiful." She gazes at the forests we're passing by. We've been driving steadily since we left London. After we cross East Devon, I turn onto a B road, and the scenery grows more wild, more untamed. There's a ruggedness and yet, a desolation, to the terrain that resonates with that darkness I'm no longer able to hide.

I glance toward her. "It is."

She turns, and our eyes meet.

"I want you to know, I'm on birth control. I decided to get a prescription when I realized we were getting married."

Something streaks across the corner of my vision. I hit the brakes, turn to face forward, and the car screeches to a halt. The impact throws me against my seatbelt. I know she's wearing her seatbelt because I checked before we left, but it doesn't stop me from throwing my arm out in front of her.

There's another flash of white as the rabbit disappears into the undergrowth.

"You okay?" I turn to find the color has leached from her features. Her shoulders tremble. I unhook my seatbelt, reach over and take her in my arms. "You're good. I'll never let anything happen to you."

She nods against my shoulder. "Wh-what happened?"

"A rabbit ran across the road. I stopped in time."

"Oh, thank god." She burrows deeper into my chest. I tuck her head under my chin and breathe in her scent. My heart thunders in my chest, echoing hers.

"I'm glad you didn't hit it," she says softly.

"You sure you're okay?"

"Yes." Her voice sounds steadier. I hold her for a few seconds more, then release her and scrutinize her features.

"I promise, I'm fine." She half smiles.

I reach for the bottle of water and hold it out. She takes it from me, screws open the top, and takes a sip. Some of the water slips down her chin, and before I can stop myself, I wipe it off.

She flushes a little, and says, "Thanks." She hands it back to me, and I take a few gulps. I put it aside, then take another deep breath.

That scared me more than I'd like to admit. If something had happened to her, if she'd been hurt—my heart crashes into my ribcage and sweat breaks out on my brow—I wouldn't have been able to live with myself. But she's fine; nothing happened to her. And I intend to make sure it stays that way.

I turn to her. "Ready to go?"

43

Mira

I hear my name and open my eyes. I yawn, then sit up and look around. Lights. The entire place is lit up. We're in queue behind a long line of cars, and the sign on the side of the road says, "Angarrack: Twelve Days of Christmas."

"I've heard of this village. It hosts one of the most famous Christmas light displays in the country."

"It does." He nods.

I sit up, take in my surroundings. Edward eases the car forward, following those in front. We make our way through the quaint village streets. The display pays homage to the Twelve Days of Christmas with the illuminations counting up from the first day of Christmas. The houses are lit across rooftops and at the sides, and there's even a display on the river over which we drive.

"It's beautiful." I can't take my gaze off the lights.

"It is," he murmurs.

I shoot him a glance, but he's focused on the driving. The sidewalks teem with tourists, families with kids, couples, all taking photographs of the lights. It's so festive. I feel like I've been dropped into the pages of a storybook Christmas. Finally, we pass the display with twelve drummers drumming, for the Twelfth Day. "Oh, I want a picture. Can I get a picture?"

Edward brings the car to a halt at the side of the road.

I grab my phone and step out, then gesture to him. "Can I take a picture with you?"

He hesitates.

"Please?"

He seems like he's going to refuse, then nods. He gets out of the car and follows me. I hold up my phone, posing for a selfie, then realize he's standing too far away.

"Come on." I hold out my arm. "I need you in the frame."

He walks over to stand next to me. I bend my head in his direction. He stands stiffly, unsmiling. I reach up on tiptoes and use my fingers to curve his lips. "There, that's better."

I look back at the screen, begin clicking, then freeze, for he's put his arm about my waist and drawn me into his side. I snuggle in, take a few pics, then show them to him. "Not bad, eh?"

He grunts.

I roll my eyes. "You are the original Grinch, aren't you?"

He says something under his breath that sounds like 'what-fucking-ever.'

"Do you want me to take your picture?" I turn to find a tiny woman, who must be at least seventy, smiling at us. She has short grey hair cut in a bob and is wearing a sparkly green dress with black wedges on her feet. "You look so cute together." Her smile increases in intensity. "Would you like me to take a picture of the two of you?"

"No, we don't—" Eddie begins, but I cut him off.

"We'd love that." I hand my phone to her, then step back. He pulls me close again. I wrap my arm about his waist, and he brings his other around the front of my shoulders, embracing me in the circle of his warmth. I draw in the crisp evening air, redolent with pine and cinnamon, and laced with his darker scent. Little goosebumps dance across my skin. I smile, placing my cheek against the steady drumming of Eddie's heart. Contentment seeps into my blood. I sigh, cuddle into his side and pose for a few seconds more.

"All done." The woman walks over and hands the phone to me. "Are you on your honeymoon?"

Next to me, Eddie tenses. "Why do you ask?"

The woman blinks.

I dig my elbow into my husband's side. "What he means is, it's so nice of you to ask. Yes, we are."

"Oh, isn't that wonderful." She claps her hands. "Young love, so amazing. Did you enjoy the lights?" She waves her hand in the air. "I head up the organizing committee for the Christmas Lights."

"They are gorgeous," I exclaim.

"This must all seem so quaint to you big city folk. Where are you from?" She beams at Eddie, who makes a snarling sound at the back of his throat.

I nudge him, then interject, "He's from London."

"And you're from the US, aren't you, dear?" She turns her smile on me.

Edward's muscles bunch further, and I rush in before he can say something else to upset her. "From New York, and I can tell you, these lights have more character than the Christmas lights on Times Square."

The woman seems taken aback, then claps her hands again. "You flatter us, dear, but I'll take the compliment."

Tension drums off of Edward. He wraps his arm tighter about me. "We have to go," he growls.

I lean forward and take the woman's hand in mine. "Thank you so much. We need to be on our way." I lower my voice. "My husband gets churlish when he's hungry."

"You mean, he's hangry." She laughs. "Please, don't let me keep you. Come again next year." She waves as we make our way back to the car.

Once we're seated, I turn to him. "You could have been a little more polite."

He sneers.

"No, really; she was just being sweet and helpful."

"She was asking too many questions." He scowls.

"She was making conversation and being nice, is all."

"She can be nice to someone else."

"Would it kill you to be a little more civil to her? She was a sweet old lady. She couldn't hurt a fly."

"Threats come in all shapes and forms, and when you least expect it." He sets his jaw. "It's my job to watch over you."

I throw up my hands. "Nothing's going to happen to me."

"You bet, it won't. I'm going to make sure it doesn't."

We set off again, and when we're clear of the village and back on the road, I turn to him. "What happened to you, Edward? What made you so suspicious of everyone and everything. Was it the incident?"

When he doesn't answer, I scrutinize his features. "It *was* the incident, wasn't it?"

"Don't." His jaw hardens. "I told you, I'm not ready to talk about it."

"When will you be ready?"

"I'm not sure."

"Will you *ever* be ready?" I know I'm pushing him, when I should be giving him space. But I wish he wouldn't shut me out. I wish I didn't have to second guess his reactions. I want to be understanding, but I'm only human. And his wife. And he's, my husband. I trust him. *Why can't he trust me? Will he ever trust me?*

Maybe I shouldn't have come. I thought spending time alone with him, away from our day-to-day cares, would help bring us close. Now, I'm not so sure.

I turn to face forward. Darkness has fallen, and the headlights illuminate the road before us. We begin to climb up a hill, the road winding its way around another village. The lights of the city below come into view, and beyond that, the darkness of the sea. Even though it's too dark to make out the scenery, something tells me the view will be spectacular in the daylight. It begins to snow again, and by the time I see the sign that says we're entering Penzance, some of my earlier anger fades away.

I'm being too hasty. We've only been married a few weeks. He's beginning to open up to me, not by much, but more than when we first met. I need to be more patient. Also, we've only just left London. We haven't even reached our destination. I can't possibly expect him to open up and spill his secrets while he's busy driving.

I need to give this... give *us*, more time. I shoot him a sideways glance, "Thank you for taking me to see the lights, anyway. Especially since, I'm sure you didn't want to be there."

He raises a shoulder.

"That's why you drove through the village," I say slowly. "You wanted me to experience the Christmas lights. You knew I'd love it. You did it for me."

He stays quiet, and anger crawls up my spine.

"Oh! You could, at least, take credit when it's due." I turn on him. *Okay, so I'm not as patient as I'd like to be.* "Why do you have to be so stubborn? Why do you have to hide behind that severe facade when you're so much more inside? Why, Edward, why?"

His biceps bulge, and his shoulders seem to swell. And when he finally speaks, his voice brooks no argument. "Because I will never be able to love you the way you should be. Nothing you tell me will convince me otherwise. I'm broken, Belle. I'm not a good man. I'm not the kind of person you want to spend the rest of your life with. I'm all wrong for you, Belle. I never should have brought you out here."

His thoughts echo my earlier thoughts, but hearing it from him sends a chill of foreboding through my veins. "Don't say that."

"You wanted to know more about me. Well, this is it. This is who I am. Cold, distant, unfeeling. Unable to appreciate the kind of woman you are. Unable to give you what you need to thrive."

"I need *you*," I insist. "I want to be with you."

He turns off the main road and onto a road that curves around the hillside and heads down toward the water. Below us, the sea stretches out, a mass of darkness, and I shiver. I wrap my arms about myself. He must notice it, for he flips a switch and the air circulating through the Jag grows warmer. He positions the vents, so they're focused on me, then presses the button for the seat warmer. That's the kind of man he is, so cued into my needs.

He won't let me get cold, will make sure I want for nothing… Except maybe, for an emotional commitment from him.

No, that's not true. Regardless of what he says, we've made so much progress. If not, I wouldn't be here. If not, he wouldn't have taken this step of bringing me with him to a place where it will only be the two of us for the next week. Another shudder rolls through me. This one is thicker, syrupy. This one is the kind that slides through my bloodstream and coils between my thighs. He reaches the level of the beach, drives down a road, that's rocky enough to make the Jag bumps as he eases it along. He finally brings the car to a stop and switches off the engine. In the silence that follows, broken only by the sound of metal cooling, he stares through the windshield. "Do you really need me, though?"

"Of course, I do."

And when he finally looks at me, the pain in his eyes shoots an arrow through my heart.

"Eddie," I whisper, "what is it? You can tell me anything."

"Are you sure?"

44

Edward

"I'm not who you think I am."

"So you keep saying."

"I can't be redeemed, Belle. There are things in my past, things I've done, things which were done to me… Things that cannot be undone."

"Tell me, Eddie, I want to know everything. I can help, Eddie."

"And if I don't want you to?"

She swallows.

"If I don't want to share them with you, what then?"

Her features pale, and her eyes take on a hurt look. And when she glances away, it's as if the sun has been hidden by an eclipse. A-n-d this is me. The bastard who cannot help but hurt her. I saw her at Angarrack, witnessed the happiness on her face, her friendliness as she spoke to that woman. Her exuberance as she skipped along to take a picture in front of the lights.

And then, I came along and spoiled it all. I was suspicious of that woman, of everyone near her. It's ingrained in me to be cautious, and she's right; it's because of the incident. *Could I come out and tell her that?*

No. Could I have been more reticent, more withdrawn through the journey? Of course, not.

I thought I'd learn to lower my walls, to give in to her wants, her needs, to share my past, the events that formed me. I want to dig out my heart and lay it at her feet. I want to shatter the last remaining barriers around my soul and give her a peek. I want to show her I can be the kind of man she'll flourish with. The kind who will compliment her, who will be her partner, her other half. Who will not hold her back. Who will be worthy of her trust. I want…a present and a future with her. The kind I could never imagine for myself. I want her. Only her. And when she finds out what I've done to bring her to me, she's going to hate me. And I have to tell her everything. It's the least I can do. If I were a better man, I'd let her leave me… But I'm not. Instead, I've brought her to the one place where it won't be easy for her to leave.

"I'm sorry," I force out the words. "Sorry I hurt you."

When she continues to stare straight ahead, I run my fingers through my hair.

"This is who I am, Belle. I'm not the kind given to romantic gestures and—"

"You took me to see one of the most famous Christmas light displays in the country when you couldn't stand being there. You gave me your grandmother's engagement ring. You picked out our wedding rings. You're wrong, Edward." She stabs a finger at me. "You are the most romantic person I know. You know, instinctively, how to please me. If you'd only let yourself be and stop hiding behind that alpha-holish, brutish, don't-give-a-damn-front."

I scoff. "I brought you to the middle of nowhere for your honeymoon. I don't think that's romantic."

"Is this place special to you or not?" She scowls.

When I don't reply, she snorts. "That's what I thought. Bet you've never brought anyone else here."

Again, I stay quiet, and she throws up her hands. "That's what I mean. Your every gesture is romantic."

"My spanking you was romantic?'

"Yes."

"My withholding orgasms was romantic?"

"You promised you'll make up for it when I earn them."

"My making you crawl was romantic?"

She swallows, then nods. "It was demeaning and derogatory and, it turned me on," she whispers.

"I didn't hear you."

"It turned me on, okay?" she yells.

Satisfaction slithers through my veins. "What else turned you on?" I ask with interest.

"Everything. Everything you did. Everything you do. How you treat my body like it's your possession. How you order me around. How your voice goes all deep and dominating when you order me around. How you eat me out like it's your favorite dessert."

"It's better than that," I admit.

"How you squeeze my tits like it's your favorite sport."

"It's more thrilling, actually."

"How you look at my butt like it's not disgusting."

"It's not."

"But I'm so big. All my life, I've been teased about it. It's why my stepmother and stepsisters didn't want anything to do with me. They acted like I was contagious. Like if they ate with me, or spent time with me, they'd become fat, too."

"And if I ever meet them, I'll set them straight. How dare they shame you like that."

"For a while, I thought I was contagious, too, you know? I'd hide in my room. I wouldn't eat in front of anyone. That old thing about a fat person caught eating…" Her eyes gleam with unshed tears.

"And your father never did anything?"

"He was never around. He was drowning his sorrows in his work," she admits.

"Just for that, I should hold back from this merger. I shouldn't transfer the funds he needs to save his company."

"No, don't do that." She reaches out and touches my shoulder, and a shot of lust zips to my groin. I move away, only because if I don't, I'm likely to unsnap her seatbelt and haul her over to me, and I don't want to ravish her here, in the front seat of a car. Also, I wouldn't be able to stick to my plan of edging her. I wouldn't be able to hold back, and I must. I need to bring her body to the brink, and then hold back, and do it over and over again, so when she finally comes, the orgasm will be the single most moving experience she's ever had. Which means, I need to hold myself back, too.

Her features crumple, and I know she thinks it's because I don't want to touch her, but that's so far from the truth it's laughable. I should set her mind at ease, but I also know if I don't, when I finally touch her, it's going to be doubly pleasurable. So, I school my features into a mask and narrow my gaze on her.

"Give me one reason I shouldn't teach that man a lesson. A man who stood by and let your life be turned into a living hell. A man who didn't hesitate to barter you."

She winces again, then sets her jaw. "Because...I would never forgive myself if his business fell apart because of me. It's his life. Besides, all of those employees depend on him for support. I will not be responsible for them losing their livelihoods."

I stare at her. And keep staring. The seconds tick by. She shifts in her seat, looks away, then back at me. Sitting here, in this enclosed space with her, her scent intensifies by the minute, and my cock extends by the second. My pants are so tight, I'm sure I won't be able to walk properly, and I need to, if I need to get her in safely.

"Fine," I snap.

"Fine?" She blinks.

"You want me to go through with the takeover of your father's company; I'll do it."

Then, I push the door open and step out. Pausing only to adjust myself, I walk around and open the door to her side. "Coming?"

45

———————

Mira

"A lighthouse?" I gape at the structure looming above us. I was so absorbed in him I didn't notice where he'd stopped. I didn't even notice the building when I got out of the vehicle. He held out his hand to help me, and I hesitated before taking it, given his reaction earlier. But he stands there, his features unmoving, his body stiff, and I know he'll stand there for hours, days if needed, until I take his hand. So I do.

Shockwaves scatter up my arm. I feel him tense further, the muscles of his forearm flexing under the ever-present suit he wears. Then, he tugs lightly and helps me to my feet. Small dots of snow float down and only melt when they touch my cheeks. A wave crashes against the shore. The sound is wild and desolate, but also welcoming. A contradiction. Like him.

"Come on." He begins to lead me over the rocky path toward the edifice standing sentry over us. It's lit by a single spotlight from the ground. It turns the tower into something out of a painting.

"Wow." I blink. "This is your secret hideaway?"

"I come here at least once a month, to get away from it all."

How like him it is. A building that has the ability to warn sailors, to look out over the sea and surrounding land, to spot a storm before it hits. To stay tall, silent, unwavering in the face of challenges. To persevere. And cut a romantic figure. If there were ever a personification of Edward brought to life, it would be this lighthouse.

We reach the door at the bottom, and he lets go of my hand long enough to punch in a few buttons on the keypad set into the wall. Of course, he has an electronic lock, paranoid as he is about security. The door unlocks with a click; he walks in, hits a switch, and lights come on. I take in the spotless space—a surprisingly spacious hallway, with the walls painted white, a carpeted floor, and two chairs pushed up against the far wall with a window between them.

"I had the place converted after I bought it." He leads me to the spiral staircase in the center and gestures for me to go up.

I climb the stairs. By the time I reach the top, I'm out of breath, and I reckon we must be at least six stories up. I step onto the floor at the top and gasp. The entire space has been converted into a very spacious, open plan apartment. On one side is a kitchen, furnished with a cooking range, an oven, a refrigerator, and even an island. It flows into the living space with a sectional, and an armchair facing a fireplace, above which hangs a massive flat screen television. On the other side is a king-sized bed, with bedposts. And there are cleats embedded into each of them. The kind used to secure ropes. O-k-a-y? I tear my gaze away long enough to notice a door nearby. He steps over to it and pushes it open. "This is an ensuite bathroom."

I follow him and peer inside. It has everything, including a large shower space.

"And here"—he walks toward a set of sliding doors and pushes them open—"is the walk-in closet." It's a miniature of the closet in his office. On one wall are his suits; on the other, women's clothes and shoes.

"Are those—"

"Your size."

"And you had these clothes brought all the way here for me?"

"I had a team get to work to have it all done in time."

I should be used to how he thinks forward, how he makes sure I'm always taken care of. A warmth invades my skin. I glance around at the floor-to-ceiling windows that form one side of the circular area. Set in front of it is a clawfoot bathtub. Everything is sparkling. Everything smells fresh. There are even flowers in a vase in the middle of the island. And there's a bookcase between the bed and the living space. One I head toward. I run my fingers down the spines and gasp. "Spicy books?"

"It's what you love to read."

"I guess you found out from Summer?" He doesn't reply, and I know I'm right. There are more books on the shelf above: Shakespeare, Harry Potter, Sun Tzu and *The Art of War*, *Brave New World* by Aldous Huxley, Kafka, Oscar Wilde, Tennessee Williams, thrillers and murder mysteries. As eclectic as the man himself. I tear myself away from the books, walk toward the floor-to-ceiling windows and peer outside. It's dark, but the spotlight illuminates the snowflakes which seem to have picked up in intensity. I turn and take in the entire space and Edward standing in the center of it watching me. Above us, there are skylights in the domed ceiling—currently dark, but I'm sure when the lights inside are switched off, I'll be able to see the stars in the sky. "This place is gorgeous." I half smile.

He doesn't smile back. His features are set in stern lines that pinch my nerves with anticipation. He prowls toward me, his steps deliberate, his gaze filled with intent, and when he stops in front of me, my breath catches. He slides his fingers around my waist, then down to grab a handful of my butt. A shudder grips me.

"You like that?"

I nod.

Then he cups my breast with his free hand and squeezes. "And this."

"Yes," I croak. "I mean, yes, I do."

"What about this?" He drags his hand down to slide it between my legs. He cups my pussy, and my heart drops to the place of contact. I open my mouth, but all that comes out is a whine.

"I believe that's a yes?"

I manage to nod. Manage to not give into the weakness invading my knees.

He releases his hold on my core, only to draw up the fabric of the skirt I opted to wear. And all I can think of is, *thank god, I didn't wear jeans or pants. But why did I have to wear stockings?*

"Hold this up." He nods to where the skirt is bunched around my waist.

I scramble to do so, my movements so quick, it's almost embarrassing. And when he grips the nylon at my crotch and tears a hole, I cry out. He shoves the gusset of my panties aside, stuffs two fingers inside my channel, and I'm so wet, and so swollen with desire, I almost come right then. He curves his fingers inside me, watching my features closely. I know he's taking note of just how responsive I am, and it should embarrass me, but I'm beyond caring. I part my legs to give him better access, begin to ride his fingers. The climax weaves up my thighs. "I'm coming; I'm—"

He pulls out his fingers, brings them to his mouth and sucks on them. My orgasm hovers there for a second, another. *Come on, come on.* I almost cry out in disappointment when it fades away. He removes his fingers with a popping sound. "Delicious."

"Is it?"

"Here, taste." He brings them to my mouth and when I suck on them, the sweet-umami taste of my cum coats my tongue. My stomach chooses that moment to growl. He tilts his head. "Hungry?"

46

Edward

"Where did you learn to cook?"

"I taught myself." I bring some of the pasta to my mouth and chew on it. I sent her to change into more comfortable clothes, and proceeded to cook. When she returned, she wore the sleep shorts and camisole I laid out for her. *Good*. She watched me as I'd cooked, and I paused to offer her small tastes of the food. Then realized watching her little, pink tongue lick the sauce off the ladle was turning the entire experience into an erotic episode. My pants grew too tight, and my balls hardened, and that wouldn't do. I needed to ensure she was fed, so I stepped away and focused on the cooking. Soon, I plated out the food and slid it over to her, and we both dug in.

"You taught yourself?" She scoops up more pasta with her fork.

"You sound surprised."

"It's really good, is all," she offers.

"I had time on my hands when I went traveling after leaving the church. After years of not allowing myself to indulge, it felt necessary to feed all of my senses, so I took some classes in different countries."

Her brow furrows. "*All* of your senses?"

I nod.

"So you were with women?"

"You know I didn't have penetrative sex with anyone for two years," I remind her.

"But you did do, uh…kinky stuff with them?"

"I watched. And I may have touched—"

She pauses with her fork halfway to her mouth.

"I was experimenting."

"Experimenting?"

"I knew my tastes ran to the extreme. I wanted to see how much."

"And what did you find?"

"That BDSM helped me deal with the trauma from my past."

"You mean inflicting pain on another helps you release your own?"

"And inflicting it on myself." I take another mouthful of the food, then nod to her plate. "You need to eat."

She places her fork on her plate. "I think I've lost my appetite."

"Are you jealous that there were other women I used before you?"

"Maybe?"

"You don't need to be."

She tips up her chin.

"You're the only woman I've wanted to bind to me. You're the only woman I've wanted to mark. You're the only one I married—"

"Fake married."

"I think we're past that, Belle."

She purses her lips. "I want to believe you. You brought me here, and I can tell this place is special."

"So are you."

She flushes, then picks up her fork and begins to eat. *Thank fuck.* The thought of her going hungry sends a physical ache through me. I plate out more food for her. She protests, but I insist she eat it. Then, when she's done, I cut a large slice of chocolate cake.

"Did you bake that?" Her eyes widen.

I allow myself a small smile. "I could've if I'd had more time, but this is from the housekeeper."

"Housekeeper?" She looks around the place, then back at me. "You have a housekeeper?"

"A caretaker and his wife who live in the village. They take care of the place and make sure it is stocked when I'm going to visit. They shopped for fresh ingredients before we arrived."

"You sent them a list, I'm assuming?"

I shoot her a glance. "And you guessed this, how?"

"You're so particular about everything. Of course, you'd make sure your favorite haunt has groceries, which you specified."

I continue to stare at her, and she raises her gaze to meet mine. "What?"

"You're not eating the cake." She looks down at the untouched slice. "I… I'm full."

"You love chocolate cake."

"How do you know that?"

"Who doesn't like chocolate?" I ask lightly.

"You don't."

I tilt my head. "That *is* true."

"You really don't like chocolate?" She gapes.

I shake my head. "Not unless it's 100% cocoa."

She makes a face. "That's too bitter for me."

"Not a big fan of sugar."

She groans. "So you also don't like cookies and apple pie, I suppose?"

"But you like them all. Which is why—" I scoop up a piece of the chocolate cake with my finger and hold it out. "Open."

"I shouldn't," she murmurs.

"You absolutely should."

"It'll go straight to my thighs."

"Just how I like it."

"It will—"

"Open. Your. Mouth. Belle."

She instantly parts her lips. Fucking gratifying. I slide my finger between them. She closes her mouth around the digit and licks off the last bit of icing.

"That is sinful." She makes a sound that goes straight to my groin. I can feel the suction of her mouth all the way to the crown of my cock. I scoop up more of the icing with my finger and smear it over her lips.

Her breath hitches, and her cheeks pink. Then she flicks out her tongue and licks it off, and every cell in my body stands to attention.

She swallows. "I shouldn't want more, but I do."

So do I.

I pick up some more of the cake and hold it out. She leans forward and licks it from my fingertips. Our gazes meet, the air thickens, grows saturated with need. My thigh muscles grow even harder. I'm fucking torturing myself. I take another dollop of the icing, lean over and drag it down her chin, her throat, to where the dark shadow of her cleavage is visible, then over her sleep camisole. She's not wearing a bra underneath, and her nipples are outlined through the silky material.

"I just showered."

"I want to shower you with my cum."

She gasps. "Is that filthy? It is. Am I aroused by it? I am. This is soooo wrong." She shakes her head.

"All the good things in life are. A lesson I learned the hard way. Come here, Belle."

She swallows, then slides off the stool and comes to stand in between my legs. I push the hair back from her flushed cheeks, and her breathing intensifies.

"There are going to be a few rules as long as we're here."

"Rules?"

I nod. "Rules to ensure your orgasms bring you the most pleasure possible. Rules to ensure you have the greatest number of orgasms in the shortest period of time."

"Oh."

Her voice is so breathless, so excited, I almost smile. This woman makes me act out of character. It's a constant surprise. One I relish. One I'd miss if she weren't around. It's the main reason I need to ensure she never leaves me. It's why I need to gratify her, ensure she's so high on endorphins, she's addicted to the sensation only I can rouse in her.

"First rule, no clothes." I snatch a knife from the counter, slide it under her camisole straps and twist.

47

Mira

The camisole strap splits. He does the same to the other. The lacy fabric slithers down my chest and stays suspended—held up only by my nipples, which are saluting at him. They're so hard, and my breasts are so heavy, I feel weighed down. I reach up to tug off the fabric, but he clicks his tongue.

"Second rule: you'll do everything I ask."

"Like I don't already."

"Third rule, if you talk back, you'll be spanked."

I swallow. The fading palm prints on my butt twinge in response. My pussy clenches down, and I know I'm already making a mess between my legs.

"Fourth rule—" He slides the knife under the waistband of my sleep shorts. He flicks his wrist, and cuts through the fabric. Does the same on the other side. He places the knife down on the table with care. His every movement is restrained, controlled. His fingers are steady—unlike mine, which tremble with need. And when he turns to face me, there's almost a bored look on his face. *Ohmigod, do I find that hot? I do find that hot.* The fact that I'm turned on, but he seems so indifferent to the million little butterflies that take flight in my belly, only intensifies my arousal. I shuffle my feet, begin to rub my thighs together, but he shakes his head. "You can't alleviate your need."

"But I itch there."

"Good."

"Just a little chafe of my thighs," I whine.

"Nope."

"It'll only take a second." I flutter my eyelashes at him. "I'll slide in a finger and touch myself once. Just once."

"No, Belle." His voice is hard. "You cannot touch yourself. You cannot get yourself off. You definitely will not allow yourself to come."

"But why?" I pout. "What harm can it do?"

"Do you trust me on this?"

As soon as the words are out, his feature grow tense. *Trust.* That word is like a boulder between us. I want him to have enough faith in me to tell me about his past. But do I have enough confidence in him, enough to hand myself over to him? To entrust my orgasms to his expertise? Do I trust him enough to spend the next few days with him doing everything he wants? Allowing him to do what he wants with me? Not sassing him? Maybe not the last… But the rest? Yeah, I do. He may not be ready to talk about himself, but with everything he does, we come closer. The more time we spend together, the more layers I unearth. And everything I find out about him only makes me want him more.

So, his question was a rhetorical one, in all likelihood. Still, when I nod, his chest rises and falls. His shoulder muscles relax. Huh? Was he tense? Did he think I would refuse him? And if I had, what would he have done? Would he have convinced me otherwise? Would he have spanked me, then kissed me and brought me to the edge, only to hold back my orgasm again? Probably. And the specter of it is not altogether unwelcome.

"Choose a safe word."

"A safe word?"

"If you need me to stop at any time, you only have to use it."

I bite the inside of my cheek, "I don't think I'd ever want you to stop whatever it is you're doing."

His eyes flash, then he cups my cheek. "Much as I am tempted to agree, it would be in your interest to choose one."

I take in the intensity on his features then nod. And don't have to think twice when I say, "Fleabag."

"Your safe word is Fleabag?"

"The series with Andrew Scott as the Hot Priest."

"The Hot Priest?" He frowns.

I peek at him from under my eyelashes. "'Course, you're hotter, Eddie."

I must say the right thing because an expression of satisfaction crosses his face. "What, am I going to do with you?" His throat moves as he swallows.

"Anything you want."

"Anything?"

My heart beats so loudly, it drowns out all other thoughts. "Anything."

I expect him to pull off my torn clothes, then throw me to the ground and ravish me. Instead, he peels my camisole down my arms, then lowers my shorts until both pieces are in a puddle around my ankles.

He grips my hips, lifts me up, kicks the fallen clothes aside, then sets me down. He does it in one uninterrupted move. His biceps bulge, his shoulders turn into rocks of delightful muscle, and his chest swells, but he doesn't breathe heavily. Or show any sign of strain on his face. Of course, he's strong. I've seen the cut of his physique, felt it's impossible wall-like planes dig into my softer curves, but just how powerful comes home to me with this maneuver.

After the years of laughs and jeers in school, and the averted glances of my half-sisters, the graffiti on my locker calling me 'fat face,' the fact that he can handle me like I weigh nothing…is the most erotic thing I've ever encountered. And now, he's going to touch me all over. He's going to fondle my tits, and squeeze my hips, and pinch my clit, and oh god, I want him to. I want him to bite my flesh, mark my thighs, rub the throbbing space between my legs and bring me to the edge. I draw in a breath, and when his scent sinks into my blood and his heat cocoons me like the soothing steam of a sauna, I sway toward him. He steadies me with a hand on my shoulder, then steps back. He reaches for his phone and swipes the screen. The haunting strains of something classical, something deep and complex and so soul stirring, it pours liquid heat through my veins, fills the space. Another sweep and the lights dim. He places his phone down on the island and holds out his hand. "Dance with me."

As if in a dream, I place my palm in his, the other on his shoulder.

He grips my hip with his big hand, the fingers so long and thick, they seem to cover most of my back. And no, my waist isn't the slimmest, and my hips are wide. I've tried to hide my figure — or lack of one — my entire life. But he seems to revel in my softness. He guides me across to the space in front of the floor-to-ceiling windows.

Outside, the dark expanse of the water is broken by the lights of ships in the distance, snowflakes float down in a dance almost as sensuous as the one he leads me through. The music flows over me. He holds me close as we move around the room. His hold on me is sure, his every step confident, yet so light I feel like I'm floating. He holds my gaze, and his own is intense, but there's also a softness around the eyes. Something that indicates he's at peace. Like he's finally coming into himself. It's why he brought me here. He might not have said it aloud — or even admitted it to himself — but having me here is like giving me an insight into his personality without speaking. It's a very Edward move. Dominant and sure and also, so passionate. So emotional. Like this song. The notes rise in crescendo, and tears prick the backs of my eyes.

When the song fades away, he slows to a stop but doesn't release me. "You're crying." He bends and licks the tear drops that skates down my cheek. "Why are you crying?"

48

———————

Mira

"It's… I'm not crying. Not really. It was the music. It was haunting and sad and hopeful, all at the same time."

"The dance before when someone you love becomes a memory," he murmurs.

I widen my gaze, but before I can say anything, he places a finger on my lips. "That was my past. Mired in darkness, filled with a yearning I thought was for my past, when it was me anticipating my future. Anticipating a curvy woman who would sweep into my life and turn my plans upside down. A future which is here. A future I want to see with you. A future which is you."

"Eddie." I move in closer.

He releases my hand only to wrap his arms about my waist. "Forgive me for everything I did to get you here."

"There's nothing to forgive."

He smiles a little. There's something sad in the turn of his lips, something that squeezes my heart. "What is it? Please, tell me."

He hesitates, when the next song comes over the speakers. The familiar notes fill the space, and "Ceilings" by Lizzy McAlpine, starts to play. I was not expecting that. Especially after that classical music piece that almost torn my heart out. Not that "Ceilings" isn't sad, but there's something about that first piece that was timeless. Something that forced my emotions to the surface. Something that made me feel I'd been afforded another peek into his soul.

"That's an eclectic play list," I murmur.

"I'm an eclectic man."

"You don't say." I loop my arms about his neck. "It suits you. You're not what I expected you to be, Mr. Chase."

"Neither are you, Mrs. Chase."

My heart stutters. My fingers tremble. I'm not used to being referred to as Mrs. Chase. At the office, no one dares call me that. I'm still his assistant, and no one has even alluded to our marriage. Either they haven't heard about it — which can't possibly be true, considering I've seen the women eyeing my ring — or he told them not to ask me about it. I frown. "Did you tell the people at the office not to ask me about our marriage?"

His features turn into that mask I'm beginning to recognize as his refuge when he doesn't want to speak.

"You did, didn't you?"

"I might have sent a company-wide email, one which you were not copied on." He continues to lead me in a slow dance, one in which his thighs press against mine, his hips cradle mine, his chest is like steel against mine, and his hands... His big palms are like a brand on the curve of my hips. He slides them down to cup my butt-cheeks and I shiver.

"You're d-distracting me," I stutter.

"Am I succeeding?"

"Almost." I look between his eyes. "Why did you do that?"

"I knew you wanted to work and be independent. You want a life outside the house. You want to find out who you really are and what your likes and dislikes are. You want to get to know yourself better, and I didn't want to stand in the way. And I wanted you to have it, without being embarrassed that you're my wife. I don't want you to work anywhere else, either. I want you with me, but also I want you to feel comfortable coming into work."

"You knew this, even though I never mentioned a word to you?" My steps slow. "And you were looking out for me in ways that never would have occurred to me." *When was the last time someone was so considerate toward me? So thoughtful, so attentive?* He might come across as cold and insensitive, but really, the opposite is true.

"Don't make me out to be something I'm not," he warns.

"I'm not. I'm drawing my conclusion based on facts."

We slow to a stop. The song over the speakers changes to The Weeknd's cover of "Jealous Guy." While Lennon was supreme, The Weeknd brings something darker, deeper, almost twisted to the lyrics, while losing none of the pain of the original. If any song embodies my hot priest, this is it.

"Don't believe everything you see. It may be different from what you interpret it to be."

"Not possible." I slide my palm down to place it over his heart. *Bam-bam-bam.* The thunder of the beats mirrors mine. "Your heart doesn't lie."

"Neither does my cock."

I slide my hands down to cup the bulge between his legs. I squeeze, and his shoulders seem to swell. The expression on his face doesn't change, though.

"Or my mouth." He bends and places his lips on mine. His mouth is hard, but his kiss is so sweet, he simply shares my breath and continues to brush his lips over mine, slowly, so slowly. I melt into him. He drags me up on tiptoe, and that bulge at his crotch feels like a boulder, only hotter, and alive, and throbbing with unspent desire. I moan into his mouth, and his grip tightens, but his lips stay barely touching mine. Fireflies seem to have taken flight in my belly. I seem to be lit up from inside, the need for him burning bright. "Eddie," I whine.

He cups my cheek and looks into my eyes. "Remember this moment, baby. Remember how much I want you. Remember how every part of me needs you. How every breath I take is for you. Only you. Remember."

There's something fervent in his gaze. Something vehement and fiery, and yet also, guarded. Something he wants me to recognize without coming out and telling me. Is it about himself? About me? About—

He looks over my head, then turns me around to face the glass window. "Look."

49

Edward

"A shooting star? No, there's more than one," she gasps.

"It's a meteorite shower."

"Should I make a wish? I definitely need to make a wish. " She squeezes her hands together while her gaze follows the blazing streaks of the stars in the night sky. Her lips move. She continues to watch the skies after the trails fade. "That was incredible." She sighs.

"What did you wish for?"

She shakes her head. "I can't tell you."

"Of course, you can."

"If I do, it won't come true." She turns and sees the skepticism on my features. "It's true. What did you wish for?"

"I didn't."

"You didn't?"

"Everything I want is here in my arms." I pull her close.

"Then you won't mind if I push this jacket off your shoulders?" I let her move it down my arms. She tosses it to the side, and it lands on a chair. Reaches for my tie, and I let her unknot it. When she pulls it off, I take it from her.

"I'm going to blindfold you."

"O-k-a-y?" I wrap it over her closed eyelids and secure it, then tug to make sure it's not too tight, but also taut enough that she can't peer through the gaps.

"This is unnerving," She laughs; the sound is nervous. A hint of anticipation, mixed with apprehension spools off of her body. I'm instantly hard. The blood in my veins begins to pump. I cup her breast, and she swallows. I tweak her nipple. She groans. And when I drag my fingers through her slit, she's already creaming.

"Fuck, you're so wet." I bring the moisture to my mouth and suck on my digits. My already excited cock stabs into the fabric of my pants.

"It's not fair, I can't see you."

"But you're going to experience everything so much more intensely." I scoop her up in my arms. She gasps in surprise, then holds on. I stalk toward the bed and when I throw her down on it, she bounces once. Her hair ripples out behind her. Her ample breasts, the fold of her stomach, her plump thighs—all of it calls to me. But I cannot give in to her siren call. Not yet. I prowl toward the closet, step inside, and walk out with a few coils of silk rope.

I ease her up to sitting, then urge her to fold her knees so her feet are flat on the bed. I pull her thighs apart, then can't stop myself from running my fingers up her exposed pussy. And when she groans, I curl my fingers around her swollen clit, before I suck her cum off my fingertips.

"Oh, god," she moans.

"God has nothing to do with this," I promise. I loop the rope around one thigh and tie it to her ankle. Then I repeat it with the other, before I position her wrist at her ankle and tie that, too, then repeat it at the other side.

"Do you want to use your safe word?" I look at her flushed features.

"No," she says without hesitation.

"Good girl."

Her breathing instantly grows choppy. Her chest rises and falls. She flexes her thighs, trying to squeeze them together and I click my tongue. "You're not allowed to alleviate your needs, remember?"

"That's a stupid condition."

"It's to help you orgasm harder."

"Yeah, yeah, that's what you keep saying. This mythical orgasm seems like something out of a fairytale."

"Only the dark smutty ones."

She gapes. "How do you know about them?"

"I read."

"Have you read my—" She gasps again, because I've finished securing her wrists to each ankle. I test the knots to make sure they don't bite into her skin but are tight enough to restrain her. Her muscles are tense, and I turn and kiss her. She begins to relax and when she parts her lips, I slide my tongue between them. I swipe it over the seam of her mouth and she whines, then melts into me.

"What's my name?" I murmur.

"Eddie," she groans.

"Such a good little slut, you are." I slide two fingers inside her slit, and she bears down on it. I press my thumb into her clit, and her entire body jolts. "Eddie. Oh, Eddie."

"I'm right here." I weave my fingers in and out of her, in and out. Her breath comes in little pants, sweat beads her upper lip. I lick it off, and she chases my mouth with hers. "So greedy for my cock."

"I am," she pants. "I want to feel you inside me."

I slap her pussy, and she cries out. "You asshole."

"That reminds me." I scoop up some of her cum, then smear it around her forbidden hole.

Her entire body shudders. Who'd have guessed my Belle has an erogenous zone in the unlikeliest of places.

"I want to come, please, Eddie," she whimpers.

"Not yet."

She pouts, then gasps when I loop the silk around her chest, and under her breast. I knot it at the back before crossing it over her shoulder and under the opposite breast. When the chest harness is done, I move way, and admire my artwork. "Beautiful."

A shiver grips her.

"If you could see yourself through my eyes, you'd know you're the most gorgeous woman in the world."

"Only in your eyes."

"That's all that matters. Your body was made for my ropes."

"Shibari; that's what this is." She lowers her chin to her chest. "Have you practiced it with anyone else?"

"No one who has your curves. No one who wears it like you. No one whose flesh will show off the marks of the ropes like you will. No one who I have fucked after tying them up."

I kneel between her bent thighs, then slowly ease her on her back. In the crab style I've tied her in, her wrists are linked to her ankles, which are up in the air. The result, all her beautiful bits are open and ready, and right there. All offered up to me in the most alluring of ways. All showcased and waiting to receive my ministrations.

I run my finger down the dip in her lips, to her cleavage, down to the hollow of her navel and when I trace the valley between her pussy lips, she mewls. When I follow the trail to her back hole, she whimpers.

"The sounds you make; they're driving me out of my head." I lower my zipper, then grab my throbbing cock. I pump it once, twice, then fit the angry head to her weeping slit. "I'm going to fuck you now."

50

Mira

That's all the warning I get before he kicks his hips forward and impales me. I'm so wet, he slides right in and hits that hidden heart of me deep inside. My breath whooshes out, and a groan boils up. He stays embedded in me, his cock throbbing, pushing against my inner walls. In this position, I am spread open and at his mercy. I can't see him, but I can feel the heat of his body as he looms over me. I feel the thickness of his thighs digging into mine. I feel the bones of his hips pressing into mine. I can sense his massive chest poised over my body like a bird of prey, a beast ready to break me.

"Eddie, please," I pant. Not sure what I'm asking for, only knowing I need more, so much more.

He presses his finger into my lower lip. "Open."

I do.

The next second he tears off my blindfold. I blink as he comes into focus. His golden eyes are almost silver with lust, his jaw hard, a fierceness to his features as he scans mine. "I want you to see this." He spits into my mouth, and I almost come undone. *No, this is disgusting. How could he do this?*

He notches his knuckles under my jaw and pushes up. I close my mouth.

"Swallow."

I do.

"Good girl."

Oh, shit. My pussy squeezes down on his cock; my nipples are so hard, they ache. Sparks zip down my body to knot with the tension at the base of my spine.

"You take everything I give you so beautifully," he growls.

I can't take my gaze off of him. Can't move, can't breathe. Pinned to the bed with his monster cock inside me, I can merely look into his eyes. See the silver-gold flares that light up deep inside. See his soul—scarred and broken and knitting itself back together. Because of me. A thrill of power barrels through my veins. I squeeze my inner walls again and am rewarded by the undulation of his muscles. He may have me tied down, but I have him at my mercy.

He reads the expression on my face, for a cunning look comes into his eyes. He pinches my nipple, turning it to the side with such suddenness, my breath catches. A blast of pain squeals down my body. Sweat slicks the space between my breasts, and I pant. So does he.

"Fuck!" He grits his teeth, then pulls out and stays poised at my opening. This time, when he slams into me, the entire bed jolts. He throbs inside of me, then pulls out again and thrusts into me. And again. As much as he's denied me an orgasm so far, something inside him seems to have tipped over the edge. And oh, my god, am I glad to be at the receiving end of all that intensity. That restrained violence. That passion that clings to every angle of his body.

He picks up even more speed, the sound of flesh hitting flesh filling the space. I am dripping, probably making a mess on the bedspread. The evidence is in the embarrassing sucking sound that sputters though the air every time he pulls back. It seems to urge him on, for he slaps both hands down on either side of my head, kicks his hips forward and drills into me. He stays there, still looking deep into my eyes. The world retreats. Everything stops, but for his gaze that holds me in thrall, and his cock that pegs me in place.

"Eddie, I love you."

He pulls back, and the next time he thrusts into me, the orgasm barrels up my body. "Come for me, Belle," he growls.

And I do. I ride the climax, all the way to the top, and when it breaks, I cry out. I hear him groan as he follows me over into the abyss. As the darkness subsides, and I open my eyes, I find I've been untied. He's rubbing a flowery ointment into my skin. I try to move, and my entire body protests.

"Stay still." He places his big palm between my breasts, and the weight of it is calming. I close my eyes and follow the gentle touch of his fingers over my ankles, my thighs, my wrists, and around my breasts.

Then he pulls the cover over me, turns me on my side and spoons me. I'm instantly in heaven. Am I smiling? Yes, my lips are curved. He wraps his arm about my waist, pulls me in and fits his knee into the space between mine. The heat of his body drugs me and pulls me down. I allow myself to float away.

When I wake, silvery light shines through the skylight and from the windows. The sight of the sea stretching out with the pink streaks of dawn on the horizon stops me. I take in the awe-inspiring sight, then pause. I'm in bed alone. I sit up, look around, and spy the open door to the bathroom. The sound of running water reaches me.

I slip out of bed, then wince as my muscles protest. Every step I take warns me of how sore I am in between my legs. I increase my speed, reach the bathroom and slip in. Steam fills the space, and beyond the fogged walls of the shower cubicle, I make out Edward with his back to me, head thrown back, as the water pours over him. Tall and broad, he could be carved out of stone. My belly clenches, and the honey of desire oozes through my veins.

I walk across the bathroom floor, open the cubicle of the shower and slip in. The steam wafts aside, and I spot scars crisscrossing his back. Pain squeezes my chest. I must make a noise, for he looks over his shoulder. His gaze widens, then that stony countenance drops over his features. "What are you doing here?"

51

Edward

"Your poor back." She traces her fingers down the scars. I pull away, but she closes the distance to me, then kisses the puckered skin.

Goosebumps pop on my skin, despite the heat of the cascade I'm standing in.

She rubs her cheek against my back. The muscles of my shoulders turn to concrete. My heart thrashes against my ribcage. My stomach twists itself in knots, and I feel dizzy. I dig my palms into the wall, forcing myself to stay unmoving. She traces the blemishes all the way to the nape of my neck.

My cock lengthens, and my balls tighten. I came inside her again last night, and it was earth-shattering. Again. And when I pulled her body to mine, buried my nose in her hair and closed my eyes, I slept deeper and longer than any other night. The last time I slept this peacefully was before the incident. And when I woke up in the morning, I slipped my upright cock inside her and finished off in a few jerks…like a teenager. She moaned in her sleep, but I managed not to wake her. Then, I crawled out of bed. I decided to take a shower because, if I stayed in bed a second longer, I'd make love to her again, and I didn't want to disturb her sleep. And it was 'making love.' I can't kid myself any longer.

I switch off the shower, and in the silence that follows, I hear her sniffle. "Who did this to you?"

"I did."

"What?" She steps back and stares at my back in horror. "You hurt yourself?"

When I don't reply, she pushes her wet hair back from her face. "Why would you do that?"

"To punish myself."

"Is this because you couldn't have her? Is that why you did it?"

"I deserved it."

"No one deserves so much pain." She reaches out and, once more, traces one of the hardened trails of skin. "No one," she leans in, but before she can replace her fingers with her mouth, I turn and catch her wrist.

"I'm tainted, Belle."

"I don't care. Whatever happened before is in the past. I'm your future—you said it yourself."

I lower her hand, then drag my fingers through my hair. "I need to get dressed."

"No, not until you tell me why you scarred yourself."

"I lost what I thought was my one chance at happiness. I couldn't face my best friend anymore."

"You mean Baron?"

I nod. "I didn't want to see any of the Seven, either. They'd been my constant companions since our school days. We went through…a lot together. It formed a bond between us. But after Ava and Baron got together, I couldn't stay in London. I wanted them to be happy. I'm the one who told Ava to go back to Baron—"

"You did?"

"It was clear she loved him more. I had my chance and I lost it when I left her. I needed time to get my head on straight. I was a priest and I'd sinned. Everything inside me told me I was in the wrong, but I couldn't reconcile it with how I felt when I was with her. It was a mindfuck."

She reaches out for me, and I hold up my hand. "Don't touch me."

Her features fall.

Fuck. I squeeze the bridge of my nose. "I just… Let me get this out while I can Belle."

She nods, then tucks her arm into her side.

"I left her. I told Baron to watch out for her and I left. When I came back, I realized they had fallen in love. I saw them together, and I knew I couldn't be all the things she needed. I knew I wasn't in any space to hold down a relationship. How could I, when I hadn't figured out who I was and what I needed? She chose me. She even moved in with me, but seeing her face every morning, realizing how much she missed him, I told her to return to him."

"You did?"

"What Baron felt for her... It was different. He adored her. He wanted to take care of her. He needed her, and she leaned on him. They turned to each other in my absence and discovered they completed each other. I couldn't stand in their way."

"So you sacrificed your own happiness?"

"I did no such thing. I knew I couldn't be happy until I'd dealt with my own devils, so I walked away from them."

"Oh, Eddie." She wraps her arms about herself, and I notice the goosebumps on her skin. I scoop her up in my arms and walk out of the shower stall.

"What are you doing?" she squeaks.

"You're cold." I manage to grab a couple of towels on the way out, and when I reach the bed, I lower her to the ground. I dry her shoulders, her breasts, her waist, her thighs, down to her feet, then back up to her core. I pat it, then say around the ball of lust in my throat, "Spread your legs."

She does.

I slide the edge of the towel over her slit and back again.

She moans.

I do it again, and she shudders. The sweet scent of her arousal bleeds into the air, and I feel my cock stand up and salute her. *Fuck.* Can't keep my hands off of her, can't keep my gaze off of her pussy. If only I could spend days buried inside her tight cunt, I might get this insane need to rut into her every time I'm near her out of my system. A-n-d, who am I kidding? The more time I spend with her, the more I want her, the more I can't let go of her. I'll never get enough of her, and that is the truth. And when she finds out my truth, she'll hate me. And I can't let that happen. I can't. I let the towel drop to the bed, then I lift her up and throw her on it.

52

Mira

"Hold yourself open for me," he growls.

Fish in the snow, his words are hard and demanding and... I can't say no. I manage to widen the space between my legs, then reach down and hold open my pussy lips.

"Good girl."

I'm not ashamed to say, I almost climax. Just from his words. The way he says it, it makes me feel like the most special person in the entire world, and the luckiest. He stares at my glistening cunt—I can feel the moisture gathering at my slit—then reaches down and squeezes his cock from base to tip. It's the first time I've seen my husband without a stitch of clothing, and the reality far surpasses my dreams. Sculpted shoulders, corrugated chest, concave waist, not to mention, the eight pack he sports like he works out every day, and those thick powerful thighs without an inch of fat on them. He's pure muscle, all the way down to his calves and his bare feet. Something about his feet shoots my blood pressure through the roof. I have a foot fetish—correction I have an Edward fetish. He widens his stance, and my gaze is drawn up to where he massages his thick cock once more, all the way to the crown. There's a vein running up it, and moisture drips from the slit.

"Put three fingers inside yourself," he commands.

"Th-three?"

He merely arches an eyebrow.

I swallow as my heart descends to the space between my legs. The blood roars so loudly in my ears, I'm sure the sea has risen all the way to the top of the lighthouse. I slide three fingers into my opening and pause.

"All the way in."

"I... I can't."

"You took my cock inside you; your fingers are nothing."

Moisture drools from my core. I thrust my fingers inside, and sensations vibrate out from the intrusion. I'm so sensitive, flickers of heat zip through my blood.

"Hold out your fingers and show me your cum."

OMG, that dirty talking mouth of his is going to make me orgasm without him having touched me. I manage to glide my fingers out and show them to him.

"You're wet enough for what's going to come, turn on your front.

I hesitate.

He glares at me, and frissons of anticipation spark up my spine. I turn over.

"Stay there."

I hear him move around, hear the slither of the silken rope over his palm. Goosebumps splatter on my skin. *Oh god. Ohgod, ohgod. He's going to use the ropes again, and I'm going to love every second of it. What is he doing to me? To think I was a virgin less than a month ago and now I can't wait for him to tie me up and fuck every hole.*

"I can hear you thinking, and I'm going to deliver on it."

A whimper escapes me. I sound so needy, so greedy. So ready for everything he has in mind.

He lifts my foot then pushes down until my leg is fully bent at the knee, then slips the rope just below the knee and above the ankle, tying me in a frog legged shape. He does the same to the other side. Then I sense him straighten.

"What's my name, Belle?"

"Eddie," I breathe.

"Such a good little slut, you are."

A shiver of pleasure swirls through my blood like cream poured in coffee. I begin to squeeze my thighs together, but he grips my knee and holds them apart. "Remember, you can't alleviate your need."

"That's ridiculous."

"That's called a frog-tie."

"What?" I blink.

"Tying your legs the way I have."

"You mean, it helps you reach any of my orifices conveniently?" I scoff.

"Exactly." He sounds pleased. Because clearly, he got the response he wanted. Because I walked into the trap he'd set me. I firm my lips.

"Aren't you going to ask me what I'm going to do next?"

I want to. Of course, I do, but I'm not giving him the satisfaction of doing what he expects. I stay silent and hear him chuckle. The bastard chuckles, which, coming from someone who has a hard time curving his lips in a smile, is enough to make me glare at him over my shoulder.

"Next is the box-tie," he informs me.

Like I need to know the name of whatever convoluted knot he's going to drape over my body?

He places one knee on the bed, then the other on the other side of my body.

"Place your cheek on the bed." He gently urges me, then when I'm positioned to his satisfaction, he begins to knead my shoulders. He digs his fingers into the tensed muscles, and when they relax, a warmth seeps through my blood. "Draw a deep breath," he orders.

I do.

"Now let it out." He guides me through a series of breathing exercises, at the end of which my body seems to have turned into a puddle. I don't even feel the knots around my legs, except for the pleasant stretch on my hamstrings. And when he pulls me up so I'm sitting on my heels, I don't protest. Not even when he twists one arm, then the other, so they're folded over the small of my back. He passes the ropes around my upper arms and chest, then loops them around my wrists. When he tightens the ropes, I realize the position causes my breasts to thrust out. Also, my knees are spread wide enough for my clit to be bared, and because I'm balanced on my knees he can access my forbidden back hole. The position feels natural enough that I could hold it for hours. Which is the effect he was going for.

"You should see how you look, tied up, with my ropes marking your skin, with your flesh curving around my knots. It's the most erotic thing ever." He walks around to the other side of the bed, so he's facing me. Then drags his gaze down my body. "Fucking hell, you're a vision, Belle."

Color heightens his cheeks. His chest rises and falls. And when my gaze is drawn to his crotch, I find him erect and hard, with his cock standing up against his stomach. It also looks even bigger than earlier. Like seeing me tied up is lending an added stimulus to his arousal. I know the way he's watching me is definitely boosting my horniness.

Then his brow furrows. "Something's missing."

53

Mira

He moves away only to return with a bowl in his hand. He scoops up something and holds it out. "Open."

My pussy clenches at once. Only he could turn that one word into something so salacious, I feel like he's talking about other holes in my body. I part my lips, and he slides his finger over my tongue. I'm overcome by the dark taste of chocolate, the tanginess of cherries, the sweet taste of brandy, the bite of citrus, and the hint of apple. "Christmas pudding?" I frown.

"I'm going to decorate you with it."

"You're joking."

He tilts his head, a serious look on his face as he takes measure of my body.

Not joking, then.

He scoops up some more of the mixture, then draws a circle around my breast, before dabbing it on my nipple. He does the same with the other side. He continues to trace sticky lines down my stomach before filling my belly button with the gooey stuff. I wriggle, but he shoots me a glare. "Stay still."

Of course, I oblige. How can I not when the dominance in his voice brooks no argument. He smears the concoction on the skin above my pussy, then down the crease of my inner thigh. I squirm, but when he makes a warning noise at the back of his throat, I freeze. He rubs some of it over the tops of my thighs, coming close to my core, but never touching my pussy.

"Eddie," I whine.

"What do you need, Belle?" He raises his gaze to mine.

"You know what I want."

"You need to ask for it."

I scowl. He dabs some of the pudding on the tip of my nose, then across my lower lip.

"Those are not the only lips I want you to touch," I plead.

"Ask me." He brings his finger to his mouth and sucks his digit. And when he pulls it out, it makes a popping sound that kickstarts a flurry of activity in my lower belly.

"Okay, fine, can you please touch my pussy?"

"And?'

"My cunt."

"And—"

I swallow. "I don't want that stuff to stain your bed."

"I'll lick it up before that happens."

"Oh," I gulp audibly. He's going to lick this off my body. He's going to lick all the parts where he's rubbed in this icky mixture. It shouldn't turn me on further, but oh god, it does. He's going to stuff his tongue into all the nooks and crevasses of my body and I…want him to. "Put it in my pussy," I mumble.

"I didn't hear you." His lips curl a little at the edges. He's smirking. Ugh, and that only makes him hotter, and I'm tired of all this teasing.

"Fuck me with your monster dick," I yell.

"As you wish." He places the bowl on the side table, then climbs onto the bed facing me. He leans in and licks the stuff on my nose, the gesture almost affectionate, then brushes his lips over mine. Just a feather light touch. Enough to make me want more, so when he pulls away, I chase his mouth.

"Greedy girl." He weighs my breasts in both of his big hands. The calluses on his fingers chafe my tender skin. The sting combines with the tension in my stomach, and the result is a sweet pain which goes to my head.

"Eddie, please," I moan.

He bends his head, bites down on my nipple, and my eyes roll back in my head. And when he pays similar attention to the other, I almost collapse. He grips my hips and holds me up, then proceeds to lick his way down my stomach, over the fold of my belly, and when he swirls his tongue into my belly button, I cry out, "Eddie. Eddie. Eddie."

I try to pull away, but his grasp is firm. He holds me captive as he licks and sucks and bites his way down the pudding tracks, which means, he circles my pussy, coming closer and closer to my aching core. My clit is so swollen, my slit so moist, the hollow in my center seems to be growing by the moment, and I try to close my legs, but he releases his hold on my hips, only to grab my thighs and splay them wide. He lays out on his front and shoves his face into my pussy. I cry out, then whimper when he slurps his way up my pussy lips and over my clit. Sweat drips down my cleavage, and my teeth snap together. I'm shuddering so hard, it's like I've caught a fever. Not that it makes a difference to him.

He lays his head on my thigh and blows on my cunt. I cry out. He slides three fingers inside me and twists, and the climax screams up my spine. I throw my head back and wait…wait for the orgasm. Only, he pulls back. The orgasm hovers there like a wave about to crash on the shore; only, it's as if someone has pressed the rewind button. It retreats.

"No, no, no," I pant.

"Yes." He raises his head, then eases me onto my back. It should be awkward, but really, the way he's tied me up, he can move me around, and no part of my body protests. I lay there with my legs bent at the knees, splayed like a frog.

He stares at my exposed center, and a flush climbs up his chest. As turned on as I am, I realize, he is, too. As needy as I am, the thick length of his cock standing to attention seems almost painful.

Then he draws his whiskered chin across my pussy, and I cry out, "Oh my god!"

He instantly stiffens. "Told you, God has nothing to do with this."

Before I can react, he lowers his head and draws his tongue up my slit.

54

Edward

I can't get enough of her. I can't. Tied up in my knots, wearing the marks of the rope I've wrapped around her, with her flesh flushed by my ministrations, she's the most beautiful creature to grace this earth. I drag my tongue up her pussy lips, and when I bite down on the swollen knob of her clit, her entire body shudders. Her thighs quiver, and her breasts swell. She makes that telltale moan at the back of her throat, and I know she's close. Not to mention, she's so wet, I can't stop lapping at her entrance. I continue to eat her out, and when full body shudders grip her, I rise over her. I fit my cock to her opening, and plunge into her.

"Eddie," she gasps.

"You're so wet, so tight." I grit my teeth, giving her time to adjust to my size. No matter how many times I take her, it feels like the first time. "Belle," I groan and push my forehead into hers. "You feel so fucking good."

She clenches down on my shaft, and the tiny flutters of her inner-walls embracing my shaft, drain the blood to my groin. I begin to fuck her in earnest. In-out-in, and again. Every time I bury myself in her, the entire bed shudders. Every time I pull out, she moans in frustration. The heat generated from us presses down on my back. Sweat drips down my forehead. The next time I slam into her, she cries out. Her back arches, and her eyelids flutter down.

"Look at me as you come, wife."

She manages to meet my gaze, and her pupils are so dilated with lust, and something else, something soft that sends me over the edge.

"Come with me." My balls tighten. "Come right now, Belle."

Her mouth opens in a soundless cry. She topples over the edge, and I follow her. My climax seems to go on and on, as I pour myself into her. When she slumps, I begin to pull out of her. The mix of her cum and mine slides down her thigh, and I reach down and stuff it back inside her cunt.

"What are you doing?" Her voice is slurred.

"Making sure you take every last drop of what's mine."

When I'm satisfied, I sit up, pulling her up with me. Then I reach behind her and untie the knots at her back, then at her legs. I ease her back onto the bed and stretch out her arms and legs. I begin to massage them with long strokes, and she sighs, "That's so nice..." She yawns.

"Sleep." I kiss her eyelids closed. Her body twitches, and I know she's out. I walk over to the bathroom, returning with a warm washcloth, and run it down her body. Then I pull the covers over her before walking back to the bathroom and tossing the washcloth in the hamper. I get dressed but can't tear myself away from her. So I pull up a chair and watch her sleep.

Can I give you my confession? I've done this before—watched her sleep. Before she even knew me. There, I've told you. Now I need to confess to her, and accept whatever penance she deems fit. But not yet. Not until I know she's bound to me in a way nothing on earth can break that connection. A few more days, is all I need... I hope.

She stretches, yawns, then her gaze finds mine. "What time is it?"

"Not even noon."

"What are we doing today?"

"Not much, considering..." I nod toward the window.

She follows my gaze, and her mouth drops open. "Whoa, it's a snowstorm out there."

"It is. And it's supposed to go on for a few days."

"A few days?" She turns to me. "So we're stuck inside here?"

"Seems that way."

"Hmm." She sits up, and the sheet falls to her waist. "I wonder how we're going to fill our time?"

Perhaps, that was a rhetorical question. There's never been any question in my mind that I'm going to use the time to get to know every inch of her body thoroughly. And she seems perfectly amenable to my plans.

I took her in our bed, again, then made us lunch. For dessert, I had her on the island. And I told her I'm not much a dessert-eater—ha! I let her catch a nap while I worked out, needed to keep up my energy for the coming days, after all. Then, it was an early dinner, for which I reheated a casserole.

Post dinner, we curled up in the settee in front of the fire while the snowfall outside was so dense, it felt like we were marooned on an island.

She stretched out, and I read to her from one of her spicy books. She began to squirm, and when she looked at me with her dilated eyes, I knew what she wanted. I positioned her on the bed, on her knees with her behind in the air and a pillow under her chest. When I pulled her arms back and tied her wrists to her ankles, she moaned with excitement. The cum running down her inner thighs, and the gleaming pink of her pussy told me how turned on she was. Which, in turn, turned me on. There was so much wetness, I scooped it up and used it to lubricate her back channel. She shuddered. I thought she'd protest, but she pushed out her butt in invitation. I checked in with her, made sure she called me by the name only she does, then I fucked her there. I made sure she orgasmed before I allowed myself to come. Then, I made sure to clean her up before I curled around her and fell asleep.

When I wake up, the light coming in through the windows is a golden yellow. It's stopped snowing, and the sun illuminates the arches of the clouds in the sky and highlights her curves. She's standing naked at the window, with her hand pressed into the glass. The light turns her hair to a cloud of spun gold, and outlines the dip of her waist, the flare of her round bottom. My cock hardens at once. Without conscious thought, I prowl toward her, then wrap my arm about her waist and bring her against my naked body. Apparently, now that I've shown myself naked to her, I feel comfortable enough to stay that way.

"Mmm." She turns around and reaches up to touch my face. "Merry Christmas."

I tilt my head, unable to bring myself to say the words. There was a time when I looked forward to this time of year, when I threw myself into the spirit of the season. When I led Advent services, led community efforts, visited the older parishioners at home to bring them the Eucharist. I also presided over the Christmas Eve Mass, and I enjoyed it. I used the season to help families reconcile differences and learn the importance of helping others. I was good at my chosen line of work.

Now? It all seems so pointless. To have believed in something and been happy at that time... I suppose, that counts for something. It certainly helped me through some tough times, providing hope when I was bereft. Only now, I question if my faith was misplaced? I believed...and was let down. This time, I'm not leaving anything to chance. Or some nonexistent or uncaring god. This time, I'm in control. I'll make sure I get what I want... Her.

I cup her cheek, then bend and kiss her lips. "Sleep well?"

"I did." Her lips curve in a smile.

So beautiful, so open, so happy, so everything I'm not. My heart catches. I tighten my grip on her.

Her forehead furrows. "And you?"

"Never better." No nightmares, no ghosts from the past haunting my thoughts. I feel refreshed and full of energy and...my cock throbs between us. "Horny."

She glances down, then up at me, her eyes wide. "Again?"

"If you're too sore —"

She shakes her head, then pulls out of my grasp. "But you'll have to catch me."

55

Mira

I saw the play of expression on his face, knew he was thinking of things he wouldn't share with me. And I'll admit, it upsets me. I want to confront him about it, but if I do, it'll cause him to shut down, which I don't want. Especially after how he took me last night. Tying me up is how he expresses his emotions toward me. Maybe he can't say the words aloud, but how he worships me with his body tells me he's halfway—more than halfway— to falling in love with me. And I don't want to spoil the intimacy that's sprung up between us.

Marooned here in this lighthouse, miles from anywhere, it's just him and me, and I want to enjoy the feeling. I want to…make him laugh, lighten the thoughts he's having. I want to just forget about the real world for a while. Which is why I slip out of his embrace and taunt him to catch up. And he doesn't disappoint. A sly look comes into his eyes, and he prowls forward.

I take a few steps back, stumble against the settee, straighten and move around it. His lips curl as he continues to walk toward me. He knows he's going to catch me. I know he's going to catch me. But… I'm going to make him work for it.

I scramble back, cursing my boobs which flap around my chest. But then, he notices them, too. His gaze locks on my chest, and it's his turn to stumble. Holy shit, he's distracted by my body. He seems to love my figure—always tells me so, shows me how much he enjoys it in how he handles my body, but I'm self-conscious enough that I need constant reassurances. And what's more of an ego boost than to have this gorgeous, confident man lose his footing when he sees my boobs?

I bring my hand up to play with my nipple, and his body tenses. He picks up his pace. I glance around, then dart around the bed. He stalks toward me and when I play with my pussy lips, he bumps into the bed. "Shit."

I giggle.

He frowns, then his forehead smoothens out. "You know what happens to little brats?"

I shake my head.

"They get taught a lesson."

"Oh." Moisture oozes out from my slit. I scoop it up, show him my glistening fingers. "Wanna taste?"

He nods.

"Too bad, you're not getting any." I bring my fingers to my lips, making a popping sound the way he's done in the past.

His gaze narrows. "Belle," he growls.

"Is that a sushi role between your legs, or are you sashimi to see me?"

He blinks. "What was that?"

"A…a…joke."

"I'm not laughing."

"How about knock-knock joke?" I hop from foot to foot. Behind me, is the wall; to the right, a glass window; and to my left, a bed. There's only one way out. I jump up on the bed. He's at the foot of the bed, and the various parts of me that jiggle once again seem to get his attention. He sweeps his gaze from the hair on my head, which is a rat's nest, no doubt, all the way down to my toes, which I dig into the mattress, then back to my face.

"Knock-knock," he says in a hard voice.

"Who…who's there?"

"Dozer."

"Dozer, who?" I ask in a cautious tone.

"Dozer some great tits you got there." His tone is still without expression but his eyes wear a glint.

I scoff, "That the best you can do?"

He slaps his palms on his hips and scowls. "Knock-knock."

Here goes nothing. "Who's there?"

"Hop on."

"Hop on, who?"

"Hop on this dick."

I make a gagging sound and begin to edge toward to the far side of the bed, away from him. I reach it, jump down, and move toward the kitchen area.

"Knock-knock," he growls.

"Who's there?" I tip up my chin.

"Iguana."

I frown. "Iguana, who?"

"Iguana touch your tits." He races toward me. I shriek, run toward the kitchen island, and circle it.

"Knock-knock." He bares his teeth.

"Who's there?" I pant.

"The dentist." He moves to one side of the island, while I dart to the other.

"The dentist, who?"

"I heard you have some cavities that need filling." He races around the counter, and I run to the side opposite him.

"Knock-knock." He rolls his shoulders. The movement is so menacing, my stomach flips up into my throat. And when he lowers his chin and glares at me, every drop of blood I have drains to my clit. "Who's there?" I gasp.

He takes a step toward me; I sidle to the side.

"Can I come in?" He cracks his knuckles. He's doing it to intimidate me, and he's succeeding. Also, I can't wait to have those thick fingers on me, in me, pleasuring me, plucking on my nipples, playing with my clit, intruding into my forbidden hole. My heart flutters like the wings of a dragon fly. "Can I—" I swallow. "Can I come in, who?"

"You!" He throws himself over the island.

I scream, turn and run away, but he's too fast. I hear him hit the floor, then footsteps race toward me. He grabs me around my waist and throws me over his shoulder. I'm breathing so hard, and my blood is pounding so hard in my temples, I think I'm going to faint. My hair tumbles over my face. I push it aside, orient myself to realize he's reached the bed. Then, he throws me on it on my back, and covers me with his body.

He stares into my face, his chest rising and falling, his eyes slightly wild. Apparently, I did the right thing by asking him to chase me; seems it not only broken the chain of his brooding thoughts, but also turned him on even more, as evidenced by the massive thing that stabs into the curve of my belly.

"I'm going to have to punish you, Belle." His voice, by contrast, is almost casual. But I'm not fooled. I know by the way his jaw tics and his left eyelid throbs, by the way the tendons of his throat stand out under his flesh, he means it. He reaches down between us and notches his cock into my slit.

56

———————

Edward

I kick my hips forward and in one sweet thrust I'm home. Inside her soft melting pussy which embraces me like it's missed me.

"I missed this," I confess.

"I missed you, too." She cups my cheek. "Missed you so much."

Her soft words are like balm on my wounds. Her eyes glisten with empathy, with tenderness, with love. She wears her heart in her eyes; she has nothing to hide, unlike me. I urge her to lock her ankles about my waist, then plunge into her and bury myself, again, to the hilt. She gasps; her mouth opens, and I stay there, pushing forward with my knees until I'm fitted into her. I stay there, and she flutters around me. "That's it, baby," I croon.

"Eddie," she gasps. She winds her arms about my neck, digging her fingernails into my back. I want her to mark me. I want to replace the scars of my past with blemishes she's bestowed on me.

"I'm here." I begin to pump my hips forward and fuck her in earnest. Her body moves forward with the force of impact, and the headboard cracks against the wall. Something falls to the ground behind me, but I ignore it. I'm too focused on the expressions that flit across her face; the heightened blush that climbs up her chest and neck; her whines and whimpers as I rut into her, over and over again. Looking into her eyes as I fuck her is the most intimate experience of my life.

"I love you," she whispers.

"I..." *love you.* I want to say it. I do. But the words stick in my throat. Instead, I tilt my hips, and sink into her with enough impact, my balls hit her inner thighs. I hit the space deep inside her, then push in further. That familiar shuddering sweeps up her hips, her back arches, and when she begins to cry out, I close my mouth over hers and absorb the sounds. She shatters around my cock, and I grunt as I come inside her. When she begins to slump, I lean back, taking in her freshly fucked features. Then, because I can't help myself, I press a kiss to her forehead before I pull out and throw myself on the bed next to her. She curls into my side, and I wrap my arm around her and pull her closer.

"I first saw you in Brooklyn a year ago."

"A year ago?" She doesn't react. *Maybe my idea of fucking her until she's so filled with endorphins she won't be able to react to my revelations is what's keeping her calm? Now you know how morally grey I am. And yes, I'm a bastard. But you know that already.*

"I was there for a work meeting. I was in my car, saw you walking home from the subway. I followed you to your townhouse."

"My father's townhouse," she corrects me. So, she doesn't think of it as her home, interesting.

"Over the next week, I trailed you to your part time job at the preschool, to meet your friends in Manhattan."

"O-k-a-y?"

"I also got access to your devices."

"What do you mean?" There's a thread of curiosity in her voice. But her muscles are still relaxed. I draw circles over her hip, and she shivers. And when I lean in and kiss her lips, she melts into me further. "I had an investigator break into your room and put hidden cameras and listening devices there."

"You put hidden cameras and listening devices in my room?" She asks slowly.

"Also, in your phone and on your Kindle."

"Why my Kindle?" She frowns.

"It's the device you spend most of your time on; more than your phone."

"And how did you find that out?"

"I saw you reading on your Kindle in the coffee shop, and on the subway, and even while walking to and from the subway, something which was so dangerous, I ended up following you to make sure you reached home safely."

"You followed me home from the subway to make sure I reached home safely?" Her brow furrows.

"It was either that or reveal myself to you, and I wasn't ready for that."

Something of what I'm saying seems to infiltrate through her subconscious, for her gaze widens. "You're saying you saw me before we met at Gio's wedding?"

I nod slowly.

"And you first saw me in Brooklyn?"

I stay quiet, letting her read the assent in my gaze.

She rubs at her temple. "And you bugged my room in my father's home?"

I nod.

"How did you do that?" The wrinkle between her eyebrows deepens. "My father's home has security."

"Nothing my team couldn't bypass. I also had eyes and ears on your apartment in London."

This time, she pushes away from me, and I don't want to let her go. I don't want there to be any distance between us, but I release her... For now.

"In my a-a-apartment?" she stutters.

I reach for her, but she pulls away. A hot stab of pain squeezes my chest; I rub at it. I knew it was going to hurt when I finally told her. But I had to tell her. Even though everything in me warned me if I did, I could lose her.

And what if I didn't tell her? I've managed not to, so far. But now, when I'm so close to her, when it feels like so many walls have come down between us, when I'm beginning to show her who I am, when she knows my darkest desires and hasn't run yet, I know it's now or never. And it has to be while we're here, when she can't run and leave me. While we're still snowbound. But it won't last forever. It's stopped snowing, and the sun has started to shine, and once it thaws, we'll have to return. And then... I won't be able to stop her from leaving. But for now, I can keep her here, even if she hates me.

"I had to make sure I knew where you were at all times."

"I don't understand. You had cameras on me and listening devices. You were tracking me; you knew where I always was?" Color fades from her cheeks.

"I had to make sure you were safe at all times."

"There was no threat to me," she protests.

"And this was the only way to be sure." I rub the back of my neck. "I know this is a lot for you to take in but—"

"So when you offered me a job—"

"I knew you needed it. I knew your preschool had gone out of business, and you were running out of options."

She pales further. "You used that to your advantage."

"I saw the opportunity and took it."

She shakes her head. "So, you already knew everything about me. You knew—"

"That I wanted you to be my wife? Yes."

"Fake wife." She swallows. "You wanted me to marry you to satisfy G-Pa's terms, so you could confirm your role as CEO of the company."

"And you still believe that? After everything that's happened between us the last few days, you still think that?" I look between her eyes.

She holds my gaze for a second, another, then looks away. "What other explanation is there?"

57

———————

Mira

He had me followed. He invaded my privacy. He's known who I was for a while. He knew everything about me when he asked me to work for him. It was all preplanned, including asking me to marry him. My head swims. And yet, somehow, I'm not overly surprised. It explains why, when I met Edward I felt like I knew him. I felt like I had seen him. It's why it always felt like he was hiding something from me. I just never thought it would be something so big.

"Everything you told me was a lie." I begin to inch toward the edge of the bed.

"Do the last few days seem like a lie?" He raises his hand as if he's going to reach for me, then lowers it. "I'm not good at expressing myself through words, Belle."

"Don't call me that."

"You can't negate everything that's happened between us just because the way it started was a little unorthodox," he growls.

I rise to my feet. "You stalked me. Bugged my devices. Had cameras on me. Had me followed. You manipulated me into working for you, knowing I didn't want to work in the role of a personal assistant. You knew I worked in a preschool. If you had so much information on me, you'd have known I've always wanted to work with kids, yet you offered me the role of your PA."

"I wanted you close to me."

"I was right outside your office, and you still had a camera trained on me."

His jaw tics. "You have to understand, I'm not good at sharing what's mine. Left up to me, I'd have had you locked at home, and not allowed anyone to see you."

I glance around the space. "Is that why you brought me here? So you could hide me away? I'd question whether you also arranged for a snowstorm, but not even you could do that."

His eyes flash, then he glances away.

I raise my hands to my mouth. "Oh, my god, you knew there was a storm on the way."

"I might have heard about it on the weather forecast, yes."

"So you planned it so that we'd be here and unable to leave."

He drags his fingers through his hair. "It's not like that."

"It is exactly that. You had it all planned. You knew my every move. You knew my past, who my father was—" I lower my arms to my side. "You knew he was going to arrange my marriage. Did you also arrange for his business to go under so you could use it as leverage?"

When his left eyelid twitches, I know I'm right. He must see the realization sink in, for he slides his legs over the side of the bed and stands.

When he moves toward me, I throw my arms up. "Don't touch me."

His features twist. A haunted look comes into his eyes. He seems helpless and forlorn, and so lonely, and... I cannot let that get to me. I cannot let the devastation in his gaze soften me. I can't allow him to get close to me again. Not after everything he just revealed.

He looks away, then back at me. "When we return, you can lead on the initiative to set up childcare facilities in the office."

It's not what I expected him to say, so I stay quiet.

"I've wanted to set up childcare services in the office for a while, and you would be the perfect candidate to drive that." He lowers his chin to his chest. "You know you want to help with this project."

"I do." I put more distance between us. "But it doesn't change what you did. Things which I may never be able to come to terms with."

Color drains from his features. "Don't say that." His voice is hoarse like he's been yelling, or maybe it's all the lies he's told me.

"You did something unforgivable. You betrayed my trust."

"I didn't have a choice."

"You could have come out and told me you liked me."

"Liked you?" He pronounces the words like they are something foreign.

"And maybe, we could have gone on dates."

"Dates?" The furrow between his forehead deepens.

"You know. Dinner, a movie...? Like normal people."

"Normal people." There is a strange look in his eyes, something I can't quite place. A mix of surprise and disbelief.

"Yes, normal people. People who respect boundaries and know they can't just plant cameras and listening devices on others. People who think of more than running a company, and who don't earn billions and make more in one day than most of the planet does in a year. People like me."

"You're wrong."

"What do you mean?"

"You're not a normal person," he says through gritted teeth.

"Of course, I am."

"You're the most genuine person I've ever met. The most honest, the most generous, the most empathetic. You care about others more than yourself, and that is not normal. Not even faintly normal. People are selfish and cruel and hurt others to get what they want."

"Like you hurt me?"

He winces. "I... I didn't want to hurt you. Quite the contrary. I wanted to make sure you got everything you wanted."

"I didn't ask for all this." I wave a hand in the air. "All I wanted was a home of my own, a family, a man who loves me."

"I—" He swallows. "I...care about you, Belle."

"You have a funny way of showing it."

"It's the only way I know."

"And I'm sure you're going to use the incident to justify the way you turned out. You're going to tell me the incident is the reason you're an uncaring, unfeeling, calculating person...who I hate."

"You don't hate me."

"I do now." I pull the sheet off the bed and wrap it around my shoulders.

His features take on a dissatisfied look. He seems like he's about to say something, then draws in a sharp breath. "Everything I did...was from a place of wanting to woo you."

"Clearly, we differ on that definition," I scoff.

"Give me one chance." He shuffles his feet. "Just one chance to win your heart."

"Why should I, when all you've done is lie to me and make me believe in a relationship which doesn't exist?"

"But it does. Everything that's happened between us—all of it is true. From the first moment I saw you, I knew there was no one else for me but you. I recognized you, Belle. I knew we had a connection. I knew I had to have you in my life."

"And me? What about me? You didn't think about what I wanted, or what I needed—"

"Only every second. I knew you didn't want to marry a perfect stranger—"

"You were a perfect stranger."

"I was your boss; you'd gotten to know me. You knew there was chemistry between us."

"Oh, so that makes it all justifiable. That you gave me a job under false pretext, a job I was woefully unqualified for—"

"And which you performed well."

"—and just because we were attracted to each other doesn't mean I wanted to marry you."

"Marriages have been built on less. And you have to admit, the physical connection between us is mind-blowing."

"But I want more." I turn on him. "I understand, you express yourself through your actions. I think it's why you wanted to tie me up. It's how you showed me you care for me, in your own way. It's how you wanted to share with me what you feel for me. But if you can't give words to your sentiments... If you can't open your mouth and elaborate what it is you feel for me... Then, I'm not sure we have a future, especially after—" I tug the sheet tighter. "After everything you just told me."

"I'm sorry, I hurt you. I'm sorry, I couldn't play by the rules. I'm sorry, I wasn't open about my intentions. But if I had been, would you have given me a chance?"

I stay silent.

His throat moves as he swallows. "I know what kind of a person I am. I know I'm not good enough for you."

"What are you talking about?" I frown.

"I spied on you, yet I couldn't tell your stepmother and half-sisters were not treating you well. I'll never forgive myself for that."

I rub at my temple. "They were subtle about how they hurt me. Oftentimes, their remarks almost seemed like compliments, but I knew they were meant to be hurtful."

"I should have paid more attention."

"It's not like you could have intervened," I point out.

"I'd have found a way. If I had been a better man, not so focused only on my own needs, I'd have stepped in. It's why you should have married someone better, someone who could be more open with his emotions and give you the emotional security you deserve. Someone 'more normal.' Someone who'd give you a white picket fence and a house in the suburbs and—"

"And you're wrong. Those are external trappings. I just want someone who loves me."

His chest rises and falls. A fleet of expressions crosses his face. He opens his mouth, and I'm sure this is it. This is when he'll say those three words that will change everything. Instead, when he speaks, it's to growl, "Nothing can change the fact that we're married." He continues in a hard voice, "The ceremony was real. The paperwork around it was real."

There's a tinge of desperation in his voice. *Edward and desperate? Nope, that must be my imagination. He's a lying, conniving, bastard. That's who he is.*

"Are you hearing yourself? I'm talking about the fact you violated my personal boundaries." That's not all he violated, but the physical aspect of it… I can't bring that into the equation, because I enjoyed it. Damn him, but he took me to heights I didn't think I'd ever reach. He showed me the kind of pleasure that's imprinted on every pore in my body—his touch is stamped into my skin and his name is painted into the most secret parts of my body, thanks to the intensity with which he fucked me. And it was *fucking*. It *wasn't* lovemaking. I might have fooled myself into thinking otherwise, but it wasn't love. It can't be love. The fact he overstepped the limits of my personal space, breached my faith… It's not something I can look past.

"And you're still my wife."

That's when his phone buzzes.

58

———

Edward

"You shouldn't have rushed back," G-Pa says from his bed. Tiny is on his haunches near him, and G-Pa keeps reaching out to pet him. The Great Dane welcomed me and my wife when we arrived, then went back to being by my G-Pa's side. The friendship between the two of them has deepened since I last saw them.

"Of course, we should have." My wife slides into the chair next to G-Pa's bed and takes his hand in hers. "I'm glad you're okay."

"There's nothing wrong with me," he insists.

"Of course, not," she says in a soothing voice.

"Don't patronize me, young lady," he says in a half-stern voice.

"Me, patronize you?" she says in an innocent tone. "As if I'd dare."

"Oh, yes, you would." His eyes twinkle, before he darts his gaze in my direction. "Of course, you have my permission to do what's needed to keep my grandson in line."

Like I'm not pussy-whipped enough? Aside from the fact I seem to lose my voice when I want to tell her I love her, I've lost all free will. I've lost the ability to do anything except stay close to her, and look at her, and touch her to make sure she's real. Which, considering the reason I took on this role in my grandfather's company was to find focus, has turned my world upside down. I found my reason for living the day I saw her, but I didn't recognize it. It was only after marrying her and realizing there was no better sound in the world than calling her 'my wife' that my world found its axis. I found my grounding. My anchor. My re-entry back into reality. My equilibrium. She is my foundation. My life. *Mine.* So why am I not able to tell that to her?

"I'm glad you're okay." She places her other hand over his and squeezes.

"It was nothing," he huffs.

"It was a fall," Knox growls from where he's standing at one corner of G-Pa's bed.

"I was barely hurt." G-Pa sets his jaw.

"You fractured your toe," Nathan says in a mild voice. He's the one who messaged me. He was trying to make amends for the fact my grandfather decided to share my veto power of the company with him. My older half-brother leans a hip against the windowsill. It's as far away from the rest of us as possible. Clearly, I'm not the only one who has issues. Nor am I the newest member to join the family fold and meet his extended family for the first time.

"It was a hairline fracture," G-Pa protests.

"It could have been much worse if Tiny hadn't found you," Knox growls.

"Tiny found you?" I glance toward the Great Dane, who looks at me with his big melting eyes.

"I didn't have my phone with me when I fell in the bathroom. Luckily I didn't lock the door. Tiny pushed the door open and came in when he heard me groan. I gestured to him to go my nightstand and grab my phone and bring it to me. I wasn't sure if he could understand me—"

"But he did?" my wife exclaims.

"He did." G-Pa pats the big dog's head, and he places his chin on G-Pa's bed and looks up at the old man with adoring eyes.

"Aww, you're a hero." She drops to her knees and hugs the dog, who looks at me over her shoulder with a smirk... No, he really has a smirk on his face. He's in her good books, while I've been banished to the doghouse. I resist the urge to bare my teeth at the mutt. He's just a dog. So what, if my wife feels more kindly toward him at the moment.

"I'll be at my desk in the office before you know it," G-Pa declares.

"You need to rest your foot," Knox reminds him.

"My foot!" G-Pa snaps.

"That's what he said," I nod.

"I second that," Nathan rumbles.

G-Pa looks at the three of us, a considering look coming into his eyes. "So, it takes me being on my deathbed for my family to form a united front."

"You're not on your death bed," I point out.

"I have a fracture," he groans.

My wife snickers at me over her shoulder. I begin to smile back, when she must realize what she's done and that she's supposed to be pissed off with me, for she turns back to G-Pa. "You were just saying you were completely okay."

G-Pa slumps back against his pillows. "I think, I'm feeling a little weak…" He ends his sentence on a moan, which is more theatrical than pain-filled.

"We could get the doctor back in. He did say if the pain got worse he could inject you with painkillers," Knox offers.

"An injection?" G-Pa pales. "That's not needed. I just need some rest, is all." He pretends to yawn.

"We should leave you." My wife locks her fingers together.

"You take good care of her, you hear me?" G-Pa glares at me from across the room. "I don't want to hear any complaints from her."

She bites down on her lower lip, probably to stop herself from slinging a host of grievances against me. Problem is, it makes me wonder how it would feel to have those lips wrapped around my cock and her fingers digging into my thigh as I grip her jaw and—

"Edward, did you hear what I said, boy?" G-Pa booms.

"Yes, you want the family together for Sunday lunch." *Kill me already.* An entire afternoon with my half-siblings is not my idea of a relaxing weekend, or a relaxing anything. Or anything approaching relaxation. The only thing I want right now is to take my wife home and find a way to make things up to her. Perhaps, she'll allow me to hold her and sniff her hair, and if I apologize enough, she might let me bury my dick inside her tight, moist hole.

"That's right. I expect to see the both of you there."

"I'm sorry but—" I begin but my wife interrupts me.

"Of course, G-Pa, we'll be there."

"But—" I begin, but she scowls at me over her shoulder. Pathetic arse that I am, I'm so grateful for the fact that she acknowledges my presence—only the second time since we left the lighthouse earlier today—that I zip my lips and watch as she turns back to Arthur.

She leans over and kisses his cheek. "You should rest up. We'll see you for Sunday lunch."

Which means, she's not planning to leave me... Yet. Which gives me time, until Sunday, to woo her back. She wanted to be dated and courted. Well, I'm going to re-invent the meaning of those words. I walk over and hold out my hand. She looks at it, then back up at me, and I'm sure she's going to refuse, but then she places her much smaller hand in mine. The stress in my shoulders leaches out. Fucking hell, if every minute of my time is going to be spent bathed in so much tension, then I'm headed for the coronary my wife predicted when she first set eyes on me. By then, I already knew everything it was possible to know about her, but it wasn't a replacement for spending time with her. For discovering her likes and dislikes, how she wrinkles her forehead when she's thinking, how she sighs when she sips her coffee, how she makes those little moans at the back of her throat when she's aroused, how her lips thin when she's angry with me.

And yet, I can't regret the fact that I invaded her privacy. That I watched her unobserved. That I snooped around her life. That, since I set eyes on her, I've made sure to have eyes on her all the time. How can I, when a part of me worries that I won't be able to prevent bad things from happening to her? Is this how it feels to love someone? When your heart feels like it's being torn out your chest, and every time you think about how vulnerable they are, your chest tightens, your lungs burn, your pulse rate shoots through the roof and you're sure you're having a panic attack?

"Ed?" She squeezes my hand. "You okay?'

She called me Ed. Not Eddie. But also, not Edward. That's another sign there's a chance here for me to put things right... Right?

When I don't reply, she grabs my collar, pulls me down, then goes up on tiptoe and kisses my lips.

59

Mira

He doesn't kiss me back. His lips are hard, his chest unmoving. He bent enough for me to reach his mouth, but other than that, I might as well be kissing a stone. Shit, what possessed me to do this, in the first place, and when I'm so pissed off with him? I'm sure it had nothing do with that haunted look in his eyes, or the granite-hard set to his jaw, or how he looked at me like it was the last time he was seeing me. Like he expected me to run out of there and never look back.

And I was tempted, don't get me wrong. But also, the part of me that's responsible and dutiful and never gives up in the face of a challenge, the part of me that already loves his grandfather like my own, the part that is still attracted to him, so help me god, the part that hasn't forgiven him for how he got me here but cannot resist the urge to be physically close to him—that part took over. Before I could talk myself out of it, I acted on the urge to take his mind off whatever he was thinking, whatever caused that despairing look in his eyes.

And now, he's not reacting. Ugh, this is a mistake. I begin to back away, but he swoops his hand around my waist, drags me close, back on my tiptoes, and regardless of the fact his family is watching, he kisses me

—not the polite peck on the lips I attempted, but a nip on my mouth until I part my lips so he can slide his tongue over mine and suck on it, and share my breath, and sip from me until I lose my balance and sway against him. At which point, he pulls me closer, wraps his arm about my waist, and announces we're leaving.

I have just enough time to register the satisfaction on G-Pa's face, the mild surprise on Nathan's, and the smirk on Knox's before we're out of there and he's hustling me toward the car.

"What's the hurry?"

He doesn't reply. He merely walks me to the car, tears open the door on the passenger's side, all but throws me in, and proceeds to snap the seatbelt around me, before he takes the driver's seat. His door slams shut, and he grips the steering wheel, but he doesn't start the car.

"Ed?" I ask softly. "What's wrong?"

"What's wrong is that you should be hating me now. You should be telling me go take a long walk off a short pier, and never set eyes on you again."

"I'm tempted," I confess.

"And yet, you kissed me."

"I, uh… G-Pa was watching, and it seemed like a good time to convince him the marriage is genuine, and you… You looked so desolate."

"I *am* desolate…without you."

I shake my head and glance away. "Don't. Please, don't make this more difficult."

"Why *did* you kiss me?"

"Told you already, it was all an act to convince your grandfather about the veracity of our wedding."

"Didn't seem like an act."

"Just because there's chemistry between us doesn't mean anything. And just because I kiss you, doesn't mean I've forgiven you for everything you did."

His fingers tighten on the steering wheel. "I'm sorry I crossed boundaries I shouldn't have. I'm sorry I hurt you. I'm sorry I upset you. I'm so sorry it's causing you so much distress, but"—he swallows—"it helped ensure you were safe and well, and given a choice, I'd do it all over again."

I whip my face in his direction. "Are you hearing yourself? Have you crossed the line so many times that you can't tell what's right and wrong? Have you forgotten what it is to be a decent human being?"

"That, I never was." He laughs without humor.

"You were a priest and served your parish; you must have been a decent human being then."

"I was, and then I wasn't."

"What do you mean?" I frown.

"I walked away from my faith. Then I turned my back on my best friend. I couldn't face the fact the woman I thought I loved chose him over me. I was envious about their happiness. I was envious of them. That's how far I had fallen."

"You were human."

"I couldn't stand to see them together."

"Understandable."

"I hid away, hoping to get my life back together, but I flitted from one focus to another, until I saw you. I saw you and my world rightened."

"You...can't tell me all this, Edward. It doesn't make what you did right."

He blows out a breath. "Then tell me how to put it right, Mira, because I have no fucking clue how to make things up to you."

"You have to stop this entire tracking me and having eyes on me and following my every movement baloney, Ed."

He shakes his head. "I... I'm not sure I can do that."

"You have to." I set my jaw. "And you need to tell me why you feel compelled to shadow my every move. Why are you convinced I am in danger? Is it because of the incident?" I scrutinize his features. "Is that what's making you paranoid about my safety enough to have me followed? Do you have to have eyes on me because that's the only way you feel reassured?"

He squeezes his lips together. "I told you I need more time to tell you about what happened."

He must see the disappointment on my features for he blows out a breath.

"Belle, I—" He rubs the back of his neck, "I want to tell you what happened. I swear, I do. And I will, I promise. Just give me a little time okay?"

A crushing sensation squeezes my ribcage. My shoulders feel heavy. I thought...he might make up for what he did by sharing more of himself. I refused to let him down in front of his family; I wouldn't walk out on him or show my anger toward him in front of them. Did I do that because I wanted to use it as leverage against him? Maybe. I think a part of me hoped it would demonstrate goodwill and encourage him to trust me. Maybe it would put enough pressure on him to reveal the secrets from his past. But it didn't work.

I know I'm not being fair. I know how painful this must be for him. I'm sure whatever happened to him contributes to his need to watch over me at all times, but if he won't tell me anything, how can I understand his actions? Then there's the fact he's been watching me for almost a year.

All this time, I've had a stalker, and I didn't even know it. And now that I do know, every rational bit of me is telling me to run away.

But there's another part of me saying I just need to listen to his explanation, and it will make sense. Maybe, it's not as creepy as it sounds. On the other hand, maybe, that's just wishful thinking. I'm just so overwhelmed, I don't know what to think… Or feel… Or do.

It's clear he cares about me, and he would never harm me. So that means he can't be a stalker, right? And sure, he wants me enough to take me to his place where he likes to hide out from the world, and he desires me enough to tie me up and mark me and fuck me. He's protective enough to be my shadow and follow my movements. And even though he hasn't been able to say the words, it's obvious he loves me. Only, that's not enough for me.

I want to be a part of his life. I want to help him, but every time I try, he shuts me down. Perhaps, he does trust me. Maybe, he doesn't want to talk about his past because his trauma is deep, and it will reopen old wounds to do so. He says he needs more time, which is understandable. I just need to be patient. Which I can't be when I'm working in such close proximity to him, and falling more in love with him every day, and becoming impatient when he doesn't open up to me. I need to find a way to get perspective on this situation.

"I need another job." I look away from him.

"No."

"I can't work in such close proximity to you. Not when I'm trying to find a way to be patient and give you the time you need to come to terms with your past."

His jaw tics. "Your life is with me."

"Not when you can't let me help you. I'm trying to be understanding, but it's difficult for me to watch you in pain and not do anything about it. I... I think we need some space."

"No, we don't." He flattens his lips.

"You asked for more time to tell me what happened. Surely, you can extend the same courtesy to me?"

He draws in a breath as conflicting emotions flit across his features. "You don't want to be my assistant?"

"I... I *can't* be your assistant. I need to find some perspective on this situation. Surely, you understand that?"

He stays silent for a few seconds, then nods. "Okay."

"Okay?" I blink.

"Instead of working for me, you can set up and run the workplace nursery, as we discussed."

I hesitate. *That's something I'd love to do.*

"You'd be helping the others who work in the building, who need childcare so they can work without this weighing on their mind."

He knows I'm thawing and he's pushing his advantage. *Of course, he is. That's the kind of man he is. You show him a weakness, and he makes the most of it. I even told him that's one of the things I admire about him, so how can I get angry?*

"Okay." I turn to him.

"Okay." His shoulders relax.

"And you'll stop monitoring my movements."

His chest rises and falls. "If that's what you want."

"I do." I swallow. "And one more thing…"

He turns to me, and there's a mixture of fear and resignation in his eyes. "What is it?"

60

Edward

"Didn't expect to see you at poker." Sinclair blows out a cloud of cigar smoke from the other side of the poker table. "Shouldn't you be on your honeymoon?"

"Been there; done that." I train my focus on my cards. The image blurs in front of my eyes. I reach for my twentieth — or is it my thirtieth? —cup of coffee of the day in a bid to clear my vision. This is what happens when you're running on three hours of sleep. I'm lucky I caught that. And only because I managed to snag her nightshirt from the laundry basket and buried my face in it. Y-e-a-p, I'm the pathetic sod who can't fall asleep without sniffing his wife's scent. That's what I've been reduced to since she moved into a spare bedroom down the hall. That's what she asked of me, and I couldn't say no. At least, she's still under my roof. That has to count for something.

It's been a week, and I've missed her every second of it. She also took charge of the on-site-nursery and had it up and running in five days. When that woman sets her mind to something, nothing gets in her way. To be fair, I'd already prepared the space and purchased the necessary supplies, but she interviewed, hired, promoted, and managed the hell out of it. I managed to watch from afar, managed not to interfere, managed to even have the cameras and bugs on her phones and Kindle de-activated, managed not to have any new ones installed in her guest room or in her new car. I can't lie to her on this again. Can't justify looking her in the eye and saying I haven't stuck to my word.

It almost killed me, but I did it. And if it means I follow her in my car to and from work, at a distance, to make sure she reaches her destination safely? Well, that's not a crime. I'm not engaging anyone else to do it. I'm doing what any good husband should do; I'm looking out for my wife.

Good thing no one around the table knows that.

"He doesn't look like he's been on his honeymoon. In fact, it doesn't look he's been on holiday at all." This, from Knox.

"Shut the fuck up," I grumble.

"It's the early days of being married, you'd be better off bonding with your other half and all that." This, from Nathan, who sounds like he doesn't give a fuck, either way.

"Who invited you here, again?" I frown.

"I did." Sinclair rolls the cigar to the other side of his mouth. "You don't mind, do you, ol' chap?"

I glare at him, but he merely shrugs. Of all the people, Sinclair should know Nathan is not on my list of favorite people, but he went ahead and invited him. Which is his way of telling me I need to build bridges with this man who's an equal decision maker in Davenport Industries. Or rather, equal decision-maker after my grandfather, considering he hasn't yet handed off full control to me. And Sinclair's right. Arthur has shown he trusts Nathan as much as me.

Given my adoptive father, Arthur's oldest son wants nothing to do with him, and my biological father who is also Nathan's father is dead, it makes Nathan his oldest grandson and the logical successor to Arthur's fortune. It also makes him my closest competitor for the position of my grandfather's heir.

Strangely, that doesn't bother me the way it might have before I met my wife.

Before I realized the most important thing in the world is taking care of her—her safety, her security, her happiness, her future. All of that takes precedence. It's disconcerting and, also, grounding, in an unexpected fashion. It's why I don't rise to the bait when Nathan nods his chin in my direction. "Trouble in paradise, I take it?"

"None of your business," I growl.

"It's affecting your performance at work, so it is my business."

I still, then glance up from my cards. "Explain?"

"You missed a crucial loophole in the takeover documentation for the Young Group. Of course, I spotted it and fixed it prior to signing the deal."

"What loophole?"

"One that would have cost us close to a million dollars, but it's been taken care of."

"I don't let loopholes slip by me."

"You did, this time." He jams his cigar between his lips. "Might have to do with the fact you leveraged this takeover for your marriage, and—"

I reach over and grab his collar, then haul him forward. "Shut the fuck up."

He smiles, the satisfaction in his eyes showing he's proven his point by getting a rise out of me.

"Let him go," Sinclair snaps.

I glare at Nathan. His smile grows wider. I tighten my hold on his collar, then release him. He sits back; so do I. But our gazes are locked.

"Thought you could control your temper better," he says in a mild voice.

"What do you want?" I square my shoulders. "Why did you accept Arthur's proposition of sharing the veto power?"

"I have enough money, thanks to my investments. What this brings me, is power...and the breadth of control that comes from being the joint CEO of the Davenport group."

"Joint CEO?" I frown. That's when my phone vibrates. I glance at the screen to find Arthur's name on the caller ID. I fix my gaze on Nathan and answer: "Arthur?"

There's silence, then, "I'm only G-Pa when your wife is around, I take it?"

It's my turn to stay quiet.

Arthur sighs. "What I'm going to tell you is going to upset you."

"You don't say?" I ask dryly.

"You're newly married, and I want you to focus on your wife, and—'

"Cut the bullshit and give it to me straight."

He blows out a breath. "I want you to share the CEO role with Nathan."

I glance up at Nathan, who's watching my reaction. He was expecting Arthur to call me, no doubt. I roll my shoulders. Somehow, I'm not as pissed off as I should be to hear this news from my grandfather. Maybe my wife is already softening me up? That must be the reason I haven't lost my temper yet. In fact, the thought of not having to shoulder the decision-making role on my own, having another ear with whom to discuss the daily challenges, is a relief. It means I'll have more time to devote to my wife. In fact, the thought of not being CEO, at all —*nope, not going there. You're not giving up the role you've been angling for because a woman, are you? Nope, no way, am I conceding defeat to Nathan already.* Not when I know Arthur's proposing this joint-CEO deal as some kind of test to ascertain who is best placed to be his successor. "Is that all?" I bark into the phone.

"Yes, I wanted to be the one to tell you—"

I hang up the phone. Yes, I hung up on my grandfather, the Chairman of the company. Yes, I should be more worried about the repercussions of my actions, but given I have him on the defensive, given he went back on his word and decided to make me *not* the CEO, but the *joint*-CEO of the Davenport group of companies, somehow, I doubt I have much to worry about. And if he's upset? I couldn't give a shit about it. Considering all I want to do is get out of here and back to my wife.

Nathan raises the cigar to his lips. "I take it, Arthur told you he's decided it's best you share the role with me?"

"I take it, you're not aware I've won this round?" I place my cards on the table, face up. It's a straight flush. Knox throws his cards down in disgust. Sinclair shakes his head and tosses his hand on the table.

Nathan slowly reveals his. I take in his Ace, King, Queen, Jack and Ten of Diamonds. "Guess it's me who wins." He smirks.

"Guess I *let* you win." I drain my coffee and rise to my feet. "I'm not giving up control of the company without a fight."

"Anything less, and it would be boring." He tilts his head.

I jerk my chin at Sinclair and Knox, then walk out of there and to my car. By the time I reach home, the anger inside me has coiled around my guts and poisoned my veins. I march up the stairs and throw open the door to her room, but she's not there. I enter, and it feels like I've stepped into a garden of apple blossoms. I'm instantly hard. My heart picks up speed. And my mind…

It begins to replay how it was to tie her up and bend her over the bed and fuck her. How it felt to fall asleep inside her and wake up and push my face in between her legs. How it felt to curve my body around hers and hold her while she snored those ladylike snores. I sit on the bed, reach for her discarded blouse and bring it to my face, and sniff. *Mistake.* My balls harden, and my pants tighten until I'm sure I'm going to come in them.

I drop her blouse and glance around the space, taking in her cosmetics on the dressing table, the half open door to her closet, the towel she's slung over the bathroom handle. Her books are on the bedside table, one of them annotated with post-it's sticking out from between the pages. The drawer below is half open. I walk around and pull it all the way, spying some very interesting gadgets.

Is this why she wanted to move to another room? So, she could pleasure herself...without my knowledge? So, she could orgasm while thinking of someone else? So, she could torture me with images of her moaning herself to sleep with some inanimate objects inside her while I'm harder than a stallion on a stud farm in the room nearby? I snatch up one of the vibrators, something thick and long and veiny, but I'm proud to say, it's not thicker or longer, or as veiny as my cock.

She could have the real thing; but instead, she's here stuffing this lifeless dildo inside her pussy... Inside *my* pussy. I bring it to my nose and sniff, and it's as if I'm back between her thighs. *Fuck.* I take another deep breath, when the hair on the back of my neck rises. I turn toward the door and find her standing there. She's wearing a pink skirt which stretches across her thick thighs, and a matching jacket with a blouse underneath that dips toward the valley of her cleavage. Color flushes the column of her throat, up her cheeks. "What are you doing here?"

61

Mira

"Give me that." My handbag falls from my grasp. I cross the floor, reach
for the stupid vibrator, but he holds it out of my reach. I jump up, and
he extends his arm. I leap onto the bed make a grab for it, but I'm
nowhere near close to touching it. "That's mine," I protest.

In response, he lowers the vibrator, and when I try to get a hold of it,
he steps away. He brings the device to his nose again and sniffs, the way
I saw him from the doorway. Goosebumps pop on my skin.

"I washed it after I last used it." I tip up my chin.

"I can still smell your cunt on it."

I gasp, "You're filthy."

"I want to be filthier." He fixes me with that glare that has moisture
rushing out from between my thighs. *No, no, no. I'm not going to let our
mutual chemistry get the better of me.*

I walk to the other side of the bed and step down. "What are you
doing here?"

"Checking to see if my wife's doing okay."

"I'm well, thank you. You can leave now."

"Not before you tell me what you're doing with these." He glances from the instrument in his hand to my open drawer.

"You're infringing on my privacy again," I cry.

He pauses. His shoulders seem to swell. I'm sure he's going to tell me off, but to my surprise, he nods. "You're right; I'm sorry."

He eyes the vibrator one last time, then slips it into the drawer with the other implements I have there. He shuts the drawer, then straightens and turns to me. "I'm sorry. I didn't mean to intrude. I came looking for you, didn't find you, then saw the open drawer and couldn't resist. I didn't mean to peek, I swear."

He apologized to me? His features are set in grim lines. His lips are flattened. He seems to mean it.

One week. I haven't seen him for a week. He's always gone when I wake up in the mornings and comes home much later than me in the evenings. At least, I think he does, because I never hear his footsteps go past the doorway of my room, no matter how late I stay up reading.

I moved out of my role as his assistant to work on setting up the childcare facilities on the second floor of the office building. I threw myself into getting it up and running. Things went smoothly, not least, because of the generous budget he allocated for the project. Turned out, he'd already organized the permits, as well as the space needed to set up the nursery.

I wanted to refuse to lead on the project, but the childcare facilities will benefit everyone, and the children deserve only the best. So, I swallowed my pride and proceeded with my plan.

Today was the first day we opened, and already, we're full, and with a waiting list. We had to turn away parents from the buildings nearby, with regret. The facilities are only for the employees of the Davenport group of companies. It's a crying shame that more companies didn't invest in such services for their staff. It only increases productivity, as many studies have proven, but big corporations still hesitate to invest in something so essential. Not Ed, apparently. I suppose I have our interactions to thank for that. If, because of me, children can benefit, then I almost didn't mind the fact that he was spying on me before we formally met. Almost.

"I think you should leave now." I cross my arms about my waist.

He nods, then stalks toward the door, pausing only to retrieve my bag from the floor and place it on the bed. He reaches the exit, when I call out, "Did you see me... take care of myself when you had cameras in my room in my father's house?"

He pauses, then nods.

Heat flushes my cheeks. That beat between my legs, which always flares to life when he's around, amplifies. "How could you do that?" I burst out.

"How could I not?" He turns to face me. "I wanted you. I knew I shouldn't; knew I was all wrong for you, but I couldn't let go of you."

"So you trapped me in this marriage?"

He curls his fingers into fists at his sides. "I wish I could say I'm sorry for influencing events so you find yourself here, but—"

"You're not?"

"How can I be, when you're more important to me than life itself."

"What you are is obsessed with me," I cry.

"I'd rather be obsessed with you than anyone else. I'd rather devote my life to taking care of you. All I want is to see you happy."

"So you'd release me from this marriage if that's what made me happy?"

He flinches, his jaw tenses, and he seems to force himself to unclench his fingers. He straightens his shoulders. "Is that what you want?"

I run my fingers through my hair. Tiredness grips me. My feet seem to wobble, and I sit down on the bed. "I don't know what I want."

He takes a step toward me, and I throw up my hand. "Actually, I do know what I want, for now. I need you to leave me alone."

"Have you eaten?"

"I don't want your sympathy. I don't want you to cook for me. I don't...want to see you, is all."

"Have you eaten yet?"

"Didn't you hear what I said," I snap.

He holds up his hands. "I heard you." He turns and leaves, his shoulders slumped. The door snicks shut behind him. And of course, I miss him. Which makes no sense. After how he treated me, how he got me to marry him under false pretexts, I shouldn't want him. I shouldn't miss him. I shouldn't go to sleep every night wanting to wake up next to him.

I'm sure it's because he's the first man I've slept with. The first man to bring me to orgasm, to show me it could be even better than my smutty books made it out to be. And for a while there, in that lighthouse, with the snowstorm raging around us, I was sure he was 'the one.' I thought I'd get my happily ever after. I didn't realize I'd fallen for someone whose heart is morally grey, and whose past holds secrets I'll never be privy to.

I climb into bed and curl up on my side. I should hate him. I do hate him… I think. But I also miss him. And there's nothing keeping me here. I could leave, go to one of my friend's places. But wouldn't that be running? Would that resolve anything? Staying under his roof is a constant reminder of him, of how it could be with him. But leaving… Images of him and our time together would only haunt me more. No, I need to weather this out the way I've done the storms in the past. On my own. Me, myself, and I. I smile. That's how I've always consoled myself. *I have myself.* And him. *Not him. Don't think of him.* I close my eyes and drift off until a knock on the door awakens me. I sit up and realize it's dark outside. I reach for my bag and pull out my phone. I've been asleep for an hour. I also have missed messages.

> Summer: Haven't heard from you since you got back. Are you ok?

> Gio: Bitch, how was the honeymoon? Why no word from you?

> Penny: Forgotten us already?

I haven't been in touch with any of them because… What am I going to say? I'm not used to having friends, let alone ones I confide in, and I want to tell them everything but… Not yet. How can I, when I don't know what to say? I drop my phone on the bed, head to the door and open it.

There's a tray on the floor, with a bell-shaped cover on it, the kind they use in hotels for room service. I look up the corridor, but the door to Ed's room is shut. I pick up the tray, shut the door with my hip, then walk to the bed and place it there. When I pull off the lid, my gaze widens. Vegetable lasagna, with a slice of chocolate cake on the side. There's even a small bottle of red wine and a glass.

I glance at the door, again. Ed must have cooked it for me — or his housekeeper might have. He mentioned to me he has staff, although I haven't seen anyone around. But someone's cleaning the house, and there are cooked meals in the refrigerator. So, maybe he didn't cook it, but he took the trouble to bring it up to me.

Tears prick my eyes, and I wipe them away angrily. Why should I feel moved by that? He's not doing anything out of the ordinary. He also didn't ask me where I was so late—I'd been working getting everything sorted at the nursery, and it was barely ten p.m. by the time I got home but the husband I know would have asked me where I'd been— No, he wouldn't have allowed me to come home on my own. And I know he wasn't tailing me because he was in my room when I walked in.

Unless he has cameras on me in the nursery? There are the usual security cameras there, but I haven't noticed anything else. *Not that I'd know what to look for.* I dig my heels into my eyes. *Argh, I have to stop thinking like this. He promised not to do it anymore, but I'm still not sure if I can trust him. And I'm tying myself up in knots. Maybe I should just go and confront him? Yes, that's it; I'll just ask him the question. Otherwise, I'm not getting any sleep tonight.* I glance at the food, and my stomach rumbles. *Let me ask him and I can come back and eat afterward.*

I march out of the room, then down the corridor. I tap on the door, but there's no answer. I knock more loudly, then wait.

When there's still no reply, I push open the door to his bedroom and enter. A bedside lamp is on, casting a golden glow over the bedroom. The sound of the water running reaches me. I walk past the bed and toward the open door of the bathroom. It doesn't even occur to me to stop. I should leave, but my legs don't heed the warning.

I slip inside the bathroom, and the heat surrounds me, embraces me, seduces me…leads me to where he's standing in the shower, fully clothed. One fist is pressed into the wall; the other arm hangs by his side. His head is bent. The water drips down his hair and plasters his clothes to his back, his butt, his thighs. I step into the shower, and he still doesn't notice me. His shoulders bunch; a shudder runs down his spine.

Is he… Nope, not possible. He's not… He can't be crying, can he? As I watch, he raises his fist and smashes it into the wall. The muffled crack splits the air.

"Ed, stop."

<h1 style="text-align:center">62</h1>

Edward

One second, the pain squeezes up my arm; the next, she's there. She slips into the space in between me and the wall of the shower cubicle, wraps her fingers around my wrist and urges me to lower my arm.

"Why did you do that?" She surveys the reddened skin over my knuckles. "Why did you hurt yourself?"

"I hurt you." I try to pull my hand from hers, but she holds on; and while I'm stronger than her physically… Emotionally, this woman is my rock. I've come to depend on her in ways I never thought were possible. I've come to need her for her sunshine, her warmth, the way she shines a light in the dark crevasses of my soul. How she illuminates the secrets of my past, treats me with compassion, and brings them to the front of my mind. She forced me to look in the mirror, to acknowledge the man I've become—bitter, unscrupulous, one without a conscience. One not above resorting to unethical means to get what he wants. A man who is the opposite of everything I ever hoped to be. A man who wants to stay true to his calling, to his vow to serve the greater good. Only, I hadn't faced the ghosts of my past.

Not until she processed all the wrong I'd done her and decided, shockingly, not to walk out on me.

Not until she reminded me—with the goodness of her nature, her generosity, her magnanimity, her kindness of spirit—to see the positive, the good in everyone and in any situation.

By being herself, she reflected back to me how in the wrong I was... I still am. How I shouldn't have let my ego get the better of me and twisted the circumstances around her to force her into this marriage with me. "I'm so sorry, Belle."

She looks up at me, and when our gazes hold, that chemistry between us heats up. The air grows thick, the heat in the air pushing down on us.

"Ed"—she swallows—"please don't punish yourself like this."

"I deserve all of this, and more, for how I changed the course of your life. You should have had the freedom to choose who you wanted to be with."

"That choice was never mine to make. Not when I was headed for an arranged marriage anyway. At least, I knew you...somewhat. I suppose, it was the lesser of evils."

I wince. "Why didn't you rebel? Why didn't you tell your father you could choose the man you were going to marry?"

"I thought about it. Perhaps, if I'd met someone else, someone I wanted to be with, I would have, but from the moment I saw you, there was this attraction, this longing, this need to be with you. And when I found out you were my arranged match, I thought all the stars were aligning. I didn't realize you'd manipulated things to look that way."

"Belle—"

She places her fingers on my lips. "And even now, after I found out just how much you engineered things so you could marry me... When I should hate you and want you out of my life, all I can think of is how much I miss you. I'm such a loser."

"You're not."

"I hate myself."

"But I love you."

Her gaze widens.

"I've wanted to tell you so many times over the past week, but I couldn't bring myself to. You...my wife, are far more courageous than I am. You're able to speak your mind, unlike me. You're able to share how you feel, while I… When it comes to the stuff that matters in life, turns out, I'm not the man I thought I was."

"But you are, Eddie. I don't know what the incident did to you, but I know it couldn't have been easy. And yet, you picked yourself up and moved on. You survived. You lost the woman you thought was meant to be your soulmate—"

"She's not; you are." I cup her cheek. "You're everything I prayed for all through those years when I was a priest."

She frowns.

"Oh, I don't mean I prayed to find a soulmate. But I prayed for peace, for a way to still the thoughts that never allowed me to sleep, the images from my past that haunt me. I asked for a way to release the hurt, the pain, the sorrow. And the only time I find any measure of stillness is when I'm with you."

The water pours down over the both of us. Her hair sticks to her forehead, long strands plastered to her cheek. I reach behind her and shut off the shower. The silence envelops us, punctuated by the drip-drip-drip of the last remaining drops of water. Then that, too, cuts out.

"Eddie, the way you twisted things around in my life—"

"Is unpardonable."

"The way you engineered the situation around me so I had to marry you—"

"Is reprehensible."

She swallows, then wraps her arms about her waist. "I should leave you."

"You should."

"But I'm not able to bring myself to."

Every muscle in my body tenses. My pulse rate shoots up further. And my heart… It stutters, then starts again.

"I hate myself for not being able to walk away from you."

"Don't." I go down on my knees. "Don't do that. I'll never be able to forgive myself if you do. You're an angel. The kind of woman I don't deserve. And I won't blame you if you hate me forever."

"I wish I could."

I take her palm in mine and kiss her knuckles. "I'm so sorry I hurt you. I truly am."

She cups my cheek. "I know what happened to you made you put up walls, so you'd come across as cold-hearted and uncaring about the consequences of your actions. It's why you pretended to be so unfeeling, when I know deep down you're anything but."

My heart booms in my ribcage; pinpricks of disgust course down my back. *Tell her, tell her.* I open my mouth, but nothing comes out. I try again, then shake my head.

Her lower lip trembles. "It's okay, Eddie. I know you'll tell me when you're ready." She half smiles, then pulling her hand from mine, she brushes past me and out of the shower cubicle.

I rise to my feet and follow her. Grabbing a towel from the shelf, I draw abreast and place it about her shoulders. "I'm sorry," I swallow. "I really am."

"Where the fuck are the sales reports? They were supposed to be on my desk an hour ago."

The woman on the other side of the desk pales. "I... I..."

I glare at her, and she takes a step back. "I... I..."

"Have you forgotten how to speak?"

"I... I..." She—whatever her name is—continues to gape at me like a dying fish. *Enough of this nonsense.* I rise to my feet. She yelps, then turns and scampers out of my office.

"Fuck!" I drag my fingers though my hair, then grab hold of whatever is nearest, which happens to be my empty coffee cup, and throw it in the direction of the doorway.

The man entering ducks—quick reflexes, I'll give you that—then straightens and smirks. "Getting your jollies by scaring your employees?"

"Get out." I point my finger at Nathan. "Out."

He prowls over to the window. "Nice view."

"I told you to leave."

"For a man who has the best office in the building, you sure don't pull your weight."

"The fuck you mean?"

"First, you almost cost us a million dollars; and now, you missed the board meeting."

"No, I didn't."

He merely stares at me over his shoulder.

Something in his gaze makes me reach for my phone and check my calendar. *What the—!*

"Exactly." He walks over and leans a hip against my desk. "You've been going to pieces."

"No I'm not."

"You also forgot poker night."

"I did?" I slump back in my seat. It's been a week since my wife walked in on me smashing my fist into the wall of the bathroom—it's intact, I didn't even scratch the surface. I did suffer some lacerations on my knuckles. Apparently, I'm not even strong enough to put my fist through a wall. Although, to be fair, it's tile. What's worse, though, is that I haven't seen her since. Her preschool is doing well; more than well. It's at full capacity, with a waitlist to get on the waitlist, or so my HR manager informed me.

I've tried to stay focused and attend my meetings and conference calls, but if you ask me what I did or said, I wouldn't have a clue.

Every evening, I get home, and after making sure she's eaten her dinner—my housekeeper has been instructed to keep meals ready and have them delivered to her room; she lets me know when she makes the delivery—I walk over to her room and stand in front of the door, hand raised and ready to knock.

But I never do. If I did, I'd be going back on the promise I made to myself to give her space. So, I stand there, knowing she's inside. Knowing she hasn't moved out—the house staff have confirmed she's there—but I never hear a sound from her room. I curl my fingers into a fist at my side to stop myself from beating down her door. I stop myself from insisting she open the door. I force myself to walk away because I'm done infringing on her personal boundaries.

Besides, what right do I have to have to talk to her or hold out hope for any kind of relationship when I haven't been able to share my past with her? She deserves to know how tainted I am. She deserves to know I'm not worth her attention, in any form. She deserves so much more, and I can't give it to her.

So, I content myself with the knowledge that she lives under my roof. She's my wife; nothing's changing that. Not even if she left me—which she hasn't. And if I still believed in a force greater than myself, I'd thank that presence. But I don't.

Instead, I bury myself in work... Or pretend to. But going by the fact I missed the meeting—which would have determined if I'm confirmed as the CEO—clearly, I'm not being successful at that, either.

Truth be told, I don't care. I curl my fingers into a fist. Enough of this pretending otherwise. *I. Don't. Care. I don't care if I'm no longer the CEO of this company. It doesn't matter if Nathan takes over my role. I no longer have to pretend to care for the things that I thought I once did.*

I loosen the tie around my collar.

"You okay?" Nathan frowns.

"Do I look like I'm okay?"

"You look like shit."

"You don't look so hot, either." I scan the hollows under his cheekbones. Not that I give a fuck, or that I want to indulge in any kind of banter, but the man's standing in my office with a furrow between his brows, and dark circles under his eyes. And clearly, spending time with my wife is rubbing off because I feel… I wouldn't say a sense of empathy, but definitely a smidgen of understanding, toward the worry in his eyes.

"What's wrong, didn't the old man confirm you as his heir yet?"

He gives me a curious stare. "As a matter of fact, he didn't."

"He didn't?"

"He's happy to keep the status quo going, with both you and me holding veto powers. He seems to think you need to be cut some slack, given you're newly married and all."

"Is that right?" I stroke my chin.

"Seems he has a heart. So much so, he insists I should be the next to marry if I want to keep my veto power."

I chuckle, then turn it into a cough.

"Something funny?" he growls.

"Funny? Of course, not."

"I was thinking…" He looks uncomfortable. "Ah—" He clears his throat. "I was thinking you might dissuade him about this notion."

"You mean, about you getting married?"

"Exactly." He nods. "Especially since, it's not like you're particularly happy after having done the deed."

"What gives you that idea?" I stiffen.

"The fact your wife is no longer your secretary—"

"We thought it best not to work in such close proximity, given we're married now. We wanted to, uh, not make things uncomfortable for those around us. Also, Belle's skills are better utilized setting up and running the childcare facilities. That job is more important than being my assistant."

"—and the fact that she takes the tube to work, while you come by car."

I stiffen. "She's an independent woman."

"And that the two of you missed Sunday lunch, despite the old man having asked you to attend."

"Fuck."

He nods. "So, it seems the two of you are struggling to figure things out."

"Early days of marriage. It's normal."

"If you say so." He doesn't sound convinced.

"In fact, the best thing the old man did was insist I get married if I wanted to stay on as the CEO."

"O-k-a-y?" He levels a disbelieving glance in my direction. "Of course, you didn't forget to send out a company-wide email letting everyone know about the child-care facilities your wife will be leading on for the company. An initiative which you should have informed me of, considering I'm joint-CEO—"

"I'm informing you now." I shrug.

"An initiative which has resulted in our employee satisfaction scores surging by fifty percent in yesterday's organization wide survey, which" —he strokes his chin— "in turn, is bound to increase productivity by at least fifteen percent. A fact which might even justify the unplanned investment behind this scheme you've already made."

My wife was right about how providing daycare services will impact productivity, after all. Apparently she's right about a lot of things. My phone buzzes. I pull it out of my pocket, glance at the screen, then jump to my feet. "I have to leave."

63

Mira

"I'm fine. It's probably because I didn't stop for lunch today." I try to sit up, the room tilts, and I find myself flat on my back again.

"You're not okay." Adela places a palm on my forehead. Demand for spaces in the preschool has spiraled so quickly, I need more help. When she volunteered, Ed signed her transfer to my department immediately.

"You're burning up," she murmurs.

"My throat did feel a little scratchy this morning," I admit.

"You need to see a doctor."

"Nothing some paracetamol won't sort out." I cough. "Just don't tell my husband."

"I called your husband," she says at the same time.

I gape at her. "Why did you do that?"

She blinks. "Uh, he's your husband? Also, he happens to be the CEO of the company, and I want to keep my job, and—"

"How is she?" Ed bursts into the reception area of the nursery, which is where my legs chose to give way from underneath me. He moves so quickly, his feet don't seem to touch the ground. He sinks to his knees next to me and rakes his gaze over my features. "Why is she so pale?"

"She has a fever…and mentioned a sore throat, and—"

"Call Dr. Weston," he orders her.

Adela looks between us, then nods and excuses herself.

He continues to stare at me, the look in his eyes so intent, that when he reaches for me, I flinch.

His throat moves as he swallows. He raises both of his hands, palms facing me. "I won't hurt you."

"I know."

"When I heard you'd fainted—"

"I was out for barely a few seconds."

All the color drains from his face. "A few seconds."

"It's probably because I'm dehydrated."

"Dehydrated?" He sways.

"Ed? Eddie?" I touch his hand, and he trembles, then seems to get a hold of himself. "I'm going to move you to the couch, Belle." He hesitates. "If that's okay with you?"

I blink. *He's asking me for permission to move me?* He didn't just scoop me up and march me over and sit down with me in his lap. And I'm grateful he queried me first, but also… I want him to do what he thinks is right for me, because I do enjoy it. I do. My head spins, and it's not just because of whatever bug I've caught. It's this constant warring inside of me where he's concerned that's tearing me up inside. I want to hold onto the independence I've fought so hard for all of my life. I want him to not give me a choice where my wellbeing is concerned. I want him to manipulate my body as he's always done because he knows what I need. And because I know when I tell him no, he'll stop.

It's because he wanted me so much, because he couldn't stand the thought of me belonging to anyone else, that he masterminded events so I ended up married to him. And while I'm not sure if I've forgiven him for that, the fact that he had such a strong yearning for me, that he desired me and longed for me enough to pull strings until I became his, is a powerful turn on.

"Belle?" His voice softens, "Please? I can't stand to see you lying on the floor."

"It's carpeted," I point out, then cough. And he seems to grow even more pale. His fingers curl into fists. "Belle, I'm begging you."

"Yes." I stop my lips from twitching. "You may carry me, but you can't place me on the couch."

"Where then?"

"Your lap would be better."

He draws in a sharp breath, then nods. "Your wish is my command." He scoops me up, then prowls over to the couch and sits down, gathering me close. I curl into his broad chest, turn my nose into his vest, and breathe deeply. That dark, spicy scent of him settles in my blood, and some of the tension drains out of my shoulders.

He balances me with one arm, then pushes the hair off my flushed forehead. His fingers tremble. Because I can't stop myself, I reach up and twine my fingers through his. "I'm fine, really."

"Really, you're not."

He places our joined fingers over my heart, as if to reassure himself that I'm here and alive.

"When I got the message that you'd collapsed, I felt like I was going to die. I felt like everything inside me had dissolved and was floating away into the ether. I felt so helpless. It's all my fault."

I stare. "How is it your fault that I'm sick?"

His lips flatten. "I should have taken care of you. I should have paid more attention to you. I should have made sure you were taking your vitamins—"

"Why would you want to make sure I'm taking my vitamins?" I shake my head. "Honestly, the last thing I want is a helicopter husband."

"A helicopter husband?" He frowns.

"Yeah, a husband who constantly hovers over you and wants to make sure you're fine."

"What's wrong with that?"

"It can be stifling?"

"It's a way of showing I care for you."

"There are other ways of showing it... Like not trying to control everything in my life."

His jaw tics. "I'm trying, Belle, I swear. I'm trying to be the kind of man you'd be proud to call your husband, but I'm a little short on practice and—"

"What seems to be the problem here?" A man bustles in. He's tall and broad-shouldered and is wearing a tux.

"Wes." Edward jerks his chin.

"You do realize I'm a heart specialist." The man stares at my husband.

"You're a doctor. I trust you. End of story." Ed sets his jaw.

"You're a heart specialist?" I blink.

"A cardiologist," he confirms.

"There's nothing wrong with my heart."

"Of course, there isn't. My friends prefer I take on the role of family doctor, when it comes to their loved ones." He gives a long-suffering sigh. "And I can't refuse. It's almost routine they call me whenever I'm at a social occasion. So much so, I never leave without carrying everything I need to attend to these house calls."

"I'm so sorry he pulled you away from whatever event you were at." I gesture to his tux.

"I don't mind, and I know the only way to put this wanker's mind at rest is if I examine you quickly." He places his bag on the floor, pulls up a chair, then reaches for my wrist and takes my pulse.

"Uh, I fainted," I offer.

Ed interjects with, "She collapsed and was out for a few seconds, and—"

The doctor glares at him. "I'm talking to my patient."

"And she's my wife," he snaps.

"And if you want to see her well and on her feet again, you'll let me have a conversation with her," the doctor says in a steely voice.

To my shock, Ed lapses into silence.

I stare at the doctor with respect. "I'm Mira."

"Dr. Weston Kincaid." He half smiles. "Let's look at your throat." He does a quick examination, then reaches for his bag and pulls out a thermometer.

He takes my temperature, then makes a *hmm* noise. *Gosh, I hate it when they do that. Like they know something you don't. Which they do. But does that make me nervous? It does.*

My nervousness must communicate itself to Eddie, for his arms around me tighten. "You're going to be okay," he whispers.

"Yes, she will. Her tonsils are enlarged, and the lining of her throat shows signs of redness. She probably has a strep infection," the doctor declares.

"A strep infection?" Eddie frowns.

"It's been going around. Some of the children had it; I probably caught it from them." I shrug.

"I need to take a throat swab to confirm it."

"Go on then, what are you waiting for?" Edward pulls me into his side.

The doc reaches for his bag, then gestures toward us, while looking pointedly at Ed. "If you can give us some space—?"

Edward only holds me closer.

"It's okay." I pat his chest. "I'll be fine."

He hesitates, then kisses my forehead, places me on the couch gently, and backs away.

The doctor takes the throat swab. A few minutes later, he reads the test results and nods. "It's as I thought. Any allergies I need to be aware of before I issue the prescription?" he asks me.

"No allergies," I say at the same time that my husband snaps, "She's not responsive to penicillin."

I turn to him. "Oh, I forgot about that, but how did you know?"

He merely tilts his head. "I made it my business to acquaint myself with your medical history.

Of course, he did. He knows everything about me, and I should definitely be pissed, but in a roundabout way, I'm also pleased he remembered.

"Oh, that's good to know. I can prescribe something in its stead." The doctor completes his examination and sits back. "I'd like you to come to my clinic tomorrow so I can draw some blood and run some tests."

"Blood? Tests?" Ed stiffens. "What's wrong with her? What are you not telling me?"

The doc sighs. "It's routine; nothing to worry about. I want to make sure she's not anemic."

"Anemic?" Ed's gaze narrows.

"It means lack of iron in the blood," I say in a soothing voice.

"I know what it is."

"Then you'll know, it's not serious, and I am prone to it. My vitamin D levels may have dropped, as well."

"What?" Ed looks down at me, then cups my cheek. "Oh, my god, that's not good."

"It happens when you're a woman." I resist the urge to roll my eyes. "Especially due to my, uh, heavy cycles."

"When did you last have your period?" the doctor asks in a casual voice.

"Uh, three… No, four weeks ago, now." I hesitate. "Maybe longer." Now, it's my turn to gulp. "You don't think… No… I, uh, I'm on the pill."

"Best to take the guesswork out of it and take a pregnancy test."

"A pregnancy test?" My head spins.

Behind me, Edward's chest hardens. "Why don't you give her a full check-up when we see you tomorrow?" Ed growls.

I slap at his chest. "Excuse me, you could ask me if I want a full check-up done."

He squeezes his eyes shut, and when he opens them, there's remorse in them. "Would you get a full check-up done? Please?" he adds in a cajoling tone. His eyes are soft, and there's a plea in them. One I can't turn down. Especially since I can feel the tension strumming under that massive chest of his.

"Okay." I turn to the doctor. "What time do you want me there?"

***

"There's no way I can be pregnant." I wring my hands.

The doctor had emailed the prescription over to the pharmacy and he'd sent his team to pick it up. He'd also warned them that it had better have reached his home before we did. I exchanged glances with Adela, who merely shrugged and told me she would lock up the place before leaving for the night.

Ed called for his car, then carried me to it, placed me gently in the back seat and got in with me. I was surprised he wasn't driving but I kept quiet. Best not to add to whatever gamut of emotions he seems to be experiencing. For a man who, until a month ago, had trouble conceding he felt anything—let alone, giving voice to his feelings—he seems to have done an about-turn. I've never seen him this perturbed.

Now, he makes me lay down in the backseat with my head in his lap. Then, he proceeds to caution the driver to go slowly, until we're barely crawling along. He made sure I downed a bottle of water and some fruit before we left the office. And only because I insisted I couldn't eat anything else.

I try to sit up, but he coaxes me to lay down again. His thigh feels like a column of steel covered with the smooth fabric of his pants.

"I really can't be. I haven't missed a day of my contraceptive pills."

"Maybe you did, and you don't realize it." He strokes my hair. I swallow around the ball of emotion in my throat. He's so tender, so gentle. So everything I need.

"I'm strict about it. I need to take them to regulate my cycle and manage my cramps. But then, I've never been late, either…" My voice fades. *Which means, I might be pregnant.* The realization sinks in. *I might be carrying a child. His child. Ed's child. A family. I might have a family of my own. The family I've always wanted.*

But Ed… He wasn't very receptive when we spoke about children. But then, he also said we wouldn't be sharing a bed, and that there would be no sex — both of which haven't held true. Of course, there are other things he didn't tell me, either. All of which now seem secondary to the fact that I might be pregnant with his child.

When I look up, he's staring out the window.

"Eddie," I whisper, "how do you feel about it?"

"About what?"

"My possibly being pregnant? My — us having a baby?"

"How do *you* feel about it?" He looks down at me, and his voice is cautious. His features are back to being that bland mask I can't read.

"You know how much I want a child."

He lowers his chin, "Does that mean you'd be happy?"

"It means if I am pregnant — and that's a big if, but *if* I am — I'd be very happy." I search his features. "And you?"

64

____

Edward

"When I found out you'd collapsed—" I look into her eyes.

"I fainted," she insists.

"—I made a deal with God."

"With God?" She frowns. "I thought you and He weren't on speaking terms?"

"We weren't, but when I saw the text message from Adela, my heart stopped. I thought I was going to die. I knew then, I couldn't go on without you. I knew then, I'd do anything to make sure you were okay. I..." I swallow. "I promised Him I'd drop the grudge I have against Him. I promised I'd believe in Him again. All he had to do was make sure you were okay when I got to you. Those minutes it took to reach you as I ran down the steps, were the longest of my life."

"You ran down twenty floors?" She gasps.

"Of course, I did. No way, was I going to wait for the elevator to arrive."

"Eddie, you—" She shakes her head. "You're the most confusing person I've ever met."

"Look who's talking. When I look at you, I see my biggest passion, my only love, my greatest regret."

"Because of you how you got me to marry you?"

"Not only." I blow out a breath. "There…there are things I need to tell you."

"About your past."

"Also that."

Her forehead furrows. "What do you mean?"

"Let's get you inside the house and make sure you eat something, then take the medicine the doc prescribed, and—"

"And you're delaying the inevitable."

I rub at my temple. "Just give me this, Belle, please." I cup her jaw. "Just a little more time for you to look at me without hate in your eyes."

She sits up. "I would never hate you."

"No more than what you already do?"

"I'm pissed at you." She narrows her gaze. "And I don't understand you. And you confuse me a lot with your actions. And I don't want to say I'm fine with your stalking tendencies and how you're obsessively into me, enough that you didn't want me to marry anyone else, enough for you to plant devices in my room and in my Kindle, but a part of me almost understands—" she squeezes the bridge of her nose, "I can't believe I'm saying this but, it's almost flattering that you want me so much. So no, I don't hate you, but I don't agree with your methodology, either."

"And I can only agree with everything you say."

"Why are you being so agreeable?"

"Why shouldn't I be?"

She purses her lips. "I think I prefer you being your usual alternating between growling at me and being cold toward me."

"All of which has always been a cover for the depth of what I feel for you."

"I know that now. So I doubt you can tell me anything more that will make me hate you."

"We'll see." I square my shoulders.

"You sound like you want me to hate you."

"Maybe your hate is easier than any other emotions. Maybe I'm scared that one day, you'll love me, and then what am I going to do?"

"You'll accept it, Eddie. That's what you'll do. You'll accept the fact that you can be loved. That you're worthy of it. Whatever happened to you in the past does not define you. Your future doesn't define you. Power and money don't define you." She places a hand over where my heart beats in erratic thumps. "This… What is inside you, this goodness, this man who has always wanted to help others, who still helps others—"

"No, I don't."

"You signed off on the quotes for the nursery, and then for Adela to help me out, without blinking an eye."

"I had a vested interest in that."

"You give away a lot of what you make from your investments to charity."

I blink.

"Don't deny it. I found out from Summer, so I know it's true."

"Hmm, I need to have a talk with her," I scowl.

"That's what I mean. You do these things and then pretend it doesn't mean much, when it does. Most people who have money use it to make more for themselves. They don't go about donating it to charitable causes."

"I don't need the money, so I donate it. It doesn't mean anything." I raise my shoulder. "Besides, it makes a difference between life and death for so many others."

"That's what I'm talking about. You don't even realize how much of a softie you are."

I blink slowly. "You sound like you almost like me."

"I don't dislike you," she murmurs.

I suppose, that's a start. And why am I trying to talk her out of it, when all I want is for her to feel a fraction of what I feel for her?

"I just wish you'd realize, it's as important for you to learn to accept as it is to give. If you can't accept what people offer you, then it's as if you look down on the people who accept from you."

"What? No. I'd never do that."

"Then why is so difficult for you to receive the concern I have for you?"

She's right. I've shunned anybody showing understanding about how the incident affected me. I hate it when people pretend to identify with what I've been through. I turned my back on any sympathy my parents tried to show me. Not that they tried particularly hard, but I rebuffed any efforts on their part. I made it difficult for them to care for me in any way. I've even kept the Seven at arms-length, despite the fact we went through the incident together. And when Baron and Ava got together, I distanced myself from both of them. I stopped communicating with Baron—the one person who knows exactly what I went through; he was there with me. He suffered almost everything I did. *Almost.* For even he doesn't know the extent to which I was hurt... But he has a good idea. More than the rest of the Seven. More than anyone else, except her. And it's not because I've told her much, but she's looked behind my facade, she...has an inkling.

"You're right." I tuck my elbows into my sides. "It *is* difficult for me to accept help from anyone."

"Including me?" She peers up into my eyes. "Will you let me help you?"

65

Mira

He scooped me up in his arms and carried me inside our—his—okay *our* home. I was feeling better, and wanted to tell him so, but I also sensed this need inside him to take care of me, so I let him. He carried me into the living room and placed me on the couch. Then, proceeded to fluff the cushions behind my head and pull a comforter over me. Then, he handed me my Kindle, along with a large glass of water he commanded me to drink and told me to occupy myself while he got my dinner.

Yep, he did order me there, like the bossy-pants he is, but it felt right. I barely read a couple of pages before he came back with a tray of food. He'd heated up the chicken soup—which he'd called ahead and asked his housekeeper to prepare. There was also crusty bread, which he buttered for me, and he made me eat it all as he watched. Then he gave me the medicine Doc Weston had prescribed—something safe, in case I am pregnant. I told Ed I was feeling better, but he'd hear none of it. He insisted I swallow it down, then offered me a cup of herbal tea.

When I finally lean back with a sigh, he slips onto the couch and replaces the cushion under my head with his thigh. For a few seconds, I lay there, once again, enjoying the feel of his firm flesh. I rub my palm over the silky material of his pants, and he places his much bigger palm over mine.

"Don't," he murmurs.

"Why not?" I look up at him.

"Because we need to talk."

"I don't want to talk," I pout.

His features soften. He pushes my hair back from my cheek and tucks the cover under my chin. "Tomorrow then."

"Okay," I murmur.

He begins to drag his thumb over my lower lip, then catches himself. "What do you want to watch?"

"Watch?"

"On the streamers. I have all of them."

"Anything romantic, like—"

He groans, "Don't tell me *The Notebook*."

"—*The Notebook*." I nod.

He rubs the back of his neck. "Okay."

I blink. "You don't mind watching *The Notebook* with me?"

"There's a first for everything, I suppose." He raises a shoulder.

"You've never seen *The Notebook*?"

"Not my normal taste, but I've heard about it, like it's the most romantic movie ever."

"It is," I agreed with a smile.

"Also I've been... Otherwise occupied for a lot of my life."

"You took your role as a priest seriously, didn't you?"

He hesitates, then rubs at his stubbled cheek. The sound of his nails over his whiskers pulses goosebumps over my skin. Oh, my gosh, I'll never not be attracted to him. And at some point, he discarded his jacket and rolled up his shirt-sleeves so the tendons of his veiny arms flex. And everyone knows, forearm-porn is the easiest way to turn on a girl. Also, he's still wearing his vest, and the way it contours the planes of his chest should be banned.

"—Belle, you okay?"

"Yes, of course, why do you ask?" I clear my throat.

"You had a dazed look in your eyes." He touches my forehead. "Your fever hasn't increased, has it?"

"Nope, the medicine I took is making me drowsy, is all."

He runs his fingers though my hair. "You should rest."

"You evaded my question again."

He sighs. "There's nothing to evade. I tried to deliver on my responsibilities toward my congregation with the utmost sincerity. I felt I was making a difference in peoples' lives. I tried to be a spiritual guide, a counsellor for couples, and I loved teaching young minds. It was deeply satisfying and yet"—he swallows—"something was missing. I knew I wasn't addressing the real reasons I was pushing myself so hard to feel needed. And when I had a crisis of faith, I left."

"You did what felt right at that time."

"I turned my back on everything that defined me." He firms his lips.

"That took courage."

"That was cowardly of me," he says at the same time.

I begin to sit up, and he doesn't stop me. "It's all about how you look at things, isn't it? It's your mindset. You think you were running away, I think you knew it was time to leave and find yourself, so you could deal with whatever happened earlier in your life."

His lips curve. "When did you become so wise?"

"I was born wise." I smile back.

Our gazes hold; the air between us shimmers and grows heavy. My thighs clench, and my pussy feels like Niagara Falls opened up between them. *OMG, I did not just think that!*

"I can read what's on your mind," he warns.

I scoff, "You cannot."

"I did, but I'm not going to elaborate because you need your rest." He urges me to pillow my head in his lap, then reaches for the remote. Between the familiar scenes of *The Notebook* playing on the screen and the gentle touch of his fingers combing through my hair and whispering down my neck—which is both soothing and a turn on—a warmth steals over me. I close my eyes and drift off. I have a vague recollection of him carrying me to bed, me protesting, and him kissing my forehead.

He slides me into bed, pulls the covers over me ,and I'm asleep again. When I wake up, dawn is breaking through on the horizon. The silver light pours through the un-curtained windows. I turn on my side and realize, he's stretched out on the bed, on top of the covers. He's still wearing the same shirt with his sleeves rolled up, and he's folded his arms over his vest. I take in his shoulders, his chest, those lean hips, the powerful thighs, his bare feet. He must have discarded his socks at some point in the night. His toes— *Oh, my god, his toes—why do I find the sight of them so erotic?* I manage to drag my gaze back to his face, and the sight of his thick eyelashes fanned over his cheekbones, that hooked nose, the mean upper lip and that plush lower lip, now parted slightly in sleep, draws me to him.

Before I can stop myself, I throw off the covers, then inch closer. I play my mouth over his, not touching him, but drawing of his breath. That scent of woodsmoke surrounds me. That sharp tang in the air, which reminds me of an incoming storm, a sensation I always associate with him, envelops me. I lean in and touch my lips to his. That's when he opens his eyes.

66

Edward

Her blue gaze holds mine. Her breath mingles with mine. She keeps her mouth on mine, doesn't back away, and I let her kiss me. She licks my lower lip, and my groin tightens. She nips on my mouth, and it takes everything in me not to throw her over on her back and plant my hips between her thighs and grind into her to show her exactly what she's doing to me. Instead, I curl my fingers into fists, push them into the mattress, and savor the sensation of her exploring my mouth. She drags her tongue across the seam of my lips, and my blood begins to thud at my temples. She takes small bites of my chin, down the column of my throat, and nudges her nose into the hollow between my collar bones. She draws in a deep breath, and it's my head that spins. I feel the beat of her heart against mine, the flutter of her fingers as she clutches at my vest, and when she reaches for the button of my waistband, I wrap my fingers around her wrist. She looks up at me, a question in her eyes.

"We need to talk."

A flutter of fear pulses over her features, then she nods. "Okay."

I cup her cheek. "I love you." I bring her forehead to mine and draw in her familiar scent.

"I love you," she whispers against my mouth.

And I want to kiss her. Want to move her on her back and press her into the mattress and show her how much I worship that gorgeous body of hers, but I will not. Not until I've come clean with her. And if she decides she never wants to see me again, then I'll have to accept it. I'll have to walk away from her and spend the rest of my life making it up to her. I'd do everything possible to win her back. I have to. I don't have a choice because without her, I'm nothing.

She brushes her knuckles over my cheekbone. "Eddie?"

"Yeah." I open my eyes. "Let me make you some breakfast."

"That was good." She scoops up the rest of the omelet with her bread and chews on it. "I shouldn't be eating like this."

"Like what?"

"Like I have a healthy appetite."

"You do have a healthy appetite."

"And everything I eat goes straight to my thighs."

I take in the faded T-shirt and sweatpants she changed into earlier and shrug. "All the more for me to bite on."

She reddens. "I can't believe you said that."

"And I can't believe you'd put yourself down. I love your curves, love the thrust of your tits, the swell of your hips, the fleshy spread of your thighs that invites me to park my head between them and close my mouth around your juicy core."

"Oh—" she swallows.

"Not to mention, your peach of an arse which I can barely keep my hands"—I flex my fingers—"and my teeth"—I snap them—"off."

She shifts in the chair. "Okay, fine, I get the picture."

I push away my half-eaten plate. "I threw your contraceptive pills away."

She laughs. "No, you didn't. I have them in the drawer of my bedstead."

"I replaced them with multi-vitamin tablets that look exactly the same."

"Eh?" She blinks. "You replaced my oral contraceptives with multi-vitamin pills?"

I nod.

"What?" She shakes her head. "Why?" She drags her fingers through her hair. "You're not making any sense." She swallows.

"I...realized I want to have children with you, after all."

"And you couldn't have simply told me that?"

"I couldn't."

"Why not?" She jumps up to her feet and slaps her open palm onto the top of the island where we're seated. "You knew I wanted them! I would have been happy that you did, too. I"—she shakes her head—"I need time to process this." She turns and begins to walk away.

"I'm sorry. I should have been upfront with you. But I was scared..." *There, I've said it. Another confession.* And, once again, I feel lighter. It took giving up the cloth to understand the power of speaking the truth.

She stops and turns to face me. "Scared?"

"Scared that when I finally tell you what happened to me with the incident, you won't want to have my child."

She scoffs. "Nothing that happened to you would ever change my mind about having your child. Since the moment I saw you, all I wanted was to be yours and have a family with you. Do you understand?"

"I was kidnapped when I was twelve."

She freezes.

"So were the rest of the Seven: Sinclair, Saint, Weston, Damian, Arpad, Baron and me. We were in the same school, in the same class, and we were targeted by the same person. We were held for ransom. All except Sinclair, whose family wasn't as wealthy as the rest of ours. He happened to be in the wrong place at the wrong time."

"Oh my god, Eddie." She presses her knuckles into her mouth.

"We were kept blindfolded and tied up. Each of us was abused"—I swallow—"in different ways. Some of us emotionally; others physically. Baron and I—" I grip the edge of the counter. "Baron and I, we"—I squeeze my eyes shut—"we were held together. We were made to do things to each other. We—"

A soft touch on my cheek makes me snap open my eyes. "—you don't need to tell me anything more."

"I do." I curl my fingers around her wrist and tug on it. And when she lowers her hand, I weave my fingers through her much daintier ones. She doesn't resist, thank fuck. "Baron and Ava know what happened, but none of the others know exactly what went down. They suspect, of course, but they've never pushed me to open up. Not the way you have."

Her eyes fill with pain and empathy and so much love, and that's my undoing. This woman—she understands me the way no one has. I've been unfair to her; the way I've treated her is all wrong, and yet, she's here for me. "You should leave; you should walk away from me."

"That would be the easy way out."

"If you stay, it's going to be harder on you."

"Maybe,"—she squeezes my fingers—"but it'll be worth it."

"It scarred me, what happened. We were held for a month—"

"A month?" she gasps.

"By the time the cops found us, we had all suffered in different ways. It bonded us together, but it also made us feel different from everyone else. We didn't feel like we belonged. It made us emotionless, angry men who pursued wealth and power to fill that emptiness inside us."

"Were the perpetrators ever found?"

"Much later, and not by the police. Thanks to the investigators we employed over the years, we tracked down those responsible. But that's not all."

I look away then back at her. "The person who provided information about us to the kidnappers, and thanks to whom the perpetrators had enough leads to abduct the seven of us... That person walked into my church for confession when I was a priest."

She draws in a sharp breath. "What...what did you do?"

I shift my weight from foot to foot. "Turned out, he went to the same school as us, which is how he was able to spy on us. But he was repentant about what he'd done. He needed redemption. He wanted to confess his sins and be forgiven. And I... I couldn't forgive him."

"Of course, not."

I look into her eyes and all I see is understanding.

"He asked me for forgiveness, and I... I wrapped my fingers around his throat and squeezed the life out of him."

67

─────────

Mira

"You took his life?" I stare.

"I thought I had but I managed to stop in time," he swallows. "The kidnappers… They made Baron and me touch each other, and bugger each other, and… I hurt my best friend." He squeezes the bridge of his nose. "And to find the man responsible for everything that happened was in my church, confessing his sins and asking me for forgiveness, felt like a cruel twist of fate." He lowers his hand and meets my gaze. "I couldn't control the anger and the hate inside me from pouring out." He curls his fingers into fists, "I thought I wouldn't be able to spare his life."

"But you did."

An expression of anguish twists his features. "I was a priest. What I did went against everything I believed in. Everything I had spent my life in pursuit of, until that point."

"What you are is human." *And what I should be is more shocked.* I should leave. After all, I'm standing in the presence of someone who almost killed another person. Someone whose life was changed forever, through no fault of his own. Someone who was forced to do the most reprehensible things, which scarred him forever. Someone who's coming clean and sharing his deepest secrets with me. It's not easy for him to do so and yet, he's doing it anyway. *If I were in his place, would I have done the same thing? I'll never know.*

What I *do* know is, this is Eddie, my husband, and I don't hate him. Far from it, I'm finally beginning to grasp the motivations behind what he does. Why he's so aloof. Why he's put up so many walls between himself and the world. Why, he's so paranoid about my safety. Everything he's been through has taken his trust in the world and forced him to be ever-alert to the dangers around him. Finally, I understand him better. I get why he's so protective of me and fears for my safety. I square my shoulders.

"You did the right thing."

His gaze widens.

"I can't even fathom how you went through everything you did and are still a functioning member of society. If what you did helped you find some peace then, so be it."

"Belle," he whispers.

"Are you surprised I'm not freaking out more?" I half smile.

"A little." He lowers his chin.

"How can I be upset when, clearly, that man was responsible for the trauma that you and your friends had to deal with?"

He shakes his head, and his features take on a tortured look, "And I was supposed to teach and uphold the sacraments of my faith. I was supposed to help individuals navigate moral and ethical dilemmas. I was meant to counsel and support my flock and help them overcome sins and make amends. Instead, I committed the most heinous sin of all. Worse, I'm not sorry about what I did."

His shoulders shudder. All the color leaches from his face. A tear squeezes out from the corner of his eye, and I swear, I can see the child he used to be peeking out from behind his watery eyes.

I can't stop myself from throwing my arms about him. "Oh Eddie, I am so sorry for what you went through."

Another shudder rocks his big frame. His arms are tucked into his sides. He seems to be curling into himself, trying to make himself smaller and occupy less space. It's a contrast to the tall, broad, confident man who always knows what he wants and doesn't hesitate to go after what he sets his mind on, and… A part of me has always known it was a front. I've known he was hiding something inside, something that changed his life and impacted him in ways that not even years of therapy can undo, but this... What he's telling me is not something I could have imagined he went through. I knew it would be awful, whatever it was he was going to tell me—because I always hoped he would eventually tell me. But this...terrible secret of his... It's so much worse than I could have ever imagined.

I pull his head into the curve of my shoulder and hold him tightly. He feels cold, and distant, and yet, the little shiver that grips him gives away just how much he's suffering. "It's okay to hold me," I whisper.

He stiffens, and every muscle in his body seems to turn to stone. Then, he releases a breath. His body slumps a little, and he wraps an arm about my waist. I turn my face into his neck and take a long breath of Ed into my lungs. That spicy woodsmoke, the tang of electricity which ripples over my skin... All of it is so familiar, so very dear to me. "Oh, Eddie." I sniffle. "I wish you hadn't had to go through that."

"Me too." His hold tightens. "I really am so sorry for how I hurt you. I'm sorry I switched out your oral contraceptives."

"Why did you do that?"

"Because—" he swallows. "Because I was sure once you found out how I'm tainted—"

"You're not." I lean back in the circle of his arms. "You're not, Eddie. You came through the challenges thrown at you. You picked yourself up again and again. You moved on. You didn't give up."

"I don't deserve your beauty, your generosity, your love." He looks between my eyes. "I don't deserve you."

"That you don't," I murmur with a little smile teasing my lips.

That divot makes an appearance at the edge of his mouth. "But I want you. I want you so much, Belle. I love you, like I've never loved anyone else before. And at the risk of you hating me, can I say, I don't regret having eyes on you before you knew who I was."

"Ed!" I slap at his chest. "Take that back."

"I apologize, again, for infringing on your life without your permission"—he looks away, then back at me—"but it's because I knew you were there that I could carry on. It's because I knew there was a goddess who makes this world a better place that I could continue living. You gave me hope, Belle. You made me realize there was more to life than just the existence I was eking out. You gave me something to look forward to. Something to anticipate, something to aspire to. I knew then, if you were connected to me in some form, if I had you in my life, if I could have your love, in any small way, if—" He slides down to his knees and takes my hands in his. "I can't live without you Belle. And I'll do anything to make you happy. I'll do anything to make up for the grief I caused you. You mean everything to me, and I know my methods of showing it so far have been unorthodox—"

"—to say the least."

"Please give me a chance. One chance. That's all I'm asking. Let me show you I can be the kind of man you'll be proud to call a husband."

I'm already proud to call you a husband.

"Let me show you how good it can be between us, Belle."

"I already know how good it can be, but... You broke my trust, Ed. How do I know you won't do that again?"

"I won't." He brings my hands to his mouth and kisses the edges of my fingers. "I can't. Not when I know how close I came to blowing it all. You're my life, my breath, my heart, my everything. What can I do to make you believe that?"

"I'm not sure."

He peers into my features, then nods. "I deserve that." He sits back in his chair, still holding my hands in his. "I'll be here for you, Belle. Always."

"I know that. I also know you're a good man at heart. Which is why this is so difficult for me."

"Take your time." He half smiles.

"Thank you," I whisper.

He brings my fingers to his lips and kisses them again. Then he turns and pushes a paper bag in my direction.

"What's that?"

"Pregnancy tests."

"Oh," I swallow.

"I had them delivered, along with your prescription."

I make no move to touch the sack.

"It's best we find out for sure," he coaxes me.

I gulp. He's right, of course. But oh, my god, this is what I've always wanted, and if I'm not pregnant, what then? And what if I am? How does that change everything?

"It's okay; I'm here." He pushes the hair from my cheek. "Whatever the result, whatever you decide, I'm here for you."

"Okay." I rise to my feet, then snatch the bag and walk toward the bathroom at the end of the corridor. When I step in, he follows. "No." I turn to him. "Please. I need to do this on my own."

He looks like he's about to refuse, then steps back. I shut the door, lock it, then walk toward the counter and pull out the pregnancy tests. The blood drains from my face. I manage to pull out one of the pee-sticks, then place it on the counter. I look at the mirror and splash some water on my face. I can do this. I can. I pull down my yoga-pants, perch on the pot and pee on the stick. Then, I place it on tissue paper, clean myself up, flush, straighten my clothes, and walk back and forth on the bathroom floor.

"You okay?" Ed knocks on the door.

"Yes, just, ah… Waiting for the results." I wash my hands again, dry them, then sneak a look at the test. "No," I whisper. "No, no, no."

68

———————

Edward

I hear her gasp, then the muffled thump of a body hitting the floor before the sound of crying reaches me.

"Belle!" I knock on the door. "Let me in."

She doesn't answer, just continues crying.

I try the handle, but it doesn't open. "Belle!" I rap on the door again. "Let me in, please."

The weeping seems to escalate, my heartbeat keeping pace. *Fuck... Fuck, fuck, fuck. It's my fault she doesn't trust me enough to be with her now when she took the test. And it's my fault she's not letting me in right now so I can comfort her. It's my fault I'm listening to my sweet wife cry and I'm not able to do anything about it.*

"Belle, please—" I swallow. "Please, baby, it's killing me to stand out here and listen to you weep. I'll do anything, anything to stop it; anything, Belle, please."

There's no response. The sound of her crying fades and there's silence. Dread is an anchor in my stomach, a twist in my guts, a burning sensation in my heart. I push my palm into the door and place my forehead against it. If this is how it feels to be helpless and not be able to do anything for the one person who is more important to you than anything in the world, I don't want to feel this again. I sink to my knees. Then, for only the second time since I left the priesthood, I beseech him, *Please, God, please help me. Give me one chance to set things right with her. I beg You, if You're there and if You're hearing me, allow me near her. Please, I—*

The door swings open. She stands in front of me. I look up into her features. Her nose is red, her eyes swollen.

"What is it, Belle?" I rise to my feet.

She shakes her head.

"Tell me, sweetheart." I move forward, and she takes a step back.

That anchor in my stomach drops to my feet. It feels like I'm drowning. I need to be strong. For her. "Belle, let me help you."

She locks her arms around her waist. "Okay."

"Okay?"

She nods.

"What do you want from me? Tell me, baby, please. I'll do anything. Anything to make things up to you. Anything to make you feel better."

"Anything?" She tilts her head. There's a feverish look in her eyes now. "Anything?" she asks in a shrill voice.

"Anything." I nod. "Whatever you want."

"I want you to fuck me."

"What?" I rear back.

"I want you to turn me over that countertop right now and fuck me. Can you do that?"

"Belle, no." I reach for her again, but she slaps me away.

"I'm not pregnant," she cries.

"You're not?"

Her features crumple, "I want so much to be a mother."

I close the distance to her, but she steps out of reach.

"I can't believe, despite your replacing my contraceptive pills, I didn't get pregnant." She hunches her shoulders. "What's wrong with me? How could I not have conceived? Why?" She begins to weep in earnest. This time, when I pull her to me she doesn't resist.

"I really wanted this child." Her voice breaks.

"I'm so sorry, baby." I kiss the top of her head, but she only weeps harder. And when she collapses against me, I pick her up, carry her out into the living room and sit on the couch with her in my lap. I rock her until she falls asleep, then I carry her to bed. I call the nursery at the office and arrange for Adela to cover for her absence. Then, I message Summer.

***

When she wakes up, I survey her features. "How are you feeling?"

"Not great," she groans and closes her eyes. "I have a headache."

"This will help." I hold out two Ibuprofen capsules. She takes them, along with the glass of water I offer her. Once she's swallowed the pills and chugged down most of the water, I place it on the nightstand.

She lays back against the pillows and takes in my features. "I'm sorry," she croaks.

"For what?"

"For my breakdown." Her lower lip quivers.

"You never have to apologize for sharing your sorrows with me. I want to be the one you turn to when things don't go the way you hoped they would. I want to be the one to help carry your burdens. I want to share your pain. Please, don't ever hide from me. To know you were suffering, and yet be unable to reach you... I felt like my heart was being torn out of my body." I catch her hand, then bring it to my mouth and kiss her fingers. "Besides, I'm as much to blame, Belle. I couldn't get you pregnant; I failed you."

She shakes her head. "Neither of us is to blame. It's not like everyone gets pregnant right away. Some women try for years and—" Her chin trembles.

"Shh, don't think about that. We'll tackle tomorrow together. For now, you need to rest and recover." I press my forehead to hers. "Close your eyes."

I let her sleep for a few more hours, not able to take my eyes off of her. My phone keeps pinging with messages from the office, but I ignore them. Funny how I thought the job and confirming my role as the CEO of the Davenport Group was a priority, when really, none of that matters. Life isn't about sitting at a desk, perusing spreadsheets, and signing mergers or steering acquisitions.

Life is a plus-size blonde with a heart so generous she could reform the grumpiest of souls. A woman whose smile lights up my soul. A woman whose gaze is like looking into the eyes of the divine. I swallow. A goddess who's shown me the error of my ways. Who's helped me make peace with Him. Something I didn't think would ever happen in my life. She swept into my life and turned it upside down.

She changed my mindset, turned my life inside out. She's shown me what it's like to be vulnerable. To share the parts of me I never have with anyone else. She…completes me, in a way I hadn't thought was possible. She makes me a better man. Someone who's rejoined the land of the living. Someone who can feel the range of emotions in their messiness and their predicaments. Someone who feels the highs and lows of being human. Of being here, in the now, and experiencing what it is to be alive. Someone who's able to see a future with her. And with our child.

When she told me she wasn't pregnant, a flash of disappointment gripped me. It surprised me because I never thought I'd have children. Not until she'd told me how much she wanted them.

For so long, the concept of a family was that of my parish. The people I served. Then, for a brief while, it was the hockey team when I had been their general manager. I wanted the best for all of them.

I function best when I'm looking out for others. I've never thought about what that means for me. Until she came along and began caring for me. She's the only one who looks at me like I'm her world. With her understanding and her love, she's changed who I am, until I no longer recognize myself. And all I want is for her to be happy. For her to get everything she wants. I take her hand in mine, then go down on my knees and place my forehead against our joined fingers.

69

Mira

The sound of a baby's crying percolates through my sleep. I must be dreaming. *Am I dreaming?*

"Oh, sorry, didn't mean to intrude," a voice says.

I fight my way up through layers of drowsiness to find Summer standing in the doorway, and in her arms, is a toddler. The baby whose crying I must have heard. Her gaze moves from my face to that of the man who's kneeling next to the bed. His fingers are twined with mine, and his forehead is pressed into the back of my palm. My fingers twitch. I want to reach out and run them through his thick hair. But before I can act on my impulse, he looks up at me. "I called Summer; I hope you don't mind?"

I shake my head.

"I thought it would be good for you to have some company—" He swallows. "—someone with whom you could talk?"

I nod, unable to speak. His features are drawn, and in the sunlight pouring in through the open window, he looks haggard. There are dark circles under his eyes, and his cheekbones are hollow. I, on the other hand, feel refreshed after having napped. Our gazes meet. There's warmth in his, and regret, and love, so much love. He catches my hand, then brings it to his mouth and kisses my fingers.

The baby yells again. Ed releases my hand, then walks over to Summer and holds out his arms. "Want to take a walk, little man?"

He blinks, then jumps into Ed's arms.

"O-k-a-y?" Summer looks stunned. "He's been stuck to my side since he woke up this morning. Which is why I brought him along."

"Can he eat blueberries?" he asks her.

"Yes, luckily, he hasn't exhibited any allergies."

He turns his attention back to the boy. "Whaddya think? Would you like some blueberries?" The kid babbles something, and Ed nods. "Blueberries, it is." He turns back to Summer. "Can I get you some coffee?"

"Yes, please," Summer says with enthusiasm.

"And tea and croissants for you, wife?" He looks at me over his shoulder.

OMG, I'll never get over how it feels when he calls me wife. Also, that's sneaky. If he continues to call me wife in that brandy-laced voice of his, I'll never be able to think straight. I'll never be able to decide what I want my future to look like. *Do I want to stay with him? How do I get past everything he's told me? How do I trust him again? And why is it, I still feel safe with him? Especially after he told me how he stalked me. How he took the life of another man.* My mind spins, and when I rub at my temples, he frowns.

"You okay, wife?"

I nod. "I'm good, just uh, still waking up, I think." I clear my throat. "And tea and croissants sounds wonderful; thank you."

He searches my features for another second, then the toddler tugs on his chin and draws his attention. "Okay, come on little man, let's get you some blueberries and milk, maybe?" He looks at Summer, who folds her fingers together in a gesture that says, *please and thank you and you are a lifesaver.* He walks out of the room, and Summer heads toward me. "He's so good with kids; he's going to make a great father someday.

Tears prick the backs of my eyes. *I know he will. Only, it's not going to be as quick as I'd hoped.*

She must notice the distress on my face, for her features soften. "Oh, Honey, how are you feeling?" She drops into the chair. "Edward messaged me. I hope you don't mind that I came over."

"It's good to see you. I suppose, I could do with someone to bounce my thoughts off of."

"Hit me, sister." She toes off her boots, then pulls up her knees and settles into the armchair.

"Did… Did Ed tell you what happened last night?"

"He just said you weren't feeling well, and it might help you to have another woman around."

I nod slowly. "I found out I wasn't pregnant."

"Okay?" She frowns. "I didn't think you two were going to try for a child right away."

"It was an accident. No, it wasn't an accident." I glance toward the doorway.

She follows my line of sight, then jumps to her feet, walks toward the door and closes it. "There, now we can talk freely." She curls up in her armchair again.

"He substituted my contraceptive pills with vitamin pills."

She freezes. "You're telling me Edward switched out your oral contraception?"

I nod.

"And you found out because — ?"

"He told me. He also revealed he spied on me."

Her gaze widens. "Edward spied on you?"

"He saw me first, in Brooklyn, when I lived in my father's house, a year ago. I had graduated and was looking for jobs in New York, and I couldn't afford to live on my own. I hated having to do it but moving back home helped me save enough to buy a one-way ticket out of there and to London."

"How did he spy on you?"

"He had someone install cameras in my room and bugged my phone. And my Kindle."

"Oh, my god." Summer presses her hands to her mouth. "And he confessed all of this to you?"

"Yep."

"Okay." She runs her fingers through her hair. "How do you feel about it?"

"I don't know," I say honestly. "When I thought I might be pregnant with his child… I was willing to forgive him for everything. Having a child, the one thing I have always yearned for, seemed to make everything right. But then —"

"—you found out you weren't."

I nod.

"And now you're angry with yourself for feeling so ready to forgive him because you thought you got what you wanted, a child?"

I nod again.

"And now you're wondering what to do?"

I raise my shoulders. "What am I going to do? Do I leave him? And go where? Do what?"

"And what is Edward saying?"

"We haven't discussed anything in great detail, but he says he's sorry for what he did. No, let me rephrase it: he's sorry his actions hurt me, but he's not sorry he did it."

"What does that mean?" She places her chin on her knee.

"That watching me saved him. That if he hadn't been able to see what I was up to on an ongoing basis, he's not sure what he would have done."

She rubs at her temples. "Babe, this is a lot to take in."

"You're telling me."

"No wonder, he thought you could benefit from talking to someone else."

"You've known Edward longer than me. What do you make of all this?"

"The fact that he turned stalker on you? That he was so obsessed with you, he had to watch you via secret cameras?"

I wince. "When you put it that way, it does sound creepy."

"Question is, why aren't you freaking out more about it?"

I throw up my hands. "Don't you think I'm not asking myself that question? Where is my self-respect, my dignity, my ego? Am I such a doormat that I'll allow him to get away with what he did?"

"Or maybe, you're flattered that he was so focused on you?"

"Eh?" I narrow my gaze.

"Are you flattered by the fact he was...*is* so infatuated by you."

"Maybe?" I wriggle around, trying to find a more comfortable place in the bed. "My mother died when I was young, and my father never paid much attention to me... And my stepmother and sisters? Let's just say, they didn't care what I did, as long as it didn't affect them. And then, to find out this man took one look at me and decided I was the one for him."

"That's what he told you?"

I nod. "Only, he didn't act on it, like a normal man. He decided to get fixated on me. And then, oh, yeah… When he realized my father's business was in trouble, he stepped in and told him he'd marry me in exchange for saving his company."

She whistles.

"Exactly."

She moves around and drapes herself sideways on the chair, so her legs hang over one of the arms. "When Sinclair and I met, he came onto me in the conference room of his office, then filmed me and used the video to blackmail me into marrying him."

"He did?"

"Also, there was this whole thing of him holding my father responsible for the incident, so he wanted revenge and decided to take it by marrying me."

"Oh." I stare at her. "Was your father responsible?"

"He gave information to the people behind the incident to save me and Karma. He didn't have a choice. And Sinclair seemed to think he didn't, either, but—" She raises a shoulder.

"But—?"

"But of course, there's always another way. Was I pissed off with Sinclair? Yes. Did I want to leave him? It crossed my mind, but I was already in love with him. I couldn't see a life without him. And then he changed. Turned out, it took the love of a good woman to reform him. And of course, he apologized and said he'd do anything to make me happy, and"—she tilts her head—"I chose to believe him. Not that I'm advising you to do the same."

"You're happy, though?"

Her lips curve in a soft smile. "Very. He's the best husband ever, and as a father, he's so devoted. He's changed his entire life for us and maintains we're the best thing that's ever happened to him. He says we help him stay grounded."

"You got your happily-ever-after." I try to keep the wistfulness out of my voice but don't think I succeed, for she leans forward and takes my hand in hers.

"Oh, honey. It wasn't easy, but I persevered. I just knew it was Sinclair or nothing. I guess, I didn't hold his actions against him. He'd been through so much, and then he showed he could change. Again, I'm not saying that's what you should do—"

"So, what should I do?"

"I can't tell you that." She shakes her head. "But what I can tell you is that you'll know, when you know. And if you can hang in there until you know… Well,"—she purses her lips—"do you think you can do that? More to the point, do you want to do that?"

70

Edward

I hold the door to the car open. My wife swings her legs over the side and places her feet on the ground. When I offer my hand, she hesitates, then takes it. The breath I hadn't been aware of holding rushes out of me. Each time she doesn't attempt to put distance between us, I send up a prayer. Yep, me, the man who decided he didn't want anything to do with HIM, apparently, can't go an hour without beseeching Him to give me a chance to show my wife how much I love her. How much I want her. How much I can't do without her in my life.

My wife straightens, and when I take in that gorgeous turn of her stocking-clad ankles, that familiar bolt of lust squeezes my groin. I shove it aside, continue my perusal up the flash of her legs, those thick thighs covered by a bright red coat that falls to below her knees. It brings out the color in her cheeks and the golden streaks in her hair.

Yesterday, when I arrived with a blueberry-sated kid, as well as a housekeeper in tow with breakfast for her and Summer, she wouldn't meet my eyes. But she didn't refuse my help when I plumped the pillows at her back, then placed the breakfast tray on her lap. She also didn't mind when I broke off a piece of croissant and fed her, and she took the cup of the tea I poured her. Then, I made sure to occupy the toddler while she and Summer visited.

After Summer left, I ran her a bath and waited outside while she bathed. Then, I insisted she take a nap while I dismissed the house-keeper and cooked an early dinner for her. We ate in front of the television, and when I pulled up another chick flick — *The Fault In Our Stars* — she didn't protest. And when I pulled her close and offered her my shoulder and a box of tissue when she cried, she accepted both. She fell asleep tucked into my side, and I carried her up to her room, tucked her in, and stretched out over the covers.

This morning over breakfast — which I'd cooked — I told her we were expected for dinner at G-Pa's place to bring in the New Year. I'd expected her to decline the invite, but she'd said she was happy to come. Of course, she said she loves the old man, and she wants to see Tiny. Clearly, the dog has a bigger share of affection than me. Not that I blame her.

It's a wonder she's even talking to me, after everything I told her. It's a wonder she hasn't told me to fuck off. But that's my wife. Sweetness and honey and all things nice... And I so want to taste her again. I want to bury my nose in her hair and take a long sniff — I confess, I manage a quick one when I help her out of the car. I also savor the feel of her deli-cate fingers in mine as I lead her up the path to Arthur's town house. And the warmth of her skin through the wool of her coat as I slide it off her shoulders. The creamy length of her throat, the nearness to her curves, the flare of her hips which pulled the dress tight across her rear... And fuck, the dress she's wearing. It clings to her in all the right places, showing off her lush figure, and when she turns to look at me over her shoulder, I have to tear my gaze away from her butt and hand the coat over to Arthur's staff. Her cheeks have gone pink. So, she noticed me ogling her, but she doesn't comment. If anything, the gleam in her eyes indicates she's pleased by my reaction. I step past her and lead her to the living room, where the rest of the family is gathered.

We step inside the room and Sinclair claps me on the shoulder. "Good to see you man." I nod.

"Glad you both made it." He looks from me to my wife, then back at me. "What are you both drinking?"

"You the bartender? Why are you here anyway?" I tighten my stare.

"Arthur's orders. Someone has to keep the peace while you Daven-ports trade scowls and looks which could tear the skin at ten paces."

"Count me out of that." I raise a shoulder.

His forehead wrinkles. "Thought you and Nathan were in competition for the CEO role."

"He can have it."

"You told him that yet?"

"I will. Also, sparkling water for me," I add.

"A glass of champagne would be nice." My wife nods.

"Coming up." Sinclair walks away.

I spot Summer across the room with her boy. She's deep in conversation with Ava. I must stiffen because my wife turns to me. "You okay she's here?"

"Are *you* okay she's here?" I scan her features.

"She's no threat to me," my wife murmurs.

"No one is a threat to you. You're it for me."

She looks between my eyes, a troubled look on her features, then she turns away. "That must be her husband. Baron, is it?"

I take in the tall man with blonde hair who has his hand around her waist and I notice the baby carrier next to Ava. I wait for the inevitable churning of my guts, that stabbing sensation in my chest, but there's nothing. Only the feel of her hand still in mine, of her presence next to me. Unable to stop myself, I wrap my arm about her shoulder; that's when she goes rigid.

At first, I think it's because of me, but then I look down at her face, to where she's eying a trio of woman gathered in a corner. The older among them has a pinched look to her features. She's wearing a dress which accentuates her too-thin figure, the kind run-way models favor and which many seem to aspire to but makes me want to offer her a thick-juicy burger. Given the lack of expression on her face and the too-smooth expanse of her forehead, she's pumped her features with botox. The two younger women, one blonde, the other brunette, sport dissatisfied frowns. Their faces are painted with an overly generous application of make-up, enough to turn them into caricatures of themselves.

When one of the staff comes by with a tray of food, the brunette waves them off with a sniff. The blonde notices my wife; her gaze widens. She leans in and whispers something to the older woman. All three of them turn to look at my wife. Tension thrums off of her, and my insides twist. I pull her close into my side, and to my surprise, she melts in, which tells me she's feeling threatened by them. And anxious. And anyone who makes my wife feel that way is not welcome here. I take a step in their direction, and she grips my arm.

"Where are you going?"

"To tell them to leave."

"You can't...you can't do that."

"I can."

"They are G-Pa's guests."

"They make you unhappy."

She looks away, then nods. "That's my father's wife and their two daughters."

"Your evil stepmother and your half-sisters?"

My poor attempt at levity must work, for she gives me a small smile.

"We don't have to be here; we can leave," I say softly.

She looks torn, then slowly shakes her head. "We came here at G-Pa's invitation. He wants us here. You want to be here."

"I want to be where you are."

She turns her gaze on mine and, again, that confused expression flits across her face.

"What is it?" I take in her features. "Tell me, wife."

"It's... " She opens her mouth then shuts it. "Nothing." She squares her shoulders. "I'd better go get this over with."

71

Mira

My heart feels like a sledgehammer. My ribcage trembles with each beat. *Am I nervous about meeting my stepmother? What do you think? And I shouldn't be, really. They can't hurt me. No, strike that. They can hurt me, but it's time I learn how to deal with it. Besides, they don't know anything about me. So what, if I grew up under the same roof as my half-sisters? They've spent their lives pretending I don't exist. That's when they weren't making fun of me. As for my stepmother... Does she hate me? Boy, does she.*

She sees me as a threat for my father's affections, and I don't know why, considering my father has found it difficult to look at my face since my mother's death. I know, I remind him of her. He's said so on a few occasions, in the days he'd make an occasional appearance in my life. But it must have been too distressing for him, given how he blocked me out of his life.

So why do I feel so duty-bound toward him? Why is it, I felt as if I were the one responsible for doing what was needed to help his business? It's what my mother would have wanted. Given she died when I was little, it's not a conversation I've ever had with her, but if she'd been alive, I know she'd have wanted me to fulfill my obligations of a daughter.

She'd have also wanted me to be happy.

Perhaps, she'd have stood up for me and convinced my father not to go through with the tradition of an arranged marriage for me. Or maybe not, considering she and my father had an arranged marriage, too, and they were very happy, by all accounts. And seeing my stepmother and half-sisters has only brought home all the insecurities I grew up with.

But I'm stronger than that now. I *have* to be. And it's best to face them now and get it over with. I begin to wipe my damp hands down my dress, then stop. The last thing I want to do is stain the fabric. When I chose it earlier, I thought—no, I knew— it looks good on me. I like how the silk clings to my curves, how it outlines my hips and stretches across my thick thighs. How it bares my neck. I knew it would capture his gaze and focus it on my figure.

I wore it because a part of me wanted to bask in his admiration. I wanted to flaunt my size sixteen figure knowing he loves it. He's told me so often enough that, for the first time in my life, I'm secure about how I look. I no longer watch what I eat. I don't berate myself for not working out every day at the gym. For the first time since I can remember, I like what I see in the mirror. And it's because of him.

The way Eddie touched me and kissed me and worshipped my body. The way he hasn't wanted to allow me out of his sight since the first day he saw me... Yes, it's obsessive, but it's also flattering. So, flattering. So, gratifying... So, pleasing that he loves me for what I am. He doesn't want me to change. He hasn't demanded anything I can't give him...

He's the first man to adore my lush figure. The first to relish my size sixteen curves. He tied me up before he fucked me. He loves how my flesh embraces the knots. He was aroused by the marks left on my hips and my thighs by the cords. He was fixated on me, but then, I'd rather he be infatuated by me and consumed by me than by anyone else. I'd rather he dominate me than any other woman.

He loves me. And I don't want any other woman to occupy this space in his life. I'd rather he focus all of his considerable attentiveness on me. That his scrutiny stops and ends with my face, my body, my soul. He's mine. I'm his. And I love him. I don't want anyone in my life, except him. He loves me. He wants me. He finds me beautiful... More than that, he thinks I am the most alluring woman in the world.

And that gives me the courage to walk up to the women who've been responsible for so much of the sadness in my life. They fall quiet as I approach. And when I reach them, all three of them stare at me. They take in my dress, Chanel, and my heels, Balenciaga. Eddie filled my closet with only the best brands, all in *my* size. And while I could have been churlish and not accepted any of it, they looked so appealing, and they looked so good on me. I may be stubborn at times, but I'm not stupid.

Maybe, he's doing it to win me over, but I'm confident it's also because he loves how I look in them. His adoring gaze when he saw me was everything. His possessive touch as he helped me with the coat, and later, helped me remove it, gives me the wherewithal to hold out my hand to my stepmother. "Matilda."

Her eyebrows rise, and she seems taken aback by my confidence. She ignores my hand and continues to study me. I place my left palm on my hip, and her gaze widens. She sees my engagement and wedding rings—good. It's the first time I'm meeting her without a trace of nervousness—because, you know what? Somewhere on the walk over, as my mind went over how much my husband cherishes me, my uncertainty faded away, leaving in its place, a quiet belief in myself.

That's what Edward has done for me. He helped me find myself. All it took was my husband showing me how much he values me, how much he wants me, how he sees me as everything he needs, for me to find my trust in myself. Seeing myself through his eyes gives me the self-assurance I thought I'd never find. He's helped me find my faith. He's changed my life. He's shown me I'm not less than anyone else. He's taught me to love myself, and as a result, I've learned how to accept love. And for that, I'm willing to give him a second chance.

"Mirabelle." My stepmother looks past me, in the direction of my husband, before turning her gaze on my features. "I suppose congratulations are in order on your nuptials?"

I lock my fingers together. *I will not be nervous. I will not allow the memories of all the way she's insulted me over the years to get to me.*

When I was a kid, and I found out she was my new stepmother, I was so excited. I threw myself into her arms when my father introduced her, and she played along. She pretended to care for me, long enough to win my father over. Enough to worm herself into his affections, enough to make him trust her to look after me while he was away on work.

It was only later, I realized, she found ways to isolate me from him. She'd worked herself into a place where most of my father's communication to me came through her, where he never had the opportunity to see me or hear from me directly. I felt so lonely. Even more so, once my half-sisters came along. I'd thought it would be wonderful to have sisters, but she shut me out.

She turned all her attention to them, and while she put me in the care of a string of nannies, she made sure none of them stuck around long enough for me to form a bond with them. In a way, it turned out to be a blessing, of sorts, for the women she chose to care for me were not exactly affectionate.

I ended up missing my mother so much, I turned to food to make up for the lack of love in my life. I was trying to fill the mom-shaped hole in my life with the rush of endorphins that came from filling my stomach. It's also when I decided I wanted a family of my own. Children I could love and make up for the lack I had in my own life.

"Uh, is that your engagement ring?" Eleanor, my older half-sister, grabs my hand. I try to pull away, but she tightens her hold on me. She peers at my finger and sniffs. "Nice stone, but why isn't it a diamond?"

"I like it." I yank at my hand again, and this time, she releases it.

She tosses her hair over her shoulder. "Of course, it was an arranged marriage, so love wasn't part of the equation." Her voice is disdainful.

Heat flushes my cheeks. My stomach twists. *My husband loves me. He does.* She doesn't know what goes on in my marriage. I open my mouth to tell her off, when a server comes by with a tray of hors-oeuvres. I reach for it, and Kate, my younger half-sister, exclaims, "Oh, honey, are you sure you want to eat that?"

Eleanor takes one of the fried mozzarella sticks from the server's tray and bites into it. "It's soo good." She smacks her lips. "But you shouldn't eat it; it has too many calories."

My guts churn. My pulse rate spikes. A crawling sensation pricks my skin, and I retract my hand. Eddie's appreciation of my curves made me so comfortable in my own skin that I forgot I hate eating in front of others.

When I hit puberty and my unhealthy eating habits meant my weight had ballooned, Matilda insisted on rationing my food. She'd serve treats to my half-sisters but tell me I couldn't have any because I was too heavy, and she was looking out for my health. She'd also serve me too-small portions, explaining she was trying to help me control my weight. All of this meant I often went to bed hungry.

Once, I'd been unable to sleep because I was starving. I sneaked down to the kitchen after everyone was asleep and stole food. She caught me in the act, and Kate teased me mercilessly about it. The result? I stopped eating with them. For years, I preferred to have my food delivered to my room and eat on my own.

Then there was the time Matilda took the three of us shopping for clothes. I was suspicious when she invited me to come along. After all, she never treated me as part of the family. But she was so sweet, and when I hesitated, Eleanor and Kate insisted I join them. I was so happy they were including me in their activities that I agreed.

We'd reached the boutique, and Matilda insisted I try on clothes that were a size too small for me. Then she looked at me with disappointment and commented that if I lost a little weight, they'd fit me better.

Eleanor and Kate tried on the prettiest dresses in the shop. They modelled them, and Matilda oohed and aahed over them. She bought them all the clothes they'd tried on, then turned to me and proclaimed, once I slimmed down, she'd buy a new wardrobe for me too. Meanwhile, she was "more than happy" to buy me my plus-size clothing, but really, wouldn't it be best if I waited? It would be an incentive for me to lose weight. With sweaty palms and a piercing pain in my heart, I agreed.

She proceeded to take us to a fast-food joint as a 'treat,' then looked at me disapprovingly when I ordered a burger. I settled for not eating, while the three of them tucked into burgers and shakes. I reached for one of the fries from Kate's plate, and she burst into tears and complained to Matilda that I was stealing her food.

Of course, she and Eleanor had looked at me with judgement. I was a fat girl; I couldn't restrain myself when it came to food. It was one of the worst days of my life—one to which I directly attribute many of my insecurities with food and my weight. Suffice it to say, I never went out with them anywhere after that.

The waitstaff moves on to serve someone else, and I heave a sigh of relief, only to stiffen when Matilda gestures to my dress. "What a lovely color, my dear." She turns to Eleanor. "Doesn't it give the illusion of taking inches off her hips?"

"It does." Eleanor beams. "In fact, it almost flattens her stomach."

"It definitely makes her look a size smaller." Kate taps her chin with a talon-like fingernail. *Too bad she hasn't stabbed herself in the eye with it.*

How many times have I heard the three of them hold a conversation about me like I wasn't there? Only I *was* there. And I was hurt. And I still carry the emotional scars from their torment. That confidence I thought I'd shored up oozes out of me.

I take a step back, only to connect with something solid. Something warm. And hard and ungiving. Something that supports my weakening knees that threaten to give out from under me. I draw in a sharp breath, and his woodsmoke scent surrounds me. That tingle of electricity, which I've always felt in his presence, loops about my shoulders. My muscles relax, and when he places his big hands on my hips, the comfort from his touch knocks away the moment of self-doubt which had crawled into my chest.

"Belle's lush figure is what I love about her. No, that's wrong." He tucks me closer. "Her big heart is what I adore about her. And her giving nature. And how she wants to take care of those around her. She is the most authentic, most unselfish, most beautiful soul I have ever met. As for her curves? They're what make her even more special. My wife is worth a hundred, no, a million of you." He turns to my stepmother. "You insulted my wife and made her unhappy today. For that and for all the times you've upset her during her growing years, I'm going to cut the salary paid to your husband by eighty percent."

Matilda laughs. "Who are you to have any say over my husband's income?"

"He's the man who owns my company," my father's voice cuts in.

Matilda looks from my husband to my father, who's walked over to join us. "What do you mean?" She scowls.

"My business needed an infusion of cash to stop it from going under. Mira's husband stepped in. As of today, he owns a majority interest in the shares. In effect, he has control over my paycheck, and hence, over our future."

Matilda's gaze widens. "You never told me."

"You didn't need to know." My father raises a shoulder.

"This doesn't change anything." She waves her hand in the air.

"Actually, it does." My father widens his stance. "Since my salary is going to be cut to a fraction of what I used to earn, we'll have to trim our monthly outgoings. No more vacations—"

"What?" Eleanor slaps her hands on her hips. "I promised my friends I'd take a trip to Barbados with them. I can't let them down,"

Our father ignores her. "No more buying new dresses," he proclaims.

"I can't do without one for my debutante ball!" Kate bursts into tears.

Matilda pulls her close then glowers at my father. "Now, look what you've done."

"As for you" — he looks my stepmother up and down — "I'm going to cut your allowance by eighty percent."

Matilda stiffens. "You're joking."

My father shakes his head. "I should have done this much earlier for how you mis-treated Mirabelle all these years. I'm seriously thinking of divorcing you."

Matilda gapes, then a sly look comes into her eyes. "We've been married long enough, that if you did, I'd be entitled to a good portion of your money."

My father smirks, and it's a look I've never seen on his features before. "Remember the pre-nup you signed?"

Matilda draws in a sharp breath.

"That's right. You don't get a penny if we divorce," my father says in satisfaction.

Matilda narrows her gaze on my father. "I am your wife; you can't treat me like this."

"And Mira is my daughter. When I married you, I told you she was the most important thing in my life. I told you I wanted you to be a mother to her. Yet you mistreated her all these years."

"I did my best," Matilda snaps.

"And it wasn't enough."

"Don't blame me for your shortcomings," Matilda says in a low voice.

"You're right, it's my fault. I was too caught up in my grief. I was so self-absorbed I didn't intervene, even though I sensed my daughter was unhappy. But thanks to Edward, I realize I can make amends." My father looks between Eleanor and Kate, "I take responsibility for how the two of you turned out. I was an absent parent. I should have intervened in how your mother brought the two of you up. For that reason, I won't disinherit the both of you from my will. But consider yourselves warned. I expect to see changes in your attitude and your behavior toward your older sister. You'd do well to remember, she *is* your sister. And I love all of my girls. You, on the other hand" — he turns to Matilda — "I'm contemplating changing my will, so you don't see a penny of my fortune."

"You can't do this." Matilda purses her lips.

"Oh, I can, and I will. Unless—"

"Unless?" Matilda frowns.

"Unless Mirabelle tells me not to."

Matilda stiffens. She curls her fingers at her sides, then slowly straightens them out, before she turns to face me. "I am your step-mother. I did the best I could with you, but you were a difficult child. Always sad, always overeating. What was I supposed to do?"

I look away. All of my life, I wanted a chance for things to change between me and my father's wife and their children. I hoped, one day, they'd accept me as part of the family. I hoped... I'd be accepted by them, get their love. Maybe that's why I decided to go home after gradu-ation, while I was looking for a job. It was a last-ditch effort to get their approval. A final bid to find the belonging I'd always yearned for. But it's not the reason I turn to my father and say, "You don't need to cut her out completely."

Edward

"You're too forgiving." Cyril takes Belle's hand in his. "Anyone else in your position would have taken the opportunity to hit them where it hurts most, but not you."

After she made that announcement, I told her stepmother and half-sisters to leave. They marched off, similar expressions of petulance and arrogance on their features. Not one of them thanked her. Not one of them acknowledged her generosity.

Her father watched them go with a resigned expression before taking my wife's hand in his. "I am so sorry for everything you went through. I knew she wasn't doing right by you. I knew the three of them were making you unhappy. I knew it was my responsibility to stop them, but I didn't. I should have stepped in earlier. I should have told them to back down. I—" His eyes gleam with unshed tears. "I failed you. I failed your mother."

"No, you didn't." My wife goes into his arms. "You did well, Daddy. You were struggling with your grief. I know how much you miss Mama. It couldn't have been easy for you."

"I knew I wouldn't be able to take care of you. I was barely functioning, myself. Barely able to get through every day. It's why I married her. I hoped she'd be a good mother to you. Instead, I ended up hurting you."

"Don't apologize, Dad, please. You did your best."

"But it wasn't enough. I am so sorry I wasn't there for you when you needed me. So sorry, I put the interests of my company before your happiness. I am so sorry I put pressure on you to fulfill the obligation of an arranged marriage. I should have allowed you to choose your own life partner. Instead, I used you as leverage. Can you ever forgive me for it?"

"There's nothing to forgive." She sniffles.

He steps back and surveys her features. "If you're not happy"—he glares at me, then back at my wife—"if you want out of this arrangement, you only have to tell me. I'll give up everything to see you content."

"I'm... I'm..." She swallows. "I'm happy."

The tension drains out of my shoulders. I'm not sure what I was expecting her to say—that she hates her life. That she's trapped. That *I* trapped her? That *I* destroyed her life? If she wants to leave me, this is the chance. With her father's help, she could start a new life. She could file for divorce, and I wouldn't contest it, *if*...that's what she wants. I'll never go a single moment without thinking of her, but *if* she wants to be free of me... I won't stand in her way.

"You sure?" Cyril looks at her closely. "If you want to leave him—"

"I'm good, really."

He surveys her face again, then nods, before turning to look at me. "If you do anything to upset her, you'll have me to contend with."

"Understood, and I appreciate the sentiment."

"There they are." Arthur walks up, Tiny by his side.

The mutt brushes against my wife, who pats his big head. "How's my boy?" she says in a soft voice. "Did you miss me?"

Tiny makes a purring noise in his throat and leans into her touch. And damn, if I don't envy him. She loves him, that's clear. Could she still love me after everything I've done?

"I see you got rid of the three witches with a 'B,'" Arthur drawls. "No offense." He glances at Cyril.

"None taken." Cyril shrugs.

"Why did you invite them?" I lower my chin to my chest. "They're not family."

"They had a role to play." His eyes gleam, but the expression on his features does not change.

I stare at him, and he meets my gaze with an innocent look. *What the —? Did he invite them, knowing they'd prompt me to come to her rescue and help her make up with her father, thus providing more common ground between my wife and me? Nah, he can't be that strategic.* I frown. *Can he?* I tilt my head. *It'll bet that's why he invited Baron and Ava.* The canny old man wanted to prove to me I'm truly over my past. It's time to move forward, and what better way to bring that home than by having my best friend and the woman who I once thought I loved over for our family dinner? For me to able to look at them without feeling an ounce of envy or yearning. It proves to me, even more, that she is my future.

I glower at my grandfather; he beams back, a look of satisfaction on his features. The man is devious with his schemes. And of course, he'd justify it by saying he did it with our best interests at heart. In this case, sadly, I must agree.

Tiny looks between us and whines.

"I think he's hungry," my wife offers.

"He's always hungry. The dog has the appetite of a horse." Arthur clicks his tongue, and Tiny rises up and walks over to him. "Let's eat."

Arthur taps his fork against his champagne glass, and the talk around the table dies down. "I propose a toast."

"Oh, no," my wife whispers. I follow her glance to where Tiny is watching the bottle of champagne, which has been placed in a bucket next to Arthur, with an unflinching gaze.

"Shit, what was Arthur thinking?"

"Thinking about what?" Nathan asks from next to me.

"The champagne." I nod toward the bottle on ice. "The mutt likes champagne."

"You're kidding." He blinks.

"Nope." I shake my head."

"Umm, maybe we should do something?" my wife interjects.

"And steal Arthur's moment in the limelight?" Knox smirks from across the table.

"What are you'll nattering about?" Ava turns to my wife. She's seated next to her with Baron on her other side. My once-best friend, with whom I parted on good terms when he and Ava had gotten married —then failed to keep in touch with him. I've also avoided meeting his eyes all through dinner. *Loser* that I am. Because what can you say to a man who was practically your brother, in all but blood, and who you decided not to talk to because you were jealous. *Face it; you hated the fact he got the girl you thought you loved.* And I'd have continued thinking that way, but for the fact I found the one I really wanted. *And then you did everything in your power to alienate her. She should leave you. She should never forgive you. You should never forgive yourself.* How am I going to repent for what I did? I reach for the flute of champagne and raise it.

"Thank you to all of you for coming here to bring in the New Year. Congratulations to Edward—the first of my grandsons to get married."

"—but not the last." Knox coughs, and Nathan glares at him. He continues to smirk and raises his flute in Nathan's direction.

"A big welcome to the family, Mirabelle. You put up with Edward every day, and I can only thank you for that."

"Hear, hear," Sinclair calls out from across the table, and it's my turn to scowl at him.

"He doesn't deserve you, my dear, and if you ever need someone to kick his arse"—Arthur smirks, —"you only have to ask."

"And me," Sinclair adds.

"And me," Nathan calls out.

"I'll be at the head of the line," Knox growls.

I glance sideways to find Baron trying to hide a smile and failing. I scowl at Tiny, wondering when he's going to make a move. So far, he's been watching the bottle, but has seemed content to sit panting, his tongue lolling out one side of his jaw.

"Which brings me to the next point of business."

"Didn't realize this was a work thing," Nathan muses.

"With Arthur everything is work." Knox bares his teeth in what he must think is a smile; he resembles a shark who's smelled blood in the water.

"What's happening?" my wife whispers to me.

"Not sure." I place my arm about her shoulder, and she doesn't shake it off. Which is good, right? To be honest, I'm waiting for the other shoe to drop. I'm waiting for her to lose her temper with me and tell me she hates me and that she'll never forgive me. But none of that has been forthcoming. I rub the spot of tightness in my chest. Shouldn't have drunk so much coffee today. In my agitation over whether she was coming to dinner with me, I paced the floor of my home office, tried to work, kept going to the kitchen, hoping to run into her, and ended up swigging too much coffee.

"I'm confirming Nathan as the CEO of the company."

Knox stiffens. My wife turns to me. "Did you know this?"

I nod.

Nathan glances at me, a look of surprise on his feature that turns to wariness. "No," he growls.

I raise a shoulder. I had a word with the old man earlier today and told him I wasn't interested in being the CEO, not when it would mean being away for work and committing to working around the clock. I intend to spend a lot more of my time pursuing the only thing important to me—taking care of my wife's needs and making sure she wants for nothing. Arthur didn't seem surprised. If anything, he seconded me and told me I was making the right decision.

Nathan turns to fix his glare on Arthur, not that it makes a difference. The old codger wears a grin on his face. His eyes twinkle. "Which means, Nathan, you have three months to get married."

"Fuck." Nathan's fingers stiffen on the stem of his flute, which cracks. The champagne spills; the glass hits the table and rolls to the end. That's when Tiny jumps up on his hind legs and snatches the bottle of champagne and downs it.

"That was eventful." I unlock the front door of my house and gesture to my wife to enter.

"I can't believe no one noticed us leaving."

"They were too busy trying to find Tiny," who, after emptying the bottle of champagne in one, dropped the bottle at Arthur's feet and grinned. No, he really grinned. There was a smile on his face, until he noticed the stunned look on my grandfather's features and realized he'd committed a booboo. Which is when he bounded into the house—with Nathan, Knox and Sinclair in hot pursuit.

I turned to find Baron at my elbow. "We need to talk," he said.

"Yes, we do,"—I looked away, then back at him—" but not now."

"Not now,"—Baron nodded— "but we will."

"We will." I held out my hand, but he bypassed that and hugged me. I was surprised, then hugged him back. Something settled in my chest.

I've missed my friend. But I'm not that selfish, bitter man who cut him and Ava out of my life. I am a husband in love with his wife. I'm ready to make amends and move on with my life. Baron must sense my thoughts because, when he stepped back, he's smiling. He walked back to Ava and I... I left with Belle.

On the ride home, I hoped she'd forgiven me. I prayed she'd find it within her to give me a second chance. I've made my peace with Him, thanks to her; and I'm not beyond turning to Him in the hope he'll work a miracle and have her forgive me.

Now, I slide the coat off her shoulders because it's a legitimate way to be close to her. As is the sniff I take of her hair. How else am I going to sleep if I don't store up her scent in my lungs?

"Did you sniff me?" She glances over her shoulder, a strange look on her face.

"I...did," I admit.

"Can I sniff you back?"

I nod, sure my mouth is open in surprise and not doing anything to hide it.

She goes up on tiptoe, places her nose close to my neck, and takes a deep breath. A shiver grips her, and I can't stop myself from rubbing her arm. "Are you cold?"

"Electricity." She looks up at me. "Every time I smell your scent, a frisson of something runs up my spine."

"And every time I look at you, every time I see you, every time I sniff you, I know I wouldn't be able to bear it if you left me. Don't leave me, wife, please." I go down on my knees. "I can't function without you. I can't see myself without you. I wouldn't know what to do with myself. My heart would stop beating; my body would stop functioning. I am nothing without you, wife, nothing."

73

Mira

"Oh, Eddie." Tears prick the backs of my eyes. His every word is like a balm on the jagged wound in my heart. One I hadn't even been aware of. Maybe I've been numb since he confessed to me. Not just about what he did to me...but what happened to him. I'm still digesting the details. That talk with Summer helped, of course. It put things in perspective. He's a complex person, my husband. So many layers to him. Layers I'm still unwrapping.

"I love you, wife. More than anything. You have to believe me."

"I do." I swallow.

He looks up at me and his eyes shimmer. "Then don't leave me."

"I need...some time, some space to decide what I want. You understand that?"

He nods. His fingers tighten on mine, then he kisses my knuckles. "Whatever you want."

"And you can't stalk me or put cameras or bugs on any of my devices, or even in my car."

He doesn't seem happy with it, but nods.

"And I'll need to move out of the house."

"No." His lips thin.

"If you love me, you'll let me have this time."

A tortured expression flits across his features, then he nods slowly.

"And I won't be working at the office nursery."

"What?" He rises to his feet. "Don't do this, wife. It's the fact that you're under my roof during the day that lets me breathe."

"Nothing is going to happen to me." I cup his chin. "I promise. I just need to be on my own, so I can think things through."

He doesn't respond.

"You helped me find myself; now give me a little time to figure out what's in my mind."

His expression grows more intense. "Wife, I—" He squeezes the bridge of his nose, then lowers his arm. "This is what you need to figure things out?"

I nod.

"What are you going to do? Where are you going to live?"

"I still have my flat."

"Didn't you sublet it?"

I nod. "To a friend who moved to London, but she's happy to share with me."

"And what are you going to do?"

"I've been saving the very generous salary you've been paying me. I'm going to invest it in the preschool where I used to work."

"I thought that shut down."

I nod. "The owners took out a loan and are going to re-open it. I'm putting my money in, so I'll have a share of it."

"Look at you." Pride shines in his eyes. "I am so proud you're doing this."

"Oh." I blink. I was sure he'd tell me he would buy out the preschool for me. The fact that he didn't, and that he's encouraging me in this venture, is a surprise. And it feels so good. I throw my arms around his neck. "Thank you, husband."

His entire body stiffens, then a shudder runs up his spine. When I lean back, he has a look of shock on his face.

"What's wrong?" I murmur.

"You called me husband."

"You are my husband, last I checked." I turn and begin to walk away, putting an extra twitch in my butt and an extra bounce in my step. Knowing he's following me, knowing his gaze is firmly fixed on my ass. I reach the kitchen, head to the kettle, and fill it. Then switch it on and set it to boil. I place my palm on my hip and turn to find he's standing by the doorway, watching me, a hungry look on his face.

"Would you like a cup of tea?"

"Sure." His voice is hoarse.

I pop out one hip; he swallows. And when I push my hair over one shoulder to reveal the low neckline on the back of the dress, he reaches up and loosens his tie. Stifling a smile, I turn and rise up on tiptoes to reach for the teabags, when suddenly he's behind me. His heat sears my back, and his fingers brush mine as he gets to the pack of teabags before me.

"Here." He places it on the counter, hesitates, then slowly backs away. *Whoa, he's really giving me space.*

I place a teabag in each cup, pour the water in, then hand him a cup.

"Want to watch the fireworks on the tele and usher in the New Year?" He holds out his hand, and I place mine in his.

He leads me over to the living room. I place the tea on the coffee table, sink down into the couch, then kick off my stilettos and pull my legs up under me. He sits down next to me, and switches on the television, before reaching for a blanket and placing it over me. I snuggle in, and when he places his arm over the back of the couch and behind my neck, I lean in and push my cheek into his chest.

The television screen shows New Year celebrations in progress from around the world. I snuggle into him, and he wraps his arm about me and pulls me even closer. As the New Year dawns in different countries, the TV beams images of fireworks and celebrations from their respective capital cities.

"I'd love to travel to all these places," I murmur.

"Anything you want." He runs his fingers through my hair. "I love you, wife."

I turn my nose into his chest and kiss his vest-covered abs. "I love you, too, but—"

The planes of his chest tighten, "But?"

"But I still need time to work out what I want for my future."

On screen, the ten-minute countdown to the New Year begins. Fireworks commence over the Thames, highlighting the London Eye, the Shard, Big Ben, the Houses of Parliament, St. Paul's Church, and other landmarks.

"It's gorgeous," I gasp.

"You are."

I glance up to find he's staring at me. Heat flushes my face. "I was talking about the fireworks."

"I only see you."

He presses a kiss to my forehead, then directs me back to the television. A dazzling display of pyrotechnics, lights, and music illuminates the night sky on screen. The fireworks are choreographed to a soundtrack that gets my blood racing. My heartbeat speeds up. My pulse thrums to the beat. Or maybe it's because of his nearness. How tenderly he holds me. How I know he stares at me like I'm the most important thing in his life.

I keep my gaze focused on the spectacle unfolding on the TV. London's skyline is transformed into a canvas of colors and patterns as the fireworks continue. It's spectacular and breathtaking and even more special because I'm bringing in the New Year in his arms.

When the final ten-second countdown begins, he notches his knuckles under my chin, stares into my eyes.

"Can I kiss you?"

74

Edward

She nods. *Thank fuck.* Without wasting a second, I lean in and gently fit my mouth over hers. I pour all of my feelings into the kiss. My love for her, my need for her, my apology for how I turned her world upside down. My regret for everything I did that upset her. I'm only a man—hopelessly, completely devoted to his wife, and I try to signal that through my lips on hers. I nip on her lower lip; she moans, parts her lips. I slide my tongue over hers and deepen the kiss. She melts into me. Every pore on my skin is alive, heat squeezes my chest, and my groin hardens. I pull her into my lap, slide my hand over her butt and squeeze.

She gasps, then leans back. "Eddie—" she swallows. "I... I'm not—"

I place my finger over her mouth. "I'm sorry." I squeeze my eyes shut. "I'm trying to be the kind of man you want, but I seem to be making a mess of it."

I release her, and she slides back onto the couch. "It's okay."

"It's not. I want to do everything right. I can't fuck this up, wife; not when it's my last chance to win you over."

"Is that what you're doing? Winning me over?" she asks with a laugh.

"Not doing a great job of it, obviously." I adjust myself, then rise to my feet. "Can I take you to bed?"

She blinks.

"I mean..."—I rub my fingers through my hair—"can I carry you to your bed? And only because I know your feet hurt after wearing those pumps."

When she nods, I switch off the television, then scoop her up in my arms. She cuddles into me, and I walk up the stairs, then place her on her feet next to the bed. I walk into her closet and emerge with the T-shirt—my T-shirt—she likes to wear to bed. I place it down, then bend and kiss her forehead. "Goodnight, wife."

Before I can change my mind, I head for the doorway.

"Eddie," she calls out.

I stop.

"You need to make your peace with Baron."

I don't reply.

"You need to move on from what happened, and this is the only way out."

I stay silent, and she blows out a breath. "For me, husband? Please."

She knows I'll do anything for her. *Even this.*

It's been two weeks since she moved out. Two very long, lonely weeks, during which I've been barely functional. I knew I was being insufferable at work, until Nathan barged into my office yesterday and barked at me to take the day off and not come back until I've gotten my shit together. I left and wandered the city aimlessly. I kept finding myself walking in the direction of her flat and barely managed to stop myself before I reached it.

Instead, I went home, changed into my running gear, and ran until I was too tired to think straight. Then I went back home, crawled into her bed, under her bedclothes, to try and find some shut eye. Still, I stuck to my promise. I had already removed all my hidden cameras and wiretaps from her devices and her car and had told my investigators to stop following her.

It feels like I cut off a part of myself, but I've done what she asked of me. I also managed to not text or call, and fuck, if that hasn't just about killed me. If it weren't for the fact that Summer is keeping me updated

—without my prompting—that they're hanging out with mutual friends and she's good, I don't know what I'd do.

I wake up very early, after managing to get a few hours of sleep, and decide to go for another run. Now, I gaze at the skyline of London spread out over me.

There are no tourists at Primrose Hill at this time of the morning. It's quiet, except for the footsteps of the jogger who runs by. To the side a couple works out. He holds onto her legs as she goes through a series of sit-ups. Then she does the same for him. They're equal partners, at least for the duration of this exercise session, and so in sync, it hints at their being together for a while. They finish their workout, and he helps her to her feet, then pulls her close and kisses her. She laughs and hugs him, before they jog down the hill.

That's when I see him. A tall man with broad shoulders wearing a pair of sweats. He begins to jog up the slope. His gait is familiar. The way he holds himself straight, his elbows tucked into his sides, his steps even as he approaches me—all of it is so very familiar. As he nears me, I focus on the view once more. He reaches the bench I'm sitting on and sinks down on the opposite side. For a few seconds, we stay silent. His breathing evens out. I reach for my bottle of water and offer it to him. He takes it without comment and chugs from it, before placing it in the space between us.

"Thanks, man," he murmurs.

I nod. "Sorry it took me a while to reach out to you."

Baron shakes his head. "Never too late. I'm glad you did."

"I almost didn't,"—I rub the back of my neck—"but she insisted."

"The wife always knows best," he says without any hint of sarcasm.

"No disputing that." I laugh. "And how's the kid?" I swallow. There, I said it. When I found out Ava was pregnant, it hurt. And I couldn't understand why my reaction was so extreme.

I'd already accepted Ava and Baron were meant for each other. He'd been looking for her since he'd first seen her as a girl. I was the man who abandoned her to find myself. At the time, I blamed her for being the reason I left the church, but time and perspective showed me I would have done so anyway. Meeting her and realizing I hadn't dealt with any of my issues was the trigger. But if not that, it would have been something else.

So, it was a shock when hearing they were having a child left me in despair. It took falling in love with my wife and realizing there's a chance I might lose her to put that in perspective. Because as much as it hurt to see Baron and Ava together, and to find out she was pregnant, nothing compares to how devastated I was when my wife asked me to give her space to figure things out.

The fact I can't see her every day, can't be in the same space as her, can't look into her eyes or watch as she works in the nursery—all of it is gut-wrenching. It feels like someone reached into my throat and pulled out my heart. For she has it. She has me. And when I can't be with her, it feels like everything is pointless. Like I've reached the end of my line. Like nothing I do has meaning without her being part of it.

"The kid's good." He laughs. "We're going through the entire sleep-less night thing, but man, Ava is so fucking good. She's up at all hours of the night nursing, and I try to relieve her, but of course, the baby needs her right now. I try to stay up with her, and she insists I get my sleep because I have to work the next day. Like that matters. She's doing the most important thing possible—the real stuff, the stuff that's messy and genuine and bloody tough. And she's still worried about me."

"I know the feeling."

He peers closely at my features. "That's good, Ed, really good."

I finally meet his gaze. "I'm sorry I didn't stay in touch with you. I… I needed time… Or maybe, that's an excuse. To be honest, I wasn't thinking straight. I didn't want to be jealous of the two of you. I know you two were made for each other, and yet… I couldn't stop myself from wanting what you had. I felt terrible about it but couldn't stop myself. I was envious of the two of you, and I'm not proud of it."

"It takes guts to accept it, and even more courage to share that with me," he murmurs.

"Yeah, well…" I scratch at my unshaven chin. "My wife told me I needed to talk to you."

"And here you are." His lips curve in a smile.

"Indeed."

"And now, you have what Ava and I do." His smile widens.

"I do." I allow myself a small smile. "What we went through, Baron, was the kind of thing that turns men into addicts and makes them do things that destroy their lives. We're lucky we didn't end up there."

"Thanks to the women in our lives who stopped us from going off the deep end. They helped us find the humanity in ourselves. They helped us get in touch with our emotions and all that shit. Which we used to look down on." He chuckles.

I rub the back of my neck. It's true, what he's saying. When the seven of us would get together, before any of us met our women and got married, we'd look down on anything to do with sentiments and feelings. And all the stuff that makes life worth living. And when the men started getting hitched, we'd mock them for being pussy-whipped. I didn't realize there's a special kind of happiness in meeting the right woman. In coming home to her every night. In waking up next to her every morning. In sharing life's ups and downs, the good and the bad, and the stuff that makes it all so worthwhile.

There's a touch on my shoulder. I glance up to find Baron watching me with serious eyes. "She's too good for you, of course."

"Of course." I half smile.

"And you're torn about something related to her?"

I'm not surprised Baron sensed that. We've been through so much together. Amongst the seven of us, Baron and I have always shared a special bond. One I didn't value until I didn't have it in my life. Wisdom truly is based on hindsight, and... When it comes to her, I'm going to make sure I never have cause to say that.

"I may have done things which caused her unhappiness. I was selfish. I only thought about myself. Now, I see I could have done things differently. She's the most important thing to me, and now, I realize... I should have approached her in a different fashion. I should have been more open, allowed her to see my foibles, my weaknesses, my fears"—I wince—"the hurt, the pain I hold within me. I should have allowed her to feel it. I should have—" I swallow around the ball of emotions in my throat. "I should have told her how much I loved her much earlier."

"But you did tell her, so don't be too hard on yourself. You're facing your feelings. You're embracing the fall-out from the incident. You're allowing yourself to be vulnerable, Edward. You're on the right path..."

"But?" I look between his eyes.

"But"—he opens, then shuts his mouth— "it's not my place to say it."

"I want to hear it." Before I ceased all communication with him, Baron was my conscience. After the incident, when my parents turned their backs on me, when I turned to alcohol and drugs as a teenager to cope with the guilt I felt about what had happened to me, it was Baron who rescued me from myself. Also, he's a successful husband and father. If anyone knows what I should be doing to ensure I don't fuck up this chance I have been given at finding true love with Belle, then it's him. "Tell me, Baron." I squeeze his shoulder. "You'll be doing me a favor."

"You need to forgive yourself for everything that happened to you."

I lower my hand and glance away.

"You know I'm right, Edward. You need to complete this journey you're on. You need to heal yourself, so you can be whole again, for her."

75

Edward

"Go on." Baron nods toward the church in front of which we're parked. I took his advice to heart. I knew what I had to do, the final step in finding absolution. When Baron realized I intended to go back to the same church where I'd served as the pastor, he immediately insisted on driving me. "I'll wait here for you," he adds.

"You're a good friend," I pause with my hand on the door handle. "I'm sorry I didn't keep in touch with you and Ava. I'm sorry I hurt the both of you."

"It's in the past." Baron cuts the air with his palm. "What you're doing is very brave, Edward, make no mistake."

I step out of the car, then head for the doorway of the church. My heart begins to hammer in my chest, and my pulse rate shoots up. My breath comes in pants, and it takes everything within me to push open the door and step inside. The scent of incense envelops me, transporting me right back to the days I spent here preaching to my flock. We hit morning rush hour traffic on the way here, but the church is still empty. And so silent, every thud of my heart feels like it's playing through a boombox. I swallow down the ball of emotion in my throat, take a step forward.

Like a tractor beam, my gaze is instantly captured by the cross on the wall at the end of the aisle. The sunlight pours in through the stained glass from above it. I step forward, and the light blinds me for an instant. I move past it, and it's as if I can see everything in relief. Dust motes dance and beckon me forward. My footsteps make a hushed thud that echoes in the space. The candles flicker in the side chapels in the distance. And when I pass the confessional where I almost took a life, the hairs on the back of my neck stand up. That's when I know, I've done the right thing by coming here. I need to face the past so I can move forward... With her.

The scent of beeswax, of wood and stone, the vibrations of all the prayers by the faithful who have passed through this church before me, embrace me and urge me on. I reach the altar and sink to my knees.

I lower my chin to my chest, press my palms together in front, and close my eyes. For a few seconds, I allow myself to flow into that space deep inside of me. The one I haven't visited since I left the priesthood behind. Oh, I prayed to Him when I found out she was unwell, and again, in the hope He'd help her forgive me. But I didn't truly face my past. I didn't ask Him for forgiveness for killing the man who facilitated the incident and everything that happened to me and the Seven.

I didn't ask Him to help me forgive myself. I didn't ask for His help to dissolve these feelings of unworthiness which have haunted me since my abuse.

I haven't allowed myself to revisit any of it since turning my back on Baron and Ava...and the Church. I left to travel.

I've spent so long running away from my past... But I'm done now. Baron's right. It's not enough to reconcile with Him, as I've barely done with my recent prayers. No, I need to ask him for absolution.

I traverse that familiar path to the deepest part of my heart, and when I think I can't go deeper, I sink even further into that nothingness I once used to be so familiar with. That emptiness where I could face myself. That sense of being here and yet, also, being in a space where all of my walls drop away. Where I, once more, stand naked before Him.

"My Lord, I am heartily sorry for having offended Thee,
     and I detest all my sins, because I dread the loss of heaven

and the pains of hell, but most of all because they offend Thee,
my God,
> who art all-good and deserving of all my love.
> I firmly resolve, with the help of Thy grace,
> to confess my sins, to do penance, and to amend my life.
> Amen."

The words pour out of me. I allow the feelings of hurt, despair, of loneliness…of guilt, of fear, of hate, and revenge—all of it—to gush forward. I open myself up and allow His healing touch to embrace me. I allow that feeling of repentance to consume me. I bow my head and surrender to His grace. To that sense of oneness that has always resided in me, since I was little. That feeling of peace which has evaded me since the incident.

I see the loathing which has become a part of me since the incident. The guilt I've carried since I almost took a life. The envy which ate into me when I watched Ava and Baron.

And I feel the relief of having found my sweet Belle. The love that overwhelmed me when I saw her but which I didn't allow myself to acknowledge, until I was shocked into realizing I could lose her.

And really, all of it is His doing. It's He who led me to her. He who brought her into my life. All I am, is His instrument. I renounce myself to His will and ask for His guidance.

Show me the way, Father. Tell me what to do next.

"Edward?"

A familiar voice reaches me. I look around to find a fellow priest and friend, who was ordained with me and served with me in this very church.

"Zephyr, Brother, I have come to confess."

"You seem lighter." Baron shoots me a sideways glance as we wait for the signal to change.

I went into the confessional and allowed myself to speak without reservation. I hadn't realized how much I needed to do that until, with every word I spoke, the load I carried lifted. Oh, I'd confessed when I was a priest, but I was a different man then. Everything I've faced since leaving the Church has changed me. I've matured, and I've fallen in love. I found her, and she helped me find my faith. In a strange way, I had to lose myself completely to find the true me again. I know, I'll need more therapy to deal with the repercussions of the incident, and my later actions. But I know, coming full circle and revisiting the Church, where I found my faith and lost it, only to be united with it again, is pivotal in healing myself.

"Thank you, Baron." I turn to him. "I couldn't have done this without you."

Baron shakes his head. "The credit goes to you for having the courage to take the first step. I didn't do anything. I—"

My phone buzzes in my pocket, and Baron pauses. I pull it out, then sit upright and answer it. "Wife, are you okay?"

76

———

Mira

"Let me through, that's my wife in there," Eddie's angry voice reaches us.

Dr. Kincaid and I exchange glances, but before he can say anything, my husband barges into the examination room. It's a tiny room with just enough space for the exam table and the doctor—who is not a small man—and with Eddie's big body in the space, it seems to shrink even further in size. He walks over to me and rakes his gaze down my features. I'm the one on the exam table, but he's the one who looks pale, like he may be about to faint.

There are dark circles under his eyes, hollows under his cheekbones, and he's lost weight. Just enough to make him look leaner, meaner, and hungrier than when I last saw him. And god, I've missed him so much. It took everything within me not to reach for the phone and call him over the last two weeks.

I left to give myself space to think, and I knew the only way I could work through my thoughts was if I focused on myself. I threw all of my efforts into the new preschool—worked on the curriculum, the staffing requirements, health and nutrition plans for the children.

We decided to revamp everything and start from scratch, doing things a bit differently this time. I was in my element, and the fact I'm building something that is, in part, my own, makes me almost giddy with happiness. I feel fulfilled, for the first time in my life. But I also miss him.

It doesn't matter that he stalked me, was obsessed with me, and used my circumstances to steer me into marrying him. No matter what he's been through, no matter the mistakes he's made, I missed my husband. And when the motorcyclist hit me this morning and I crumpled to the road, my only thought was that if I died then, it would be without telling him how I feel about him. That I love him and want to spend every moment with him. Apparently, it took my life flashing in front of my eyes for me to realize he's in my corner. He's my ride or die. He's the man for me.

He takes my hand in his, then brings it up and kisses my knuckles. "Wife, you're, okay?"

"I'm okay, honestly. The motorcycle just brushed me."

"You were hit by a motorcycle?" He sways.

"I'm fine; nothing is hurt."

"You have scratches on your cheek." He surveys my features. And when he brings his fingers to the bandage on my forehead, his fingers tremble. "Your poor face."

"It's nothing, really."

"It's not nothing." The skin around his lips tightens. "And your legs--" He looks down at the expanse left uncovered by my skirt.

"I know, I have a few scratches there, and a wound on my knee, for which I had to receive a couple of stitches, but really, I'm fine."

"Fuck!" He drags his fingers through his hair. "Stitches? You had to have stitches?"

"Just two," the doctor says in a dry voice.

"Don't make it out to be less than what it was." He turns and points a finger at the doctor. "You're supposed to make it all better. Instead, you're standing there doing nothing."

"I'm a doctor, not a magician," Dr. Kincaid protests. "Also, she's a little shaken, but the wounds are minimal. The man who ran into her called for an ambulance right away. In fact, he's waiting outside, and—"

"He's waiting outside?" My husband pivots and stalks toward the door, but the doctor steps in his path. "Easy, Tiger. Accidents happen."

"Not with her, they don't," my husband growls.

"It would have been a lot worse if he'd gone on his way without bringing her in," the doctor says in a soothing voice.

"That's no excuse."

"That's true." He hesitates. "All I'm saying is, don't go out there and beat him up. And not in a hospital, for chrissakes."

"Alright then, I'm going to drag him out and smash his face in, and—"

"Fleabag!"

He stiffens. Is it because I used the safe word? I've never used it, but it seemed like the only way to stop him. But I didn't expect to see the shock on his face when he turns to face me.

"Wife?" He swallows. "Did you just—"

"Say fleabag?" I nod. "Didn't see any other way of stopping you. It was my fault. Honestly. I was in my own world and crossed when the pedestrian cross sign was red. It was *my* fault."

He draws in a breath, then slowly walks back to me. He takes my hand in his again and holds my gaze. "I'm sorry, I lost my temper. Seeing you hurt and helpless is more than I can bear. I've been berating myself ever since Weston called me and told me you were in hospital. It's a good thing I was with Baron when I got the call, or I might not have made it here."

I stare. "You were with Baron?"

"You were with Baron?" Dr. Kincaid asks at the same time.

"Yes, I was." My husband flushes. He releases his grip on my fingers, then stuffs his hand in the pocket of his sweatshirt.

A sweatshirt, people! Not that I don't find his three-piece-suited-and-vested look sexy, but Eddie unshaven and in a hoodie, and in grey sweatpants that outline that appendage between his legs, is drool-worthy. I squeeze my thighs together. My husband darts me a look. A gleam comes into his eyes as if he senses my reaction to his presence, but he doesn't comment. Instead, he gives me that half smile which brings out the divot in his cheek. "I took your advice."

"I'm glad you did," I murmur.

"About time the two of you made up," Dr. Kincaid growls.

"Someone talking about me?" Baron walks in. "Weston." He and the doctor bump fists, then he fixes his gaze on my husband.

"I spoke with the man outside who was responsible for the accident."

My husband begins to speak, but Baron raises his hand. "The man was digging a groove in the floor with his pacing. He was extremely sorry and apologetic. And at the risk of being beaten up, by all counts, it wasn't his fault."

"It wasn't. I was the one who ran into his path. I crossed when I shouldn't have."

"Glad you're doing okay." Baron smiles at me.

A nurse walks in, then stops when she sees all three men. And whoa, the three of them together are like a rugby defense team, with their height and broad shoulders. Lord alone knows how it is when all seven of them are in the same room. It probably results in an overload of pheromones that attracts all the women within a square mile of them.

"Oh, I'm sorry, Doctor Kincaid. I didn't realize you were still here. I wanted to check if the patient is being admitted?"

The doctor looks at me, then shakes his head. "I'm discharging you. You need to take it easy though, get some rest, lots of fluids… And stay warm."

"I'll make sure she does," my husband vows.

"Thank you, doctor" I tell him.

He smiles and nods at me, claps Baron on his shoulder, shakes Edward's hand, and leaves.

Baron looks between us. "Can I give you both a lift home?"

77

———————

Edward

I walk toward my wife and scoop her up in my arms, leaving Baron to get her bag.

"I can walk," she murmurs.

"Not when I can carry you."

To my surprise, she doesn't protest. She snuggles in, and I take her to the car. I place her in the back seat, then walk around and slide in next to her.

"Where to, folks?" Baron looks at us in the mirror.

"Her address is—" I begin, but my wife cuts me off. "We're going to your place."

"We are?" I jerk my chin in her direction.

"We are," she confirms with a soft smile on her face.

Baron meets my gaze in the rearview mirror, nods, then eases the car forward. In the forty-five minutes it takes us to reach home through traffic, she falls asleep on my shoulder. I manage to text my housekeeper and let her know she can finish up for the day and leave. I want my wife all to myself when I get her home. She opted to come with me, probably because she feels weak and shaken, and while I never want to see anything like this happen to her again, I'm not going to waste this opportunity to hold her. We draw up at my place. I thank Baron, then hook her handbag over my shoulder and carry her inside. When I approach her bedroom, she stirs. "Are we home?"

Home. She called this home. *I hope she thinks of my home as her home, too.* She's probably out of it; that's why she called it home.

"We are." I walk into her room, but she shakes her head.

"Your room." She looks up at me with her big blue eyes. "I want you to take me to your bedroom."

I swallow. "Are you sure?"

She nods.

"I don't want you to feel beholden to me for anything. I know I rushed to the hospital, and I know I was worried about you, but I don't want this to make you feel compelled to want to be with me."

"And what if I do want it?" Her gaze intensifies. "What if I told you I've missed you and couldn't wait to be with you. And when I was run into and fell to the ground, all I could see was your face in front of my eyes. And I realized that if I can't be with you, my life will be incomplete."

"Then I have to say, He's listened to my prayers." I start toward my room.

"You've been praying?"

"Not daily, and nowhere near as much as I did in my past life as a priest. But I admit, I've been beseeching Him to give me a second chance with you." I glance down at her. "You have to know nothing is worth seeing you hurt. I'd rather you be safe and unharmed than have you here with me, having almost been run down."

"It was just a nudge, honestly." She rubs her cheek against my chest. "And the guy who was on the bike was really sorry. I was sure he was going to burst into tears when he helped me up on the sidewalk. And I told him I was okay, but he insisted on calling the ambulance. And then Dr. Kincaid happened to be at the hospital as they brought me in—"

"I'm glad he was, and that he called me."

"I'm glad he did, too. The only person I wanted to see then was you."

I place her on my bed gently, then sit down next to her. "How are you feeling? Do you want something to eat? Maybe some herbal tea?"

A buzzing sound fills the air. I pick up her bag and bring it over to her. She pulls out her phone and answers it. "Hi, Summer. No, I'm okay."

I can hear the woman's voice rise in pitch on the other side.

"No, I'm good, really. I'm here with Eddie."

The voice on the other side says something, and my wife blushes. "I'm sure, I don't want you to come and get me. Honestly, I'm good. Yeah, I'm spending the night here." She nods. "Thanks, I'll keep you updated." She switches off the phone and slides it into her bag. I place it on the nightstand.

She leans back against her pillows and yawns again. "I'm so tired."

"The shock must be wearing off." I pull the sheets up to her chin. "You should rest."

"That was Summer. She asked me if I was moving back with you."

My heart somersaults in my ribcage. Sweat pools under my arms. I'll never take what we have for granted. Never take the fact that she's my wife and in my bed as a *fait accompli*. Never stop myself from telling her how much I love her, every day, for the rest of my life. And if You're really up there and watching over me, then please, let her say yes, please. I swallow, and when I don't say anything, she lowers her chin to her chest.

"Don't you want to know what my reply was?"

78

———————

A week later

Mira

"What made you decide you wanted to be with him?" Summer peers through the huge floor-to-ceiling windows at the snowflakes that float down to the ground. It's been snowing since the morning, enough to cover the trees with white and disrupt the trains in the city. Enough for the weather people to predict that this will be the heaviest snowfall in the last fifty years, or something like that. Truth is, I'm happy to snuggle up on the couch in the living room and watch the snow from here. I'm happy for my husband to wait hand and foot on me. He insists on carrying me everywhere in the house, and on bathing me and feeding me. He's given the housekeeper—who I finally managed to meet and say 'hi' to—the week off so he can tend to me alone.

He also hasn't gone to work; hasn't even checked his phone. So much so, Nathan finally called *me* and asked to speak to him. He must have invited himself over because, a few hours ago, he arrived at our doorstep. Summer was right behind him. I convinced Edward I'd be fine with her for company for a few hours. He told Summer to keep an eye on me and retreated to his study with Nathan to catch up on his office related matters, but only after I insisted he leave us.

She turns to me. "He does seem cray-cray about you."

"He is." I nod.

"And you're sure you want to do this?" She waves in the direction of the doorway he disappeared through.

I nod again.

"What made you decide to forgive him?"

"It wasn't just one thing." I wind a strand of hair around my fingers. "Or maybe, it was the way he knew I was resistant to Penicillin, something I tend to forget."

"But he remembered?"

"He did…when the doctor asked. If he hadn't, I'm sure he'd have recommended Penicillin for me, and that wouldn't have any impact. Frankly, that shook me a little. That he knew it and had the presence of mind to bring it up to the doctor, when"—I swallow—"when my own father doesn't know that about it."

"Oh, honey." She walks over and sits down on the couch next to me. "I'm so sorry."

"Of course, he seems to be coming around. He did stand up for me at Arthur's New Year party."

"The one where the Witches of Eastwick were kicked out of?"

I laugh. "The same. And he came to my rescue when they were horrible to me, too."

She nods.

"No one has been in my corner for so long. All those years growing up and feeling on my own, trying to win my stepmother's approval. It's only after meeting Eddie that I realized I was looking for a place to call my own. I was looking for…" I glance about the living room with its elegant, yet comfortable couch; the deep armchairs; the fireplace he lit earlier; the Christmas tree up in the corner, which he hasn't taken down yet, at my request; the windows that look out on the garden; the floor lamps lit at intervals; the lush carpeting on the floor—all of it is so Eddie and yet, also, so me. If I'd picked out the furniture for the place, I'd have probably ended up with the same look. "Home. I was looking for somewhere to belong to, but meeting Eddie made me realize home is wherever he is."

"You realized all this while you were away?"

I nod. "I know it should have taken me much longer, but for that small accident I had. It shook me, and all I wanted was Eddie by my side, holding my hand and telling me it would all be okay."

She smiles a little. "And you've forgiven everything he did?"

"Do I forgive him for spying on me without my permission and for replacing my contraceptive pills?" *And for almost taking the life of a man who was responsible for what happened to him and his friends. A man whose actions emotionally scarred a twelve-year-old boy for life?* I shake back my hair. "I do."

Besides, who's to say what's right and wrong. Aren't these rules made by man, after all?

She begins to speak, and I hold up my hand. "All I know is, good or bad, he's mine. He stalked me because he wanted me. He replaced my birth-control pills because he thought he was tainted by the incident. He was sure if I found out what he'd been through, I'd never want to be the mother of his child."

"And now?" She tilts her head.

"Now, I believe he loves me enough to never do anything to hurt me again."

She looks into my features and her smile broadens. "I'm so happy you and Ed found each other. I always worried about him. Of all the Seven, he's the one the incident affected the most. He's the one who seemed to carry the most secrets. He's also the most sensitive, though he never showed it. I always hoped he'd find a woman who'd love him as he is and you, my dear friend, are the perfect foil for him."

She throws her arms about me, and I hug her back. When the doorbell rings, she sniffs and breaks away. "I invited Gio and the girls. I hope you don't mind. It felt like the right time to celebrate."

She walks away and opens the door, and when my friends join me, I can't stop myself from smiling widely. I've found my tribe, and my man, and oh my god, it's everything I hoped for, and more.

"Is there a party in progress?" My husband walks past Gio, sprawled in one of the armchairs, and Penny, in the other. Both are holding glasses of champagne. Summer and Abby are in the kitchen, getting us all some snacks. He approaches me, leans a hip on the arm of the couch, then leans in and kisses my forehead. "How's my wife doing?"

"I'm perfect." I beam up at him.

He holds my gaze, and when that tiny divot appears in his cheek, I fall for him all over again. He leans in and kisses me. I allow myself to sink into his embrace, to draw in his scent and curl my fingers around that rock-like bicep of his, when the sound of someone clearing their throat infiltrates my subconscious. My husband softens the kiss, surveys my flushed features, and a smirk curls his lips.

"I'm off then, Ed," Nathan rumbles from his position in the doorway of the living room.

"Don't forget the site visit tomorrow," my husband says without taking his gaze from my face.

"Site visit?" Nathan frowns.

"It's one of Arthur's new pet projects. A bakery he's set on acquiring."

"A bakery?" Nathan stiffens. "The fuck does he want to do that?"

"You know the old man," Eddie manages to tear his gaze from mine and train it on Nathan. "Once has his mind set on something, he's not going to veer from it."

Nathan snorts, "More like, he's going senile."

"And his befuddled image is just that." My husband raises a shoulder." A front. He's a canny bastard who knows what he wants."

"Which is to get his grandchildren married off," Nathan says in a bitter tone.

"Not that I'm complaining." Eddie pulls me closer.

Nathan looks between us, and a strange look crosses his face. A mixture of longing and jealousy, if I'm interpreting it correctly. "You're a lucky wanker—sorry about the swearing ladies." He apologizes to my friends.

"We've heard worse." Gio waves a regal hand. "We're married to men who were all growly-faces like you at one point—"

"Then they fell for the right woman and reformed," Summer says with a sunny smile.

Nathan squares his shoulders, and his expression morphs into one of resolution, like he's making up his mind. "You mean, they're hooked to the ol' ball and chain?" He coughs.

"We heard that," Abby sings out as she and Penny enter the room with a bowl of popcorn, another of nachos, and a third one with salsa.

"A fate I intend to avoid at any cost," he growls.

My husband and I share a quiet smile. Gio and Penny, on the other hand, have no qualms, bursting into laughter.

"Poor man." I shake my head. "I feel sorry for what's coming."

"Something I'm missing?" Nathan frowns.

"No, nothing." Eddie stifles a grin. "Just as long as you make it to the bakery tomorrow."

Nathan drags his fingers through his hair. "Feels like a waste of my time. What do I know about the bakery business, anyway?"

To find out what happens next read Nathan and Skylar's story in The Unwanted Wife

Read an excerpt:

Skylar

"I can't do this." I lock my fingers together and narrow my gaze at my reflection. I'm in the tiny bathroom adjoining my office at the back of my bakery—my baby, my enterprise into which I've poured my lifesavings. And now, it's going to shut down. Unless I find the money for the rent next month, and for the utilities to keep the lights on so the sign on the shopfront continues to be lit up in pink and yellow neon, and for the supplies I need to continue baking. Etcetera. Etcetera. *Cutie Pie* is more than my dream; it's my whole life. What I've worked toward since I was sixteen and knew I was going to become the most phenomenal baker in the world. And now, I'm going to lose it.

"Sure, you can." My brother encourages me from the doorway. He grins. "You can do anything you set your mind to."

"That's what I used to think. It's why I started this pastry shop." That was six months ago. Followed by weeks of working eighteen-hour days and barely getting any sleep in my little apartment over the shop. Days of churning out my favorite cakes and pastries, showcasing the best ones on social media, and in short, doing everything possible to get my business off the ground. All, to no avail.

"Don't give up. You have to believe this can take off," Ben murmurs.

"Oh, trust me, I want to believe. But blind faith in yourself can only take you so far, apparently." Despite having viral posts take off on social media and having a surge of customers over the past month, I'm still not making enough to salvage my business.

"Success is what's beyond the dark night of the soul," my brother, ever the wise one between the two of us, remarks.

"Is that a saying among you Royal Marines?" I scoff.

"It's—"

The bell over the door at the front of the shop tinkles.

"—your destiny." His lips curve in a smile.

"What?" I blink.

"The bell—it's your future calling."

I roll my eyes. "If you say so."

"Go on, your customer is waiting." My brother walks over and kisses my forehead. "Good luck. Remember, when one door closes another one opens."

"If only I still believed that." I make a rude noise.

He steps back and wags a finger under my nose. "You'll see; it will work out." He turns me around and points me in the direction of the doorway leading to the shop." Go on, now."

"Whatever you say, big brother." I was ten when my father passed, and Ben became the de facto father figure in my life. I'm fifteen years younger than him, an "oops baby," born when my mother was in her early forties. I hero-worshipped Ben who, in turn, allowed me to tag along to all of the activities teenaged boys indulge in. He stepped into my father's shoes. He took care of me and never let me feel the loss of my father. "If I don't find a way to pay off my debts today, I'm shutting down," I insist.

There's no answer. I turn to find my brother has left the shop. Not that I blame him. He only has a two-week break before he has to ship out again. I suspect he's gone to meet his current squeeze. Ben never lacks female companionship.

As for me? I need to face whatever's in my destiny. Ben's right about that much. With a last tug at the neckline of the blouse which dips a little too low in the front, and which I wore to try and cheer myself—big fail there—I march out behind the counter, and all the air whooshes out of my lungs.

The man standing on the other side is so big, he seems to take up all of the space in my little bakery. He's tall enough, his head almost grazes the ceiling. And his shoulders—those shoulders I once held onto—are wider than I remember. They're broad enough to block out the view of the rest of the space.

His biceps stretch the sleeves of his suit, which must cost my entire annual rent to buy, given its tailor-made finish. He's wearing a black silk tie, and his jacket is black. A suit? I've never seen him in a suit before, but OMG, does he do it justice. I take in that lean waist, and those massive thighs, which seem ready to burst the seams of his pants, and between them, the tent that was the object of my obsession for so long.

"There was no one at the counter when I walked in. No wonder, you need a cash infusion," a familiar voice growls.

What the—? How dare he say that! I tear my gaze from the part of him that has always turned my insides to mush, and train my gaze on his face, and all remaining thoughts in my head drain away. I was prepared to give him a piece of my mind, but all of the pieces have scattered.

Those eyes. One piercing blue, the other an amber brown. Those heterochromatic eyes, which have always had the effect of reducing me to a mindless blob of need, stare into mine. My entire body hurts. My shoulder muscles turn into cement blocks. My stomach twists. It feels like I've run into a wall. Frissons of shock reverberate down my spine, and when he rakes his gaze down to my chest, his entire body seems to tense. He brings his gaze back to my face, and it feels like I've been punched in the guts. Again.

"What are you doing here?" I manage to croak around the ball of emotion in my throat.

"I might ask you the same question." His jaw tics, a muscle spasms at his jaw, and he curls his fingers into his sides. There's so much tension radiating from him, I feel faint. Apparently, he doesn't like what he sees.

That makes two of us. Nathan-fucking-Davenport. My brother's best friend. The man I've had a crush on for more than half of my life. The man who turned me down when I threw myself at him the day of my eighteenth birthday party. Not before he kissed me, though.

He hauled me to him, thrust his tongue in between my lips, and ravaged my mouth. He squeezed my ample butt and drew me against him, and I felt every inch of what he was packing. The kiss seemed to go on and on. My head spun. My knees gave way underneath me. I stumbled, and he straightened me. Only to tear his mouth from mine and stare into my face. His chest heaving, his breath coming in gusts that seemed to swell his shoulders. He raked his gaze across my features, like he was seeing me for the first time. Like he wanted to throw me down and mount me right there.

"Nate…" I breathed his name, and he released me and jumped back.

A look of confusion, then regret, then anger swept over his features.

I felt his rejection even before he blanked all expression from his face. "I'm sorry, I shouldn't have done that." He turned on his heel and walked out of my birthday celebration, and our house. And my life.

That was it; he cut off all communication with me. I never saw him again. Over the last five years, I've heard about his progress in the navy from my brother, but I never set eyes on him. Until today.

"You're the last person I want to speak to." I cross my arms over my chest, thereby pushing my breasts up higher. His eyes move down before he forces them back to my face. *It's not that I want to flaunt my double-D tits. Okay, okay, maybe I do. Maybe, I want to make him realize what he's been missing.* I'm proud of my assets. I might be a size sixteen, but I've never tried to conceal my full figure. So, what if I want to turn and hide right now?

"The feeling's mutual," he growls.

He actually growls. I draw myself up to my full height. Not that it helps, considering I'm only five feet four inches tall, and he's a good foot taller than me. Still, this is my space. "This is my shop, and you need to leave."

"Trust me, I wouldn't be here if I had any other option."

"What's that supposed to mean?"

"You're looking for a bailout."

"Excuse me?" I gape at him.

"Your business is in trouble. You need money to pay off your debts."

My flush intensifies. Heat crawls up my cheeks, all the way to the roots of hair, followed closely by anger. *How dare he walk in and throw my failure in my face? How dare he not talk to me all these years, only to reappear at the worst possible moment? And right after my brother told me it was my destiny come a-calling when the bell to the shop rang.*

"Wait, did Ben put you up this?"

"Eh?" He stares at my lips. His gaze is so intent that frisson of awareness, which has crackled up my spine since he arrived, flares into a full-blown shiver. I shake my head, ignoring the buzz of electricity that has always hummed between us. "Are you here because Ben asked you come by and help me out?"

A weird look comes into his eyes. He rubs at his temple. "I'm here because my grandfather is the chairman of the Davenport group of companies, and he thinks your bakery would make for a good investment."

"He does?"

"I'm yet to be convinced," he sneers.

So that's how it's gonna be, eh?

He glances toward the counter, taking in the various desserts on display, and his frown deepens. I follow his gaze and take in the tray of cupcakes displayed: Sp1cy Scene, Red Room, Velvet Ties, Purple Patches, Cave Wonder, The Vanilla Vajayjay, The Earth Moved. You have to admit, they're innovative names for the treats.

I named the first one in jest, but it proved to be a hot topic of discussion among fellow spicy book readers like me. Before I knew it, I ended up naming all my desserts in a similar vein.

In fact, the dessert shaped like the backside of a woman and called Spanking New keeps selling out. And then my other hit, a chocolate cake shaped like a vibrator and called C1itasaurus. Yep, they loved that one. Also, another raspberry-infused one in the shape of a fig called Moist Goodness. And finally, the doughnut-shaped tr. eat called—you guessed it—Alphah0le, which is always a hit when I cater at book events.

"Is this a joke?" He stabs his forefinger at the display.

A-n-d that was the absolutely wrong thing to say. No one insults my baby— my bakery, my dream—and expects to get away unscathed.

"I can assure you; they are popular amongst my customers."

He turns those searing eyes on me, and it feels like I'm looking into the coldest depths of a frozen lake. The surface seems able to bear my weight, but one wrong step, and I'm going to fall right through and never find myself again. I try to breathe, but all of the oxygen in the room has been sucked out by his presence. My pulse crashes in my ears, and my nerve endings are so tightly stretched, I fear they'll snap any second. And when he stabs a hand in his pocket, pulling the fabric of his pants taut over that bulge between his legs, a slow thud flares to life between mine.

I *cannot* find him attractive. Cannot risk acknowledging this chemistry that thickens the air between us. Not when I need his help to save my business. Not when I know who he is, and he's definitely out of bounds. Forbidden. Sirens go off in my mind. *Back away. It's not worth taking on the humungous backlog of complications that're going to come with having anything to do with him.*

Then a look of boredom crosses his face. He yawns, and my pulse rate shoots up.

Strike out everything I felt earlier. It's definitely worth taking on every challenge that comes with getting him to cough up money, because by god, he needs to realize the world doesn't revolve around him. How can anyone be this full of himself? This insensitive.

Anger squeezes my chest. Adrenaline laces my blood. *And how dare he turn the most important meeting of my life into…into…something that doesn't merit even a few seconds of his attention?*

"I've seen everything I need to see. Goodbye." He turns to leave.

Think! You need to say something to stop him. You cannot afford to piss off the one guy who might be able to help save your bakery.

"Wait, don't you want to taste my wares?" I burst out.

He freezes mid-step. His shoulders seem to swell. The planes of his back rise and fall, and the jacket pulls even tighter. *Is he going to burst out of his skin and go all Hulk on me?* I swallow. And when he turns slowly and makes a growling sound at the back of his throat, I have to stop the yelp that almost spills from my mouth. Every single cell in my body has woken up and is doing the hula. *Stop that. You can't feel this drawn to this… to this arrogant beast who rejected you.*

But I also need his help. I have to save my business from going bust. And if that means swallowing my pride, then so be it. I tip up my chin and straighten my back. "I… I mean, maybe you want to taste my Honey Pot?" *Ugh. Didn't mean it to come out like that.*

His left eyelid twitches, and he seems one step closer to either having a breakdown or walking away. Neither of which is desirable.

"Oh, shoot. What I meant to say is, you'll definitely like the Purple Patches." I point to the range of cupcakes showcased under the counter. "Or of course, you could try The Clitasaurus?"

"The whatasaurus?" He tilts his head. His gaze is, once again, fixed on my mouth. My thighs clench, and moisture laces the flesh between my legs. I push away the burst of awareness which seems to have stuck its claws into my skin. No way am I going to give in to his magnetism, which has only multiplied in the years since I last saw him. Especially not when his jerkhole factor hasn't reduced either.

It's always been a mystery to me why I found his arrogance such a turn on. Now, I'm also reminded of how he always managed to get on my nerves. Not that it stopped me from throwing myself at him. A mistake I'm not going to make again. When I named that particular cupcake, it seemed like a stroke of genius. Having to pronounce it aloud in front of the Hulk, however, negates any laughs I've had about it so far.

"Uh, you know what I mean?" The color of my cheeks deepens and spreads to my chest. My entire body seems like it's on fire.

"No, I don't," he says in a low, hard voice.

I shiver. "You know that…that… pink pastry between the blue cakes that looks like…" I glance around, then slide open the glass door to the under-counter area. I pull on a pair of gloves, reach in and, instead of the C!itasaurus, slide one of the fig-shaped desserts onto a plate. I place it on the counter. "Actually, I think you should eat my Moist Goodness, and everything will be clear to you, and—"

I hear a gnashing sound, and when I dare to peek a glance at Mr. Grouchy Face, the muscles of his jaw ripple. *Oh no, at this rate he's going to crack a molar. Or two.* I blink rapidly, "Maybe we should start afresh?"

"Start afresh?" he asks in a tone that implies he'd rather have never met me.

Yeah, me too. Unfortunately, I don't have that luxury. "You know, pretend we don't know each other. Pretend the last few minutes never happened?" Pretend *that kiss* is not seared into my brain, and into other parts of my body I'm not going to think about.

I hold out my hand. "Skylar Potter." Then, because I hate my life and because, apparently, the connection between my brain and my mouth has been lost under the force of his glower, I smile. "No relation to Harry, as you're aware."

"Harry?" He looks at my slim, pink-tipped fingers, then back at my face, and makes no move to shake my hand.

I set my jaw. *Oh, my god, he's so rude, I should slap one of the pies baking in my oven into his face; only, they're too good to waste. Also, I can't risk messing up a pie when I need every sale I can get.* Every part of me wants to turn and run out of here. But I can't. *I owe it to myself, to my dream, to give this one last shot. I will not give up easily. I will not. I will stay polite, even if it kills me.* I manage to bare my teeth in the resemblance of a smile. "You know, Harry Potter? Boy wizard? *Evanesco.*" I pretend to flick my wand in his direction.

His jaw hardens further.

He looks pissed. The tips of his ears have turned white. Also, the end of his nose. Also, the vanishing spell on him didn't work. His Royal Dickness is still here, larger than life and glowering at me.

"I'm totally immersed in the Potterverse. Oh, and Taylor Swift. I love Taylor Swift." I beam at him.

His frown deepens.

"I'm guessing you're not a Swiftie?" I nod.

"What's that?" he asks in a contemptuous tone.

"Those of us who love Taylor Swift call ourselves Swifties."

"Sounds contagious," he sneers.

I ignore his cantankerous attitude because I need to charm him. And because I do need him to fork over the money I need. "I love her songs, don't you?" I chirrup.

His fingers curl into fists at his sides. Which is not a good sign. Then, because I love to go from the sublime to the surreal, I smile even wider. "Guess which Hogwarts's house Taylor Swift belongs to?" I toss my hair over my shoulder.

"Hogwhat?" He seems like he's about to have a cardiac event. Or like he went to sleep and woke up in an alternate reality. This is bad. So bad. And I have to go and put my foot in it by prompting him, "Hogwarts."

"Hogwhat?" he snaps again.

This time, the light goes on in my brain. "Oh, you haven't heard of Hogwarts." I snicker. "That's okay, I wasn't alive when man landed on the moon." *Don't say it, don't say it.* "Unlike you."

He blinks slowly.

Zip your lips. Just shut up already. "Not that I'm implying you're old or anything. The grey in your hair adds to your distinguished appearance. Besides, you're only fifteen years older than me." *Oh shoot, I don't think that makes it better.*

The veins on his throat stand out in relief. I try to swallow, but my throat is so dry, it feels like sharp knives line my gullet. I flick out a tongue to wet my lip, and his eyes gleam. He watches my mouth with a predatory gaze. Every part of his body seems to have turned to stone, watching me with such intensity, he seems to have turned into a predator who's planning every possible way to jump me.

The silence deepens. It doesn't stop me from shaking a finger at him. "You, mister, need a crash course in pop culture. Although, I suppose I shouldn't expect someone who has grey at his temples to have a sense of the zeitgeist."

"The fuck you talking about?" he bites out through gritted teeth.

"Whoa, hold on, no need to show me your horns now." *Although, I'd love to see the one between your legs.* "In fact, you look so angry, I'm expecting you to breathe fire at any moment." *You can turn into a dragon and carry me away anytime.* "And seriously, you should taste this." I push the plate with the moist, pink and purple, fig-shaped cake in his direction. It has a silver button between the lips and there's glitter around it.

"My desserts are awesome; one bite, and you'll be a convert." I nod.

He stares.

"Unless you're worried, you'll get addicted to my sweet bits." I tip up my chin.

Did I say *my* sweet bits? I did say *my* sweet bits. *Somebody kill me.* But he must see the challenge in my eyes, and alpha male that he is, of course, he doesn't back down.

Without taking his gaze off of my face, he licks the cream from the hollow in the center. A thousand little fires flare to life under my skin. I swallow; my breath grows shallow. He bites down on one of the plump lips, and a shiver grips me. I clutch at the edge of the counter. The pulse at the base of my throat speeds up. And when he pops the other lip into his mouth, I gulp. He brings his thumb and forefinger to his mouth and sucks on them, and a breathy moan leaves my lips.

"Not bad." He shrugs.

I stare. "What do you mean, 'not bad'? *That* is my bestseller."

"It was okay." He looks down his nose from his superior height, "I admit, the names you give your baked goods are creative, but I'm not sure that's enough for me to approve the takeover."

"Takeover?" I stiffen. "Who's talking about a takeover?"

"It's the only way I'd consider investing in your business."

"I only need help," I say through gritted teeth.

"That's putting it mildly. I reached out to the bank you took the loan from —"

"You reached out to my bank?" I burst out.

"You don't think I'd be here without due diligence —"

I cut in, "The terms of my deal with them are confidential." I lock my fingers together.

"Not when you're about to go bankrupt. When they realized the Davenport group was considering an acquisition —"

"An investment; a loan; that's *all* I'm looking for. Something to tide me over and buy me some time until I get back on my feet."

"Keep fooling yourself. You might be a good baker —"

"So you did like my dessert?" I declare in a triumphant voice.

"—but you're not a businessperson, by any stretch of imagination."

Oh, my god! What I wouldn't give to wipe that smug look off his face.

"There are ups and downs in any business." I lock my fingers together. "Things will bounce back."

"There are ups and downs, and then, there are downs and more downs," he drawls.

Anger thuds at my temples. *I will not lose my temper. I will not.*

He slides his hand into his pocket. "Not that I don't understand your reluctance to sell out."

"You do?"

"Of course. You've invested your sweat and blood, and likely, your entire savings into the venture. Too bad, you didn't have a financial person advising you."

Of course, he'd say that. Nate's always been a numbers whiz. I heard that from Ben. It's why, even when they were in the navy together, Nate was quickly put in charge of strategy. He was the person coming up with the game plan, while Ben was always on the front lines. And Nate's sharp brain helped him always stay ahead of the enemy. He saved Ben's life many times, or so my brother informed me over the years. Too bad, his best friend's temperament leaves much to be desired.

"I would be willing to consider a merger instead of an acquisition of your little business." His gaze flicks about the place and back at me.

"*Little* business?" I curl my fingers into fists. *Breathe, count back from ten. Do not give into the impulsive need to throw a pie in his face.*

He wipes his thumb under his lip, a considering look in his eyes. "Of course, I don't have to do anything. But given you're Ben's little sister, and he wouldn't want me to leave you in the lurch, I might have a proposition that could help both of us."

"Of course, you do."

My sarcasm is lost on him, for he looks me up and down. "Marry me."

TO FIND OUT WHAT HAPPENS NEXT READ NATHAN AND SKYLAR'S STORY IN THE UNWANTED WIFE

HERE'S AN EXCLUSIVE BONUS EPILOGUE FEATURING EDDIE *&* BELLE

Belle

"Does it bring back a lot of memories?" I turn to my husband. We're in the Church where he wants us to get married. The same Church where he served as a priest. The one where he went to confession a month ago and prayed for forgiveness. He's been a changed man since.

There's a lightness around his eyes, and his shoulders don't seem so heavy. Facing his past has helped him find peace. Still, when he shifts his weight from foot to foot, I realize, it must not be easy for him to be here.

Eddie runs his finger under the collar of his shirt. The white is a contrast to the golden-yellow tie he has knotted around his throat. His jet-black suit fits his broad shoulders, the sleeves of the jacket tight around his biceps. His trim waist is shown off by the cut of his suit, not to mention the powerful thighs which strain the fabric of his pants. He slicked back his hair, so his cheekbones stand out in relief. The hollows under them lend an almost ascetic look to his features. His gaze is fastened straight ahead on the altar that awaits us at the end of the aisle.

I know he didn't sleep much last night. He fucked me to sleep, and when I woke up, the mattress next to me was cold.

I went into the kitchen to find him standing on the adjoining deck. Seeing the empty coffee-cup on the counter I knew he'd been awake for a while. Also, he was smoking. It's the first time I've seen my husband smoke in all the time we've been married. It gave me pause. I knew he was thinking things through.

If I asked him whether he was worried, he'd deny it. So instead, I walked over to him and wrapped my arms around his waist. I pressed my cheek into his naked back and enjoyed the feeling of his skin against mine. I flattened my palm against his flat stomach and relished the feel of the hard planes. I didn't say a word, but he understood, I was offering him my support. He placed his hand over mine, put out his cigarette, and flicked the rest of it into the make-shift ashtray.

Then, he turned and lifted me up in his arms. He kissed me thoroughly, and before I could recover, he'd stalked back to the bed. This time, he made love to me. We fell asleep, and the next time I awoke was to find he'd brought me breakfast in bed. I took a sip of the coffee—delicious in a way I'll never been able to brew myself—and once I felt awake enough, I told him: "We don't have to do this."

"Yes, we do." He poured himself a cup, then scanned my features. "I'm not a coward."

"I know, you're not."

"I thought it would be easier coming back, now that I've found some measure of peace—"

"—but it isn't?"

"It's easier than before, but it does bring back scenes from my past," he admits.

"It doesn't have to be here. It doesn't have to be now." I placed my cup of coffee on the tray and pushed it aside. Then I reached over and cupped his jaw. "You can take your time on this."

"I need to do this, here and now. I want to marry you in the place where I committed myself to Him. I need to face my past fully, so I'm one-hundred percent committed to you and our future together."

I peered into his eyes. "You are a hundred percent committed to me. You have been since the day you first saw me. No other man would have gone to the lengths you did to ensure we were together."

"Do you resent what I did? Do you hate me for becoming obsessed with you? For continuing to fixate on you? To have my life revolve around you?"

I laughed. "I'd rather you be obsessed with me than anyone else. I'd rather I be the center of your attentions. If you dare look at another woman, I'll ensure she never comes near you again."

It was his turn to laugh. "What have I created?"

"A single-minded woman whose entire world revolves around her man. If you're preoccupied by me, I'm consumed by you."

His eyes flashed. "I love you." He placed his cup on the tray then pulled me into his lap, effectively silencing me.

Then, it had been a rush for me to get dressed; this time, in a gown Karma designed for me from scratch. This time, we had enough time to plan the kind of wedding my husband wanted. I confess, I still don't have a better vision of what I want my wedding ceremony to look like. I already snagged the man I want to spend the rest of my life with. Everything else is moot.

But Eddie... He wants to do this to put his past to rest. And a part of me understands it. I think it's brave of him to want to get married in the same Church where he was once a priest. He even asked one of his friends, someone who served with him in the clergy, to officiate. He's coming full-circle, and I understand the significance of it. Eddie's closing out that chapter of his life completely.

It's why I asked Baron to give me away. I also asked Ava to be my maid-of-honor; because it's not about me. This time, it's about Eddie. They were a big part of his life, and it's only right they have a starring role in the ceremony.

It's not like I couldn't have asked Gio or Penny or Summer to be my maids of honor… But it feels significant that it's Ava.

If she hadn't appeared that day at Eddie's office, I wouldn't have realized I had nothing to fear from the woman who once played such an important role in his life. She's moved on, and so has he. There will always be a connection between them, but it's become a friendship, and Ava's happy with Baron. I have nothing to worry about, in that respect. They're so happy, their contentment is a beacon that lights up any space they're in. And she played a pivotal part in reuniting Edward with his best friend.

His brother, in all but name and blood. The man who went through things with him that no teenaged boy should ever have to go through. They survived and supported each other—and fell for the same woman. And then, Eddie walked away. Perhaps, a part of him knew, even then, that there was someone else waiting for him. Perhaps, on some level, he knew he'd find me. Perhaps, deep down, he knew he was yet to meet the love of his life. It was my destiny that this man see me, fall for me, and pursue me. And while I don't condone his style of courtship, I'd be lying if I said a part of me doesn't revel in how thoughts of me occupied his every thinking moment since he first saw me. No, it's not the norm. But then, we aren't an average couple either. He's a former priest, and I'm the woman who was so focused on standing on my own two feet, I wasn't prepared for him to sweep me off of them.

"Baby?" Now, I link my arm through his. "You ready?"

Eddie

"With you by my side, I'm ready for anything." I peer into her eyes.

"Oh—" Belle swallows. "You spoil me."

"It's true." I wrap my arm about her waist and haul her close. "From the day I first set eyes on you, my world changed. From the moment I decided to make you mine, I found purpose. From the second you came into my life, I knew I was redeemed."

"Eddie," she whispers. A tear rolls down her cheek, and before I can stop myself, I lower my head and lick it up. "So sweet. Every part of you is a siren call that tugs on my heart and turns me into a raging mass of need only you can satisfy."

She swallows, then half smiles. "Who'd have thought the angry former priest I met would turn out to be such a sweet talker."

"That's what you do to me, baby. You turn my perspective upside-down."

"In a good way, I hope?"

"The best." I lower my lips to hers, when the sound of someone clearing their throat reaches me.

"I'm aware you guys are married, but considering we're in church and you two are set to exchange vows in the house of God, perhaps you should save the gestures of love for later?" Nathan rumbles from somewhere behind me.

"Fuck off," I say without heat.

Belle's eyes round. "You swore in church?"

"I'm no longer a priest."

"Still,"—she blinks rapidly—"you should maintain a modicum of respect for being in a place of worship."

I cup her cheek. "You're right, wife. It's thanks to you my belief in Him was restored."

"It was?"

I nod. "I'm not egoistical enough to think I had any part to play in our paths crossing. You becoming my wife, you being by my side, you lighting up my life and banishing my dark thoughts, showed me there's a possibility for miracles in my life… And I have no doubt, He had a hand in it. Why else would I have been driving up that street in Brooklyn the very moment you were walking home?"

"Aww, you two are so sweet." Nathan sounds like he's about to throw up in his mouth.

I glare at him over my shoulder. "Don't make me regret I asked you to be my best man."

"Not saying it's not an honor." He holds up his hand. "Besides, I'd rather be best man than the bridegroom."

My wife chortles, then turns it into a cough. I exchange an amused look with her. "He thinks he has a choice in these matters."

"Of course, I do."

"Has he met G-Pa yet?" she murmurs.

"Poor sod, believes he's going to continue in his merry single ways."

"I heard that, and you bet, I'm going to stay single. I have no intention of falling into the marriage trap."

"Whatever you say," I murmur without turning around.

"So sorry we're late." Ava strides in through the front door and into the vestibule.

She's followed by Baron, who walks over to us and claps me on my shoulder. "Looking good, ol' chap."

"Thanks." I turn a quizzical glance in my wife's direction.

"Surprise. Ava's my maid-of-honor, and I asked Baron to give me away."

I feel a rush of emotion for this woman who knew what I needed when I didn't know it myself. "That's wonderful," I manage to talk around the ball of emotion in my throat. "How're you holding up?" Baron searches my features. "You don't seem nervous." There's a thread of surprise in his voice.

"We're already married," I point out.

"I thought it might be difficult for you to get married here." He nods in the direction of the altar.

"It's not easy, but it's necessary," I glance toward where our friends and family occupy the pews. In front of the altar, stands Zephyr. He was thrilled when I asked him to marry us. I also spot some of the parishioners from my congregation.

When word spread, I was getting married here, they reached out to me and congratulated me. It was a huge surprise, one which helped settle something inside of me. Perhaps, a part of me will always feel a thread of regret at leaving my calling. But the more mature part of me knows, it wasn't meant to be. I also understand, I had to go through that phase of my life to make peace with the impact the incident had on me. My future, though, is with her.

"You'll never take the easy route, will you?"

I turn to face him.

"Would you?"

He shakes his head "It's why I respect you."

"And I, you."

I pull my wife into my side, then, without letting go of her, I grip Baron's neck and haul him close. "Love you, man."

"Me too, bro. Me too." He squeezes the back of my neck. "I couldn't be happier for the both of you. You take care of her now, you hear me?"

"With everything I have," I vow.

"Time to take our places." Nathan nods toward the front of the church.

Baron steps back, and I turn to my wife. "Ready for the rest of our lives together?"

Nathan

"How does it feel now that you married her in the same house of worship where you were once a priest?" There's a ten-year difference between Edward and I, but given what I've heard about his past and what he's been through he seems older than his years.

Not the same as serving in the military and being posted in god-forsaken places and having to see friends die in front of you, but as gut-wrenching in a different way. I've gotten to know Edward better in the past month and in one of our conversations he'd hinted at the incident which had changed his life and that of his friends forever. It took a strong man to weather what they went through and come out on the other side without turning into an addict or doing something to hurt yourself. God knows I'd seen my share of teammates and friends turn to alcohol and stronger substances in a bid to drown out the voices they carried out of battle with them. God knows I'd come close when I'd lost my entire battalion and emerged as the only man alive. But I'd known the risks going in. I hadn't done it only for glory or the thrill—it had been my calling. Since I was five, I'd known I was going to serve in the armed forces. There was a need in me to dedicate myself to a calling bigger than mine. I'd found it in the navy. Just as Edward had found it in the church. When my best friend Ben, had decided to join the navy with me I shouldn't have been surprised. We'd been buddies since high school, and it was only natural Ben followed me in enlisting. Still the fact he had been able to leave his sister behind was unexpected.

After their father passed away Ben took on the male role model in Isa's life. Little Skylar with her big green eyes that looked at Ben with adoration. She'd been crushed when Ben had decided to leave but also mature enough to tell him she understood he was devoting his life to a higher purpose.

Little Skylar who had been all grown up the last time I saw her.

The no longer little Skylar who had bloomed into a woman with the most luscious curves I'd ever set eyes on. I'd been thirty-three when I'd made it back to Sugar Valley, the town near London where I had grown up with Ben. We'd been on a break between tours, and Skylar was cele-brating her eighteenth birthday. She'd sparkled with life and hope and an optimism which was a contrast to my jaded self. I'd seen enough on my tours, felt my heart break when I'd had to make decisions which involved the loss of innocent lives. I'd never be that idyllic soldier who'd started his career with the naïve notion of serving his country. It was so much more complicated than that. The life I lived meant making decisions which would always put me in the shadowed side of life.

Coming off a particularly difficult tour it had been difficult to understand that the life I had left back home had continued. That acquaintances had gotten married and had children. That my foster mother had died. That Skylar was all grown up and kissing me. And I kissed her right back. I had pulled her into me hoping to absorb some of her innocence, her freshness, her dreams. I wanted some of her zest for life to rub off on me. I won't deny I'd almost thrown her down right there in the back garden of her house with her brother and mother not more than a few feet away from us. I won't deny I'd wanted her with a helplessness that had swallowed my commonsense. I won't deny that when I finally managed to tear my mouth from hers, I was horrified at what I'd done. I wouldn't be able to live with myself if things had gone further. She was Ben's little sister. I had watched her grow up. And now I wanted to fuck her? Disgust had curled my guts. I barked out an apology, then turned and ran out there. And kept running. Until my last mission had gone wrong. I'd been injured and had to take early retirement.

I'd returned home to my empty place, and not known what to do with myself. I'd taken to running and working out every day, a fervor which saved me from sinking into depression. Then I'd begun volunteering at a veterans' charity. Which is when my biological grandfather had shown up.

Seeing him had brought home just how much I didn't know about my past. Hearing from him about my biological father and seeing pictures of the man whose features were so like mine had made me realize how much I didn't know of myself.

Listening to Arthur had made it clear how much of a stranger I was to myself. It had brought home how much I didn't belong where I was. And I wanted to, in some form. Perhaps it was the lessons I'd learned from my military career or the fact that at thirty-eight I was tired of being on my own—either way when Arthur asked me to join him and take over as the CEO of the company I had agreed.

Besides it's not like I was doing shit with my life. And I could help the veterans more if I took over as the CEO of the Davenports.

I could use my power to address the failings of the system I had once been proud of. And if there was the little matter of Arthur insisting, I get married, well that didn't mean much to me. I'd go through the motions give the old man what he wanted, get what I needed out of this arrangement. Everyone would be happy. No way was I going to fall in love with a woman and become as hen-pecked as Edward. I follow his gaze to where his wife is laughing with one of her friends.

We're in a pub not far from the church. One owned by the Davenports. Arthur had diversified his holdings it seems. He had interests in media, in food products and also in a chain of gastropubs like this one, among others.

"You're pussywhipped, mate," I snicker.

"I am," Edward tosses back his whiskey, "and I'm fucking grateful for that."

He turns to me, "what about you?"

To find out what happens next read Nathan and Skylar's story in The Unwanted Wife

Want more bonus excerpts? Go to https://authorlsteele.com/ebooks-bonus-content/

Want to read Edward, Ava and Baron's story? Get The Billionaire's Sins

Read an excerpt

Edward

"I have taken a vow." I step back from her. "I have promised to live a celibate life. I have completely given my life to Christ and the people I have been called to serve."

I turn away from her, head for the clothes that I'd placed on the pool-chair.

The hair on the nape of my neck prickles.

I glance over my shoulder to find her staring at me. Her gaze runs down my back, then back to my face, as I snatch up my shirt and shrug into it.

"I... I don't understand."

"Me neither." I grab my towel, then head for the guesthouse that I occupy whenever I stay over at the Sterlings', which isn't often. But when I'd wanted to leave yesterday, the rest of the Seven wouldn't hear of it. With Arpad getting married, it means all of us are now hitched... Well, except me... And Baron. I stiffen. *Why the hell am I thinking of him?* The friend who'd turned his back on us and left. Not that he hasn't been in touch. He's communicated through snail mail, writing on occasion, like when Damian was hesitant about getting married to Julia. Or when there is a specific investment that Sinner or Saint aren't sure about, though how he knows this is beyond me. The two of them run 7A Investments, one of the leading financial services firms in the country. Between them, they've managed to invest our money such that we'll be living off the wealth created for this entire lifetime. Not that I am going to touch a penny of it.

My investments go toward FOK Media, aka Full of Kindness Media, the non-profit that the Seven set up to finance upcoming talent in return for a portion of their earnings. I'd also put money toward my own trust that supports the most vulnerable and those in need.

As for myself, I stay in a small two-bedroom home, owned by the parish I am devoted to serving. The place where I need to return before things get further out of hand. It had been wrong to approach her in the first place. I'd seen her watching me, had recognized her— Of course, I had. I couldn't have missed her—and then I had approached her. I should have walked away, but I couldn't resist. I had to see her once more. And now I have to atone for the sinful thoughts I entertained.

I clench my fists at my sides.

"Wait." Her footsteps approach me, and I increase my pace.

I cannot be alone with her, not for one more second.

"What are you trying to tell me, Edward?"

I reach the guesthouse, twist open the door and step in. I turn to find her hesitating at the entrance and beckon her in.

She hesitates and I tilt my head. "Come on, I have something to show you."

"You do?" Her forehead furrows.

"You need to see this."

She blows out a breath and follows me. I head inside, to the bedroom, take my collar from where I'd placed it on the bedstead. I slip it on, then turn to find her poised at the doorway.

Her face pales; her jaw drops.

"You're a…a—"

"Priest." I nod.

"B…but," she opens and shuts her mouth, "you weren't wearing a collar at the wedding yesterday."

"I'm a diocesan priest. I wear the collar when I have anything pastoral to do. I don't usually wear it when out with friends."

"I see." She shrugs off her blanket, folds it over her arm. Her gaze skitters away. "I knew it was too good to be true. Of course, it is." She retreats into the living room, drops the blanket and her book on the couch and begins to pace. "I mean, just once, things couldn't be easy for me, right? Everything has to be complicated. Just this once, couldn't things have worked out the way they do for everyone else? Of course, not." She throws up her hands. "This is not fair, not fair at all."

"Are you…" I follow her as she stomps back-forth-back, across the length of the floor of the living room. "Are you talking to yourself?"

"Shh." She turns to me and frowns. "I'm trying to figure this out."

"By talking aloud?"

"Hey, don't mock it until you try it. Did you know talking to yourself helps you organize your thoughts?" She shoves her purple-tipped hair back from her face.

Who dyes their hair purple? Ava does, that's who.

"According to psychologists, talking out loud to yourself helps you clarify your thoughts," she mumbles. "It helps to figure out what's important, and firm up any decisions you're contemplating."

"Ah," I allow my lips to tip up, "and what decision are you contemplating right now?"

She flushes. "I am not sure you want to know."

"Don't I?"

She shakes her head. "I don't think it's right for me to share what I am thinking with a priest… Not unless I was in confession, but then, wouldn't you have to keep it secret? I mean, aren't you bound by a code of conduct of some kind? And damn, but I admit, I may have eyed you up a little out there earlier. Does that even count as sin? Is it made worse by the fact that you are priest? Is it—"

"Stop." I hold up my hand.

She purses her lips together, then draws in a breath. "Sorry," she mutters, "I tend to babble when I'm nervous."

"I didn't notice." I allow my smile to widen. This girl—she's adorable. She twists her fingers together, hunches her shoulders, then snaps them back. "Uh, guess I should…go then?"

She turns to leave, and something hot stabs at my chest. Okay, so I can't have any kind of relationship with her… What the—? How had I even allowed myself to think that? Since becoming an ordained priest eight years ago, I've focused on my role, the routine, the discipline. The simplicity of my existence means everything to me. It helps me ground my thoughts, allows me to focus on what is important: serving others, helping them, listening to them, and helping to alleviate their worries.

In their comfort, I draw comfort. By easing their pain, I breathe easier. When I help a soul cross over, a part of me opens up to possibilities, and when I baptize a newborn, look into their clear eyes and welcome them to the house of the Lord, I redeem myself.

That... The regiment of how I live my life, gives me the framework upon which to anchor myself. When I am in that space, I don't have to worry about what happened to me, how the incident affected me, how I had fallen apart after the kidnapping, when the Seven and I had been taken and held in captivity for a month; how I had pulled myself together, only to fall apart again.

Boys join the army to learn discipline... For me, it had been the calling from God that had saved me. And surely, it is God who sent this girl, this absolutely stunning, untainted-by-life soul to me.

Or is it the devil trying to lure me away from Him?

No, not possible. I shake my head. This... It doesn't feel wrong. There's nothing unnatural about what I feel for her. Surely, it has to be the Lord wanting me to learn something from her? That's why he sent her.

What is this test that I am facing? And do I have the courage to go through with it?

Can I rise to the occasion; face the fears that her proximity evokes in me?

And if I don't—if I chose *not* to accept this ultimate trial... Would that not mean that I have learned nothing from all the time I have spent in serving the Lord?

If this is his way of testing me... And surely, it has to be. There could be no other explanation for why, out of everything I've encountered thus far, she stands out like a beacon...

The air around her crackles with a vitality, a strange sensation... Almost one of hope, of life, of joy... Emotions I've seen amongst my parishioners, that I have studied from afar, even joined them in celebrating... But never once, experienced personally. Not until now.

Is this why you sent her my way, my Lord? Is it a sign that I need to open myself further, allow the emotions in, sense their sting, revel in how they torture me with everything that I cannot and will not allow myself to feel? So be it, then. I follow your command.

"Ava," I call out as she opens the door, "wait."

Ava

His voice stops me. I pause at the threshold.

"Ava."

I turn, wait for him to speak.

"I ..." He shoves his hands inside his pockets. "I'm sorry," he finally says.

"For what?"

"For giving you the wrong impression earlier." He stares at me. "Perhaps some of the fault is with me too."

"Oh?" I stare. Is he going to apologize to me? Why? Because I was drawn to him? *Please, don't... Please, please, don't.* My cheeks heat, and I glance away, "I mean, seriously, it was nothing." I hold my blanket in front of me. Can I hide under it, maybe? No, that would only look silly... As if anything could be worse than our earlier encounter? Gosh, how could I have been attracted to him? He's a priest... Someone sworn to not sleep with anyone, and I can't stop staring at his perfect features. Those high cheekbones, his dark hair cut short at the sides, long on top, that hooked nose, the mean upper lip...that gorgeous throat I want to lick, the width of his shoulders that fills the doorway, cutting out the sight of the room behind him. He draws in a breath and the sculpted planes of his chest stretch the fabric of his shirt. Not that I am staring or anything. Of course, not.

I clear my throat, then glance away.

"I should be the one apologizing." I clutch at my blanket with palms that are slippery with sweat. *Dear God... What's wrong with me? And by the way, I need to have words with You. It's not fair that You dangle someone as luscious as this man in front of me only to claim him and tell me that I can't have him.* OMFG. I am seriously losing it, if I am having conversations with the Power Above in my head. "I shouldn't have sneaked looking at you earlier, and well... It's just, you're so damn gorgeous to look at, and well, I couldn't help it."

"Did you just tell me that I'm gorgeous to look at?'

I glance up to find him staring at me with surprise and bemusement.

"Yes," I shuffle my feet, "I guess I did."

"Do you always say everything that comes into your head?"

"Kind of," I hunch my shoulder, "though honestly, I seem to have even less of a filter when you're around."

"Do I make you nervous?" One corner of his lip curls...just a tad.

Holy hell, he smirked. No, he totally did. And damn, if that isn't the hottest thing I have seen. Right after the Edward I'd read about in Twilight and imagined myself as Bella.

And here I am as Ava, and this is my Edward right here. Except, this scenario is all wrong. Shit. I'm tying myself in knots. I stare at him. "Are you sure you're a priest?"

He chuckles, "The last time I checked." He glances down at me, something like amusement and regret lacing his features. "Are you a…?" He tilts his head, "What do you do, Ava?"

"I'm a, uh, dancer."

"A dancer?" He frowns.

"Not ballet," I add quickly because that's what most people assume automatically, "more like, the exotic kind."

"Exotic kind?"

"A belly dancer." I twitch my hips, more out of habit than anything else. Okay, so maybe not completely… Maybe it's to take in how his nostrils flare as he lowers his gaze to my hips and stays there, as if fascinated by what he sees.

"A belly dancer, huh?" He finally raises his gaze to meet mine and those gorgeous golden-brown eyes of his blaze at me. Then he lowers his eye lashes, and when he raises them, all emotion is shorn from his features.

"I, uh, dropped out of university. I'd joined to study medicine, but somehow…half-way through my first year, I lost interest. Turns out, becoming a doctor requires a strong stomach. The first time I saw a cadaver, I fainted and then had nightmares for days. I couldn't enter the laboratory after that. Also, the smell of formaldehyde — the solution they use to preserve specimens? Turns out, I am allergic to it… So…"

I swallow.

"Shit. Uh… Shoot, I am sorry. I'm blabbing." I shuffle my feet. "All that untapped energy, you know, it needs an outlet. It's why I turned to dancing, and then started my own studio teaching belly dancing. It makes me happy, you know — dancing?" *Stop it, what the hell are you doing? Pouring out your thoughts in a stream of consciousness?* "In fact, my dream is to one day to have a home big enough to have a studio in it so whenever I want to dance, I'll have my own space. A place where I can just be myself… You know?" I bite the inside of my cheek. So much for trying to appear calm and composed. OMG, what's wrong with me? I wipe my clammy palms against the fabric of my dress.

"So, I make you nervous?" He quirks an eyebrow, curls his fists at his sides, and whoa, his knuckles are white. I tilt my head, take in the nerve that throbs at his temple, the way his chest rises and falls. Maybe... I'm not the only one affected. Maybe, he feels it too—the connection, this strange chemistry between us that's crackled since his gaze met mine. Only... It means nothing. It can't... He's a priest...and I? I'm a hot mess.

"You do." I step back. "You make me very unsure of myself, Ed—" I bite down on the inside of my cheek. Should I call him Edward? Father? Damn, this is not cool, not at all. "I really should go."

He lowers his chin, "Guess I'll see you for breakfast at the main house then?"

"Breakfast?"

"You are going to eat breakfast with Sinclair and Summer, I assume?"

"Ah," I swallow, "yes, of course."

He nods, then holds out his hand, "It's nice to meet you, Ava."

Nice? Okay, not the word I would have used, but if he wants to play it that way, well, so can I.

I tilt my head, "And you, Father."

His jaw tics. A mask seems to form from his features as he draws himself up to his full height. He's so tall that I have to tip my head all the way back to see his face. How can someone so big, so vital, someone whose every inch of his body is packed with sex appeal... How the hell could he have dedicated himself to a life where he'll never experience pleasures the likes of which I want to share with him?

And then, there's his personality... The intensity of his gaze, the depth I sense underneath that tightly controlled exterior. The strength of his dominance that he wears about himself, tightly cloaked, held back, as if he doesn't dare give in to the power of his complete self...because it would be too much for everyone around him. For the man he is, and make no mistake, he is one-hundred percent alpha male, would outshine anyone around him. Is that the depth of his sacrifice? The depth of what he'd given up to pursue his calling?

He holds my gaze, then nods. "Goodbye, Ava."

To find out what happens next, read Edward, Ava and Baron's story in Billionaire's Sins

Read Summer & Sinclair Sterling's story HERE in The Billionaire's Fake Wife

READ AN EXCERPT FROM SUMMER & SINCLAIR'S STORY

Summer

"Slap, slap, kiss, kiss."

"Huh?" I stare up at the bartender.

"Aka, there's a thin line between love and hate." He shakes out the crimson liquid into my glass.

"Nah." I snort. "Why would she allow him to control her, and after he insulted her?"

"It's the chemistry between them." He lowers his head. "You have to admit that, when the man is arrogant and the woman resists, it's a challenge to both of them, to see who blinks first, huh?"

"Why?" I wave my hand in the air. "Because they hate each other?"

"Because," he chuckles, "the girl in school whose braids I pulled and teased mercilessly, is the one who I—"

"Proposed to?" I huff.

His face lights up. "You get it now?"

Yeah. No. A headache begins to pound at my temples. This crash course in pop psychology is not why I came to my favorite bar in Islington, to meet my best friend, who is—I glance at the face of my phone—thirty minutes late.

I inhale the drink, and his eyebrows rise.

"What?" I glower up at the bartender. "I can barely taste the alcohol. Besides, it's free drinks at happy hour for women, right?"

"Which ends in precisely—" he holds up five fingers— "minutes."

"Oh! Yay!" I mock fist pump. "Time enough for one more, at least."

A hiccough swells my throat and I swallow it back, nod.

One has to do what one has to do... when everything else in the world is going to shit.

A hot sensation stabs behind my eyes; my chest tightens. Is this what people call growing up?

The bartender tips his mixing flask, strains out a fresh batch of the ruby red liquid onto the glass in front of me.

"Salut." I nod my thanks, then toss it back. It hits my stomach and tendrils of fire crawl up my spine, I cough.

My head spins. Warmth sears my chest, spreads to my extremities. I can't feel my fingers or toes. Good. Almost there. "Top me up."

"You sure?"

"Yes." I square my shoulders and reach for the drink.

"No. She's had enough."

"What the—?" I pivot on the bar stool.

Indigo eyes bore into me.

Fathomless. Black at the bottom, the intensity in their depths grips me. He swoops out his arm, grabs the glass and holds it up. Thick fingers dwarf the glass. Tapered at the edges. The nails short and buff. *All the better to grab you with.* I gulp.

"Like what you see?"

I flush, peer up into his face.

Hard cheekbones, hollows under them, and a tiny scar that slashes at his left eyebrow. *How did he get that?* Not that I care. My gaze slides to his mouth. Thin upper lip, a lower lip that is full and cushioned. Pouty with a hint of bad boy. *Oh!* My toes curl. My thighs clench.

The corner of his mouth kicks up. *Asshole.*

Bet he thinks life is one big smug-fest. I glower, reach for my glass, and he holds it up and out of my reach.

I scowl. "Gimme that."

He shakes his head.

"That's my drink."

"Not anymore." He shoves my glass at the bartender. "Water for her. Get me a whiskey, neat."

I splutter, then reach for my drink again. The barstool tips in his direction. This is when I fall against him, and my breasts slam into his hard chest, sculpted planes with layers upon layers of muscle that ripple and writhe as he turns aside, flattens himself against the bar. The floor rises up to meet me.

What the actual hell?

I twist my torso at the last second and my butt connects with the surface. *Ow!*

The breath rushes out of me. My hair swirls around my face. I scramble for purchase, and my knee connects with his leg.

"Watch it." He steps around, stands in front of me.

"You stepped aside?" I splutter. "You let me fall?"

"Hmph."

I tilt my chin back, all the way back, look up the expanse of muscled thigh that stretches the silken material of his suit. *What is he wearing? Could any suit fit a man with such precision?* Hand crafted on Saville Row, no doubt. I glance at the bulge that tents the fabric between his legs. *Oh!* I blink.

Look away, look away. I hold out my arm. He'll help me up at least, won't he?

He glances at my palm, then turns away. *No, he didn't do that, no way.*

A glass of amber liquid appears in front of him. He lifts the tumbler to his sculpted mouth.

His throat moves, strong tendons flexing. He tilts his head back, and the column of his neck moves as he swallows. Dark hair covers his chin —it's a discordant chord in that clean-cut profile, I shiver. He would scrape that rough skin down my core. He'd mark my inner thighs, lick my core, thrust his tongue inside my melting channel and drink from my pussy. *Oh! God.* Goosebumps rise on my skin.

No one has the right to look this beautiful, this achingly gorgeous. Too magnificent for his own good. Anger coils in my chest.

"Arrogant wanker."

"I'll take that under advisement."

"You're a jerk, you know that?"

He presses his lips together. The grooves on either side of his mouth deepen. Clearly the man has never laughed a single day in his life. Bet that stick up his arse is uncomfortable. I chuckle.

He runs his gaze down my features, my chest, down to my toes, then yawns.

The hell! I will not let him provoke me. Will not. "Like what you see?" I jut out my chin.

"Sorry, you're not my type." He slides a hand into the pocket of those perfectly cut pants, stretching it across that heavy bulge.

Heat curls low in my belly.

Not fair, that he could afford a wardrobe that clearly shouts his status and what amounts to the economy of a small third-world country. A hot feeling stabs in my chest.

He reeks of privilege, of taking his status in life for granted.

While I've had to fight every inch of the way. Hell, I am still battling to hold onto the last of my equilibrium.

"Last chance—" I wiggle my fingers from where I am sprawled out on the floor at his feet, "—to redeem yourself…"

"You have me there." He places the glass on the counter, then bends and holds out his hand. The hint of discolored steel at his wrist catches my attention. Huh?

He wears a cheap-ass watch?

That's got to bring down the net worth of his presence by more than 1000% percent. Weird.

I reach up and he straightens.

I lurch back.

"Oops, I changed my mind." His lips curl.

A hot burning sensation claws at my stomach. I am not a violent person, honestly. But Smirky Pants here, he needs to be taught a lesson.

I swipe out my legs, kicking his out from under him.

Sinclair

My knees give way, and I hurtle toward the ground.

What the—? I twist around, thrust out my arms. My palms hit the floor. The impact jostles up my elbows. I firm my biceps and come to a halt planked above her.

A huffing sound fills my ear.

I turn to find my whippet, Max, panting with his mouth open. I scowl and he flattens his ears.

All of my businesses are dog-friendly. Before you draw conclusions about me being the caring sort or some such shit—it attracts footfall.

Max scrutinizes the girl, then glances at me. *Huh?* He hates women, but not her, apparently.

I straighten and my nose grazes hers.

My arms are on either side of her head. Her chest heaves. The fabric of her dress stretches across her gorgeous breasts. My fingers tingle; my palms ache to cup those tits, squeeze those hard nipples outlined against the—hold on, what is she wearing? A tunic shirt in a sparkly pink... and are those shoulder pads she has on?

I glance up, and a squeak escapes her lips.

Pink hair surrounds her face. *Pink? Who dyes their hair that color past the age of eighteen?*

I stare at her face. *How old is she?* Un-furrowed forehead, dark eyelashes that flutter against pale cheeks. Tiny nose, and that mouth— luscious, tempting. A whiff of her scent, cherries and caramel, assails my senses. My mouth waters. *What the hell?*

She opens her eyes and our eyelashes brush. Her gaze widens. Green, like the leaves of the evergreens, flickers of gold sparkling in their depths. "What?" She glowers. "You're demonstrating the plank position?"

"Actually," I lower my weight onto her, the ridge of my hardness thrusting into the softness between her legs, "I was thinking of something else, altogether."

She gulps and her pupils dilate. *Ah, so she feels it, too?*

I drop my head toward her, closer, closer.

Color floods the creamy expanse of her neck. Her eyelids flutter down. She tilts her chin up.

I push up and off of her.

"That… Sweetheart, is an emphatic 'no thank you' to whatever you are offering."

Her eyelids spring open and pink stains her cheeks. Adorable. Such a range of emotions across those gorgeous features in a few seconds. What else is hidden under that exquisite exterior of hers?

She scrambles up, eyes blazing.

Ah! The little bird is trying to spread her wings? My dick twitches. My groin hardens, *Why does her anger turn me on so, huh?*

She steps forward, thrusts a finger in my chest.

My heart begins to thud.

She peers up from under those hooded eyelashes. "Wake up and taste the wasabi, asshole."

"What does that even mean?"

She makes a sound deep in her throat. My dick twitches. My pulse speeds up.

She pivots, grabs a half-full beer mug sitting on the bar counter.

I growl, "Oh, no, you don't."

She turns, swings it at me. The smell of hops envelops the space.

I stare down at the beer-splattered shirt, the lapels of my camel colored jacket deepening to a dull brown. Anger squeezes my guts.

I fist my fingers at my side, broaden my stance.

She snickers.

I tip my chin up. "You're going to regret that."

The smile fades from her face. "Umm." She places the now empty mug on the bar.

I take a step forward and she skitters back. "It's only clothes." She gulps. "They'll wash."

I glare at her and she swallows, wiggles her fingers in the air. "I should have known that you wouldn't have a sense of humor."

I thrust out my jaw. "That's a ten-thousand-pound suit you destroyed."

She blanches, then straightens her shoulders. "Must have been some hot date you were trying to impress, huh?"

"Actually," I flick some of the offending liquid from my lapels, "it's you I was after."

"Me?" She frowns.

"We need to speak."

She glances toward the bartender who's on the other side of the bar. "I don't know you." She chews on her lower lip, biting off some of the hot pink. How would she look, with that pouty mouth fastened on my cock?

The blood rushes to my groin so quickly that my head spins. My pulse rate ratchets up. Focus, focus on the task you came here for.

"This will take only a few seconds." I take a step forward.

She moves aside.

I frown. "You want to hear this, I promise."

"Go to hell." She pivots and darts forward.

I let her go, a step, another, because... I can? Besides it's fun to create the illusion of freedom first; makes the hunt so much more entertaining, huh?

I swoop forward, loop an arm around her waist, and yank her toward me.

She yelps. "Release me."

Good thing the bar is not yet full. It's too early for the usual office-goers to stop by. And the staff...? Well they are well aware of who cuts their paychecks.

I spin her around and against the bar, then release her. "You will listen to me."

She swallows; she glances left to right.

Not letting you go yet, little Bird. I move into her space, crowd her.

She tips her chin up. "Whatever you're selling, I'm not interested."

I allow my lips to curl. "You don't fool me."

A flush steals up her throat, sears her cheeks. So tiny, so innocent. Such a good little liar. I narrow my gaze. "Every action has its consequences."

"Are you daft?" She blinks.

"This pretense of yours?" I thrust my face into hers, growling, "It's not working."

She blinks, then color suffuses her cheeks. "You're certifiably mad—"

"Getting tired of your insults."

"It's true, everything I said." She scrapes back the hair from her face. Her fingernails are painted... You guessed it, pink.

"And here's something else. You are a selfish, egotistical jackass."

I smirk. "You're beginning to repeat your insults and I haven't even kissed you yet."

"Don't you dare." She gulps.

I tilt my head. "Is that a challenge?"

"It's a..." she scans the crowded space, then turns to me. Her lips firm, "...a warning. You're delusional, you jackass." She inhales a deep breath before she speaks, "Your ego is bigger than the size of a black hole." She snickers. "Bet it's to compensate for your lack of balls."

A-n-d, that's it. I've had enough of her mouth that threatens to never stop spewing words. How many insults can one tiny woman hurl my way? Answer: too many to count.

"You—"

I lower my chin, touch my lips to hers.

Heat, sweetness, the honey of her essence explodes on my palate. My dick twitches. I tilt my head, deepen the kiss, reaching for that something more... more... of whatever scent she's wearing on her skin, infused with that breath of hers that crowds my senses, rushes down my spine. My groin hardens; my cock lengthens. I thrust my tongue between those infuriating lips.

She makes a sound deep in her throat and my heart begins to pound.

So innocent, yet so crafty. Beautiful and feisty. The kind of complication I don't need in my life.

I prefer the straight and narrow. Gray and black, that's how I choose to define my world. She, with her flashes of color—pink hair and lips that threaten to drive me to the edge of distraction—is exactly what I hate.

Give me a female who has her priorities set in life. To pleasure me, get me off, then walk away before her emotions engage. Yeah. That's what I prefer.

Not this... this bundle of craziness who flings her arms around my shoulders, thrusts her breasts up and into my chest, tips up her chin, opens her mouth, and invites me to take and take.

Does she have no self-preservation? Does she think I am going to fall for her wide-eyed appeal? She has another thing coming.

I tear my mouth away and she protests.

She twines her leg with mine, pushes up her hips, so that melting softness between her thighs cradles my aching hardness.

I glare into her face and she holds my gaze.

Trains her green eyes on me. Her cheeks flush a bright red. Her lips fall open and a moan bleeds into the air. The blood rushes to my dick, which instantly thickens. *Fuck.*

Time to put distance between myself and the situation.

It's how I prefer to manage things. Stay in control, always. Cut out anything that threatens to impinge on my equilibrium. Shut it down or buy them off. Reduce it to a transaction. That I understand.

The power of money, to be able to buy and sell—numbers, logic. That's what's worked for me so far.

"How much?"

Her forehead furrows.

"Whatever it is, I can afford it."

Her jaw slackens. "You think… you—"

"A million?"

"What?"

"Pounds, dollars… You name the currency, and it will be in your account."

Her jaw slackens. "You're offering me money?"

"For your time, and for you to fall in line with my plan."

She reddens. "You think I am for sale?"

"Everyone is."

"Not me."

Here we go again. "Is that a challenge?"

Color fades from her face. "Get away from me."

"Are you shy, is that what this is?" I frown. "You can write your price down on a piece of paper if you prefer." I glance up, notice the bartender watching us. I jerk my chin toward the napkins. He grabs one, then offers it to her.

She glowers at him. "Did you buy him, too?"

"What do you think?"

She glances around. "I think everyone here is ignoring us."

"It's what I'd expect."

"Why is that?"

I wave the tissue in front of her face. "Why do you think?"

"You own the place?"

"As I am going to own you."

She sets her jaw. "Let me leave and you won't regret this."

A chuckle bubbles up. I swallow it away. This is no laughing matter. I never smile during a transaction. Especially not when I am negotiating a new acquisition. And that's all she is. The final piece in the puzzle I am building.

"No one threatens me."

"You're right."

"Huh?"

"I'd rather act on my instinct."

Her lips twist, her gaze narrows. All of my senses scream a warning.

No, she wouldn't, no way—pain slices through my middle and sparks explode behind my eyes.

READ SINCLAIR AND SUMMER'S ENEMIES TO LOVERS, MARRIAGE OF CONVENIENCE ROMANCE IN THE BILLIONAIRE'S FAKE WIFE

READ LIAM AND ISLA'S FAKE RELATIONSHIP ROMANCE IN THE PROPOSAL WHERE TINY FIRST MAKES AN APPEARANCE.

READ AN EXCERPT FROM THE PROPOSAL

Liam

"Where is she?"

The receptionist gazes at me cow-eyed. Her lips move, but no words emerge. She clears her throat, glances sideways at the door to the side and behind her, then back at me.

"So, I take it she's in there?" I brush past her, and she jumps to her feet. "Sir, y-y-you can't go in there."

"Watch me." I glare at her.

She stammers, then gulps. Sweat beads her forehead. She shuffles back, and I stalk past her.

Really, is there no one who can stand up to me? All of this scraping of chairs and fawning over me? It's enough to drive a man to boredom. I need a challenge. So, when my ex-wife-to-be texted me to say she was calling off our wedding, I was pissed. But when she let it slip that her wedding planner was right—that she needs to marry for love, and not for some family obligation, rage gripped me. I squeezed my phone so hard the screen cracked. I almost hurled the device across the room.

When I got a hold of myself, for the first time in a long time, a shiver of something like excitement passed through me. *Finally, fuck.*

That familiar pulse of adrenaline pulses through my veins. It's a sensation I was familiar with in the early days of building my business.

After my father died and I took charge of the group of companies he'd run, I was filled with a sense of purpose; a one-directional focus to prove myself and nurture his legacy. To make my group of companies the leader, in its own right. To make so much money and amass so much power, I'd be a force to be reckoned with.

I tackled each business meeting with a zeal that none of my opponents were able to withstand. But with each passing year—as I crossed the benchmarks I'd set myself, as my bottom line grew healthier, my cash reserves engorged, and the people working for me began treating me with the kind of respect normally reserved for larger-than-life icons—some of that enthusiasm waned. Oh, I still wake up ready to give my best to my job every day, but the zest that once fired me up faded, leaving a sense of purposelessness behind.

The one thing that has kept me going is to lock down my legacy. To ensure the business I've built will finally be transferred to my name. For which my father informed me I would need to marry. Which is why, after much research, I tracked down Lila Kumar, wooed her, and proposed to her. And then, her meddling wedding planner came along and turned all of my plans upside down.

Now, that same sense of purpose grips me. That laser focus I've been lacking envelops me and fills my being. All of my senses sharpen as I shove the door of her office open and stalk in.

The scent envelops me first. The lush notes of violets and peaches. Evocative and fruity. Complex, yet with a core of mystery that begs to be unraveled. Huh? I'm not the kind to be affected by the scent of a woman, but this... Her scent... It's always chafed at my nerve endings. The hair on my forearms straightens.

My guts tie themselves up in knots, and my heart pounds in my chest. It's not comfortable. The kind of feeling I got the first time I went white-water rafting. A combination of nervousness and excitement as I faced my first rapids. A sensation that had since ebbed. One I'd been chasing ever since, pushing myself to take on extreme sports. One I hadn't thought I'd find in the office of a wedding planner.

My feet thud on the wooden floor, and I get a good look at the space which is one-fourth the size of my own office. In the far corner is a bookcase packed with books. On the opposite side is a comfortable settee packed with cushions women seem to like so much. There's a colorful patchwork quilt thrown over it, and behind that, a window that looks onto the back of the adjacent office building. On the coffee table in front of the settee is a bowl with crystal-like objects that reflect the light from the floor lamps. There are paintings on the wall that depict scenes from beaches. No doubt, the kind she'd point to and sell the idea of a honeymoon to gullible brides. I suppose the entire space would appeal to women. With its mood lighting and homey feel, the space invites you to kick back, relax and pour out your problems. A ruse I'm not going to fall for.

"You!" I stab my finger in the direction of the woman seated behind the antique desk straight ahead. "Call Lila, right now, and tell her she needs to go through with the wedding. Tell her she can't back out. Tell her I'm the right choice for her."

She peers up at me from behind large, black horn-rimmed glasses perched on her nose. "No."

I blink. "Excuse me?"

She leans back in her chair. "I'm not going to do that."

"Why the hell not?"

"Are you the right choice for her?

"Of course, I am." I glare at her.

Some of the color fades from her cheeks. She taps her pen on the table, then juts out her chin. "What makes you think you're the right choice of husband for her?"

"What makes you think I'm not."

"Do you love her?"

"That's no one's problem except mine and hers."

"You don't love her."

"What does that have to do with anything?"

"Excuse me?" She pushes the glasses further up her nose. "Are you seriously asking what loving the woman you're going to marry has to do with actually marrying her?" Her voice pulses with fury.

"Yes, exactly. Why don't you explain it to me?" The sarcasm in my tone is impossible to miss.

She stares at me from behind those large glasses that should make her look owlish and studious, but only add an edge of what I can only describe as quirky-sexiness. The few times I've met her before, she's gotten on my nerves so much, I couldn't wait to get the hell away from her. Now, giving her the full benefit of my attention, I realize, she's actually quite striking. And the addition of those spectacles? Fuck me—I never thought I had a weakness for women wearing glasses. Maybe I was wrong. Or maybe it's specifically this woman wearing glasses… Preferably only glasses and nothing else.

Hmm. Interesting. This reaction to her. It's unwarranted and not something I planned for. I widen my stance, mainly to accommodate the thickness between my legs. An inconvenience… which perhaps I can use to my benefit? I drag my thumb under my lower lip.

Her gaze drops to my mouth, and if I'm not mistaken, her breath hitches. *Very interesting.* Has she always reacted to me like that in the past? Nope, I would've noticed. We've always tried to have as little as possible to do with each other. Like I said, interesting. And unusual.

"First," —she drums her fingers on the table— "are you going to answer my question?"

I tilt my head, the makings of an idea buzzing through my synapses. I need a little time to flesh things out though. It's the only reason I deign to answer her question which, let's face it, I have no obligation to respond to. But for the moment, it's in my interest to humor her and buy myself a little time.

"Lila and I are well-matched in every way. We come from good families—"

"You mean rich families?"

"That, too. Our families move in the same circles."

"Don't you mean boring country clubs?" she says in a voice that drips with distaste.

I frown. "Among other places. We have the pedigree, the bloodline, our backgrounds are congruent, and we'd be able to fold into an arrangement of coexistence with the least amount of disruption on either side."

"Sounds like you're arranging a merger."

"A takeover, but what-fucking-ever." I raise a shoulder.

Her scowl deepens. "This is how you approached the upcoming wedding… And you wonder why Lila left you?"

"I gave her the biggest ring money could buy—"

"You didn't make an appearance at the engagement party."

"I signed off on all the costs related to the upcoming nuptials—"

"Your own engagement party. You didn't come to it. You left her alone to face her family and friends." Her tone rises. Her cheeks are flushed. You'd think she was talking about her own wedding, not that of her friend. In fact, it's more entertaining to talk to her than discuss business matters with my employees. *How interesting.*

"You also didn't show up for most of the rehearsals." She glowers.

"I did show up for the last one."

"Not that it made any difference. You were either checking your watch and indicating that it was time for you to leave, or you were glowering at the plans being discussed."

"I still agreed to that god-awful wedding cake, didn't I?

"On the other hand, it's probably good you didn't come for the previous rehearsals. If you had, Lila and I might have had this conversation earlier—"

"Aha!" I straighten. "So, you confess that it's because of you Lila walked away from this wedding."

She tips her head back. "Hardly. It's because of you."

"So you say, but your guilt is written large on your face."

"Guilt?" Her features flush. The color brings out the dewy hue of her skin, and the blue of her eyes deepens until they remind me of forget-me-nots. No, more like the royal blue of the ink that spilled onto my paper the first time I attempted to write with a fountain pen.

"The only person here who should feel guilty is you, for attempting to coerce an innocent, young woman into an arrangement that would have trapped her for life."

Anger thuds at my temples. My pulse begins to race. "I never have to coerce women. And what you call being trapped is what most women call security. But clearly, you wouldn't know that, considering" —I wave my hand in the air— "you prefer to run your kitchen-table business which, no doubt, barely makes ends meet."

She loosens her grip on her pencil, and it falls to the table with a clatter. Sparks flash deep in her eyes.

You know what I said earlier about the royal blue? Strike that. There are flickers of silver hidden in the depths of her gaze. Flickers that blaze when she's upset. How would it be to push her over the edge? To be at the receiving end of all that passion, that fervor, that ardor… that absolute avidness of existence when she's one with the moment? How would it feel to rein in her spirit, absorb it, drink from it, revel in it, and use it to spark color into my life?

"Kitchen-table business?" She makes a growling sound under her breath. "You dare come into my office and insult my enterprise? The company I have grown all by myself—"

"And outside of your assistant" —I nod toward the door I came through— "you're the sole employee, I take it?"

Her color deepens. "I work with a group of vendors—"

I scoff, "None of whom you could hold accountable when they don't deliver."

"—who have been carefully vetted to ensure that they always deliver," she says at the same time. "Anyway, why do you care, since you don't have a wedding to go to?"

"That's where you're wrong." I peel back my lips. "I'm not going to be labeled as the joke of the century. After all, the media labelled it 'the wedding of the century'." I make air quotes with my fingers.

It was Isla's idea to build up the wedding with the media. She also wanted to invite influencers from all walks of life to attend, but I have no interest in turning my nuptials into a circus. So, I vetoed the idea of journalists attending in person. I have, however, agreed to the event being recorded by professionals and exclusive clips being shared with the media and the influencers. This way, we'll get the necessary PR coverage, without the media being physically present.

In all fairness, the publicity generated by the upcoming nuptials has already been beneficial. It's not like I'll ever tell her, but Isla was right to feed the public's interest in the upcoming event. Apparently, not even the most hard-nosed investors can resist the warm, fuzzy feelings that a marriage invokes. And this can only help with the IPO I have planned for the most important company in my portfolio. "I have a lot riding on this wedding."

"Too bad you don't have a bride."

"Ah," —I smirk— "but I do."

She scowls. "No, you don't. Lila—"

"I'm not talking about her."

"Then who are you talking about?"

"You."

To find out what happens next read Liam and Isla's fake relationship romance in The Proposal where Tiny first makes an appearance.

Read Michael and Karma's forced marriage romance in Mafia King

Read an excerpt from Mafia King

Karma

"Morn came and went—and came, and brought no day..."

Tears prick the backs of my eyes. Goddamn Byron. His words creep up on me when I am at my weakest. Not that I am a poetry addict, by any measure, but words are my jam. The one consolation I have is that, when everything else in the world is wrong, I can turn to them, and they'll be there, friendly, steady, waiting with open arms.

And this particular poem had laced my blood, crawled into my gut when I'd first read it. Darkness had folded within me like an insidious snake, that raises its head when I least expect it. Like now, when I look out on the still sleeping city of London, from the grassy slope of Waterlow Park.

Somewhere out there, the Mafia is hunting me, apparently. It's why my sister Summer and her new husband Sinclair Sterling had insisted that I have my own security detail. I had agreed... only to appease them... then given my bodyguard the slip this morning. I had decided to come running here because it's not a place I'd normally go... Not so early in the morning, anyway. They won't think to look for me here. At least, not for a while longer.

I purse my lips, close my eyes. Silence. The rustle of the wind between the leaves. The faint tinkle of the water from the nearby spring.

I could be the last person on this planet, alone, unsung, bound for the grave.

Ugh! Stop. Right there. I drag the back of my hand across my nose. Try it again, focus, get the words out, one after the other, like the steps of my sorry life.

"Morn came and went—and came, and... and..." My voice breaks. "Bloody asinine hell." I dig my fingers into the grass and grab a handful and fling it out. Again. From the top.

"Morn came and went—and came, and—"

"...brought no day."

A gravelly voice completes my sentence.

I whip my head around. His silhouette fills my line of sight. He's sitting on the same knoll as me, yet I have to crane my neck back to see his profile. The sun is at his back, so I can't make out his features. Can't see his eyes... Can only take in his dark hair, combed back by a ruthless hand that brooked no measure.

My throat dries.

Thick dark hair, shot through with grey at the temples. He wears his age like a badge. I don't know why, but I know his years have not been easy. That he's seen more, indulged in more, reveled in the consequences of his actions, however extreme they might have been. He's not a normal, everyday person, this man. Not a nine-to-fiver, not someone who lives an average life. Definitely not a man who returns home to his wife and home at the end of the day. He is...different, unique, evil... Monstrous. Yes, he is a beast, one who sports the face of a man but who harbors the kind of darkness inside that speaks to me. I gulp.

His face boasts a hooked nose, a thin upper lip, a fleshy lower lip. One that hints at hidden desires, Heat. Lust. The sensuous scrape of that whiskered jaw over my innermost places. Across my inner thigh, reaching toward that core of me that throbs, clenches, melts to feel the stab of his tongue, the thrust of his hardness as he impales me, takes me, makes me his. Goosebumps pop on my skin.

I drag my gaze away from his mouth down to the scar that slashes across his throat. A cold sensation coils in my chest. What or who had hurt him in such a cruel fashion?

"Of this their desolation; and all hearts
Were chill'd into a selfish prayer for light..."

He continues in that rasping guttural tone. Is it the wound that caused that scar that makes his voice so... gravelly... So deep... so... so, hot?

Sweat beads my palms and the hairs on my nape rise. "Who are you?"

He stares ahead as his lips move,

"Forests were set on fire — but hour by hour
They fell and faded — and the crackling trunks
Extinguish'd with a crash — and all was black."

I swallow, moisture gathers in my core. How can I be wet by the mere cadence of this stranger's voice?

I spring up to my feet.

"Sit down," he commands.

His voice is unhurried, lazy even, his spine erect. The cut of his black jacket stretches across the width of his massive shoulders. His hair... I was mistaken — there are threads of dark gold woven between the darkness that pours down to brush the nape of his neck. A strand of hair falls over his brow. As I watch, he raises his hand and brushes it away. Somehow, the gesture lends an air of vulnerability to him. Something so at odds with the rest of his persona that, surely, I am mistaken?

My scalp itches. I take in a breath and my lungs burn. This man... He's sucked up all the oxygen in this open space as if he owns it, the master of all he surveys. The master of me. My death. My life. A shiver ladders along my spine. *Get away, get away now, while you still can.*

I angle my body, ready to spring away from him.

"I won't ask again."

Ask. Command. Force me to do as he wants. He'll have me on my back, bent over, on my side, on my knees, over him, under him. He'll surround me, overwhelm me, pin me down with the force of his personality. His charisma, his larger-than-life essence will crush everything else out of me and I... I'll love it.

"No."

"Yes."

A fact. A statement of intent, spoken aloud. So true. So real. Too real. Too much. Too fast. All of my nightmares... my dreams come to life. Everything I've wanted is here in front of me. I'll die a thousand deaths before he'll be done with me... And then? Will I be reborn? For him. For me. For myself.

I live, first and foremost, to be the woman I was... am meant to be.

"You want to run?"

No.

No.

I nod my head.

He turns his, and all the breath leaves my lungs. Blue eyes— cerulean, dark like the morning skies, deep like the nighttime...hidden corners, secrets that I don't dare uncover. He'll destroy me, have my heart, and break it so casually.

My throat burns and a boiling sensation squeezes my chest.

"Go then, my beauty, fly. You have until I count to five. If I catch you, you are mine."

"If you don't?"

"Then I'll come after you, stalk your every living moment, possess your nightmares, and steal you away in the dead of night, and then..."

I draw in a shuddering breath as liquid heat drips from between my legs. "Then?" I whisper.

"Then, I'll ensure you'll never belong to anyone else, you'll never see the light of day again, for your every breath, your every waking second, your thoughts, your actions… and all your words, every single last one, will belong to me." He peels back his lips, and his teeth glint in the first rays of the morning light. "Only me." He straightens to his feet and rises, and rises.

This man… He is massive. A monster who always gets his way. My guts churn. My toes curl. Something primeval inside of me insists I hold my own. I cannot give in to him. Cannot let him win whatever this is. I need to stake my ground, in some form. *Say something. Anything. Show him you're not afraid of this.*

"Why?" I tilt my head back, all the way back. "Why are you doing this?"

He tilts his head, his ears almost canine in the way they are silhouetted against his profile.

"Is it because you can? Is it a… a," I blink, "a debt of some kind?"

He stills.

"My father, this is about how he betrayed the Mafia, right? You're one of them?"

"Lucky guess." His lips twist, "It is about your father, and how he promised you to me. He reneged on his promise, and now, I am here to collect."

"No." I swallow… *No, no, no.*

"Yes." His jaw hardens.

All expression is wiped clean of his face, and I know then, that he speaks the truth. It's always about the past. My sorry shambles of a past… Why does it always catch up with me? *You can run, but you can never hide.*

"Tick-tock, Beauty." He angles his body and his shoulders shut out the sight of the sun, the dawn skies, the horizon, the city in the distance, the rustle of the grass, the trees, the rustle of the leaves. All of it fades and leaves just me and him. Us. *Run.*

"Five." He jerks his chin, straightens the cuffs of his sleeves.

My knees wobble.

"Four."

My pulse rate spikes. I should go. Leave. But my feet are planted in this earth. This piece of land where we first met. What am I, but a speck in the larger scheme of things? To be hurt. To be forgotten. To be taken without an ounce of retribution. To be punished… by him.

"Three." He thrusts out his chest, widens his stance, every muscle in his body relaxed. "Two."

I swallow. The pulse beats at my temples. My blood thrums.
"One."

Michael

"Go."

She pivots and races down the slope. Her dark hair streams behind her. Her scent, sexy femininity and silver moonflowers, clings to my nose, then recedes. It's so familiar, that scent.

I had smelled it before, had reveled in it. Had drawn in it into my lungs as she had peeked up at me from under her thick eyelashes. Her green gaze had fixed on mine, her lips parted as she welcomed my kiss. As she had wound her arms about my neck, pushed up those sweet breasts and flattened them against my chest. As she had parted her legs when I had planted my thigh between them. I had seen her before... in my dreams. I stiffen. She can't be the same girl, though, can she?

I reach forward, thrust out my chin and sniff the air, but there's only the damp scent of dawn, mixed with the foul tang of exhaust fumes, as she races away from me.

She stumbles and I jump forward, pause when she straightens. Wait. Wait. Give her a lead. Let her think she has almost escaped, that she's gotten the better of me... As if.

I clench my fists at my sides, force myself to relax. Wait. Wait. She reaches the bottom of the incline, turns. I surge forward. One foot in front of the other. My heels dig into the grassy surface and mud flies up, clings to the hem of my £4000 Italian pants. Like I care? Plenty more where that came from. An entire walk-in closet, full of clothes made to measure, to suit every occasion, with every possible accessory needed by a man in my position to impress...

Everything... Except the one thing that I had coveted from the moment I had laid eyes on her. Sitting there on the grassy slope, unshed tears in her eyes, and reciting... Byron? For hell's sake. Of all the poets in the world, she had to choose the Lord of Darkness.

I huff. All a ploy. Clearly, she knew I was sitting next to her... No, not possible. I had walked toward her and she hadn't stirred. Hadn't been aware. Yeah, I am that good. I've been known to slit a man's throat from ear-to-ear while he was awake and in his full senses. Alive one second, dead the next. That's how it is in my world. You want it, you take it. And I... I want her.

I increase my pace, eat up the distance between myself and the girl… That's all she is. A slip of a thing, a slim blur of motion. Beauty in hiding. A diamond, waiting for me to get my hands on her, polish her, show her what it means to be…

Dead. She is dead. That's why I am here.

A flash of skin, a creamy length of thigh. My groin hardens and my legs wobble. I lurch over a bump in the ground. The hell? I right myself, leap forward, inching closer, closer. She reaches a curve in the path, disappears out of sight.

My heart hammers in my chest. I will not lose her, will not. *Here, Beauty, come to Daddy.* The wind whistles past my ears. I pump my legs, lengthen my strides, turn the corner. There's no one there. Huh?

My heart hammers and the blood pounds at my wrists, my temples; adrenaline thrums in my veins. I slow down, come to a stop. Scan the clearing.

The hairs on my forearms prickle. She's here. Not far, but where? Where is she? I prowl across to the edge of the clearing, under the tree with its spreading branches.

When I get my hands on you, Beauty, I'll spread your legs like the pages of a poem. Dip into your honeyed sweetness, like a quill pen in ink. Drag my aching shaft across that melting, weeping entrance. My balls throb. My groin tightens. The crack of a branch above shivers across my stretched nerve endings. I swoop forward, hold out my arms, and close my grasp around the trembling, squirming mass of precious humanity. I cradle her close to my chest, heart beating thud-thud-thud, overwhelming any other thought.

Mine. All mine. The hell is wrong with me? She wriggles her little body, and her curves slide across my forearms. My shoulders bunch and my fingers tingle. She kicks out with her legs and arches her back, thrusting her breasts up so her nipples are outlined against the fabric of her sports bra. She dared to come out dressed like that? In that scrap of fabric that barely covers her luscious flesh?

"Let me go." She whips her head toward me and her hair flows around her shoulders, across her face. She blows it out of the way. "You monster, get away from me."

Anger drums at the backs of my eyes and desire tugs at my groin. The scent of her is sheer torture, something I had dreamed of in the wee hours of twilight when dusk turned into night.

She's not real. She's not the woman I think she is. She is my downfall. My sweet poison. The bitter medicine I must partake of to cure the ills that plague my company.

"Fine." I lower my arms and she tumbles to the grass, hits the ground butt first.

"How dare you." She huffs out a breath, her hair messily arranged across her face.

I shove my hands into the pockets of my fitted pants, knees slightly bent, legs apart. Tip my chin down and watch her as she sprawls at my feet.

"You… dropped me?" She makes a sound deep in her throat.

So damn adorable.

"Your wish is my command." I quirk my lips.

"You don't mean it."

"You're right." I lean my weight forward on the balls of my feet and she flinches.

"What… what do you want?"

"You."

She pales. "You want to… to rob me? I have nothing of consequence.

"Oh, but you do, Beauty."

I lean in and every muscle in her body tenses. Good. She's wary. She should be. She should have been alert enough to have run as soon as she sensed my presence. But she hadn't.

I should spare her because she's the woman from my dreams... but I won't. She's a debt I intend to collect. She owes me, and I've delayed what was meant to happen long enough.

I pull the gun from my holster, point it at her.

Her gaze widens and her breath hitches. I expect her to plead with me for her life, but she doesn't. She stares back at me with her huge dilated pupils. She licks her lips and the blood drains to my groin. *Che cazzo!* Why does her lack of fear turn me on so?

"Your phone," I murmur, "take out your phone."

She draws in a breath, then reaches into her pocket and pulls out her phone.

"Call your sister."

"What?"

"Dial your sister, Beauty. Tell her you are going away on a long trip to Sicily with your new male friend."

"What?"

"You heard me." I curl my lips. "Do it, now!'

She blinks, looks like she is about to protest, then her fingers fly over the phone.

Damn, and I had been looking forward to coaxing her into doing my bidding.

She holds her phone to her ear. I can hear the phone ring on the other side, before it goes to voicemail. She glances at me and I jerk my chin. She looks away, takes a deep breath, then speaks in a cheerful voice, "Hi Summer, it's me, Karma. I, ah, have to go away for a bit. This new... ah, friend of mine... He has an extra ticket and he has invited me to Sicily to spend some time with him. I... ah, I don't know when, exactly, I'll be back, but I'll message you and let you know. Take care. Love ya sis, I—"

I snatch the phone from her, disconnect the call, then hold the gun to her temple, "Goodbye, Beauty."

To find out what happens next read Michael and Karma's forced marriage story In Mafia King

Read JJ and Lena's ex-boyfriend's father, age-gap romance in Mafia Lust

Read Knight and Penny's, best friend's brother romance in The Wrong Wife

Read Dr. Weston Kincaid and Amelie's forced proximity, one-bed Christmas Romance in The Billionaire's Fake Wife

Download your exclusive L. Steele reading order bingo card on www.authorlsteele.com

Did you know all the characters you read about have their own book? Cross off their stories as you read and share your bingo card in L. Steele's reader group on Facebook

Want to be the first to find out when L. Steele's next book is out? Sign up for her newsletter on www.authorlsteele.com

From the author

Hello, I'm L. Steele. I write romance stories with strong powerful men who meet their match in sassy, curvy, spitfire women.

I love to push myself with each book on both the spice and the angst so I can deliver well rounded, multidimensional characters.

I enjoy trading trivia with my filmmaker husband, watching lots and lots of movies, and walking nature trails. I live in London.

Follow me:
On Amazon
on BookBub
on Goodreads
on Audible
On TikTok
On Threads
on Pinterest
My YouTube channel
Join my secret Facebook Reader Group
Read ALL my books

SECOND BONUS PROLOGUE WITH EDWARD

MARRIAGE OF CONVENIENCE BILLIONAIRE ROMANCE FROM L. STEELE

The Billionaire's Fake Wife - Sinclair and Summer's story that started this universe... with a plot twist you won't see coming!

The Billionaire's Secret - Victoria and Saint's story. Saint is maybe the most alphahole of them all!

Marrying the Billionaire Single Dad - Damian and Julia's story, watch out for the plot twist!

The Proposal - Liam and Isla's story. What's a wedding planner to do when you tell the bride not to go through with the wedding and the groom demands you take her place and give him a heir? And yes plot twist!

CHRISTMAS ROMANCE BOOKS BY L. STEELE FOR YOU

Want to find out how Dr. Weston Kincaid and Amelie met? Read The Billionaire's Christmas Bride HERE

Want even more Christmas Romance books? *Read A very Mafia Christmas, Christian and Aurora's story HERE*

Read a marriage of convenience billionaire Christmas romance, Hunter and Zara's story - *The Christmas One Night Stand HERE*

FORBIDDEN BILLIONAIRE ROMANCE
BY L. STEELE FOR YOU

Read Daddy JJ's, age-gap romance in Mafia Lust
Read Edward, Baron and Ava's story starting with Billionaire's Sins

ABOUT THE AUTHOR

Hello, I'm L. Steele.

I write romance stories with strong powerful men who meet their match in sassy, curvy, spitfire women.

I love to push myself with each book on both the spice and the angst so I can deliver well rounded, multidimensional characters.

I enjoy trading trivia with my husband, watching lots and lots of movies, and walking nature trails. I live in London.

FOLLOW ME:
ON AMAZON
ON BOOKBUB
ON GOODREADS
ON AUDIBLE
ON TIKTOK
JOIN MY SECRET FACEBOOK READER GROUP
ON PINTEREST
MY YOUTUBE CHANNEL
READ ALL MY BOOKS
SPOTIFY

ACKNOWLEDGMENTS

Edited by: Elizabeth Connor

Cover Design: Jacqueline Sweet

Huge thank you to Li Iacobacci, Danielle Vale and Rachel Kroeplin, my alpha readers.

Huge shout out to everyone in L. Steele's Team Facebook reader group, you guys are awesome!